LADY
OF
SHADOWS

Also by Breanna Teintze

Lord of Secrets

LADY
OF
SHADOWS

BREANNA TEINTZE

Jo Fletcher
BOOKS

First published in Great Britain in 2020 by

Jo Fletcher Books
an imprint of
Quercus Editions Ltd
Carmelite House
50 Victoria Embankment
London EC4Y 0DZ

An Hachette UK company

A CIP catalogue record for this book is available
from the British Library

TPB ISBN 978 1 78747 646 2
EBOOK ISBN 978 1 78747 648 6

10 9 8 7 6 5 4 3 2 1

Typeset by Jouve (UK), Milton Keynes

Printed and bound in Great Britain by Clays Ltd, Elcograf S.p.A.

Papers used by Jo Fletcher Books are from well-managed forests and
other responsible sources.

To my kids:

This one's for you.

(You can't read it until you're older, though. Sorry.)

ONE

The ghosts had been following us for about an hour when we finally reached the lapidary's house. There were at least two spectres vying for our attention, dodging from shadow to shadow as we moved through the twilight streets. There could have been more, or less; it's hard to be sure about illusion magic at the best of times, and this wasn't the best of times. I hadn't slept in three days and was feeling about as coherent as your average dirt-witted farmer.

We had just reached the outskirts of Varriel's alchemy works district, with its narrow houses, thousand fume-belching chimneys and reputation for black-market magic. No one had tried to rob us yet, but the ghosts meant that was about to change. In the royal city of Varriel it seemed even knifepoint thieves could buy a bit of cheap street conjuring.

'Ignore them,' I said, resisting the urge to turn and stare as a ghost flitted at the edge of my vision. 'They just want to herd us down some blind alley to make the thievery more efficient. They aren't really there.'

'I *know* they're not really there.' Brix hunched her shoulders against the cool air, her hair gleaming in the half-light like a pale, fluffy halo. She had eyes the colour of copper, more freckles across her nose and jaw than I'd ever been able to accurately count and a limited store of patience. 'I wish *I* wasn't really here. Can we just get this over with?'

We stood in front of a green-shuttered house. It had a flying bird carved into the granite capstone above the door and a neat brass plate on the wall that read *F. Jaliseth, Alchemical Lapidary*. Brix leaned forwards and hammered on the door with a closed fist. 'Hey! There's customers out here with the smoke ghosts!'

'With the cheap street illusions,' I said.

She rolled her eyes and knocked again. 'Open up!'

The door swung open to reveal a woman like an overgrown barn owl, blinking at us over the top of a pair of magnifying spectacles. She held a slender bronze carving tool and did not look best-pleased.

'Get out of here!' She advanced on us, holding the tool like a dagger. 'Guild pigs!'

I twisted backwards, and the magic under my skin moved.

'Neyar's teeth, Jaliseth!' I hated it when I could *feel* the spells written into my body. They were the entire reason Brix and I had spent two weeks on the road to get to this horrible soot-streaked city. I bit down on the disgust that rose in my throat. 'You treat all your buyers this way?'

'I craft within regulations.' Jaliseth scowled uncertainly, first at Brix and then at me. 'The Guild doesn't have any reason to keep harassing me like this. It's persecution. First you send your spies around, then these gods-damned smoke illusions to drive my customers away, and then—'

'I'm *not* Guild,' I interrupted. 'I'm Corcoran Gray. Acarius' grandson?' This was always the worst part: convincing people who had known my old face that I was still myself. 'The last time I saw you was five years ago. Acarius bought a wardstone, something shiny – malachite maybe. You slipped me a half dose of yavad when Acarius wasn't looking and then we stayed up telling jokes and eating green apples. I threw up in your fireplace.'

Jaliseth lowered the chisel. '*Gray?*'

'As I've been telling you. New face. I'm not used to it either.' I pointed at Brix. 'And this is my partner, who dislikes the Guild even more than I do. Can we come in?'

'Holy saints.' Jaliseth moved to one side, holding the door open wider while she scanned the street. 'Get inside, both of you. Hurry.'

The house was small, just the room she led us into and a closed door that presumably led to another. Apart from the tiny hearth, every bit of wall space was crammed with stone-laden shelves. Crystals rubbed shoulders with pearly opal, undulating agate and blue-hearted geodes. The carvings were evenly split between things like the respectable row of tiny beryl house-saints and the unlawful cluster of polished, rune-carved sodalite flowers.

The little lapidary shut the door firmly behind us and ran a hand through her grey hair. 'I don't think they can get past the wards I've carved into the foundation stones.'

'Who can't?' Brix said, eyeing the bolted door.

'The Guild.' Jaliseth shuffled over to one of the many shelves and began sorting through the stones on it. 'At least, I think it's them. There was a scandal about three months ago, downriver, after one of theirs was arrested for causing an accidental death. Made no end of stir, and they've been cracking down on all the ancillary magic businesses since to prove to the throne they're still in charge, that the Charter is still important. They've been watching my place for weeks. Although I can't understand how . . .' She stopped and shook her head. 'But that can wait until Gray explains himself. Is Acarius in town?'

'No.' We had left Acarius at the cabin in the mountains we shared with him and Brix's sister, Anka. My grandfather thought this trip to Varriel was a fool's errand, that I didn't need outside help to solve my problems. But he wasn't the one who had to live with them. I stuck my hands in my pockets. 'Acarius does let me out of the house by myself occasionally.'

3

'I heard about the trouble last year.' Jaliseth eyed my face. 'But I had no idea things were so . . . severe. What happened?'

Now *that* was a hell of a question. A year ago I'd nearly died killing the false god Jaern, and ended up inhabiting the custom-built body he had been using. It turns out the world doesn't much notice when you kill a god – it's only your own universe that shatters, and you're left trying to patch the cracks with study, or work . . . or illegal alchemy.

'Necromancy,' I said.

Jaliseth examined me, from my feet to the crown of my head. 'It's not so bad,' she offered. 'You're lucky. At least you're lucky for me. I have use for a wizard tonight.' She glanced at Brix. 'And . . .?'

'And this is Brix,' I said. 'Brix, Jaliseth.'

Brix nodded. 'Hello.'

Jaliseth nodded back, then gave a dimpling smile. 'Congratulations, my dear. I didn't think this rascal would end up partnered.'

'Gods,' I said. 'I am a dangerous criminal, wanted by the Guild on charges whose penalty, at a minimum, would involve the loss of my tongue. Cats who steal butter are rascals.'

Jaliseth ignored me and gestured to two low chairs beside the hearth. 'Sit, if you please.'

'Listen, I'd like to get this done quickly.' I glanced at Brix, who was choosing a chair like we were there on a social call. I liked Jaliseth, but I didn't want to stay long.

'Why?' Jaliseth put her tool down on a shelf between a piece of jade that was half-formed into the head and shoulders of a beautiful young man and a polished, dark wood bowl. 'Does the Guild know you're in town?'

'Of course not, or I wouldn't have walked straight up to your door. The Guild wouldn't bother trying to scare me with smoke ghosts, they'd have hit me with a paralysis spell. I'm here to have something made. I need to buy a set of silencing stones.' To my relief the words sounded relatively matter-of-fact. 'As strong as you can make them.'

'Simple enough,' Jaliseth said. 'And who are you silencing?'

'Me.' I forced the muscles in my jaw to unclench. 'I talk in my sleep. It's causing disturbances. Anyway, I thought *you* were in a hurry. Are you going to tell us why somebody's running smoke illusions around your house?'

Jaliseth considered me for a moment before taking off her spectacles and placing them neatly beside the chisel. 'I think I may be going mad,' she said, quietly. 'Please sit down, Gray. I'll make you whatever wardstones you want. Just . . . hear me out.'

The hair on my arms lifted. I sat.

The lapidary's hand rested on the chunk of quartz beside her, fingers moving absently over the stone. 'I admit I was thinking of sending for Acarius. I don't even know how to . . . you'd have to look at it. I'm an alchemist, not a wizard. I don't dabble with incantations. I don't like how toxic spells can be.'

'Only if you don't know what you're doing,' I said, but she lifted a hand.

'So all you wizards say. All I know is that magic poisoning means your fingernails turn black and fall off, and that's just for starters. But this—' She reached inside the wooden bowl and pulled a chain and pendant out, and I went cold.

The pendant looked like a teardrop-shaped black gem in a tin setting, but I knew it wasn't. It was a crystal vial of black liquid, with a purple spark at the centre that pulsed like a heartbeat. The vial hung from a ring-topped metal stopper, strung on a leather lace.

An almost identical pendant hung around my own neck, nestled between my breastbone and my shirt.

'*That's* your problem?' I said.

'It started with this.' Jaliseth's eyes lingered on the vial. 'About two months ago, I became very ill. Magic toxicity, I think, in spite of all my precautions.'

'You should have been able to sleep it off,' I said. 'It goes away on its own.'

Jaliseth shook her head. 'That's your sort of toxicity. When you snuff a spell you're not in contact with the poison any more, but when I'm carving I'm touching runes all day, every day. It doesn't hurt at first. And then you think it's just a headache, just a lingering cough.' She glanced at her shelves. 'It took me too long to realise how sick I was. I went to Healers, to shrines . . . there's no proper Ranara-temple in Varriel – it's all Farran-worship here, thanks to the Guild and the king's shrine – but I would have travelled to the nearest one and sacrificed as many doves as they wanted if it would have done any good. I couldn't keep food down, couldn't do anything. You can't understand what it's like to know you're dying.'

Brix shot a quick look at me. Last year, I'd bled out in her arms.

'It must have been enough to make you desperate,' I said gravely.

'And then at one of the saints-shrines by the river, I heard a rumour.' Her brow furrowed. 'A cure, offered by a potion-seller. Black-market, off record. He said he was only passing through Var-riel for one night. His cure was supposed to heal anyone, as long as they could pay. I paid.' Something in my face must have shown what I was thinking, because Jaliseth's voice turned defensive. 'I know how it sounds, but I was at the end of my wits. I was skin and bones, coughing up bits of my lungs. I would have tried anything. And besides, it *worked*. There was no recovery to speak of. He hung this amulet around my neck, said a few words, and that was it. One moment I was dying, and the next I was whole. He said as long as I kept wearing it, I'd stay well.'

'You're not wearing it now,' Brix said.

'No.' Jaliseth looked down at the pendant, her thumb lingering on the metalwork. 'I didn't stay well. After a while I started to lose time.

I still lose time, if I wear it. Hours go by and I can't account for them. I find cuts and scrapes I don't remember getting. I can tell I've been doing things – carvings, even. But I don't remember it, any of it. The hours are just gone, as though someone snipped them out of my memory with scissors. And things are getting worse – shadows follow me on the street, there are strange smells in the neighbourhood, and . . .' She paused. 'I think someone has been watching the house. Interfering with my things. I wake up and my tools or furniture have been moved. Why would anyone do that?'

'Wait,' Brix said. 'You think the Guild knows you have this necklace?'

Jaliseth shrugged. 'I don't know. The shadow illusions have been here for the last three days, but if it's them I don't know why they don't just arrest me. I've known something is wrong for weeks. You don't know what a relief it is to hear you say you saw the shadow illusions, too. I've been so afraid that I was growing more ill, imagining things.' The lines in her face looked deeper than when I'd seen her last, her shoulders more stooped. 'This whole business has got beyond me, Gray. I need to know what this thing is, where it came from – what it's *doing* to me. This is wizard's business. I don't have anybody else to ask. And you're a . . .' She paused, probably searching for a diplomatic way to put it.

'Talent,' I suggested, and took the pendant out of her hand.

'Indeed.' She gave a taut smile. 'So you do the divining, and I'll get your wardstones ready. Is it a bargain? Do you really want the stones keyed to you? Plenty of perfectly normal people sleeptalk.'

'Yes to both.' I rifled through my pockets for a pencil. It wasn't as though I really had a choice. I wasn't normal, and my sleeptalk wasn't harmless. The magic under my skin saw to that.

Jaliseth released her breath. 'Thank the gods.'

'If the Guild really is watching the house, it would be better to get this over with quickly,' Brix said.

'I have a set of wardstones that are mostly finished.' Jaliseth moved to the shelf closest to the hearth and picked up two small, round grey stones, polished to a high sheen and covered in careful spirals of runes. 'All I'll have to do is add your name to them. I can do that while you're divining.'

'Then that's settled.' I knelt and began to scribe runic characters in a spiral on the wooden floor, trying to put everything else out of my mind. Divination is a particularly fickle incantation. It requires a lot of attention to avoid nasty hallucinations and uncontrolled expansions of the magic, and even if a divining spiral doesn't go bad it can still taint your perceptions for hours. But there was nothing else for it. Jaliseth needed answers, and to tell the truth, so did I. The amulet I wore had been Jaern's. The fact that a copy of it had turned up with a random Varriel potion-man did not bode well.

Jaliseth rustled through the stuff on her shelves, collecting a couple of chisels and several other tools I didn't recognise.

Brix moved to stand behind me. 'You want help?'

I shook my head. Difficult as the divining could be, sharing the toxicity from the magic would only ensure that both of us were rendered sick and useless. 'Just pull me off the spiral if I begin to gibber.'

Brix frowned. She did not go back to her seat.

I counted the runes as I wrote, slipping into the quiet place in my mind where the magic is always not quite asleep, and soon the spiral was finished except for the focus at the centre. I dropped Jaliseth's pendant into the middle, then pushed my sleeves up and added two strings of runes from the bases of my thumbs up to the insides of my elbows. It had to be a very precise line; only Jaern had known exactly which spells my body carried, and it had taken a lot of experimentation for me to find a blank piece of skin to scribe on.

I put the grease pencil back into my bag and let my thumbs overlap two painted characters. One by one, as I pronounced them, the characters in the spiral lit. The spell came together and swirled around my hands. My vision narrowed, darkness closing in until only the pendant was left. As I pronounced the last symbol, I saw the woman.

She was dead.

Cold. I was cold?

Focus.

No, *she* was cold, the dead woman, cold and breathless. She was stretched on her back in a coffin. Or, no, that wasn't quite right. Nobody filled coffins with liquid, and this was sloppy with purple-black goo.

Focus, I said again, as much to myself as to the spell. *Where?*

People tend to think that divination is like dreaming, or the visions the Temples priestesses get while praying and drinking yavad. I've been stoned on yavad and I've had too many dreams, and divination isn't like either. For one thing, it's fast – you lose most of the real world in a breath, and then it's just you and the vision. Pushing the vision in the direction of your query is more difficult than you'd think. Jaliseth had wanted me to ask *where*, but I kept getting distracted by *who*.

The dead woman was young, maybe in her early twenties, with black hair, high cheekbones and the kind of knobby fingers that go with scrubbing floors and splitting firewood. She looked peaceful. You might have thought she was asleep if it wasn't for the blue cast to her lips.

And the *cold*. Gods, she was like ice.

There were other people moving around her, shadowy figures I couldn't quite see. Scraps of chants floated in the air; prayers, maybe. A pendant like the one I was using for a focus rested on her chest, glowing dull red. The liquid she wasn't quite floating in lapped at her tattooed chin.

You're Tirnaal.

Her eyes snapped open, as though she'd heard me – which was impossible.

If her amulet was the same as the one I was scrying with, I was fairly certain I was seeing the past. It's not unusual for divination to stray into memory, but history doesn't interact with you. Yet here she was, the dead woman, staring right at me with bloodshot eyes.

Help me, she said.

Pain crept up my spine. I had written my spiral with shielding runes, but the toxicity inherent in magic could never be entirely avoided. I wouldn't have long until this incantation sharpened into a migraine.

Who are you? I said.

Moyra. Stop this, the dead woman said. *Make them stop this.*

The sweet stench of rot pressing in around me, the cold, the claustrophobic stasis of the vision – surely I couldn't be mistaken. *Aren't you dead?*

Not dead. Kept. Her eyes wandered. *Hurts.*

The edges of the vision blurred. My own pain sharpened into spikes against the backs of my eyes. The magic was cracking.

This was worse than no answers at all, just the knowledge of someone's suffering. *Where are you?*

She didn't answer. Her pendant flared red, blinding.

My spine exploded in agony.

A heartbeat filled my ears, hammering with slow, heavy thuds, drowning out the vision. This wasn't Moyra; someone else was trying to enter my divination spell. Brix wouldn't have done anything so reckless, and Jaliseth was too afraid of magic poisoning to interfere. This consciousness was efficient, professional, and inserted itself like a knife into my mind, twisting, searching. I wrenched my attention around to focus on the heartbeat's owner, but the vision wouldn't extend far enough to allow me to see them. There was something in the way, too bright. I couldn't quite find the person, just their outline, like watching someone through shadows.

The incantation radiated pain like an ember sheds heat. The toxicity of my spell was mingling with some other magic the interloper carried with them, poison boiling through my veins, speeding up my heart to the point it might burst. I had to get whoever this was off my spiral quickly or both of us could die.

Let go, I said, in case it was that simple.

The interloper's mind shied away from mine. Not only did whoever it was not remove themselves, they were actually trying to pry into what I was seeing, pushing at my mind, aggressive. Could they really not feel it? Were they oblivious to the danger they were in?

Let go, or you'll die.

The consciousness ignored me, busy forcing its way into my perceptions like a rat running through an attic, heart creaking with strain. I was going to have to pull myself off the spiral.

Breaking contact with the runes all at once would cut off the invader's access to the vision, but it also meant losing my control of the spell. I had to hope that Brix would realize something was wrong and wipe out the spiral. Otherwise, I might not wake up for weeks, if I ever woke up. In a worst-case scenario, I'd stay unconscious until I starved to death. But if I didn't—

Hells, I thought, annoyed. *This is going to hurt.*

TWO

I fell into the dark for a long time before I found my own throbbing heart, and the pain where my lungs should have been. Even then, when I opened my eyes, what I saw made no sense: there was nothing there.

I sat up and found myself in an entirely white room without walls, or a ceiling, or a floor – like I was hovering at the centre of a white orb. Such rooms don't exist. Ergo, I was either inside someone's illusion spell, or still stuck in my own divination. I didn't think it was the divination, though – my arms were smeared with dried, itchy flecks of pigment, as if someone had wiped out my spell without taking the time to actually wash the paint off.

I was also naked.

'Your spell doesn't even have a floor,' I said, in case I wasn't hallucinating.

Holy saints, a voice said, from beyond the blazing white nothing, a voice I had never heard before.

Not that you can really hear or see when you're inside an illusion. The sense-altering effect of the magic is part of why it's useful for disorientating people. Illusions are the Guild's bread and butter, the way they 'handle' prisoners for the king. Jaliseth had said the Guild was watching her, so I was probably in a normal cell in a

Guildhouse's stinking nether regions, awaiting a trial that would end with the removal of my tongue.

The question was how I had got there.

I pulled myself to my feet and kicked. My foot bounced off a spot in the air in front of me, like someone had made a jar of cold, elastic glass and plopped me inside it. The bounce caused a tiny jolt of pain. That meant that regardless of what I was seeing, in reality I was probably in a runic prison circle. Whoever had written it apparently didn't know how to alter temperature, though. I was freezing.

'You could have just searched my clothes for spells instead of taking them,' I said. 'Where am I? What happened?'

No answer. I kicked towards the spot again and watched my bare foot bounce, sorting through my own mind with growing panic. I'd had spells go wrong before, but never badly enough to make a blank in my head. Had Brix and Jaliseth been captured? I should have some memory of being picked up by the Guild, if that was who was holding me. I should know whether Brix and Jaliseth were safe. How had a divination spell caused this kind of damage?

'Am I under arrest?' I said, and waited until the silence got irritating. I kicked the edge of the spell again, hard.

'Stop that.' This was a voice I could hear with my ears, versus feeling it twang on the air like a lute string. Someone had pulled the illusion spell back a little. We were progressing. 'Yes, you're under arrest, if you're awake enough to understand me.'

'I make it a policy not to understand when I'm arrested,' I said, 'and I'm disinclined to cooperate unless I get some trousers. Who are you, where am I, and where are the women I was with?'

'I'll ask the questions.' The voice sounded male, and exhausted. 'You gave us enough problems that you're lucky to be waking up at all.'

I glanced down at myself. They'd left me my amulet, but nothing else. Something was going on, and it was even more disturbing than a regular arrest would have been. I folded my arms, which didn't help me feel less naked at all, and tried again. 'Look, I'm tired, and cold, and you've proved to yourself that I don't have any spells scribed on my skin, so can we just get me some trousers and get going? I'd rather not waste more time breaking the illusion.'

'You're not in a position to make demands,' he said. 'We'll do it this way.'

At the moment, he had a point. I couldn't cast unless I could break the illusion. Only a murderer throws spells into the dark. I turned in a slow circle. Visual illusions are fairly fragile, if the subject knows that they're being fed one. 'I'm not going to answer questions when I can't see you,' I said, hoping he'd answer and let me pinpoint his location.

'You will when you get hungry enough.' He was to my right.

'You're just going to leave me in a prison circle until I get peckish?' I scanned the floor near the sound. He would have left himself a thin place in the spell, an easy way for him to see me. 'I'm a little disappointed. Your predecessors threatened to break bones.'

'Well,' he said, dryly. 'My predecessors wound up dead, so it would seem foolish to emulate them. What makes you think you're in a prison circle?'

'The way I can kick and connect with thin air.' There. It was almost imperceptible, just a ripple of white on white, like the flicker of a candle flame seen through a window. I took a couple of steps towards the ripple, which grew into a narrow, dark line. I concentrated on it and forced my mind to accept that it was real, not the white room. Breaking illusions is uncomfortable, pulling your eyes out of focus, but it can be done if you're stubborn. I managed to keep my attention steady until the line widened and I could see through it, like a tear in a curtain, to a tiny portion of a flagstone floor. A bitter, alchemical scent simmered into the air.

Footsteps scrabbled on stone. He was backing up. 'What the hells are you doing?'

The illusion shattered and the white orb vanished. Instead, I stood in an entirely normal room with stone floors, a massive wooden workbench and several high, narrow windows spilling late daylight. Shelves and skinny tables lined the walls, stuffed with papers and clay jars of reagents. A Guild laboratory, then, which was a point in my favour. I had been expecting a cell.

I was still naked, though.

The speaker stood some six feet from me, looking disconcerted and a little annoyed. He was somewhere in his early thirties, with dark hair, a shadowy hint of a beard and eyes of an ambiguous light colour. A silver licence sigil gleamed on his left wrist. He was a Guild wizard, then, albeit without robes and the tell-tale curve in his upper spine that would have marked him as a scholar. That, and his tan, made me think he was a field officer or enforcer of some kind. He had the look of someone who would excel at arresting granny apothecaries for selling contraceptive philtres.

He blinked. 'How—'

'See?' I pointed at the floor, where a twelve-foot circle of glowing greenish-gold runes had been painted around me by someone who evidently wasn't thinking through the possibilities very well. 'Prison circle. Can I have my clothes?'

'We're still examining them to find out how you're running that damned persistent illusion.' He swept his hand in an arc that encompassed my whole body. 'If you were hoping to pretend to be someone else, there's no point. I divined to locate you in the first place, and then again with your blood during the arrest.'

'My *blood*?' I said.

'You were passed out on the floor of a shop when we found you,'

15

he said, impatient. 'I could hardly confirm your identity any other way. The point is, you're Corcoran Gray, and we know this isn't what you really look like.'

I didn't have time for this. 'We at least know that I'm not the one with the nudity obsession and the piss-poor scribework. If you won't tell me what happened, how about your name?'

'Dace Craxen, not that that's important,' he said, watching me. 'The women who were with you are under arrest, too, in case that makes a difference in how cooperative you're prepared to be. You've been unconscious for two days. We wanted to move you out of the laboratory after we had examined you, but the younger woman insisted you shouldn't be moved.'

I had been under for *two days*? If I got out of this alive, Brix was going to kill me. What in the hells had happened? I needed to understand, and quickly. 'What am I being charged with?'

'Nothing, at the moment, despite your deviant practices.' Dace spoke with the kind of determined evenness that usually means someone is getting very annoyed. 'The Guild needs information we believe you possess and there isn't time to take you through a normal trial process.'

'Deviant practices?' If Brix and Jaliseth were stuck somewhere inside what I was beginning to fear was a large Guildhouse, then we were in serious trouble. There weren't many options for me. My captors knew my name, which meant they knew what had happened last year. 'Writing a better spiral than you qualifies as deviant?'

'Gods and little saints.' He pinched the bridge of his nose. 'Are you still spell-shot, Master Gray, or are you always like this?'

'Like what?' What in the hells was I going to do? Once I got out of the prison circle I'd have to go out through the doors, since the windows were too high up to reach easily and I didn't know where Brix was. That made the clothing issue even more pressing.

16

'Answering direct questions with other, stupider questions,' Dace said.

I brought my concentration back to him with difficulty. Whether I liked it or not, this self-righteous Guildie was all I had to work with. 'I want to see the women who were arrested with me, and I want clothes.'

'After you answer my questions.'

'If I don't get anything for answering, I don't see why I should.'

'Self-interest,' he said. 'We know everything about you. You're an unlicensed wizard who's stolen numerous pieces of Guild and Temples property and been involved with at least one necromancer. You travel with an escaped slave, whose contract is still held by various ecclesiastical offices. There have been fatalities connected with you. I could go on, but I think that's enough to make the point.'

I found my name among the sinuous runes that formed the prison circle, which explained why my foot had been bouncing off space earlier. With the circle keyed to me, I couldn't cross the runes nor touch them to wipe them out. Anyone else could, though.

'Don't you have anything to say?' Irritation vibrated in Dace's voice. He took a step towards me. 'I've just accused you of serious crimes.'

'Am I supposed to deny it?' I slid my palm up my own forearm, brushing off the flakes of old paint and thinking about the sigils hidden there, under the skin. It would be a matter of whether I could pronounce them and get out of the room before the fire spread too far. I forced myself to look up. 'So you can torture a confession out of me?'

'The Guild doesn't use torture.'

I tilted my head to one side. 'What would you call letting someone slowly starve in a prison circle, then? Not vigorous enough to qualify?'

'Look.' He bit off the word. 'Can we stop wasting time? I've read the reports about the necromantic debacle in Cor Daddan. All the survivors named you as the one who outmatched both Keir Esras and whoever the wizard was who was pretending to be the god Jaern. Evidently, then, you know something about necromancy. That alone should be enough to silence you and put you in a cell for the rest of your life—'

'He wasn't pretending,' I said.

'—but as it happens, I'm instructed to offer clemency.' He frowned. 'What do you mean, he wasn't pretending?'

'What do you mean, offer clemency?'

'No, damn you, stop it!' He moved closer. 'Answer me!'

'If it makes you feel better,' I said, stepping backwards, 'Jaern wasn't actually a god, just extremely good at necromancy. *That* part was pretending.'

'We don't have the time for this kind of foolishness. Lives are at risk. There has been a murder.' The annoyance in his voice was deepening into fury. 'And you're standing here acting like you think I'm gullible enough to believe you learned necromancy from the Lord of Secrets himself?'

'Of course I didn't,' I said, in my most patronising tone, which is more difficult to achieve while naked than you'd think. 'I don't study necromancy. I don't kill people.'

Indeed, that was what made the spell on my forearm such a tricky option. I couldn't hit him with it or he'd burn like a candle and join my rotating selection of nightmares. I would have to use the shackle-bright variant I carry on the inside of the skin around my navel. It was more difficult to aim, but there would be less chance of accidentally killing him.

'*Thirty* people died that day,' he said. 'Guildmates. Men and women I knew, some of them. That's down to you.' He was wrong, but I wasn't going to correct him. I had to keep goading him, flicking words like a whip.

'Maybe they shouldn't have been so careless.'

'Bastard.' He took another step, hands bunching into fists.

And then he halted, a glimmer of uncertainty crossing his face. He looked down at the toe of his boot, where it had smeared out the runes spelling my name.

'So,' I said.

A shade of colour dropped out of his face. He backed up. 'You're in a building full of two hundred Guild wizards. You can't do anything to me.'

I dragged my heel across the circle, which without my name was now entirely touchable. 'According to you, I'm the bastard who killed thirty people.' I pronounced the runes for the shacklebright spell and waited for it to gather in my hand, a ball of red lightning that made the hair on my arms lift. I stepped over the runes towards him and shrugged. 'It *seems* like I could.'

'I'm telling you to stop, before you make things worse for yourself.' He backed up a few steps towards the workbench, his body turning sideways, presenting a narrower target. At least I didn't have to worry about a spell; if he was going to cast, he'd be doing it now. Instead, he stared at my belly and the rune spiral that glowed on my skin. 'How did you do that?'

There was nothing on the workbench behind him but a few scraps of parchment and a large inkwell, but I still didn't like the way he'd backed straight up to it. Maybe there was a penknife hidden somewhere in the parchment?

'Quit moving, please,' I said.

'Stop this, or—'

'Or you'll hurt me. Yes. The Guild doesn't use torture. I remember.' I took careful aim. Shacklebright is, essentially, like binding and gagging someone with lightning. Hurts, too, which I probably should have felt bad about.

His voice rose. 'Or people will die! The Guild needs your help. I'm offering you a deal.'

I lifted an eyebrow. 'The Guild is asking me for help? You stuff me into a prison circle and sit there spewing threats and accusations because you secretly want a consultation?'

'Just *wait*, damn it!' He pushed up both sleeves, revealing arms covered in elaborate, barely healed wounds. All of the scabs were shaped like letters – initials, I thought. Some looked fresh. I recognised them: mourning cuts, a scarification ritual that wizards only do for their own. Dace had apparently, in the last few weeks, attended a lot of funerals. 'People are dying. Wizards at first, but it's spreading to others. We've got to stop it, and, gods help us, you're the only lead we have. Please, just – just listen to me.'

I had the uneasy sensation that the prick might actually be telling the truth, or at least part of it. Cutting your arms to deceive a prisoner seemed extreme, even for the Guild. But I wasn't going to snuff my spell.

'After what you lot did last year,' I said, 'what makes anyone think I'd trust you as far as I could spit?'

'After what *we* did last year?' In spite of the fear humming through his voice, Dace managed to sound indignant. 'You're Unguild, Master Gray, and a murderer. If we're not acting in good faith, I'm curious why you think we're attempting to bargain at all. You've been unconscious for two days. If I wanted you hurt, you'd be hurt.'

I didn't lower my hand. 'I'm naked. If you wanted to bargain in good faith, you could have left me my clothes and not tossed my friends into a cell. Your kind lie, and think they're upholding the law while they do it.'

'We can talk about this,' he said. Then I saw his foot move, and I let the spell go a split second too late.

He tripped the wire strung between the legs of the table and dove sideways as alarm bells clanged. The ball of lightning smashed into the workbench, shattering the inkwell and sending ink flying. The toxicity from the spell climbed up my spine and into my joints with a low, hot surge of pain.

The doors opened and four other people, these wearing proper Guild robes, burst into the room. Two of them had crossbows, bolts nocked.

'Don't!' Dace flung himself between me and them. 'Don't, he's cooperating!'

'Like the hells he is,' I said.

Dace turned, whip-fast and too close to me. 'Shut up.' He was panting, but had regained his calm. A spatter of blue ink shone, still wet, on his jaw. 'You want to see your friends?' There was no hesitation in his voice. 'Cooperate, and I'll take you to them, and see that they aren't charged. I can even promise the escapee legal, valid freedom papers. Refuse, and I'll charge them with every Charter violation I can find.' His eyes didn't drop. 'And I'll also let *my* friends shoot you. Do we have a bargain?'

I didn't like the chances of getting another incantation out of my mouth before the Guildies shot me, and Dace seemed entirely untroubled by the prospect of watching me bleed out on the flagstones.

'When you put it that way,' I said, 'apparently, we do.'

THREE

Three of the armed Guildies left after they produced my clothes, thoroughly picked over. They had even slashed the lining of my coat, presumably looking for spells scribed on the inside of the fabric. I fingered the tear. 'You didn't have to ruin my things like this.'

'You're dangerous. We can't take risks.' Dace stood by while I dressed and didn't take his weird, light-coloured eyes off me. In another man, I might have mistaken this for lust. As it was, I recognised his scowl as professional frustration. 'You're going to tell me how you did it,' he said, at last. 'Casting without having runes scribed.'

'After you take me to my friends.' All that mattered was getting to Brix. And Jaliseth, too, who was probably frightened to death and furious with me. This whole thing was starting to feel like more than just a pain in the backside.

'Very well.' Dace opened the door and gestured me through it. 'You first, if you please, in case Nyree has to use the crossbow.'

Outside was a dank hallway, all stone walls and gritty floors and the sharp smell of alchemical paint, which argued for a Guildhouse of some size. There was also a creeping stink that I couldn't quite identify, but then I had a fair bit of magic toxicity running through my veins and my senses weren't giving me accurate information. Dace must not have bothered to wipe out his illusion spell, wherever it was scribed. Even though I'd broken it, I could still feel the magic

pulling at me, trying to recapture my perceptions. It was like walking in a bog and constantly getting your boots stuck in the mud.
Every few steps my vision flickered in and out, blank white periodi-
cally replacing the dark corridor.

Dace and Nyree herded me along in an awkward procession until
we reached a double-barred wooden door with a stronger stench
seeping around it. The unsmiling man standing beside it paid no
attention to us beyond fondling the long knife that hung at his
waist. He wasn't dressed like a wizard. He looked more like a mer-
cenary, or even Royal Police. I slowed.

'No.' Dace shoved me forwards. 'Not here. I didn't let them put her
in with them, a kindness you can thank me for later. She's three
doors down.'

'In with whom?' I said.

'Shall I shoot him?' said Nyree.

I started walking again, but I wondered whether she actually
would have. Given the list of crimes they believed I had committed,
why hadn't Dace bound me? A bit of knowledge shouldn't have been
enough; they could have used magic to crack my memories and
extract the information they were looking for. Cracking me would
have left me mindblown, though, and a mindblown person is almost
not a person at all – just a warm, empty body, with no personality or
wit. They wanted me for something more complicated. They wanted
me thinking. That realisation should have been reassuring, but it
wasn't.

We halted just before the hall reached a broad downward staircase, in front of an unguarded door. Dace drew a key from his pocket,
unlocked it and swung it open. Once again, he waited for me to go
first.

The room I entered was lush with the scents of parchment, leather and ink. Low shelves ran along the walls, crammed with folios,
scrolls and the odd, bound codex. There was a writing table and a

chair and a worn, leather-covered settee under the window, where the light would fall advantageously for reading.

'Brix?' I said, doubtfully. 'Jaliseth?'

'Saints, Gray,' Brix said, from behind the door. She slipped around it, one hand clutching a heavy book. 'Are you all right?'

It took a moment to reassure myself she was all right. She seemed rumpled, but unhurt, and *solid*, from the top of her blonde head down to the delicate blue tattoos that crossed her feet just above her toes, like sandal straps. 'Corcoran,' she said, and I realised I had been staring, trying to pierce the echoes of spoiled magic that kept falling across my vision like a particularly annoying bit of cobweb. Brix frowned. 'You're spell-shot.'

'Yes. A little. It's not—' The significance of the way she was holding the book, knuckles white against her tawny skin, finally dawned on me. 'Did they try to hurt you? Where's Jaliseth?'

'Not yet. And I haven't seen Jaliseth since they picked us up.' Her eyes flicked to Dace. 'Have they told you what's going on?'

'I'm employed, sort of,' I said. 'Assisting the Guild with their enquiries, so they don't shoot me.' I glanced around. 'What is this place?'

Dace made an irritated gesture and Nyree and her crossbow went back out into the hallway. He shut the door and then stood there with his hand on the latch. 'The lapidary is being held separately, but quite comfortably. This is my office.'

'For an office it's awfully close to the cells,' I said.

'They aren't cells,' he said. 'They're normal administrative rooms that had to be repurposed during an emergency. Have I answered enough questions to be getting on with things, or are we going to have problems?'

'No.' I rubbed at my eyes again. Brix was right. Dace's failed illusion was bothering my eyes, but I was mostly feeling the toxicity of my pointless shacklebright spell. This was why I hated using Jaern's spells – he hadn't included anything so mundane as shielding runes in the pattern of his incantations. They were extremely effective, but intensely poisonous.

'He needs to lie down,' Brix said.

Dace pointed to the settee. 'He can sit.'

I sat, then slid down until I was on my back, my head throbbing. It only helped a little. Dace was talking, not that I could understand what he was saying. The sound felt like ants, frantic and more overwhelming than even the nausea whirling in the pit of my stomach. I was going to have to risk speaking, despite a vague feeling that the sound of the words would split me in half.

'You haven't even told me what I'm supposed to do,' I said.

Sure enough, my own voice sliced through my head, sending ripples of agony swarming into the tight places of my sinuses. But at least he went silent. I pried one eyelid open.

He was scowling at me. After a moment I realised he was puzzled. 'You're . . . you are spell-shot, aren't you? You're not pretending.'

'I told you he needed to rest,' Brix snapped.

'But it was just shacklebright, and he has you . . .' Dace's voice trailed off, embarrassed, which meant he knew Brix was Tirnaal.

Everyone who handles magic has to deal with toxicity and the possibility of death. Some, like Jaliseth, absorbed so much of it over such long periods of time that their bodies could no longer clear the toxicity naturally during sleep. If a wizard doesn't use shielding runes, there are only two ways to keep from killing yourself with your own spells. You can sharply limit the number of incantations you do in a day, or you can use a Tirnaal person to dump the poison into. Tirnaal absorb magic toxicity and, by some quirk of their bloodlines, don't feel pain. Instead, they lose the solidity of their bodies, go ghostly like djinn or wraiths – which is what led to the legend that somewhere in the misty past they were sired by liaisons between djinn and humanity. Pour enough poison into a Tirnaal person and their bodies become so unreal that they can be compressed into a bottle. Convenient for the bastard wizard who wants to carry a person around in his pocket; miserable for the Tirnaal.

Given that the Tirnaal ability to absorb and deflect magic toxicity provided the engine of a major portion of the slave trade, the fact that Brix didn't have proof of freedom did not exactly make our lives easier. We'd been operating with forged papers for nine months.

'Rather obviously it's not the same kind of shacklebright you'd write.' I forced myself to squint so I could at least attempt to look him in the eye. 'And some of us don't cheat by dumping our toxicity on innocent people.'

He flushed, but ignored the insult. 'And when did you write it, precisely?'

I shrugged. 'I use a flesh-coloured alchemical paint sometimes. I had it scribed back at the shop where you arrested us. You just didn't notice it when you stripped me.' This was not a terribly convincing lie. There's no such thing as flesh-coloured alchemical paint, at least not paint the colour of my flesh. Still, the Guild has all sorts of ridiculous legends about unlicensed wizards, and I was betting that Dace would accept the idea of odd paint more easily than *actually, Jaern wrote the spell. I just carry the latent runes under my skin and puke when I have to use them.* For all people say they believe in the gods, tell them anything new about a given deity and they treat you like you're crazy.

Dace pinched the bridge of his nose. 'I don't have time for you to be spell-shot, Master Gray.'

'Gods, it's *just Gray*,' I said, from my back. 'If you don't have time for me to sleep off this toxicity, you shouldn't have thrown shitty illusion spells at me.'

Dace turned to Brix. 'What exactly are you to each other, then? Tirnaal don't practise magic, so you're not his apprentice. If he doesn't use your toxicity absorption—'

Brix picked up one of my wrists, her fingers cool against my pulse. A rush of well-being flooded the centre of me, my vision clearing, poison leaving my veins, pain vanishing as completely as if it had simply been rinsed off. I grunted, but couldn't quite bring myself to twist away.

'Dammit, Brix,' I muttered. She was supposed to warn me before she did that.

'*He* doesn't,' Brix said, to Dace. 'Sometimes *I* choose to. The rest of it isn't your business. Now, since you're so almighty anxious to talk, talk.'

But he didn't at first, watching as I sat up. Brix remained standing and rested her hand on my shoulder, the weight of it real, and warm, and safe.

Dace leaned against the door, his forehead wrinkling as he tried to make sense of us. 'I'm instructed to offer clemency to Mas−' He broke off, correcting himself. 'To *Gray*. You'll forgive me. I'm trying to decide where to begin.' Another silence built and went by, while he picked at a scab that showed just beneath his cuff. Abruptly, I remembered the cuts on his arms, the names. 'About three months ago, we lost everyone at one of our Guildhouses in Ten Rivers to what we initially thought was some kind of poisoning. Mushrooms, tainted water. We couldn't think of anything else that could kill fifty people so quickly.' He crossed his arms, a gesture that didn't quite obscure the fine tremble starting in his hands. 'But then it happened again, to another Guildhouse, eighty miles away. It's happened several times since, always Guildhouses with Tirnaal servants. Wizards catch this sickness, start coughing and are shortly dead. Follow so far?' He paused, as if he believed I might not. Which, I supposed, came of dealing with Guildies all day.

'Wizards dropping like rain, yes,' I said. 'But I don't see what that has to do with us.'

'I've read the reports from the Cor Daddan survivors.' His eyes lifted.

'They all mentioned two things: you consorting with a Tirnaal woman, and you wearing a distinctive amulet and not dying. It's actually a vial, correct? With a dark liquid inside, and a silver stopper? Clearly magical, or at least alchemical. You're wearing it now.' He nodded towards the silver chain visible at my collar. 'The pattern has been the same in each town. The plague starts with two or three people in a Guildhouse.' Dace pointed at the floor with one hand, as if pinning the infected Guildhouse on a map. 'No one knows where the amulets come from. They just appear, in use as plague charms. Amulets that are almost exactly like yours.'

A sour taste started in the back of my mouth. I swallowed it down. I got the feeling that Dace expected some sort of denial, but I wasn't even sure what I was being accused of. A systematic catalogue of the spells written into my body was difficult – I had managed to learn some because I'd watched Jaern cast them, back when the god had inhabited this body. Others I had found accidentally, when I scribed them with paint and discovered a portion of my skin lighting up as I pronounced them. I had seen Jaern use the amulet, too, but it had been quiet the whole time I'd owned it, as if its magic died with the god.

'Why does the existence of these amulets matter?' I said.

'At first some of us dismissed them as superstition,' Dace said. 'Or the kind of charlatan "cures" you always see with disease outbreaks. We assumed the amulets came after the illness, and the people who used them did seem to keep well, at least for a while. But a couple of weeks later, they weren't in their right minds. They were hostile, forgetful, paranoid. And then . . .' He paused, swallowing. 'They died anyway.'

'And it's all wizards who are getting sick?' Brix said. 'You're telling me that a plague selects people to infect based on their profession?'

'There is some speculation that it's not so much the plague that's selecting people.' Dace was still watching me, like a cat with a bird.

'In Varriel the amulets were here before the first death. Because
Gray's was the first amulet of this sort that we had heard of, some
believe he made the thing, somehow planted the plague. That you're
both part of a plot to exact revenge on the Guild by murdering us,
inch by inch.'

I straightened. 'You believe we're causing a plague? With
jewellery?'

'Some of my colleagues believe that.' Dace shrugged, a motion
halfway between apology and impatience. 'I didn't say I agreed with
the notion.'

'Thanks,' I said, warily. 'I think.'

A wry smile crossed his face. 'I don't exactly believe you're innocent, either. Your . . . *talents* are well-documented. I've been tracking
you for almost a year. Your background doesn't support random
action. If you were going to kill us, I think you'd choose a method
less scattershot and unsure.' He paused. 'Which is why I argued for
allowing you the chance to cooperate, instead of hauling you to
judgement straightaway.'

'You can't sort out your own mess, so you need Gray's wits.'
Brix's fingers tightened so far into the meat of my shoulder that
they hurt.

'You've summed it up admirably.' Dace's eyes were steady.

'Lovely,' I said. 'What in the windy hells makes you think I *can*
help?'

'Because you have to.' Dace crossed the floor. 'The plague is here,
in Varriel. We've kept the deaths as quiet as we can, but it's spreading. Quarantine isn't helping – that room we passed is a dormitory
full of twenty people, all of them coughing up red strings that used
to be lungs. Two weeks ago, we discovered that the amulets were
spreading in town. Two days ago, in what is entirely too convenient to be a coincidence, my divining finally located you: visiting
Varriel.' He jabbed a finger into my chest, stabbing at the lump that

showed where my pendant hung against my breastbone. He wasn't gentle. 'You're wearing an amulet like the suspect ones. You're not dead. So you know something we don't, which means you can help.'

I pushed his hand away. I needed time to think about this, and I didn't have any. You couldn't package a plague in an object. Even if you could, and even if it was plausible for Jaliseth to be involved in a mass murder plot, why would she ask me to divine my way into the middle of it?

'And if we refuse?' I said. It seemed like a logical question, even though I thought I knew the answer.

Dace stepped backwards. 'In that case, I haul you before a tribunal and you both stand trial with me testifying against you. Combined with the deaths already to your account, it would be enough for execution, I should think.'

Every Guildie I had ever met had, on some level, been afraid of me. Dace wasn't. I tried to decide how he'd respond to the truth. *I died last year in Cor Daddan. I still have the nightmares. My amulet just came with the body, I don't know how to use it and I don't have the faintest idea how your damn plague works.* Yes. That would just about ensure I'd spend the rest of my abbreviated life scrubbing Guild floors without a tongue.

'Say we were going to help,' I said slowly, feeling my way into a plan. Whatever happened, Brix and I had to get away from that room and out from under Dace's eye. 'What would you want us to do?'

His shoulders relaxed, almost imperceptibly. 'Us?'

'Me, Brix and Jaliseth,' I said. 'It's us, or nothing.'

'Yes, the mention of Madam Jaliseth brings up another point,' Dace said. 'What were you doing at the lapidary's?'

'Trading,' I said. 'Jaliseth doesn't know I'm unlicensed.' If Jaliseth hadn't admitted she knew who she was dealing with, then the Guild didn't have proof she'd done anything illegal and would have to release her. I hoped.

'And what were you trading for?' Dace said, patiently.

'Wardstones. She wanted a spell done for the barter.'

'Indeed?' Dace said.

'Yes, I am aware that it's illegal for Unguild to trade in wardstones,' I said, relieved that he hadn't asked what kind of stones. I still needed some way to silence myself before I could sleep – it was either that or make a big enough fuss to get them to lock me up separately from Brix, where I couldn't do any damage. 'But, like I said, Jaliseth doesn't know I'm not licensed. You don't have to –'

'They took Jaliseth,' Brix interrupted.

'I've been tracking Gray for months. That you went straight to the house we already suspected of being one source of amulets in Varriel . . .' Dace shrugged.

'The shadow illusions,' I said. 'They *were* the Guild spying on her, weren't they? I thought they probably belonged to a cheap knifepoint thief, trying to drum up victims. Why do you think Jaliseth has anything to do with spreading amulets?'

Dace flinched a little at *cheap knifepoint thief*, but went on. 'When we raided the place, it seemed sensible to arrest everyone there. A search of the house this morning turned up only a few legally questionable carvings and a locked door hidden in a storage closet – a warded door, in fact. Which begs the question of who wrote the wards, and why.'

He was trying to back me into a corner – either accuse Jaliseth or admit to writing the wards myself. Neither was true, of course; Jaliseth was a specialist, not a wizard. I had no idea what she had behind her rune-carved door or who she had traded with to place the wards, but that didn't matter. I didn't think Dace was lying, which meant that Brix and I had a chance at a way out.

'Well, that's simple, then,' I said, ignoring the sharp look Brix gave me. 'I'll open the door for you.'

Dace's eyebrows lifted. 'I'd be satisfied to know the ward key, thanks.'

'I won't know which key to try until I've seen the spell.' I kept my gaze steady. 'I use different rune sets than the ones the Guild sanctions. It'll be a lot faster if you just take me there and let me open it.' All of which was, of course, a lie. But I was gambling that Dace wouldn't have mentioned the thing if the Guild hadn't been trying, and failing, to get the door open for the last two days. As I watched his brow furrow, I knew I was right. 'So I do this for you,' I said, 'and then you let Jaliseth and Brix go. Is it a bargain?'

The Guild officer seemed to be struggling with himself. 'Yes,' he said, finally. 'The Roys have been riding my heels for the last eighteen hours and we need to get into that door. But I do need to take appropriate precautions.'

'Precautions?' I didn't like the sound of the word. The Guild's idea of reasonable care could include anything from admonishment to shackles.

'Among other things, Brix will be accompanying us. I don't intend to let either of you roam about outside my personal supervision.' Dace's eyes travelled up and down my body. 'Do you have pierced ears?'

'Yes.' I also had a pierced nose, for that matter – one of many modifications that Jaern had seen fit to make in the body that I now occupied. I was relatively certain that the dead god had made the change for adornment. Dace had more practical purposes in mind. From one of the desk drawers he produced a tiny, engraved pewter ring, which he proceeded to clasp in my left ear.

'A tracker,' Brix said, her nose wrinkling with distaste.

'Of course.' Dace fitted an identical earring into his own ear, and pronounced a low incantation. The spell curled around me like a corset.

'The Guild thinks I'll run away,' I said, fingering my new jewellery. A tracker ring is really only useful if it doesn't have to be activated very often – magic fatigues metal over time until it breaks. Trackers are also more effective if your subject doesn't know the somewhat obscure incantation to remove them. 'They want a way to catch me and bring me back to stand trial so they can hang me.'

'They,' Dace said, 'are not idiots. Come on.'

FOUR

On our way out of the Guildhouse, Dace collected Nyree from one of the common rooms we passed. Now that I could see her more clearly, she looked very young indeed; I would have mistaken her for an apprentice without the looping journeyman's embroidery in cobalt blue on the edges of her sleeves. She was still awkwardly carrying a crossbow with a bolt nocked. 'Guildlord Trist has been in to talk to all of us, asking if anyone has plague symptoms. She says the prisoner is infected, and—'

'If he is, he's putting on a very good show of health.' Dace pointed at me. 'Walk behind him. If he begins to cast or tries to run, shoot him.'

Nyree nodded and positioned herself behind me with anxious determination.

'Don't shoot me *unless* I run or cast, if you please.' I was suddenly doubtful about this whole situation. If Dace trusted us so little, did it really make sense for him to remove us from a secure location just to open a door? 'Where's Jaliseth?'

'She'll stay in our custody until the terms of your service are met. There are limits to how far I can meddle with the Charter without ending up Unguild like you.' Dace led us through layers of dark, flagstone-floored passageways. We met nobody else before we turned through a small, narrow door and found ourselves out in the street again.

I glanced back at the building we had exited and halted, impressed in spite of myself. I had known that we were in a large Guildhouse, but I hadn't anticipated finding myself in *the* Guildhouse, the oldest and most important one ever built. The Grand Guildhouse of the Royal Mages' Guild stood five storeys tall, in mixed brick and reddish stone, its significance evident in the king's coat of arms displayed above the door. Most of the upper windows were filled with oiled parchment, but two long, skinny ones facing the street glowed with stained glass bearing the insignia of dead Guildlords. It lacked the carvings on the façade that ecclesiastical buildings would have boasted, but made up for it with heavy ward sigils cut into the huge double doors that were the main entrance. Brix halted beside me, but she wasn't staring at the building.

A highly decorated, rune-carved gibbet stood between the Guildhouse and the broad part of the street. There were no bodies at the moment, but the gibbet wasn't merely symbolic – the ragged gang of crows sitting on the crossarm of the gallows told me as much.

I forced confidence into my voice. 'If they were going to hang me, I think I'd be on it already.'

She glanced at me. 'You don't really believe that, so don't say it. It doesn't help.'

'Keep moving, if you don't mind,' Dace said. 'Our time is not unlimited.'

Brix and I followed him, and behind us walked Nyree and her crossbow. Dace may have been of two minds about whether I was responsible for unleashing a plague; Nyree clearly wasn't. As we made our way back to Jaliseth's house, she watched me like I was a foam-mouthed dog.

A bored officer of the Royal Police stood beside another young wizard at Jaliseth's front door. The wizard wore journeyman's embroidery, but the line of apprentice's cross-stitch at the bottom of his sleeves hadn't even faded to pale blue yet. When he saw Dace, palpable relief flashed across his face.

'Any trouble?' Dace said.

The journeyman shook his head. 'No, sir. But there is a' – he glanced at the Roy, uncertain – 'smell.'

Indeed, the stench seeping from the house was robust and instantly recognisable. If the journeyman hadn't ever smelled it before, he'd lived a sheltered life. Dace turned to the wizard. 'You can go home, but talk to no one outside the general staff, understood?'

The journeyman nodded, swallowed hard, and set off back the way we'd come.

'I take it this is the Guild's idea of safe prisoner transport?' The Roy eyed Nyree and her crossbow with distaste. 'We could have sent you a couple of lads.'

'And yet we managed to stumble here without an escape,' Dace said coldly. 'You lot say the door has to be opened, here the prisoner is to open it. If you'd unlock the house, please, Lieutenant Trath?'

Trath turned to the door, pulled a key from his pocket and unlocked it. Inside, we all stood in a clump in front of Jaliseth's shining wares, trying not to vomit. The stench sat in the room like a live thing, although I supposed *live* wasn't exactly the right word for it.

There, on the floor, was a pinkish smear where I'd scribed my divining spiral. Dace, who had an odd, fidgety air of discomfort, picked up a half-finished chunk of jade from the nearest shelf. It was the delicate piece of work I'd noticed earlier, the bust of a lovely, rune-chased young man. 'Listen, before we go further, there's something you should know.'

'We Unguild call that an aphrodisiac spell,' I said. 'Costly, for the magical equivalent of getting yourself and your partner very drunk, but some people like the art of it, and the superstition is that jade makes it more effective.'

'I know what it is. That's not what I'm talking about.' Dace put the carving down. 'There's been a death.'

'Yes, we can smell as much for ourselves,' I said, trying to force my voice to stay even.

'What happened?' Brix had one hand over her nose. 'What did you do?'

'We didn't do anything to anyone,' Dace snapped. 'The Royal Police found a storeroom in the back, and a closet, and they believe there's a body inside. I'm trying to warn you that the contents of the closet might be unsettling. Going by the smell, whoever it is has been rotting for a while.'

Behind me, Nyree gave a heaving lurch, turned and ran outside retching, the door swinging behind her.

Trath stared after her with a grim smile. 'The other two lads are guarding your unsettling closet, Examiner. If we could get going?'

Examiner. It was the first time I had heard Dace's title. 'You work for the Examiner General?'

'We really don't have time to educate you on the internal workings of the general staff.' Dace gestured towards the only interior door, like the interruption hadn't happened. 'If you please? I want your opinion.'

'I thought we were supposed to be here to open a door,' Brix said, leaning against one of the crowded shelves. 'I don't know why we are looking at dead bodies.'

'I don't know, either.' Trath folded his arms. 'I don't know what good the Guild is if they don't know enough about magic to explain a magic murder. At this rate I suppose we'll have the priestesses in here, too, to check for divine vengeance before they let us determine whether anyone is even dead.'

'You'll be telling me everything you do as you deactivate this ward.' Dace pointedly addressed me, ignoring the Roy. 'I don't truck

37

with unsanctioned incantations, but it's my business to understand them.' His voice took on a hint of malice. 'After you.'

Dace had a positive affection for making me precede him into rooms. I strode into the back room and halted, overwhelmed. This wasn't the first time I'd smelled a dead body, but this was somehow worse than even a two-day-rotted corpse should be, mingled with some other bitter, earthy smell. There was no body to be seen. Instead there was just a tidy bedroom, with the narrow bed in the corner still made up and clothes hung neatly on their pegs. In one corner was another door, standing open and revealing more shelves stuffed full of chunks of unpolished rock – the storeroom. The only thing out of place was the stench.

I forced myself to take a couple of steps inside, to notice things. I had been hoping for something like a door leading to an outdoor privy – any kind of a way out that wasn't being guarded by Royal Police or a puking Guildie with a crossbow. There was a window, its shutters thrown wide to let fresh air into the room. The chances that Brix and I could get through it before someone killed us weren't good. There were two more Roys in here, one on either side of the storeroom entrance. Inside the storeroom, in the dust and cobwebs and hulking pieces of stone, was the warded closet door.

'Well?' said Lieutenant Trath, behind me, impatient. 'Do you need special tools or something to get started?'

Even from here I could see the wards on the door weren't going to be simple to break. At least my nose seemed to be going numb.

'The door.' Trath planted his palm between my shoulder blades and tried to push me forwards. I didn't move, and he grunted, startled. Sometimes the strength that Jaern put into the muscle and bone of this body came in handy.

'Don't shove me,' I said, sweetly.

Trath stared at me for a moment, his hand creeping towards the hilt of his short sword. 'Kirra,' he said. 'Lin.' The other two Roys straightened, alert.

'He's not threatening anyone,' Brix said, beside me, in what I recognised as her most threatening tone. Her fingers plucked at my sleeve. 'He just doesn't want to be shoved. Come on, Gray.'

Which was, I suppose, her way of saying *don't start a fight, you idiot, there's three of them.*

The Roys watched uncertainly as Brix and I moved towards the closet. I stood in front of it and studied the runes hacked into an untidy spiral on its surface. The ward shimmered silver, active, hungry. I touched the nearest rune and a jolt of electric pain shot through my fingers. I shook out my hand and considered. The runes were rendered without much skill, but the construction of the spell itself was intricate, old-fashioned. Scorched places on the wood testified to the Guild's failed attempts to break the ward by force, which was typical, because what this needed was finesse. I looked over my shoulder at Dace. 'Can I have paint, then, or a pencil?'

'Explain first.' Dace carried a small reagent bag slung across his body. He didn't approach me, but he touched the bag protectively. 'Why can't you just deactivate it?'

'Nonstandard incantation, I think you'd call it,' I said, as blandly as I could. 'I can break it for you, if you'll give me a pencil.' Of course, if I had a pencil, I could scribe other things, as well.

'Go on, then,' said Trath.

Dace shook his head. 'Lieutenant,' he said, 'I don't think you appreciate exactly how dangerous this prisoner is. Last year—'

'You lot have been trying to open this closet for eighteen hours and getting nothing but sore fingers for your trouble,' Trath growled. 'I have my orders, and I'm telling you to give him what he needs. If he's as dangerous as you say, what do you care if he burns on the wards?' He drew his sword. 'Besides, I'll be standing by to make sure he doesn't get tricky.'

Dace's jaw worked, but he crossed the floor and gave me the pencil. 'I want this back.'

'Noted.' I started scribing a half-circle of runes around each of the door's hinges and the latch. It took me longer to finish than I'd have liked; it's difficult to maintain your concentration when a Guildie is staring over your shoulder and a Roy is standing ready to open up your belly. 'Now I need to cast,' I said, to Dace. 'Tell him not to kill me, please?'

Dace frowned, studying my runes. 'That doesn't make any sense. They don't even interact with the main spiral.'

'You told me to open the door,' I said, 'not break the wards. This will open it. My runes don't need to interact with the main spiral. You can see that they're not going to hurt anyone, yes?'

'Well, yes.' He was still scowling, inching towards me. 'But I don't see—'

I was tired of this. I extended both hands and pronounced the runes.

They came to life, searing their way into the wood. The colour of the magic in that particular breaker is dark green, but the heat it causes quickly makes the runes look red. The counterforce ran through my wrists and tumbled me backwards against Dace, who tangled awkwardly with me.

Snap. Snap. Snap.

The sharp scent of woodsmoke and hot metal overlaid the reek of old blood. The door hung as it was for a couple of seconds, then tilted drunkenly and fell towards us, hinges and latch sheared in half.

I looked at Dace, who was more or less holding me in his arms. 'Hello.'

'Get off!' He shoved me away and stepped backwards, brushing at his clothes as though I might have infected him with unsanctioned incantations. 'Those wards weren't keyed to you. You didn't even place them, did you? How in the hells did you break them?'

'An ironbiter breaker.' I straightened. 'A dangerously illegal spell that makes it so you don't have to uncouple a ward. Instead, you break the unwarded hinges. You're welcome.'

Brix had been quiet throughout this entire business. I kept my gaze on Dace, not wanting to risk turning my head and reminding him to look for her. Out of the corner of my eye, I watched her move closer to the window. I had to keep the Roys and Dace focused on the closet I had just opened and give her a chance to slip over the sill.

Except that it wasn't a closet.

Instead of the shelves full of special carvings or chests of money I had expected, there was nothing but a hole in the floor and a narrow set of stairs leading downwards.

Well, that and the intensification of the death smell. The stench leaped out at us, as if it had been crouched in the closet, waiting to be released. I coughed, eyes watering, and fell back a couple of steps in spite of myself.

'I thought so.' Trath studied the stairs with a satisfied expression. 'I knew there had to be more to this business than another plague death.' He gestured to the other two, his eyes roaming the room and catching me, Brix and Dace. 'Lin. Kirra. Bring them.'

'Why?' I said. One of the Roys took my arm while the other started towards Brix. Our chance of escape was evaporating. The last thing I wanted was to be stuck in some cellar. What on earth had Jaliseth been mixed up with?

'Because you seem to know more than this one.' Trath jerked a thumb towards Dace. 'And I want to know if magic killed whoever is rotting down there.'

'It would be better to take precautions.' Dace folded his arms. 'There could be other wards.'

Trath pointed with his sword at Brix. 'Very well. You first, then.'

I moved forwards, opening my mouth to protest, but Brix shook her elbow free of Lin's grip and lifted her chin. She grabbed my hand

and led me as we picked our way down the narrow wooden stairs. 'Let me go ahead of you,' I said. 'I know what to look for.'

'You always know everything, don't you?' she muttered. 'Shut up and think of a way to avoid that gallows back at the Guildhouse, please.'

At the foot of the stairs was a narrow cellar that must have, at one time, been a place to store wine or potatoes. Now it held nothing but a burned-out candle, a long table, and, barely visible in the faint light from upstairs – a corpse.

'Gods,' Brix said beside me, unsteadily. 'He's *sticky*.'

The man, who seemed to be wearing the remnants of a Royal Police tunic, was indeed sticky, and starting to bloat. The corpse lay stretched on the table, his chin and open mouth haloed with a weird pinkish luminescence, eyes staring. An amulet like the one Jaliseth had given me to divine with was around his neck, resting on his breastbone, glimmering through his shredded shirt. He must have been hurt at some point, because a line of stitches ran along an old wound on his wrist. There was so much blood that at first I thought his throat had been cut. He had actually haemorrhaged from his mouth and nose – and for all I knew, from other orifices as well; he was lying in a puddle that had congealed to a thick, chunky shadow.

Brix glanced at me. 'Are you going to be sick?'

I swallowed hard. It wasn't just the corpse and the fact that I had thought the word *orifices*, though those were bad enough. There was something almost familiar about the situation. Something about the waxy cast of the dead man's skin, some odour lingering underneath the grand, overwhelming putrescence of decay. I knew that smell, deep in the visceral part of me. It was the stink of magic gone bad.

'Who would do something like this?' Brix muttered. 'I think *I'm* going to be sick.'

Sweat had collected at my hairline and now a bead of it rolled down my neck, clammy, too cold. I turned, panting, half-blind with fear. Brix's hand closed on my wrist.

'Corcoran, stop.' Her voice was quiet, excessively so, and she was using the name I don't like. It got my attention, like touching a horse with a heel. In Brix's mouth, I usually find it endearing. Just at that moment I resented it like hells.

'Don't tell me to calm down,' I said. 'I've seen this before, Brix. Hells, I've smelled it before. It's like—' I bit the words off. Talking was counterproductive. Brix knew what had happened last year and how broken I was, and against all the odds she was still with me. But I couldn't stand there in the stink and risk losing control of myself. 'Let me go,' I said. 'Please, Brix.'

'They'll kill us if we charge up the stairs without permission,' Brix whispered. 'Get them down here and we might have a chance to get out while they're distracted.'

'What is it?' called Trath impatiently, down the steps.

'A plague body.' Even to myself I sounded strained and unpleasant. 'One of yours, I think – Royal Police. No traps, but there's not a lot of room down here, so can we get out, please?'

'One of *theirs*?' Dace came down the stairs and halted when he was still two steps from the bottom. 'You're sure?'

'Don't believe me if you don't want to.' I pointed at the body. 'But he's obviously coughed himself to death, and he's wearing an amulet.' I paused, but Brix and I needed out of that place, and nothing but the truth would serve. 'Jaliseth had me divine with one like this.'

'Why?' he said.

'Because,' I said, trying to keep my voice level, 'she didn't know where it came from and she was afraid. My point is that it's like the ones you're worried about, right?'

'Like the one you're wearing,' Dace said.

I very much doubted that. The metal case of Jaern's amulet was silver and it didn't have engraving visible anywhere on it.

43

The amulet Jaliseth had given me to divine with had been a cheap tin thing crawling with a pattern, albeit an illegible one under its heavy coat of tarnish. This, I thought, was yet a third, and was pewter by the look of it. Gods, I hated this.

'Stop talking jargon.' Trath shouldered his way past Dace and then stopped, blanching, when he saw the corpse. 'That's . . . that's Cellyth. He's been missing for a week. So this *is* a magic murder?'

'Of sorts. This is something new. That pink glow around his mouth – that's a late-stage plague symptom.' Dace moved down off the steps and paused, rifling through his bag. He found a pencil, scrawled runes on the inside of one wrist and cast illumination, sending a sickly blue flame to flicker near the cobwebby ceiling.

'Can we go?' I repeated. If worst came to worst, I could use some of Jaern's spells to get us out of there, but they would render me sick and useless. I hated using Jaern's spells – they reminded me of him, and they reminded me that I was dangerous.

'What's the matter with his hand?' Brix said.

She was more observant than I was. The palm of the corpse's hand had been cut. I hadn't noticed it at first because the cut was filled with some kind of growth. It looked hard, like coral or bone or –

'Crystals?' I said. A cluster of small, lavender spikes protruded from the cut in the dead man's palm, growing like the crystals at the heart of a geode. As I watched, a new one formed on the dried track of blood on his wrist. Two of the crystals had fallen out of the cluster and tumbled into the puddle he was lying in, perfectly formed obelisks.

'It would seem so.' The blue flame flickering above Dace's head lit up the cellar, revealing not only the grotesque details of the corpse but the items on the workbench.

Arranged neatly to one side of the body was a set of sharp-edged rock carving tools. One of them, however, was obviously a scalpel, and there was also a spool of thick black thread. Trath picked up a chisel and gingerly pushed the tear in the corpse's shirt open.

The amulet rested on his breastbone. On the pallid flesh around it spiralled a network of what had once been carefully scribed runes. They must have been active for a long time before they'd burned out, because the alchemical paint used to scribe them had eaten lesions into the corpse's skin. 'What's it done to him?' Anger glittered in Trath's voice. 'What *is* this thing?'

'The same sort of thing that's been killing wizards, though we haven't seen one fuse to flesh before.' Dace studied me, impassive. 'We need to find a way to retrieve and identify that amulet. If Gray managed to divine with it once . . .'

'That's not the same amulet,' I said. 'Jaliseth's was tin and tarnished black. And I'm still waiting to go upstairs.'

'You're not leaving this cellar.' Trath's flat voice cut through the dank air. 'Nobody is, not until someone can tell me what killed Cellyth.' He drew his dagger and in another instant was standing beside me, the point hovering at the level of my liver. 'Retrieve it. *Now.*'

'No need to get pushy.' I edged away from the blade, though there wasn't far to go. Brix stood on my other side, close enough that her quick, anxious breath rasped in my ear. Beyond her Dace blocked the exit, arms crossed.

I turned my attention to the amulet. Between the bad light and the decayed condition of the runes, it was difficult to tell what the spiral had been meant to achieve in the first place. The jewellery seemed to be stuck to the corpse's flesh, so maybe the runes had been some way of binding it to him, similar to the incantation Dace had used to affix the tracker earring to me. I squinted and began to count the runes under my breath.

'But it's wrong,' I muttered. 'It doesn't even look like a spell. The runes that haven't eaten themselves are religious, Temples stuff. It should be possible to just . . . lift it off.'

'Then *get it*,' Trath said, prodding me with the knife.

'I am. Get that thing out of my ribs.' I reached towards the amulet.

'No,' Brix said suddenly, her eyes fixed on the half-gone runes. '*No!*' She moved before I could react, shoving my hand aside just before my fingertips could brush the metal. Her sleeve caught on the pendant and yanked it free of the corpse's chest with a horrible tearing sound. The runes that had surrounded it surged to life, glowing violet.

The amulet whirred, its pewter setting opening up into four delicate claws that let it climb Brix's sleeve like a spider, runes blazing along its metal limbs. She shrieked, jerking backwards.

'Drop it!' I shouted, which was useless because *of course* Brix dropped it, slapping the wicked little thing off her arm even as Trath lunged across the table towards her. I suppose the poor fool thought we were trying to destroy evidence.

The amulet hit the workbench with a bright *ting!* like a bell. It should have bounced, or, failing that, shattered and spilled its fluid. It should not have skittered across the workbench until it found the closest hand – that of the appalled Trath. It should not have climbed his arm, while he screamed, and burrowed under his shirt.

It sure as the hells should not have exploded.

FIVE

When you're terrified enough that time slows, that's a gift. You have a few heartbeats to watch yourself choose. My gift was a moment while the trap spell chewed into Trath's belly.

Run, or cast?

I could run, but I didn't know how long we had to get up the stairs. The magic growing in Trath's wound was green, reaching upwards and out from the gash in him like a flower, petals unfolding. The air in my lungs crisped and sizzled, and I watched the flower quiver. It almost seemed to pause.

Cast.

The trap spell threw tendrils into the air, reaching for us as I shouted the incantation under the skin at the base of my neck, the one I knew would wreck me. The pain hooked into my throat. I turned, wrapped my arms around Brix and Dace, and dropped the three of us to the ground just as the tendrils found us.

The explosion thudded and squeezed around us. I heard a scream and belatedly remembered the other two officers in the bedroom above. But I couldn't think about them for long; maintaining the thin, glistening shell of magic took every dram of concentration I could muster.

An icy, sharp-toothed ache spread over me. I'm not sure how long we crouched in our fragile refuge. It was probably only a matter of seconds before a high, whistling tone started in my ears and I knew I was within inches of losing consciousness again.

The poison of the spell was much more intense than it should have been, almost as if it was being multiplied or reflected. *This* was what had happened before, what had made the toxicity strong enough to knock me out of my divination. This time, I had the wit not to double down and hang on to the magic. If I kept the reflection spell running I'd black out, and Brix would have to drag me up the stairs. I forced myself to let the spell fade. Dust tickled my nostrils. I lifted my elbow and felt Dace get up. The dome around us flickered, flexed and tore.

I cringed, waiting for another wave of force to throw me against a wall. It didn't.

Brix took her time standing. Dace darted across the room to the fallen Roy lieutenant. I think he had in mind to try to help, though what good he thought he could do for a man who'd nearly been sheared in half by magic I don't know.

I staggered to my feet. Then the toxicity hit me, and I bent double and puked. My stomach hurt.

Gods, my *teeth* hurt.

'What in the hells . . .' Dace stared at me.

I stayed bent over for a while, swallowing bitter strings of spittle and trying not to retch again while fiery poison flooded my veins. It's not something you get over, living in a body that isn't yours. At times like this I missed my old self intensely, even the skinny, inadequate frame, even the lame knee. I hadn't exactly been normal then, but at least I hadn't been dangerous, walking around with magic stuck under my skin that even I couldn't stand to be near. Doing Jaern's magic without his blessing had its price.

Brix laid a hand between my shoulder blades. 'Hells to pay doing reflection without shielding runes, isn't there? I thought you said—'

'Annoying,' I said, while the blood pounded in and out of my ears.

'But all I could think of. And something is amplifying the toxicity in here, so don't touch me, please.' When I did unshielded magic, the poison it created curled through my veins, gave me headaches, slipped like a parasite into my gut. If I kept going it would loosen my joints, leave lesions on my arms and hands. Over enough time it would damage my eyes, too, ruin my voice, kill me. I had been asking the question too much lately, but I couldn't keep from peering towards Brix. 'Are you all right?'

'No.' She was breathing hard, her left hand tucked against her body, blood dripping from the series of cuts where the amulet had clawed her.

I finally got control of the dry heaves enough to straighten and try to make sense of the situation. The stairs had survived, and the stone walls. The workbench still stood, but the body had been reduced to sludge. Everything was covered in a fine, scarlet splattering of gore, and I realised, slowly, that someone was chanting. I twisted on my heel. 'Wait. Listen—'

'Stand still or I'll put you on the ground.' Dace was watching me, a ball of green light gleaming between his knuckles. It was tetany, one of the spells I hated most. 'A man has just died. I want to understand what's going on, *now*. You didn't have anything scribed. I know you didn't.'

My head was spinning so merrily that I couldn't think of anything better to say than: 'You do not know that.'

'Yes, I do,' Dace hissed. 'Magic doesn't just appear out of nowhere. I—'

'Gray just saved our lives, you idiot.' Brix pointed towards the shattered, stinking remains on the ground. 'You've had us in custody for the last two days. How do you think we could have set something like that up?' She snorted. 'Plague, indeed. Plagues don't leave hexes behind. They sure as the hells don't explode.' She paused, then glanced at me. 'It *is* called a hex, right? Heavy warding with intent to maim—'

'You know it is,' I said. 'Your terminology is better than mine, sometimes. We should make sure that the trap sigil written on that amulet didn't release anything that could have caught the Roys upstairs, or Nyree outside.'

'Damn,' Dace said, softly, glancing at the stairs. 'Why didn't they come down to see what the sound was?'

An uncomfortable silence fell, all of us simultaneously realising that the Roys were probably dead.

'Do you think there's any more danger inherent in the amulet?' Dace said, carefully. Talking about technicalities wasn't going to make me forget that my odds of overpowering him with magic had just significantly improved.

I took a deep breath. 'Whoever set the trap couldn't have known that I would have a reflection spell prepared. It doesn't make sense wasting your time writing two hexes, especially on something that's going to be blown apart.' I paused. 'It has been blown apart, hasn't it?'

'No.' Dace extended one foot towards the heap of blood and bone on the floor and nudged a glimmering chunk with the toe of his boot, separating it from the rest of the mess. The amulet looked more or less intact, if inert – its delicate limbs folded back into the case, once again an innocent piece of alchemical jewellery. It had survived the blast unscarred, which meant that the spell that had been used to make the hex had to be one with an affinity for human flesh, not just blind force.

'Jaliseth didn't do this,' I said.

'I see.' His voice was icy. 'There must be another explanation, then. She just kidnapped a Roy a week ago, stuck an amulet on him and warded him into a cellar for non-murder purposes. Gods, he must have been lying here dead when we arrested you.'

'No, or we would have smelled him then. I mean I can't see how Jaliseth *could* do any of this.' Toxicity rippled through my belly again, cramping. I forced myself to breathe through it. 'Even if she was the sort of person to kidnap Roys, she's unmagicked. Can't pronounce half the runes she carves. She's *afraid* of magic, for the gods' sake.'

'So she learned,' Dace said. 'I need to know why.'

'Then it seems foolish to be standing around in the muck asking us things instead of her.' Brix moved to brush a lock of hair out of her eyes, then grimaced at the sight of her own dust-and-blood-smeared fingers and turned to Dace instead. 'Look, do we really not know anything about how whatever this is spreads? Has there been contact between the sick and the well in any of these Guildhouses? A trader, a message sent from one to the other, anything? You said there were always Tirnaal servants.'

'But the Grand Guildhouse doesn't use Tirnaal,' Dace said. 'The amulets are the only real commonality. That, and, until now, the profession of the sick. But this man was not a wizard. It's getting worse, and this proves it's not accidental. Someone is spreading these amulets and starting outbreaks wilfully, in multiple locations. And you're right about one thing: it can't have *only* been the lapidary. She's never left Varriel in her life. We've checked.' His attention shifted to me. 'You were able to divine with a plague amulet before we arrested you. Do you think you could do it again?'

A jolt of distaste shot through me. 'Why?'

'I want to know where it came from.'

'Jaliseth said she bought it from a travelling potion-man,' I said.

'Yes, she told us as much, although she couldn't explain why there was more than one amulet in Varriel. And she couldn't explain where the potion-man got it from. Said she couldn't *remember*, if you please.' Dace's jaw tightened. 'We need to be *certain*.'

'I think you've got unrealistic expectations about my helpfulness,' I said. 'We've done enough, and we're leaving.'

'I can't let you, of course.' Dace sounded tired. The green tetany spell still curled around his fingers, moving gently like a living thing.

'You don't have a choice.' I considered my options, searching for an incantation I could pronounce before Dace threw his tetany spell and immobilised me. *Fire? Or force?* 'You're alone, and you're outmatched. Say I threatened you, if you need an excuse. Blame the deaths on me – it won't make my record any worse than it already is.'

'You're not understanding me.' Dace wasn't looking at me anymore, staring instead at Brix. 'I think we're beyond that, now.'

I didn't want to hurt him, but I had no intention of letting myself or Brix be dragged back to that obscenely decorated gibbet. We'd have to think of some way to help Jaliseth when we were free. *Force, then.*

I swallowed, and took aim. 'Step aside, Dace.'

He didn't move. 'Undoubtedly whatever method you have for scribing spells without me seeing is very powerful, which probably means that you could kill me if you like.' He nodded towards the smear that had once been Trath. 'In every Guildhouse we've found one decayed like this – though I will admit nobody had witnessed the precise, explosive nature of the decay before. It is a plague, albeit not a natural one, and it's spreading. The point is, now you have a personal reason to help us.'

'I don't follow,' I said, although I instantly, sickeningly, did. There had been that pewter claw reaching out from the plague amulet, towards Brix's hand. There was the weird, electric feel on the air, that crisp almost-burning smell that meant thunderstorms, and pressure, and trouble. There was the blood.

'One of us,' Dace said, 'touched the amulet while it was still active – while it was still dripping, in fact.'

Brix looked down at the still-oozing claw marks in her skin, the lines of her shoulders tightening like a bowstring. 'Are you saying—'

'I'm saying that you most likely have a few days, a couple of weeks at the most, before you start showing symptoms,' Dace said, quietly. 'Most people are dead in three days once the cough starts. I think this thing can be stopped. But we have to move quickly.'

Brix's lips pressed together. 'How quickly?'

'He's lying.' I took a convulsive step towards Dace. 'Like Guild spelldogs always lie. You can't threaten us with that damn gibbet anymore, so now you're saying Brix has the plague. Gods, and you have the gall to lecture me about ethics? Even if Brix was infected, how can we possibly know that rushing around doing what the Guild wants will stop anything?'

'You don't,' Dace said. 'I don't either, really. But I know that people don't survive it by staying home and using healing herbs. If it was someone I cared about, I would want to try, at least.'

'No,' I said, as if repeating the word could keep the sickness away and silence the rattling panic threatening to burst its way out of my chest. Dace was lying, and if he wasn't lying, he was wrong. He had to be. I wasn't going to watch Brix cough her lungs to pieces. It wasn't going to happen. I wasn't going to *let* it happen. '*No,*' I said, between my teeth.

'Corcoran,' Brix said. 'Listen.' She put a hand on my sleeve.

If I listened, I would have to believe it. I'd have to accept that we were cornered, standing there in that stinking charnel. I'd have to think about Brix coughing. Suffering. Smothering. I shook my head. 'You want to *accept* this?'

Worry, frustration and calculation chased each other across her face. 'If we leave,' she said, 'what's your plan for when the whole Guild starts hunting us in earnest? We could get this bounty off our backs forever. I could get my freedom papers.'

'None of that is our major concern just now,' I said, more harshly than I meant to. 'If you're really sick—'

Her hand clenched into a fist. 'If I am, then it's my decision, isn't it?'

The words landed like a punch. My eyes stung. I blinked, hard.

'All right.' I turned to Dace. 'But we have to figure out how to transport that thing, if you want me to divine with it. I'm not doing it here.'

53

Dace's shoulders loosened. The green light around his fingers faded. 'I'll carry it. If it activates again, I'll be the one it hits.' He took a handkerchief from his pocket, bent and picked up the inert amulet between his thumb and forefinger. 'I have enough ethics for that, at any rate.'

The Roys in the room above us were not, as it happened, dead, although they had been thrown against the wall hard enough to have the wind knocked out of them, and one had hit his head and was dazed like a stunned bird. Nyree was already there when we emerged from the cellar, shakily trying to help Lin and Kirra to their feet, her crossbow abandoned in one corner. Dace satisfied himself that she wasn't hurt, then gave terse instructions that amounted to him locking the house and all of us wandering back to the Guildhouse in a gruesome, bloodstained row.

Our arrival didn't go unremarked. Standing in the courtyard was a knot of wizards arguing with each other, in spite of the shadow of the gallows that should have squelched all talk. When they saw us, the group broke up and surged forwards, eddying like leaves on a river. The young journeyman that Dace had dismissed earlier was among them.

'Damn,' Dace muttered. He reached backwards and grabbed my sleeve at the same time I felt Brix's grip latch on to my elbow. In short order we were hemmed in on all sides and Dace was dragging Brix and me towards the building. The crowd parted to let us through. Hostile eyes followed our every move, but instead of shouts all I heard were the whispers: *Necromancer. Poison. Killer.*

'What—' I said.

'Don't. Speak.' Dace didn't let go of my sleeve. He stalked forwards until he could confront the journeyman we had seen before. 'Parr? What's the meaning of this?'

The journeyman didn't seem able to meet Dace's eyes. 'I'm sorry, sir. Guildlord Trist was here when I got back, and she ordered me to tell her where I'd been.'

'We'll discuss your interpretation of discretion later,' Dace said. 'Nyree has two Royal Police officers with her that need to be taken to Farran-temple for medical attention. Go with them and help. Now.'

Parr slipped away, his ears bright scarlet, and Dace led us into the building and back through the warren of passageways to his office. It was, in the failing light of the afternoon, a rather miserable little room. The hearth was cold, and a lad half-heartedly poked a broom at the floor in one corner.

'What in the hells is going on?' Brix demanded. 'You said you wanted to bring us back here for Gray to divine. What was that mess outside?'

Dace ignored her, crooking a finger at the sweeping lad. 'Can you please take a message to the Guildlords that we've returned?'

'Brix asked you a question.' I watched the boy leave, new apprehension leaping in my gut. Having Guildlords interested in you was never, ever a good development. 'And why do the Guildlords care that we're back? Is this a trial?'

'If it was a trial, you'd be silenced. The rest of it isn't your business.' Dace slipped his bag of reagents off his shoulder and spilled the contents on to the desk, including the handkerchief-wrapped amulet. 'Come on, quickly. We won't have long before the Guildlords arrive, and I want to have something more to tell them than my conjectures about exploding corpses.'

'Then why send someone to get them?' I glanced at the door, where the boy had disappeared.

Dace blew air out of his nose, a bit like an irritated horse. 'Because they already know we're back, thanks to Parr, and I have no wish to be accused of collaborating with or hiding you. Some of the Guild-lords still believe you're responsible for this whole business.'

'Meanwhile I'm not convinced that you disagree with them,' I said. 'Answer Brix's question.'

'Gods, I just said we're short on time.' He met Brix's eyes. 'Very well, since you insist: Valera Trist is one of the Guildlords. She's a traditionalist. Believes only Varriel-educated wizards should be pro-moted to the rank I currently occupy. I am not Varriel-educated. There was, therefore, disagreement about my recommendation that we offer clemency to you. There is an argument being made for a more rigorous enforcement of the rules. That "mess" outside – as you put it – was the result of her interfering with my staff.'

'You talk like a gods-damned royal proclamation,' Brix said. '*An argument being made*, like arguments make themselves.'

'However I talk,' Dace said stiffly, 'I'm the one that's against split-ting Gray's wits open and simply extracting whatever it is he knows. Jaliseth, who is the only other person of interest in Varriel, is talking a lot of paranoid nonsense about the Guild moving her things around and damaging her memory. Now we've found a body in her cellar. Valera isn't going to be impressed by your insistence that Jaliseth didn't put it there. She'll ask the council to use . . . traditional inter-rogation methods.'

'The Guild doesn't use torture, I thought,' I said.

His jaw tightened. 'As long as I'm deciding, they don't. But I'm not the only one with authority over this investigation. Either we pro-duce some evidence that the amulets came from outside Varriel, or it will be difficult to argue that we shouldn't crack the wits of every-one involved.' He gestured to the items on the desk. 'So can we get started on the divination? What do you need?'

I needed answers. Arguing wasn't getting me anywhere. I had to know if Brix was really at risk of getting sick, and where the damn amulet had come from. I had to know how it was connected to the one that hung around my own neck, inert. I scanned the reagents and tools on the table, trying not to get distracted by how expensive most of them were. 'I want a . . . plate, or a bowl, or . . .' I took an unlit candle off the flat plate that it had been standing on. 'Can I use this? And red paint with pyrite in it. Do you have any?'

'Of course.' Dace handed me a tiny clay jar of paint and a brush. 'But why? Red paint isn't used for–'

'I'm *thinking*,' I muttered. 'Let me think.'

I shoved the items to one side of the desk and picked up the amulet gingerly with the handkerchief. I put it in the candle dish and began to scribe on the wood around it. If Brix's health and our freedom depended on figuring out the provenance of an amulet that had already killed two people, I had to be smarter than last time. Divination wasn't going to work. 'You just want to know where they're coming from, right?'

'Yes, but what are you doing?' Dace loomed over my left shoulder – or rather, beside my left shoulder. I always forget that I'm taller than I used to be.

'Little saints. And here I thought that Guild wizards were good at identifying spells on sight.' There was something in Brix's voice under the easy courage, a worried note that plucked at my own fears. The last time she'd made a bargain with the Guild it hadn't worked out well. I wished there was a way for me to let her know that I hadn't forgotten. But I couldn't see a way forwards that didn't involve cooperating with Dace. I had to find some way to get an inch of breathing room, the tiny sliver of opportunity we'd need to escape.

'That's a nonstandard incantation,' Dace hissed.

'I know.' I forced my voice to stay calm. 'I assume that's why you wanted the Unguild scum to be the one to write it. You can look at the runes and see for yourself I'm not going to set you on fire or make myself invisible, so relax.' I started counting again.

'You can't make people invisible,' Dace said.

Gods and little *saints*. I didn't have time to explain and, anyway, Acarius and I had invented that incantation. The Guild didn't need to know about it. I pointed my brush at him. 'Right, you can't. Good catch. Shut up.' I started over, counting for the third time. Dace fidgeted, but managed to keep quiet until I finished. If there was a flaw in the spell, I couldn't find it. I worked hard to keep my voice steady. 'May I cast, then?'

'No.' He hadn't taken his eyes off my spiral. 'That's not a divination spell.'

'I know,' I said again, trying to bite back my frustration. 'Last time divining with an amulet nearly broke my mind and landed me in a prison circle, and all I got for my trouble was a vision of a dead woman. No location. Nothing helpful.'

'Dead woman.' Dace glanced up sharply. 'What dead woman?'

'She was wearing one of these amulets, in a casket, full of some kind of liquid. I assume she was another plague victim.' I pushed my hair out of my eyes. 'Listen, this amulet was probably damaged, at least a little, in the explosion, right? If we can get the vial open, examining whatever's inside might provide some clue as to how it works or where it came from.'

'Yes, we're not completely dull-witted.' Dace shifted his weight impatiently. 'We've confiscated some from the sick and tried opening them, with a hammer and chisel. They're not—'

'They break the chisel and you can't get at the fluid inside,' I said. 'Because what's holding it together isn't the metal and glass itself, it's got to be an incantation. Like what you have on this.' I touched my earring.

'We're not blind, either,' Dace said. 'Why do you think we wouldn't have found any runes on the amulets by now?'

'Because the Guild took a whole year to find *me*,' I snapped. 'Logically, the incantation has to be there, even if you can't see it. It's scratched on the inside of the glass, or written between the case and the bottle, or any number of other illegal places. I don't know why it isn't behaving like a normal spell and fatiguing the metal. It could be something in the incantation. It could be something alchemical. The only way to find out is to open the damn thing up. I'm going to break the static sequence holding the bottle together. Then you can analyse the incantation, and your alchemists can look at the fluid. And then all of you can conclude that Jaliseth, Brix and I had nothing to do with these murders, and let us go.'

'That . . . could work,' Dace said slowly. 'But it's a risk.'

'You're the one who says you'll hang us if I don't help.' I put my hands on either side of the spiral and positioned my thumbs to overlap two specific characters. I exhaled; it came out shaky. What if the thing amplified the toxicity again, knocked me back into the dark? What if, gods forbid, I dreamed?

'Gray,' Brix said. 'It's all right. You don't have to do this.'

But, of course, I did.

The runes in the spiral lit as I pronounced them, one by one. More importantly, the pewter case of the amulet began to glow like someone had held it over the fire in a forge. For just a heartbeat the magic resisted me, and then, with a low *snap*, the bottle that formed the heart of the vial tumbled loose of its case, its neck broken through.

Brix sucked in her breath.

I jerked my hands away from the runes. A strange, acrid smell filled the room as the black fluid from the bottle formed a small puddle on the candle dish. It was much more viscous than I had expected, seeping out of the break in the glass like old honey. As I watched, a cluster of small purple crystals was revealed, pulsing gently inside the bottle. And the inside of the pewter case was scored with marks, hair-like in their fineness. It *was* a spell, its runes written in miniature. They were damaged, though, battered enough by the explosion that I couldn't make out what sort of incantation they had been.

'There,' I said. 'I don't know what the fluid is, but—'

'It's drin.' Tension rippled under the matter-of-fact surface of Brix's tone.

'What did you say?' Dace's head snapped around.

'Drin. It's a drug. I recognise the smell, from when I used to walk past the vats where they cooked it. It's only made in Genereth.' An unfamiliar expression danced across Brix's face, a pain that wasn't quite sorrow or regret. With a jolt, I recognised it. Standing in the middle of a Guildhouse, with blood still stuck to our shoes, my partner was *homesick*. 'I was born there.'

'I see.' Dace's complexion had taken on a faint greenish tinge. He spoke with perfect, polished, fake calm. 'A folk medicine, isn't it? I wouldn't have thought it had alchemical properties.'

'Is anybody going to tell me why this is important?' I said, trying to watch them both at the same time. There was something going on that I didn't understand. Genereth was a city to the south, where Brix and her sister had lived when they were small children. Beyond that and its reputation as a destination for religious pilgrims, I didn't know much about it. 'Does this mean we go amulet-hunting in Genereth?'

'You don't—' Dace took a deep breath and stepped back from the desk. 'It's plausible. Genereth is a week's ride from here, but it's only about thirty miles from where the first deaths were. And the runes on the corpse, back in the cellar. They weren't a spell.'

'They were a *prayer*.' Brix's voice vibrated with fury. 'A Generethi *prayer* to Ranara, a Temples ward. You recognised them, too? And you were just going to stand there and let Gray touch the bloody thing and call down judgement on himself?'

'Bastard,' I said. 'You weren't planning on letting us go at all, were you?'

'Keep your voice down. I can't go to Genereth.' Dace seemed to catch himself. '*You* can't go to Genereth, not unless I can find some way—'

'That's why you were in such a gods-damned hurry.' Brix took a step towards him, her jaw clenching. 'You never cared about Jaliseth, or Gray. It was just another spelldog lie, another excuse to take and use somebody else's magic. And now you get to look brilliant in front of the Guildlords, and we get to rot in a cell, and—'

'No,' Dace said. 'That's not—'

A peremptory knock sounded on the door to the passageway. It sprang open and a knot of people all burst into the room at once.

There were only five of them, but it seemed like more because they had been arguing before the door opened. Once they noticed me and Brix, they went silent, some of them mid-sentence, staring. They all wore the heavily embroidered dark blue robes of senior wizards.

'What is *he* doing here?' one of them said, eventually – a woman with short dark hair, hazel eyes and an intense, bony face like a stork. Under her disgusted inspection, I felt a little like a frog.

'This involves him.' Dace had drawn himself up, straightening his spine and lifting his chin. 'It seemed appropriate to have him here to answer any questions. Did you want to sit down, Valera?'

'No,' Stork Lady said. 'Our business won't take that long to conclude, I trust.' The other wizards had sidled into the room by this point, most of them ignoring Brix and me. Dace glanced at me and gestured towards the leather settee with a hand that tremored, just a little. I hesitated. None of this felt right – what *was* I doing here? For that matter, what was Dace doing at a meeting of the Guildlords? A field enforcer shouldn't have had the rank necessary.

'Sit,' Dace said, when neither Brix nor I moved. 'You want a way out? You want your lapidary friend to have a way out? This is it.'

Stork Lady – Valera – snorted. 'Since when do road conjurers have friends?'

Road conjurer? That annoyed me and I sat. After a moment, Brix did too.

'Now, my lords.' Dace took one step sideways, putting himself between us and the other wizards. 'Instead of harassing my staff, perhaps you'd like to tell me your objections directly. You'll understand that I am somewhat pressed for time, between dealing with the Unguild and trying to halt a plague.'

'We've just had a report that there were two more deaths today,' said one of the wizards, a fellow with a salt-and-pepper beard and calloused fingertips. 'This thing is getting out of hand, Craxen.'

'This thing has been out of hand for three months,' Dace said. 'But yes, there were two more deaths. We were lucky that there weren't five, including me.' He paused. '*Lucky* is perhaps inaccurate. Gray managed to keep a hex from harming us with an unsanctioned incantation.'

Valera crossed her arms. 'Unlicensed wizards know how to protect themselves from their own foul spells? An unlikely flash of fortune, indeed. I had hoped you were holding an emergency meeting to discuss strategy. I take it you don't have any new information, and you just called us here to inform us about the murders.'

'On the contrary.' Dace's voice was like ice. 'We've got good indications that the amulets originated in Genereth.'

'Good indications?' This wizard was younger, skinny, with smears of alchemical paint on her sleeves. 'From what?'

Dace stepped sideways and swept a hand towards the desk. 'From examining the contents of the amulet that caused the deaths. Crystals that the alchemists will need to examine, and what is certainly drin – a honey-based narcotic that is only made in Genereth.'

Valera's lips compressed. 'Have you gone mad enough that you let this maniac cast?'

Dace turned towards Valera. 'Guildlord Trist, are you questioning my competence?'

'No, my lord. Your record is quite good.' Valera rearranged her embroidered sleeves – intricate stuff, the kind of work that would have kept a tailor stitching for a month. 'For a wizard who studied so provincially.'

'Then,' he said, evenly, 'it must be my loyalty to the Guild that troubles you?'

Valera flushed. The other Guildlords all seemed a bit bored with the turn the conversation had taken. Dace's loyalty was apparently something that was not in doubt.

'You misunderstand me,' she said. 'I am only concerned about the effect on the Guild's reputation if we allow all sorts of unsanctioned magic to be done in our presence, by all sorts of . . .' She glared at me. 'People.'

'The prisoner opened one of the plague amulets. We couldn't do as much, not without unacceptable risk to Guild lives.' Dace seemed to gather himself. 'Which is why I think he should come with me when I travel to investigate in Genereth.'

Beside me, Brix tensed. 'What?'

'Out of the question.' Valera quivered with disgust, resembling an annoyed stork more than ever. 'This man works outside the Charter. Dancing Farran, you're admitting as much. If we let him do that under our authority, what's to stop the throne from considering the Guild itself outside the Charter? What's to stop us from being counted as Unguild? What's to prevent a war?'

'Well, all of you,' I said.

The room, which had been full of muttered side conversations and sighs, went dead silent. Apparently, I hadn't been supposed to speak.

'Nobody's going to mistake me for Guild,' I said. 'If I do anything that you'd rather disavow, all you have to do is claim that you were transporting me, and then give me up to the Royal Police as a rogue wizard that you were trying to bring to justice.' I looked at Dace. 'That's the idea, isn't it? You get the benefit of my skills, but you also keep deniability.'

His odd, pale eyes met mine, steady. 'Yes.'

'Do I understand,' said an elderly male wizard, 'that you want to assist this investigation? Why should we trust you?'

'You don't have to trust me.' I stood, and touched the tracker in my ear. 'Add another one of these, or tie me to you with an ankle hobble if it makes you feel better. Whatever you want, but you're taking me and Brix. People are dying. We're not waiting around here for weeks for some operative to send word about a possible cure. Hang me afterwards, if you have to.'

'They won't hang you,' Dace said, with a dry sort of amusement that didn't really match this conversation. 'The Examiner General would have to recommend execution, and unless you commit some particularly heinous crime in front of him, he won't.'

'That does not fill me with certainty,' I said. 'The last time I met him, Keir Esras tried to take my heart out with a pair of shears.'

'Keir Esras is no longer the Examiner General,' Dace said. 'He was found guilty of at least four murders and hanged.'

I frowned. I knew I had been isolated at the cabin and distracted with my own problems, but apparently I was *very* far behind on trade gossip. 'Then who's the Examiner General now?'

'I am.' Dace pointed. 'Sit down.'

A thin rope of fear like ice threaded itself through my chest. That meant that Dace's entire purpose was running down people like me, silencing us, putting us on a gallows. 'No,' I said. 'I want some assurance that the Guild isn't going to go back on its bargain.'

He crossed the floor quickly until we were nose to nose. 'I said *sit down.*'

The ring in my ear sent a jolt of tingling, electric, terrible pain down the side of my neck and into my arm and leg. Before I really knew what I was doing, I had collapsed back on to the settee. I only just managed not to writhe. When the hideous sensation faded, I saw Dace watching me, calculating. The rest of the council was staring at me with wide, impressed eyes. Brix was reaching towards me.

'I'm all right,' I croaked, twisting away before she could touch me and absorb the pain. 'Dace is just a prick. This damn earring isn't a tracker, it's a regulator.'

'Yes.' Dace ignored Brix's indignant cry, and turned to Valera. 'A regulator – a provincial tool for prisoner transport you may have heard of.' A polite but pointed note of challenge rang in his voice. 'Corcoran Gray is *useful*. With the regulator spell running I don't anticipate having trouble. Elias Thane has been in Genereth for the last three weeks testifying regarding the accidental death that occurred there – he's the best alchemist I know of, and he should have a chance to interrogate them both. You can't disagree that Gray is worth more this way than he would be after extraction, particularly since it would leave him mindblown.'

'Then we should get this business in Genereth over with promptly,' said the wizard standing behind Valera, holding his hand up formally. 'So voted.'

The vote went around the room like an unpleasant draft of cold air. For people who disliked unsanctioned incantations so much, they were very anxious to use mine. In the end only Valera stood opposed.

'I still think the council will regret it.' Valera shrugged. 'I suppose it's your neck, Examiner.'

Dace shook his head. 'It's his neck. And hers.'

After the meeting broke up, Dace had us locked into a 'guest' room – mostly empty and only marginally nicer than a cell. A tiny guttering oil lamp lit up the plain stone walls and a small rope bed shoved into the corner, barely wide enough for two people who didn't mind cuddling. I halted just inside the door as the bolts ground home.

'This was a mistake,' I said. 'I'm sorry, Brix.'

She sighed. 'For what?'

'I never should have allowed us to be brought to this godsforsaken spelldog deathtrap.'

'Windy hells, stop.' She shook her head and eased herself down to sit on the bed. 'Stop apologising for everything. Next you'll tell me that it's too dangerous for you to sleep tonight, and go on making yourself so exhausted that you're useless. It gets tedious.'

I had got used to fatigue dulling my thoughts, but I was never prepared for the way it could make my emotions bounce between fear and anger. '*This* is what we're arguing about? After everything that's happened today?'

'I *know* what happened today.' Her voice buzzed with irritation. 'I'm trying not to think about it until there's something we can do. In the meantime, we can at least get a few hours of sleep in the deathtrap before dawn. Or do we have to argue about that, too? Again?' She drew her knees up to her chest, while the bed underneath her squeaked alarmingly.

'That isn't fair,' I said, through my teeth.

'I wasn't the one who laid down ultimatums.' She rested her chin on her knees. 'You decided, by yourself, that it was get the wardstones or be done with each other – all because you have deemed yourself too hazardous to share my bed. *That* wasn't fair.'

'You aren't the dangerous one,' I said. 'I know what I am, Brix. I'm a made thing, a monster like everything else that Jaern crafted. This amulet I'm wearing, what happened at the cabin, gods, the *fire*–'

'Was an accident,' she hissed. 'Monsters kill people for the pleasure of it, hurt people because it's convenient. That's not you. Don't tell me I'm not dangerous. Don't act like I don't understand. I could be infected with whatever it was that killed that Roy. I could sprout crystals. I could infect you. I could be dying, for the gods' sake, but *I'm* not calling myself names and running away from *you*.' She rummaged in her pocket and proceeded to chuck whatever it was she found at me. '*Fix it!*'

Two small grey stones clattered to the floor at my feet. It took me a moment of staring at them to remember to speak. 'Saints,' I whispered. 'The wardstones. Where—'

'I took them from Jaliseth's.' She wasn't looking at me. 'I saw them sitting there on the shelf while you and Dace were still arguing over that jade thing. Somebody had to do something.' She was shivering, as though she was freezing. Or terrified.

I was terrified, I realised, with a dull throb of surprise. I was terrified enough that if I didn't check myself, in another few heartbeats I would be snapping and clawing like an animal in a snare.

I could be dying.

After the cough started, Dace had said people died in three days.

I picked up the stones and sat down beside her. After a moment she leaned one shoulder against mine. I slid my thumb across the filigree of delicate, pointed sigils that curled across the pewter-coloured rock. The silencing sequence was less toxic on stones than it would be if I painted it, although the stones would eventually wear out. Imperfect solutions were the only ones I had left. I'd managed to work free of gags, fight my way through sedatives – I had done everything I could think of to fix myself, and none of it had worked. I was not, in short, the ideal sort of person to choose as a soothing presence for someone who might be dying.

'It'll work,' she said. 'We'll be okay.'

'I know,' I lied.

We stretched out on the bed together and she pushed the hem of my shirt up, the flat of her palm brushing across my belly. She traced the lines of my ribs with her fingers, watching as my goosebumps and the sigils underneath both rose to meet her touch. 'They saved us. You know that, right? There was no chance to scribe anything in that stinking cellar. If you hadn't been rune-written we would have died.'

'I love you,' I said. 'But please don't make me count my blessings.'

She snorted, but continued the caress. I let myself sink into it for a few seconds, letting my mind empty out. The characters skittered across my flesh, not glowing or active, just . . . following her, like ripples in a pond.

'I still can't quite believe they do that,' she said, softly, breaking the trance. 'It's like magic.'

'*Is* magic,' I murmured, dragging my fingertips along the back of her hand. 'We at least know that.'

'You think it's because I'm Tirnaal?'

'Mm,' I said, because she knew I did, and because analysing the vagaries of Jaern's magic wasn't what I needed to do at that moment. 'About Genereth.' Her hand stopped moving. 'Will you be all right?'

She looked up at me, a slight frown between her eyebrows. 'I was born there.'

'I remember.' It was almost the only thing she'd told me about the city, except for the fact that she and her sister Anka had been kidnapped into slavery when Brix was thirteen. As far as I knew, she hadn't seen her Generethi family since – if they were even still alive. The few times I'd tried to talk to her about it she had been evasive, almost embarrassed.

'And the only question you're asking now is whether I'll be all right?'

'All the other questions seemed . . .' I shrugged, uncomfortable. I didn't know much about Tirnaal society, but I knew they had complicated beliefs about magic and sin. Bringing a wizard partner home might make a family reunion somewhat fraught. What was I supposed to say? *Will your family try to stone me, you think, or just spit at me?*

She grinned. 'Just when I think you've stopped surprising me, here's Corcoran Gray, large as life, trying to be *delicate*.'

Heat rushed up the back of my neck. It wasn't delicacy. It was cowardice. What I wanted was for her to tell me about her family without me having to risk asking, which was so manifestly unreasonable that I stuffed the desire down and forced myself to focus on more immediate concerns. 'Seemed better than bluntly pointing out that you recognised the runes on the corpse. You said it was a prayer.'

'A prayer to Ranara. Yes. It was written on the wall of the building where I grew up. My clan still lives there. If nobody's knocked it down, I could take you there, put your hand on the sigils . . .' She trailed off.

'We could have gone back before now,' I said, before I could think better of it. 'We could have gone to see them, this clan. You must have missed them. You could have . . .' *Trusted me.* I cleared my throat. 'You could have said something to me.'

She was silent for a long time, long enough for me to realise that I'd spent most of the past year having nightmares and making ultimatums. When she spoke, she wasn't looking at me. 'It's different, in Genereth. Most wizards aren't like you, Gray. My clan wouldn't . . .' She stopped, but I knew well enough what the words would have been. *My clan wouldn't understand.* 'I don't know what the prayer means. I don't know whether I'll be all right in Genereth. I don't know about anything.'

She went silent, and I let the quiet pool around us. Maybe if we didn't talk, neither of us would have to feel the fear.

I turned inside her embrace and curled against her, forcing myself to keep awake while I waited for her eyes to shut and her breath to lengthen out. Even afterwards, for a long time I just listened, willed myself to concentrate on the regularity of it. It was steady, strong, just like her. If I didn't let myself think, I could convince myself it was impossible for it to ever stop.

When I was sure that she was asleep I moved carefully away and crossed the room to sit on the floor as far from her as I could get, against the wall. I put a wardstone in each hand, then stuck my fists in my pockets for good measure, so I couldn't drop them. I recited the runes and magic stitched itself into my jaw, clamping my mouth shut.

When it was finished the runes pulsed like cold needles against my palms, and I couldn't even grunt with pain.

It would have to do. I leaned my head against the wall.

The nightmares always ended the same way: the knife, and the pain, and the blood – and then the burning. It made a kind of sense. In real life I had died because I shoved a dagger up under my breastbone. Jaern died because his soul was tied to my life. I was resurrected because Acarius, my grandfather, was a genius who knew enough about necromancy to improvise. My waking mind knew that this was the best outcome you could logically hope for.

My dream-self, on the other hand, would frantically try to find a way to save people, so determined to *not die* that my real self thrashed his way out of bed, screamed in his sleep . . . cast spells. It was breathtakingly dangerous.

And it was pointless. Thirty-two people – and Jaern – died the day I died. Nothing could change that. The problem was the things I had done and not done a year ago. The problem was that Jaern had been a monster, and now I was wearing his rune-written skin, so what did that make me?

I shut my eyes, but for a long time there was only the dark, and the quiet, and the cold weight of Jaern's amulet against my breastbone.

Cold. I was cold?

I slept.

No, she was cold.

Save me, the dead voice whispered. *Your spell could have saved me.*

The nightmares were always the same, but that night the dead woman from the divining was there, among the ones that I couldn't save.

Help us, Moyra said. *Hurry.*

SIX

When Dace had talked about 'a week's ride' I assumed he meant horses, but as it turned out, we charged down to Genereth on a crowded nightmare of a flat-bottomed river boat. We shared its inadequate deck and tiny sleeping cabin with Valera and Dace and six other Guild wizards. I admit that I should have learned their names, but none of them would talk to me, and I was worried about Brix. The trip downriver took eight seasick, hurried days, during which the boat never stopped moving, and it was difficult to find a way to use my wardstones without Dace seeing. The Guild officer never took his damn eyes off me. I didn't sleep all that much.

What sleep I did get was fitful, and risky. On the fourth day out from Varriel I woke in the dark, red flashing behind my eyelids. The bitter edges of a flame spell pressed against my tongue, heady, the terrified rage of it catching me like wine or desire. The sigils on my arm pulsed.

She was dead.

I needed to find the people who were hurting her and burn them. I needed . . .

You divined for her and she was dead.

No. That was the dream.

I was gripping the wardstones so hard that my hands were cramping. The magic in them was thrumming, keeping me quiet. I hadn't

71

cast. Brix was settled between me and the wall, sleep-heavy, her warm skin brushing mine. She wasn't dead. The sigils on my fore-arm stood out sharply, pressing upwards against my flesh – but I hadn't cast.

I forced myself to slow my frantic panting. After too long, I man-aged to release the stones.

She's all right. It's all right. You didn't hurt her.

Trembling and sweat-slick, I listened to the boat creak as it rolled easily against the current of the river. It was all well and good for Brix to cram herself into my bunk to make a point about not being afraid of me. She didn't have to feel this sick, guilty panic.

I disentangled myself cautiously from her body and eased my way up to standing, slipped out the cabin door and made my way on to the deck. There was probably a Guildie on watch and I'd have to deal with their suspicion, but at least the air would be cooler.

When I got outside, however, I didn't see anyone. A breath of wind caught the perspiration on my neck while I stood, listening to the *cloop* of water against the hull and trying to pull my wits away from dreams and back to real life.

The nightmares seemed to grow more vivid with every league we travelled. The dead woman from my vision was always there now, intermixed with memories from last year, begging for help, tighten-ing every panic-noose around my throat, twisting every knife of pain. Half of me believed that I could rest if I could just understand what Moyra was trying to tell me. The other half, more sensible, knew that this was just a deterioration, like someone with a cough taking a turn towards fever. If my dreams kept worsening, I wasn't going to be sane by the time we got to Genereth, let alone able to hunt down the origins of a plague. The wardstones had been the only solution I could think of. If they didn't work–

'You're supposed to be in your bunk,' Dace said.

He rose from where he'd been sitting on a coil of rope in the prow, barefooted with his shirt untucked. Without his tunic he looked like a dark, scruffy-haired boy, tumbled out of bed to feed the chickens. He was palpably ill-at-ease, pupils blown wide and dark in the starlight.

Not ill-at-ease, I realised, startled. *Guilty.* I had caught the Examiner General off-guard.

'I don't sleep well on boats.' I picked my way towards him, trying to work out what Dace would consider shameful. 'Don't worry about it. I'll sit up and keep watch for any catfish that might be contemplating a nonstandard incantation.'

My instinct was wrong, though: he didn't so much as flinch. Whatever he was feeling guilty about, it wasn't fiddling with an illegal spell. He raised a hand to stop me when I was three feet from him.

'Do you sleep?' There was something odd in his voice, an undercurrent of half-repulsed curiosity.

'Yes,' I said. 'I sleep, and eat, and shit, as is the way of entirely normal folk who are not necromancers. May I sit?'

He made an abrupt sound. It was almost a laugh. 'Yes.' He resumed his seat on his coil of rope, still at that careful distance. 'In spite of what you might believe, I'm not a fool. If I thought you were a necromancer, we wouldn't be having this conversation.' He drew up his knees and rested one forearm across them. 'You are an abomination, though, aren't you?'

'Thank you.' I sank down on the deck.

He shook his head. 'I told you, I read the reports about the debacle last year. I admit I was sceptical. Survivors can tend towards exaggeration through no fault of their own.'

A normal Examiner General's duties involved exterminating death-magic and curses. I didn't like where I thought this was going. 'Not being a Guild wizard, I suppose I'm not up to date on what constitutes an abomination.'

'And I suppose this works for you most of the time,' he said softly.

'Talking fast, telling lies and throwing insults to distract people if they don't buy it. But, as I said, I'm not a fool, Gray.'

It occurred to me that Dace might have inconvenient ideas about how abominations should be dealt with. I shifted the position of my shoulders, as if finding a comfortable spot would make the situation less hazardous. 'I don't know what you want from me. I'm not doing anything illegal at the moment. I'm *behaving*.'

'You have to behave, at the moment,' he said, almost amused. 'There's too much at stake for you and your partner.'

I stiffened. 'How—'

He snorted. 'Was it supposed to be a secret? And about that – you'll pardon the familiarity, but how do you have a partner?'

'And what,' I said, 'leads you to think I'll pardon the familiarity?'

He didn't seem rebuked. In fact, he was more relaxed and confident than he had been since I'd met him – almost drunk, not that I could imagine him ever consuming anything stronger than barley-water. 'I'm very good at my work,' he said. 'To do it well, I need to understand exactly what I'm dealing with. The Guild position is that Tirnaal are not constitutionally suited to magical practise. They absorb too much toxicity when they're the ones casting spells, take too long to recover for it to be practical.' He paused. 'And their abilities could be exploited by their teacher.'

'Constitutionally suited.' I snorted. '*Nobody* is constitutionally suited to magic, or it wouldn't hurt so much to cast.'

'Wizards don't generally marry,' he said, declining the change in subject. 'It's the work, the toxic residue the spells leave on us, the fertility difficulties.' He tilted his head to one side. 'But if they do marry, I've never seen one married to a Tirnaal.'

Gods and little saints, *fertility difficulties*. My ears went hot. At least it was dark. With an effort, I kept my voice flat. 'If it makes you feel any better, we haven't had a real ceremony. And Brix doesn't practise, so she's not really your concern.'

'The Tirnaal position,' he went on, 'is that practising magic is a sin, going against nature, meddling in the fabric of reality in a way that's reserved for the gods. The tattoo-work is either imposed by exploitative business partners—'

'Or kidnappers,' I interrupted.

'—or is taken voluntarily, as a religious act. So you can see how you two would strike me as unique. A purchased Tirnaal companion at your disposal could explain why you haven't killed yourself with your incantations yet, but I don't think that's how it is – you using her to mitigate the toxicity. I also don't think you bought her.' He watched as I forced my hands to unclench. 'I'm not trying to insult you. I'm trying to discern exactly what she is. What you are.'

Dace wasn't a fool. It was a problem. 'I'm an unlicensed wizard. Next question.'

'No. You cast without scribing runes. That's supposed to be impossible, according to all the magical theory that I've ever read. You look different than the description on your bounty papers, but you're still easily identified with focused divining. If your looks are an illusion it continues even while you're unconscious, which is also supposed to be impossible. So you're something else. Something new.'

'I don't see that it matters,' I said, 'seeing as I'll probably end up with a Guild noose around my neck regardless of what I am.'

'You did save my life,' Dace said. 'I'd like to return the favour, if possible. But I have to understand.'

So that was the price of survival. Dace had neatly manoeuvred me into a corner. I should have resented it, but I just felt an odd sense of relief. The only people I had talked to about my death were the people who loved me – Brix, Acarius – and I hadn't told them everything. I couldn't. I always had to be thinking about how to keep them from being hurt. But Dace didn't care about me at all, except as an interesting professional problem. It was unexpectedly liberating.

I ran a hand through my hair – a pale hand, and silver hair, neither of which had been mine a year ago. How to explain that? 'What do you know about necromancy?'

For the first time, his voice acquired an edge. 'We've already established that you're not a necromancer.'

'Right, I'm not, I died in good faith.' That didn't sound as reasonable as I had hoped it would. Why was the truth so *stupid*? 'I didn't survive "that business" last year. I died, next to a necromancer. Things happened, and I wound up inhabiting his body. This body. It has modifications. And don't tell me again that something I am currently demonstrating in front of you is impossible, or we'll never get through the rest of this conversation.'

There was a short silence.

'You're undead?' Dace said, politely.

'No. Just had my soul moved.' I hesitated, but he wasn't going to believe me without evidence. I pushed my sleeve up to my elbow and extended my arm. Since I always look like I've been bleached, it was fairly visible in the moonlight. 'Look, there's nothing written on my skin.'

'I can see that.'

I pronounced the illumination spell that circles my left wrist, as slowly as I could without letting the spell fade. One by one, the characters lit, soft blue showing through my flesh, like a bracelet. 'See *that*?'

His face, in the wash of light that now surrounded us, was stuck in that strange expression between laughter and horror.

'I have spells written under my skin,' I said. 'I don't actually know how many, and they're not all in the style I would choose – they hurt more than the ones I can scribe for myself. So there you have it: nothing impossible is occurring. I don't cast without scribing runes, it's just that sometimes they're already written when I want them. And I'm not running an illusion. This, unluckily, is just what I look like now.' I let the spell fade. 'And you don't believe me, so we're back where we started.'

Somewhere on the river, a fish jumped. I waited for my eyes to adjust back to the darkness and wished I could see the man who sat so still opposite me, as though seeing him would help me guess what he was likely to do.

'Well,' Dace said. 'You do smell like necromancy. If you'll pardon me saying it.'

'You are very optimistic when it comes to me pardoning things.' My eyes itched with fatigue. 'You stink like alchemy.'

His voice went taut. 'So?'

'So what does helping the Guild stop a plague buy you, if you're an abomination?'

Another silence. It had the thick feel that silences get when some-one who isn't used to lies has to try to compose one.

'Her freedom,' he said. 'I can give you my word on that, at least.'

'*Her* freedom.' A bright ribbon of anger wove its way through my veins. It was a trick, and I'd been foolish enough to fall for it. He'd already given me his word about the very thing he was taking away. This was probably the part where he would say something along the gutless lines of *now, then, if it was up to me . . .*

But when he spoke, he sounded almost as weary as I was. 'I was hoping my suspicions wouldn't be confirmed, but . . . little saints, I have never seen *anything* as dangerous as you are. I have a duty, and not just to the Guild. The common people – even the king himself – trust us to keep them safe. You understand?'

In a way, I did. A normal wizard had to take the time to scribe magic before attacking, give his opponents at least a few seconds to respond. A normal wizard could be reasoned with, or, failing that, have his scribing tools taken away. I didn't even have to be awake in order to hurt people. I *was* an abomination of sorts; it didn't matter whether I'd asked to be one. A wolf doesn't ask to be born a wolf, but nobody wants one in their goat pen.

'I'll keep my end of the bargain,' I said. 'In return, you don't tell Brix about this, you help me find treatment for her and you draw up freedom papers for her as soon as we stop. Right?'

'Of course. That was already the agreement.'

'And Jaliseth—'

'Stays in a Guild cell until I have proof of the extent of her involvement.' He lifted a hand, eyes glittering in the dark. 'Valera Trist and her like may be overbearing, but they're not entirely wrong. Untaught spells hurt people. Magic has rules for a reason. Practitioners like you and Jaliseth are why half the population thinks we're in league with demons and the other half thinks we're grifters. At the moment the hypothesis that makes sense is that your associates are slightly better at harming Guild wizards than you, not that you or they are innocent.'

'Then it doesn't matter whether I understand.' I stood. 'You built a good trap, Examiner. I'm caught in it. Be satisfied with that.'

Towards the end of the journey the riverbank went from being mostly trees dipping their branches in the water to a steady progression of villages, which eventually merged into each other and sprouted wharves. By the time we got to the city docks themselves, even the air had a populated feel to it. I kept slapping at mosquitoes.

Genereth, City of Gods, sprawled on the banks and delta of the river like a lady half out of her court dress, pale docks gleaming in the sun. The buildings looked like nothing I had ever seen, whitewashed halfway up and then painted in many-coloured murals to the roof line. They were all on foundations that seemed to be sitting up on wooden legs, propped above what I guessed was a river that flooded regularly. In the distance, red domes on the largest structures shone in the afternoon light.

Beside me, Brix stared at the skyline. There were bruise-like smudges under her eyes, exhaustion in the set of her shoulders, unspoken tensions running through her like fault lines. Dace had originally said we had a couple of weeks before the plague started to hurt her in earnest, and we'd spent eight days of it getting down the river. We were running out of time. At least no weird crystals had grown on her overnight.

'I thought Genereth was supposed to be the Tirnaal mother-city,' I said, with a bad attempt at lightness. 'Full of beauty and religion and so forth. You never mentioned the mosquitoes. Did you and Anka live near the docks?'

She pointed towards the red domes. 'There's beauty and religion. They grow the trees for cinnamon inside glasshouses, did you know that? The incense and the honey for Temples are both made in the city.'

I flinched. The dismissal was clear. She was treating me like an acquaintance, the kind of guest one ferried around the city while reciting historical facts. Then again, maybe she was just avoiding talking about anything real for the same reason I was. I had been debating how to tell Brix that my nightmares were changing and worsening, but last night I had caught her doing something she insisted was 'clearing her throat', not coughing. Another argument might split that illusion open and force us both to feel the full measure of our fears. I wasn't sure she'd forgive me if I did that.

'Cinnamon,' I said, after a moment. 'Fascinating.'

She glanced at me. 'It's more complicated than you think,' she said, softly. I didn't think she was talking about incense.

The Guild wizards bunched around us, too close, and the regulator ring in my ear was warm, its magical connection tugging at me every time Dace moved. But none of the Guildies were really paying attention to us as we stepped on to the dock and into the brown city-haze. The docks were weirdly quiet. Apart from our party, the only people I saw were a crew of workers unloading a barge full of apples, a covered booth with a group of club-toting Royal Police and a few ferrymen waiting beside empty boats and cooling themselves with elaborate embroidered fans. The damp, hot air stuck to my skin. It carried an odd smell, foul even compared with the rank scent of a city river – oily, the stench of something burning that shouldn't have been.

I didn't like it, any of it, especially the Roys. The place made me feel vulnerable, defenceless in a way that even Dace's regulator hadn't managed. I didn't have anything to scribe with, unless you counted whatever grease pencils and tubes of paint the Guildies might have been carrying. I would be going into a strange city unarmed, with just my wits and the poisonous spells under my skin.

Dace had finished some discussion with the dockmaster. He strode to Valera and gestured towards the police booth. 'That took more time than I would have liked. We'll register with the Royal Police now, then get to the Guildhouse and figure out how we're going to talk to the drinlords.'

'Drinlords,' Valera said. 'We're actually going to have dealings with those Tirnaal addicts?'

'Some of them just make the stuff,' Dace said. 'Not all of them use it. I'm not anxious to talk to them either, but whoever is making the amulets has to be buying the drin from somewhere. It seems like a necessary course of action. Can we get moving? The police are checking everyone who comes into the city. The dockmaster said there's a trial verdict being announced and sickness in the town, although I'm not certain it's the same illness we've been tracking.' He looked at me. 'I would prefer you to keep your tongue between your teeth during this business.'

The Roys I had dealt with in the past had always been a bit bored by the idea of magic unless they were interested in having a prophylactic spiral written. Royal Police answer to the king and the chancellor, and never have much time for the Guild, Unguild, or what they view as petty squabbles between the two. As we approached, however, these Roys seemed unhealthily alert. There were ten of them, a lot of bodies if this was supposed to be an administrative task. A dull roar rose from the city behind them.

'Greetings,' Dace began, pushing up his sleeve to show his Guild sigil. 'My name is—'

'I don't care about your name. I'm just here to make sure no upriver foreigners can bring the plague into the city.' The Roy pointedly ignored Dace's extended hand. He had a scar across the bridge of his nose, and officer's rings in his right earlobe – a lieutenant, I thought. 'All we need is your papers.'

'What sort of papers?' I said, before I remembered that I wasn't supposed to talk.

The Roy's eyes, flat and cold, swivelled to me. 'You lot get inspected by a Healer and they sign a note saying that you're not infected.' He pointed at Brix, his finger angling downwards towards the tattoos on her feet. 'She'll have to go to quarantine for a couple of days, regardless. All Tirnaal have to, until it's proven they're not sick.'

Dace's smile didn't falter, but it had frozen into a set mask. 'And who, exactly, is running quarantine?'

'We are, of course,' the officer said. 'With the help of the Healers and the priestesses – Ranara-temple is the only place with enough room for the sick. Why, you think your kind ought to be in charge of it? Wizards and Tirnaal carry the sickness, and it's in the king's interest to prevent more unrest.'

'We thought it was only wizards who've died,' Dace said. 'You say *Tirnaal* are carrying the plague now? That doesn't make sense.'

'Nothing in Genereth makes sense these days,' the Roy said. 'All you need to understand is that anyone who so much as brushes against magic seems to end up coughing, so you' – he pointed to Dace's licence sigil – 'and yours will turn over your magic tools and show your papers, or you'll come with us.' He got to his feet.

My stomach went hollow. The stick I had seen at his belt wasn't a club. He was carrying a kind of long-handled metal hook. It looked almost like a shepherd's crook, if a shepherd's crook could be used to decapitate your foes. It was stained.

'I don't think you understand who we are,' Valera said. 'We're here on official Mages' Guild business, and–'

'And?' The Roy's hand dropped to the haft of his hook. Watching a set of pampered Guild wizards encounter official resistance for the first time in their lives should have been amusing, but I was too busy panicking to appreciate it. This man wanted to shove Brix into some filthy quarantine house, and once she was locked away with the dying there was no guarantee that I could ever get her out again. There were eight wizards against ten Roys, and odds were the Roys had some way to summon help. And the Guildies couldn't use force unless they wanted to bring the Charter crashing down around their ears, but the Roys could. I was unimpressed by our odds.

'Well then,' I said, with as much cheer as I could. At least if we were moving through the streets there might be an opportunity to slip away from the Roys, although I'd have to find a way to haul Dace and his earring with me. 'If you're going to take us somewhere, we should get going.'

Dace's head turned. 'What do you think you're doing?'

'Cooperating with the authorities,' I said, mildly. 'You should try it, since you're all so worried about the Guild's standing.'

I think he would have argued with me, but two of the Roys had come out from behind their booth, and their attitude had improved to the point that they now just looked annoyed. 'Come on, then,' said the lieutenant. 'You're the third group we've had to shepherd today. Let's get it over with.' He held his hand out, and reluctantly the wizards gave him various combinations of pencils, paintbrushes and jars of pigment, which he tucked into his pockets. Dace reached into his satchel and produced a single half-used green pencil, so docilely that I was sure he had kept some back.

There was a low wall separating the docks from the city streets, with a triple-barred gate. Maybe I'd made a mistake in agreeing to go into the town. That gate looked like the kind of thing you'd close during a siege – or a riot. When the lieutenant pushed it open, he slipped the hook out of its loop at his belt and held it low, his knuckles white on the haft.

'Stay together,' he barked, 'keep your heads down, and don't fall behind.'

Brix and I walked behind Dace, hemmed in by the wizards and the Roys. The narrow streets wound between buildings that seemed too tall, their gaudy paint and elaborate balconies leaning claustrophobically over the lane, crowding around us and limiting the field of vision. Even the damn cobblestones were wrong, hexagonal instead of square, rough on the feet and interrupted at what seemed like random intervals by multicoloured pavement murals. After a while I recognised them as being dedicated to various deities, although Ranara, the Moonmother, seemed to be the most honoured. Somewhat ominously, the stones tended to depict her in her role as Lady of Shadows, Queen of the Eclipse. The air was full of distant voices, shouts of fear and command, the clatter of horses' hooves and wagon wheels, but the streets themselves were strangely empty. I wondered exactly how foolish we were being, running directly towards what sounded like a riot. The roar seemed louder here, closer, and the smoke was thicker, stinging my eyes.

'Is it normally like this?' I whispered. 'Where is everyone?'

'Of course it isn't.' Brix was looking upwards as we moved. 'Everyone is hiding, or they're gathered in Godstown for whatever this trial is.' After a moment, I saw what she was looking at: just under the ridge formed by the terracotta tiles on the roofs, most of the buildings had a line of looping red script in a language I didn't know – street names, maybe.

'And what in the hells is Godstown?' I said.

She rolled her eyes. 'The Temples district, biggest in the province, bigger than the king's temples in Varriel. And you should try not to blaspheme before you've even seen it – we're almost there.'

The sound that had been a dull roar at the docks was now the overwhelming ocean-murmur of a large, angry crowd, rising and falling as we emerged into the beating heart of Godstown. I halted in spite of myself, startled.

The sky-filling vastness of Ranara-temple spread out over half of the square, hovering over the houses of the other gods like a mother hen above her chicks. Walls of pale, creamy stone glowed in the afternoon light, and the roofs rose in a series of domes, blood red. A large, brass-plated statue of Ranara dominated the largest gate, seated on the crescent moon and beaming down at the people below. What looked like the entire population of Genereth was packed into the large open square beneath the goddess' eyes, moving in eddies against the cobblestones.

'What's going on?' Dace said. 'Why are they all here?'

I glanced at the lieutenant, but he didn't seem to have heard the question, staring at the large fountain in the middle of the square. It was another representation of Ranara, this one in gold, the statue and pool perched in the middle of a large, round platform that must have been intended as a site for public address. Steps led from the square up to the platform, where a man wearing elaborate green-and-black livery had just ascended above the crowd. He was flanked by a trumpeter and a woman in the plain linen garb of a doctor or a scholar. They all looked like they would rather have been anywhere else.

'No,' the lieutenant muttered. 'Not now. Why couldn't the bastards wait ten minutes?' The lieutenant turned to the other Roy. 'We've got to get across the square before they announce the verdict. The people are spoiling for a riot.'

'What verdict?' Dace was insistent. 'If you tell us what's happening, then it's possible that we could assist you.'

The lieutenant snorted. 'You do magic in this crowd, spelldog, and they'll have all of our throats. Wizards are not popular in Genereth just now. Come on.' He prodded Dace with the haft of his hook. 'Move.'

We had edged our way perhaps a quarter of the distance across the square when the trumpeter gave a squall of the ram's horn. The crowd quieted, barely. The Roys never stopped moving, dragging the bunch of us with increasingly frightened speed.

The man in livery was bellowing: 'The Council of Generethi Houses and the Mages' Guild have reached a verdict in the matter of the death of Moyra Behrel.'

I halted.

Moyra. That was the name of the dead woman from my vision, the one who had appeared in all the nightmares I'd had on the riverboat. This couldn't be the same person, could it? I couldn't see the platform well anymore, jammed as I was against Dace, with both the Roys and the movement of the crowd itself shoving me forwards against my will.

'After a lawful trial the Guild has ruled the death accidental. The wizards involved will not be –'

The silence broke like a dam. The howling crowd surged towards the platform, carrying me, Dace and Brix with it. I reached blindly for Brix, but she found me first, her fingers locking on my wrist.

'Don't let go!' I shouted.

'I'm not a bloody idiot!' she shouted back.

The man in livery was still bellowing, even as the trumpeter and the woman had withdrawn to the middle of the platform, watching the crowd with alarm. It was impossible to make out exactly what he was trying to say, but it seemed to be various repetitions of *calm yourselves* and *disperse to your homes* and *the officers of the Royal Police*. I glanced around, looking for our officers, but I couldn't find them.

A spasm burst in the crowd then, near the platform, and I was able to distinguish a group of shining helmets. As I watched, one of the men in helmets went down in a knot of people who immediately indulged in a frenzy of kicks – another set of Royal Police, in danger of being beaten to death by the maddened crowd. I saw the pair of Roys who had been accompanying us then, diving frantically through the sea of bodies and laying about them with their hooks, making their way to the aid of their fellows.

'We need to go,' Dace screamed, in my ear.

'No shit.' I craned my neck. 'Which way?'

'Out of Godstown.' Brix yanked me sideways, hard. 'Follow me.'

She stopped the next minute, stymied by an unmoving wall of writhing, shouting humans. She lowered her head and began shoving her way forwards. I kept my hold on her, almost too distracted to notice how close Dace was sticking, near enough that I could both smell his fear-sweat and hear what he was shouting.

'Pardon,' the idiot was yelling, over and over again. 'Pardon, we need to get through. Make way.'

Nobody was moving, at least not in the direction we wanted. I leaned forwards, my chin almost on Brix's shoulder. 'Which way?'

She pointed at an alleyway between Neyar-temple and the house of the Lord of the Afterlands, but it might as well have been on the moon. A heaving mass of humanity milled about between us and the exit, slowing any progress to a painful crawl. If we stood still, the unsettling slow push of the crowd would carry us towards the violence at the centre of the square, exactly where we didn't want to be. I squirmed my way in front of Brix, and stuck my elbow out in front of me.

'PLAGUE,' I shouted, gambling. 'We need to get to quarantine!'

The people who had been pressing so close around us all fell back a pace. It was enough to get my bearings and take a breath, although–

'I don't think that was smart,' Brix said, moving forwards under the horrified gazes of the crowd at speed. I followed, almost jogging, fleeing the wave of high-pitched exclamations that burst around the crowd noise in a weird kind of harmony. Dace was running close behind me; in another moment I realised he was actually grasping the hem of my coat.

We were almost to the edge of the square when the first person threw something hard and heavy enough to raise a bruise. It hit my shoulder, and for a second I couldn't draw breath. Brix paused, glancing back at me, uncertain. Another stone struck her then, and she stumbled, putting one hand out to the cobblestones to catch herself. A bright scuff of blood appeared on the stone.

I lunged forwards, grabbing her under the armpits. I dragged her back up to her feet and slapped back at Dace's hand. 'Let go of me – you're going to make me fall.'

His grip tightened. 'I'm not going to lose an infected fugitive because of bad luck.'

'Are you all right?' I said.

Brix was staring down at her skinned hand and shaking her head. I saw what she was looking at in the next moment: a drop of blood running down her wrist. In it, glimmering like a jewel, a perfect little clear obelisk crystal was forming.

No.

No, I wasn't going to admit this was happening. We'd stop the bleeding and she'd be all right, but first we had to get out of there. I grabbed for her hand and doubled her fingers over her palm.

Another missile struck me then, this one soft and damp, an old vegetable or something even more unsavoury. Brix broke into a run.

'Dirty spelldogs!' someone shouted. 'Killing the rest of us with your magic!'

Then another rock, this one clipping my hip just as I caught up with Brix.

We made the entrance to the alleyway and stumbled our way along it in a panting, horrified knot. Dace was there, and Valera, but I only counted four of the six Guild wizards who had been with us on the boat.

'We've got to find them,' Dace said, gasping for breath. 'That's Kula and Fyn, they're only journeymen, alone in that mess. The crowd will hurt them. We've got to think of something.'

'*Think* of something?' Valera's voice danced between disgust and terror. She did not, I noticed, stop pushing her way down the alley. She didn't even slow down. 'How do you expect to find them in that mess without losing the prisoners? This would never have happened if you weren't forever *thinking* of things. Any Guild wizard from a proper background would never have risked taking these criminals out of Varriel in the first place.' She jostled past me and Brix. 'You'll just have to go back. I'll go on to the Guildhouse and find help.'

'How useful of you.' Dace flapped my coattails like the reins of a horse. 'What's your suggestion for him, then?'

Valera didn't look back towards us. 'If you had properly neutralised him when I advised—' She halted, her voice stopping like someone had torn it in half.

Ahead of us, half-hidden by the smoke and twilight that swirled through the alleyway, what I had taken to be a heap of refuse stood up.

It wasn't refuse. It wasn't a beggar in rags, either, which was my second thought. The thing shambling towards us looked only vaguely human, with extra joints in its arms and no lower jaw. Its face just ended beneath its nose in a pulpy red mass. It probably had eyes somewhere under the matted mass of hair that hung down over its face, but it was impossible to be sure. My mind, with the cheerful thoroughness of horror, took in the lines of thick black stitches around the wrists, and the neck, and circling what I could see of the ankles and knees.

Necromancy. Has to be.

It didn't, though. I didn't know anything about Genereth. Just because necromancy was the only explanation I could think of for this monstrosity didn't make it the correct one, and I needed to be correct. There were spells that worked against dead constructs, and other, quite different ones that worked against the living. If the thing wasn't dead—

I tried to smell for decay, but the smoke and the stench from who-ever had last dumped their chamber pots into the street overwhelmed my senses. Valera staggered backwards, behind us, her ragged breath puffing like a blacksmith's bellows. Dace was still at my shoulder, his eyes fixed on the creature, and I hadn't let go of Brix's hand.

'Is there any way out if we go back?' I said, as calmly as I could.

'No.' Dace glanced over his shoulder, then at me. 'Do you know what it is? What's holding it together, something like witchclay?'

'I have no idea.' I disentangled myself from Brix's grip. 'It looks necromantic, but . . .'

'Can you help us put it down or not?' Dace's voice rattled.

'Only if you give me something to scribe with.' Which wasn't strictly true, but using one of Jaern's spells and making myself spell-shot in a narrow alley staring down that stitched horror seemed like the worst possible move.

No. I could feel the word vibrating off of Dace, but he didn't say it. Instead, his hand crept towards his shoulder bag. 'What would you cast?'

The thing's hands twitched around in front of it, glinting in the smoke. I squinted.

'What's the matter with its fingers?' Brix said. 'It looks like . . . metal?'

Indeed, the creature's fingers were tipped in short, sharp, steel claws, as though its fingernails had been torn out and replaced with knife points. I couldn't see how you'd attach steel to someone's fingerbones without killing them, but the thing had advanced several steps and I still couldn't smell rot. Instead there was the flat, metallic tang of fresh blood and a sweet, earthy odour, half-familiar in its oddity. It was almost like . . . honey?

I went cold.

'That tetany you nearly threw at me, back in Varriel?' I said. 'Please tell me you were worried enough about me getting uppity today that you're carrying it.'

'I have it scribed,' Dace said, reluctantly. 'But this is necromancy, isn't it? Necrotic muscles won't respond to tetany.'

'The thing isn't—'

—*dead*, is what I meant to say, but at that moment it stepped towards us, arms spreading wide.

'Cast now,' I said, backing up. 'Now, Dace, now!'

He was chanting as Brix dropped into a crouch, her hands scrabbling at the ground. She found a loose cobblestone and flung it at the creature. It hit it squarely on the shoulder, sending the thing into a reeling spin. Dace's tetany spell went wide, crackling harmlessly against the brick and plaster of the alley wall.

Then thing steadied itself. It lunged.

There was no time. I pronounced the force spell on my arm. It left my fingers even as the poison flooded my veins, a ball of orange magic that struck the thing's head with a splat. It stumbled back against the wall, clawing at its own face, bucking in a way that would have meant screaming if it had had a mouth. I only had a split second to feel appalled before something bumped against me.

'Out of my way!' Valera sprinted past me and Brix and Dace,

making for the gap that had opened when the creature went down. The other four young wizards followed. The creature reached towards Valera as she ran past, a pleading motion. Valera gasped and kicked out, catching the thing's wrist with her heel before disappearing into the smoke down the rest of the alley.

Brix's hand latched on to my collar.

'*This* way,' she hissed in my ear, and dragged me sideways into the shadows.

SEVEN

I don't know why I had assumed that Generethi alleys would run straight with no turnings when nothing else about the city made sense. I realised my mistake a few steps down the damp, stinking lane that Brix had chosen. 'Where—' I began, then put my toe in something wet and had to jump closer to the brick walls that hemmed us in on both sides. *'Shit!'*

'Yes. Don't be a baby,' she snapped. 'This is basically a middens, but that means nobody else is using it. Unless you'd rather go back and face that . . . whatever-it-was, just don't step in the ditch. Come on.'

I was about to open my mouth and point out that putting a magic-drunk wizard and a ditch full of sewage together was bound to be a bad idea, but a jolt of agony from my ear stole the words – stole even the ability to think. I stopped dead, reeling.

It probably only took a few seconds for Dace to catch up. I couldn't be sure; I was only capable of blinking at him while I tried not to stumble into the muck.

'Gray!' Brix had halted a few steps away. The confusion on her face cleared. 'The damn earring.'

'Sorry.' Dace reached up and touched his earlobe. He was panting, a slick of blood under his nose.

'Bastard,' I said, when I could speak.

'That wasn't . . .' He swallowed, looking as nauseated as I felt. 'The

92

ring is distance-dependent; it just activates when the conditions are met. I didn't—'

Brix wheeled towards Dace. 'Move,' she said, her voice low and dangerous. 'Now, or gods help me I will knock you over the head, cut that ring out of your ear and leave you here. I will not die in an alley in shit because of you. Move!'

Dace moved.

The midden-lane, blessedly, didn't go on much further, spilling us out into a proper road after about a hundred yards. Navigation got a little easier when we left Godstown behind. Outside the pretty white walls separating Temples from the rest of the city, the smoke was thinner, the riot confined to moving knots of looters who could be avoided. After we'd walked for about an hour, we came to a starburst of streets ending in a plaza. The area centred around a fountain where a smiling, verdigris-speckled figure of Ranara stood on an eclipsed moon. Water burst from her hands like a benediction, the sunset highlighting her metal smile. Dace halted, trembling, beside the fountain.

'We can't stop.' Brix's hand was still closed in a fist.

'I know.' Dace dug in his pocket. 'I only need a second.' He produced a squat bottle, turned his back on us and took a large swallow. Liquor, I thought, or maybe yavad.

I couldn't get away from the image of that bright little crystal falling out of Brix's hand. 'Your hand.' I turned to her. 'It was cut. You should wash the dirt out.'

'You mean I should wash the crystal out.' She opened her hand gingerly, examining the drying tracks of blood. 'There's no point in acting like we didn't see it. And anyway, you don't wash in a prayer fountain. You drink. Even you should know better than that.'

A hot wave of irritation pulsed over me. 'I know that crystals can be alchemy catalysts and that these particular crystals can apparently cause explosions – is that better?'

She crossed her arms. 'Rocks don't spread disease. You're panicking.'

'I am not panicking. We don't *know* what spreads this disease. It doesn't seem to follow any normal rules, so why in the hells shouldn't it be rocks? Your blood never grew crystals before that thing cut you.'

'We don't *know* anything, so stop telling me what to do.' Brix's voice rose. 'Stop acting like I don't know we have to take precautions, like I'm too sick to know what's good for me. You behave as though I'm already dy—'

'No,' I said, between my teeth. 'That's not going to happen.'

'Stop arguing with every damn thing I say!'

'I am—' *not*. I caught myself before I could prove her right, turned and scooped water from the fountain. I mumbled half-remembered phrases about help and healing before slurping the prayer from my cupped palm. After breathing smoke for so long, the water tasted sweet. 'There. I prayed. Now you can wash, and then you can go back to ignoring what I say and not telling me anything.' I turned towards her, chin dripping. I couldn't keep my voice steady. 'Please?'

She opened her mouth to retort and coughed instead, a long, grinding fit that took too long to stop. When it ended, she didn't look at me. 'I caught smoke in my throat.'

Three days, Dace had said. We had three days.

'I know.' It felt like the wrong thing to say, but I was damned if I was going to hurt her again. 'Smoke's bothering me, too.'

Her lips quivered for a moment before she pressed them together. She still didn't look at me, but she let me take her hand and plunge it into the fountain. Once the dried blood and the dirt were cleaned away, the cut looked normal.

'Right.' I breathed out, suddenly light-headed. 'Where are we going?'

She was looking at the script on the top of the buildings again. 'I could— I was taking you home. To my clan. They'd help me, and you

94

as long as I vouched for you.' She glanced at me, hesitant. 'I *was* going to tell you. We just haven't had time.'

Genereth is different. I had been expecting something like this, but it was startling how much the situation hurt. This wasn't a simple matter of being invited home to meet Brix's elderly relatives. A clan was an entire community, a whole village of people that we had apparently been avoiding, for reasons that Brix didn't trust me enough to tell me. Maybe they were cruel or unreliable. Maybe, with her people's safety on the line, she was finally realising how danger-ous I was. I couldn't quite force myself to consider the other option that kept bubbling to the surface of my mind.

Maybe she's just ashamed of you, spelldog.

'Sure,' I said, swallowing the ache and pasting on the most reassur-ing smile I could. 'Perfect. Makes sense.'

Her eyes narrowed. 'But now it's no good.' She gestured to the pil-lars of smoke rising in the sky all around us. 'I'm not sure how we could even get there. The riot's spreading. We'd have to make it all the way to the city wall.'

'Are you talking about the wall chapels?' Dace gave a short bark of laughter. 'Me, with a Guild tattoo on my wrist, asking a Tirnaal aunt for shelter? You might as well cut my throat here. Unhappily the magic would prevent you cutting the regulator out of my ear, and Gray would be bound to my corpse.' He didn't seem spell-shot anymore, just brittle. 'I don't think it's what you want.'

'You don't know anything about what we want,' I said.

'If you let me take us to the Generethi Guildhouse, we can wait out the riot and I can protect you from the Guild wizards.' Dace spoke rapidly. 'Unless and until Valera and the others arrive, I'll out-rank anyone there.'

Let me. It took me longer than it should have to realise why the Examiner General was asking Brix and me for permission.

'You think I'll kill you.' My stomach churned, but he wasn't looking at me. 'People are still dying. Brix still needs a cure. And you think—'

'Stop talking about the damn cure,' Brix hissed. 'We don't even know if it exists, and at the moment I just want to get off the street. Dace, do you even know where the Guildhouse is? Have you been to Genereth before?'

'I never said I hadn't,' Dace muttered. 'I know *roughly* where it is.'

Out of the corner of my eye, I saw a figure detach itself from the shadows at the foot of one of the stilt-legged houses. I spun towards it, unsure what we'd do if it was another stitched thing – but this was no abomination. It was an exhausted-looking woman in a linen shirt and a pair of loose blue trousers.

'Excuse me,' she said, halting about ten feet from me. 'I heard you mention the Guildhouse. Are you heading that way?'

'None of your business,' I said, automatically. 'Who are you?'

'She was there,' Dace said, behind me. 'In Godstown. She was on the platform, beside the court herald.'

'My name is Tynan. Yes, I was there. I had to give testimony at the trial.' She swallowed, and now that she was closer I saw she was filthy, her clothes and hands and face smeared with dirt and something that might have been ash. 'I'm a doctor. I work at the Guildhouse. I've been trying to get back—' She looked over her shoulder, helplessly. 'Every turn I take the streets are filled with people, and they all think I'm carrying the plague or spreading it – too many of them saw me in the square. I thought maybe we could help each other. I'll show you the way to the Guildhouse, if you'll protect me from the rioters.' She eyed Dace doubtfully. 'You look like a Guild wizard. Am I mistaken?'

'No. I'm a Guild wizard. But I don't think my magic is going to be the most useful in this situation.' He glanced at me. 'Are you in condition to cast if we need it?'

96

'Yes.' I should have been annoyed that Dace was again asking me to do work he found distasteful, but we needed to get Brix someplace safe whether she admitted it or not. 'Whatever it takes. Show us.'

Tynan led us away from the plaza, with Godstown behind us and the sun sinking beneath the tops of the buildings to our left. We walked for what seemed like hours on uneven streets crammed between pastel buildings. Darkness had fallen by the time the street terminated in a sturdy, blue-painted wooden gate. Tynan drew a key from a ring on her belt, opened it and ushered us into a wide courtyard. Pink-and-green houses stood on three sides, wrought-iron balconies running their length and windows shuttered tightly against the night air. In the centre was a well surrounded by dark, feathery ferns.

'This can't be the Guildhouse,' Brix said. 'Where are the people?'

'Quarantined,' Tynan said, striding towards the tallest building. 'We were the first group in Genereth to have deaths. It's not as though anywhere else in Genereth is safer, but ...' She glanced backwards. 'Are you sure you want to come in?'

'I don't have a choice,' Dace said. 'I need to speak to Elias Thane as quickly as possible.'

'Elias Thane is dead.' Tynan halted in front of the door and rapped three times. 'He died two days ago. It's why I was at the trial – he was supposed to be there. I was there to deliver the testimony he gave me on his deathbed.' After a moment, yellow lamplight spilled out on to the ridged cobblestones as the door opened, puffing overheated, incense-scented air out to meet us.

I put a hand over my nose. 'Is that supposed to keep the stink down? It isn't working.'

'The incense keeps the plague ghosts away, so the priestesses tell us.' A young man was blocking the door, staring at me. He wore homespun Guild robes and apprentice's embroidery. In one hand he held a long, thin-bladed knife; in the other, a small clay dish of white powder. 'Doctor?' he asked.

'It's all right, Sannet.' Tynan's voice had dropped into such a soothing cadence that it might as well have been a lullaby. 'These people are from the Varriel Guildhouse. They're here to help us.'

'Has Valera Trist arrived yet?' Dace said, only to be greeted with a blank look from Sannet.

'Nobody has arrived here for months,' he said. 'And you can't come in unless you're clean.'

'*Clean.*' Dace's whole body was taut. 'That's not the sort of language I would hope for from a Guild wizard, apprentice, especially when I'm asking after a missing colleague.'

'He doesn't mean anything by it.' Tynan had the decency to sound apologetic as she took the knife and dish from Sannet and turned to us. 'We've had to take precautions. I'll need a drop of blood from each of you to confirm you're not infected. It's not a perfect test, but it's the one they're using to grant papers in the city right now.'

Not infected. I stiffened, but Brix slid past me and put her hand out. 'Here. I'm Tirnaal, if that makes a difference. The guards at the gate said it might.'

'Superstitious fools.' The doctor did not remove her attention from Brix's finger, carefully nicking it with the blade. 'This test will work. It can, rarely, look a bit different with Tirnaal.' A crimson drop welled on Brix's finger. I tensed, but no crystal formed. The blood dripped into the powder in the dish with a sizzle and small puff of smoke. 'There,' Tynan said briskly. 'You're all right.'

Brix shot me a triumphant look, but I couldn't smile back. There *had* been a crystal back in the alley, and she *had* been coughing. Things were still too uncertain, whatever this test showed. The blade caught my fingertip next, drops hissing into the powder.

'You're clean.' The doctor turned to Dace. 'Sir?'

Dace extended his hand with uncharacteristic reluctance. When the test showed the requisite puff of smoke, his shoulders relaxed, almost imperceptibly. It was a strange display of anxiety for a man who hadn't seemed worried about the plague until now.

'Come in, then.' The doctor was already moving, her face tight and watchful. 'Before the night gets any worse.'

I licked blood off my sore finger and followed her into the lamplight. Besides the huge, smoking incense brazier near the door, there were also smaller ones beneath the windows. The apprentice was standing in the cinnamon-heavy haze against the wall, watching me.

'Is there something wrong with my face?' I said. 'You keep looking at me.'

'No. I'm not looking at you.' He turned and walked rapidly down the hallway, as if I'd threatened to spit on him.

'It's not personal. Sannet hasn't been himself recently. You have to understand, they've been dying for weeks.' Tynan passed a hand over her eyes. 'Months, I suppose it is, now. We're all exhausted. Sometimes I've been so tired I can hardly remember what I've been doing.' The doctor gestured down a hall. 'If you'll follow me.'

We were taken through dank, white-plastered passageways to a dim, high-ceilinged hall that held about thirty people. Judging by the scattered pieces of cutlery on the tables and the lingering odour of shrimp, they had just finished dinner. None of them wore the heavy embroidery of senior wizards. The plague must have hit hard. A Guildhouse this size should have had a master. In normal times, Guild hierarchy would ensure that an assistant would be ready to take his place. But now it seemed like the only person in charge was a short man with a receding hairline, ink-stained fingers and his sleeves pinned back. He stood on a table, hoarsely trying to talk over the chatter in the room.

It, and he, went quiet when we came in. Thirty pairs of eyes stared at us.

'Tynan?' said the short man. If he was a Guildlord's lieutenant I'd eat my left boot – more like a librarian, judging by the ink.

'These people are from the Varriel Guildhouse.' Tynan looked at Dace, and then, unsettlingly, at me. 'They're here to help, so they say.' She moved forwards and took a seat near the back of the room. The apprentice, Sannet, plopped himself down alone at a corner table, scowling.

Dace cleared his throat. 'My name is Dace Craxen. I'm here by orders of the council.' He paused until the wave of whispers that this inspired died back.

'Craxen? The new Examiner General?' The probably-librarian clambered down off his table in a rush.

'Yes.' Dace looked a little uncomfortable with his own title. 'I'm investigating the plague that's been spreading through our houses in the province, and seems to have begun here. This is Corcoran Gray and Brix, who are assisting the Guild.'

'Thank the gods, my lord,' said the librarian. 'We sent a message to Varriel by pigeon to ask for assistance, but that was only three days ago. We never thought you'd get here so soon.'

'We've seen a number of disturbing things since we arrived,' Dace said, 'including some evidence of necromancy. I think you'd better tell me exactly what has been happening here.'

The librarian scratched at his bald spot. 'I don't rightly know where to start.'

Brix, who was looking tired, sat. I straddled the bench behind her and tried not to listen too closely for the rasps in her breath.

'Start when the first person died,' she said. 'We'll get to the stitched things later.'

The librarian blinked, then lowered himself into a chair. 'Four months back or so. First to die was that Moyra, leastways that's how Temples is counting.'

Moyra.

Not dead. Kept.

For a second I saw the woman from my vision, on her back in the tank, asking me to help her. Even in that hot, oppressive room I went cold.

But the librarian was staring at me with gentle expectation. I think it's the silver hair. Once people really notice it, they pin me as either an exotic sort of consort-slave or an oracle. The librarian had evidently chosen 'oracle'. For the record, I hate my hair. 'She died of the plague?' I said.

'Oh no.' The librarian sounded surprised. 'No, she caught a spell.'

'There was an unfortunate incident between Temples and a Guild wizard.' Dace spoke carefully. 'The wizard was acting contrary to regulations and when confronted by Guildmates began to cast. In the confusion a field officer aimed a paralysis spell at the Guild wizard. He missed, and struck this Moyra, who died before the altercation could be resolved and the ley broken. She was a Ranaran acolyte.' He was looking at the floor. If he was feeling guilty, it was justified. It's not possible to reverse a spell, but you can wreck the ability of magic to take hold, in a small area, for a short time. Of course, any ley-breaker would ruin all the magic in a given area, stripping the wizard who cast it of their weapons. Even such a limited amount of impotence seemed to terrify the Guild, so ley-breakers were illegal. In this instance, the regulation had caused a death. 'I was involved in the original investigation. We saw the outcome of the trial back at Godstown.' He glanced up at the librarian. 'The verdict was not guilty. That's why the riot, I suppose. Why in the hells didn't you wait for the Guild representative before you let them announce? None of this was supposed to have been entered into without input from the council.'

The librarian shook his head helplessly. 'It wasn't our decision, my lord. Temples has the duke and the Royal Police by the ears. They demanded the trial be expedited, and insisted that a verdict be announced today. It was all we could do to try to testify, protect our own—'

'The Guild does *not* merely protect its own,' Dace said, sharply. 'Not when a woman has been killed.'

So Moyra was a Ranaran acolyte, the Guild had killed her, and they were still defensive about their failure. None of this explained why Moyra was in my divining or showing up in my dreams.

'And we're certain she's dead?' I said, before I could stop myself.

'It would be odd to have a trial if we weren't,' Dace said. 'All the eyewitnesses that I interviewed agreed that she died, and the Ranarans collected her body for burial. Short of checking her pulse myself, I don't see how I could be more certain. Unless you're implying something?'

Brix's body stiffened. She was listening for my answer, and I realised with a flash of guilty certainty that she knew I'd been keeping something from her.

'No,' I said. 'Just wanting to get my facts straight.'

'Well.' The librarian shifted his weight. 'A week after the whole sorry business, we heard that plague had struck the Guildhouse in Ten Rivers. The sickness reached Genereth, and . . . well, perhaps you know the rest. Our Guildhouse lost twenty, before Temples had the Royal Police confine us. If there's someone playing at necromancy they must have begun after we were shut up.'

'And why do the police and the duke do as Temples tells them?' Brix said.

'Precautions.' The doctor hadn't spoken since sitting down. Even now she didn't move, sitting with her head resting against the wall and her eyes shut. 'Temples – Ranara-temple, to be specific – has been able to contain the disease somewhat. They even claim that they've cured a few. After the first couple of deaths here, we started being careful. The incense, the tests . . . the wizards have even stopped doing incantations, on my advice.'

The hair on my arms lifted. 'Stopped incantations?' I said.

'The plague appears to be accelerated by magic.' The doctor opened her eyes a crack, watching me with a gleam of interest. 'Everyone who's done active spells in the Guildhouse for the last couple of months has fallen ill.'

The image of the Roy in Jaliseth's cellar flashed across my mind, pink light still on his lips, rune-written and cold in his puddle of gore. 'But others have died in Varriel. Non-wizards.'

'It does spread from person to person,' she said, 'but very slowly, and only if there's contact with blood or spittle. Magic done around the infected acts like fuel on a fire, and there are enough black-market spells sold in Genereth to fill a warehouse.'

'This would have been ideal information to share with us,' Dace said. 'I've been operating with a flawed premise.'

'We *did* try to tell you,' Tynan said, through her teeth. 'Like Gerrick said, we sent a message to beg for help. But we were stuck here under quarantine, with no way of knowing if it ever reached the docks, let alone Varriel. They barely let me out of the Guildhouse long enough to testify. If I could get the Royal Police to *listen* to me—' Tynan broke off, frustrated. 'They're not interested in stopping it with logic. They'd rather put their faith in luck-charms and the priestesses. But the theory holds, Master Gray. The magic makes it worse. I just can't explain why. Can you?'

'Maybe,' I said.

'You're a liar.' It took the room a moment to realise who had spoken. The apprentice who had met us at the door, Sannet, got to his feet. He spoke with an odd, mellifluous accent, staring at me, ashen and swaying like a drunk. 'You're not who you say you are.' He pointed at me. 'I know you. Your *voice* . . .'

I stood like a thread had pulled me. I already knew what he was going to say.

Necromancer. Poison. Murderer.

'This man *stinks* of magic.' Sannet came towards me. 'He's killing all of you, every second he stands there. People like him are the reason the plague goes on, him and his filthy incantations.'

It took me a heartbeat more to understand what he was accusing me of. Not necromancy, not the deaths I had been unable to prevent last year. He thought I was . . . a plague carrier?

'Sannet,' the librarian said, 'now then, the doctor tested them. They don't have the plague.'

'*Tests.*' Sannet spat the word. 'Meaningless.'

Out of the corner of my eye, I saw the doctor pull herself to her feet, halting, grimacing with pain. 'We're all tired, and it's late.' She was smiling reassuringly, but her hands spread out from her body like a fencer's. I wondered how many times in the last three months she'd had to pull someone out of fear-laced madness. 'We can figure it out in the morning.'

Sannet hadn't taken his eyes off me. 'Tell them, my lord.' His sleeve pulled up, revealing a glimpse of the curling line of runes painted around his bony forearm. His palm flattened, taking aim. 'Tell them what you really are.'

'Gray,' Brix said, behind me.

'I see it.' But I had to keep as still as I could. If I moved, it might tip him into action. I met Sannet's gaze. 'Listen. You don't even know me. Other people in this room are your friends, and you just heard the doctor say that magic will accelerate the plague. Whatever problem you think you have with me, this is a foolish way to solve it.'

'I don't have time or patience to waste with these games. Admit who you are, now.' Pinkish light shone on Sannet's teeth as he spoke, as though he'd swallowed a piece of the sunset. 'Or I'll cast.'

'If the rest of you would get against the walls, please, where it's safer.' Dace's cool voice sliced into the conversation. 'I think this has gone far enough. Apprentice—' He stepped forwards.

'*No!*' Sannet lunged towards me.

Tynan grabbed for him, but he twisted away from her, yelling an incantation. Sigils lit on his arms, glowing in the hollows formed where his sleeves belled around his elbows.

Two leaps took me across the floor, too slow to stop him.

My shoulder caught him in the chest, but he didn't fall. He was strong – absurdly strong for someone so young and spindly – and he was still chanting. I shoved my hands against his mouth to interrupt the spell, hard enough to force his head backwards. It should have hurt. He fought like he couldn't feel it, clawing at my arms with fingers that were already flickering with green light, the last three syllables of the incantation trapped between his teeth.

'Hold him,' Tynan said, scrambling to catch hold of Sannet's elbow. 'Hold him!'

Sannet went limp against us. It almost worked – Tynan stumbled backwards, and I lost my grip on his mouth, grappling at his arms to control him and keep my footing.

He grinned, blood on his teeth.

'*Get down!*' Dace shouted.

But, of course, it was too late for that.

EIGHT

The spell gathered in Sannet's cupped hands, green and foetid and full of searing malice, so close I could smell the sulphurous heat of the magic against his flesh.

His limbs were still snarled around mine, bone thudding against bone as he tried to free his arms enough to choose his target. Sound tumbled past us – a bench squeaking as someone kicked it over, a burst of appalled cries, and Dace, shouting something that sounded like a curse in a language I didn't know.

The apprentice's elbow caught me under the chin and a starburst broke inside my skull, blotting out my vision. I flung myself forwards, scrabbling to catch hold of him. My clawing fingers brushed his sleeves and I shoved his elbows upwards as a sheet of green energy blasted from his fingertips. The spell burst over the heads of the people in the room, curling harmlessly against the tops of the plastered walls and ceiling.

Sannet howled and charged, sweeping me backwards and off my feet like a riptide. He snatched a two-tined fork off the table beside him and then threw himself on top of me, sobbing, a ragged, painful sound that smothered everything else. His ash-stained fingers dug at my neck and face, nails scoring my flesh. 'It was all right.' He jabbed the fork downwards. A spike of fire lanced across my ear. 'Until you got here, it was going to be all right.'

I grabbed his forearm and shoved the fork away from me, alchemical paint smearing under my palm. Footsteps clattered across the wooden floor and a pair of boots planted themselves next to my head, and someone was yanking at Sannet's hair and clothes – the librarian, I thought. 'Stop it! Stop this madness!' Sannet only grunted. There was something very wrong with his skin; a weird blue tint that climbed his throat as I watched. He forced the fork towards my face, chopping at my elbow with his free hand. He was stronger than he should have been and utterly focused on killing me, his bloodshot eyes fixed and unblinking. I had to hit him somewhere else, had to . . .

I stuck my thumb in his eye. It was wet, and soft.

He twisted away, screaming.

Quite a lot of people seemed to be screaming, actually. I scrambled backwards as his weight lifted off me.

'Gray!' Brix crouched beside me. 'You're bleeding.'

'Just the ear.' I pulled myself unsteadily to my feet and looked over to where Sannet was on his knees, coughing, one hand pressed against his injured eye and the other clutching at his heaving chest. His eyes – well, eye – never left me. The wizards in the room had begun to converge on him, but the pink foam he was spitting sent them scurrying away.

'I don't know,' Sannet moaned. 'I don't *remember*. What—'

Only Tynan was left beside him. She held the apprentice, making soothing noises I could hardly hear over Dace's scolding.

'What in the hells did you think you were doing, you Unguild idiot?' He sounded shaken. 'That spell . . . you should have let me handle it.'

I frowned. Sannet was tugging at a lump under his shirt, frantic, pained. 'I can't—' He coughed up another gobbet on to the floor. His voice rose to a high, keening wail. 'I can't get it off!' He slumped over sideways, the wail cutting off when his face thudded into the floorboards.

'Gray, stay where you are.' Dace edged forwards. The doctor was on her knees, her hands moving near Sannet's mouth.

My ear was starting to hurt in earnest. I didn't have time for Dace. 'Sannet has an amulet. That means he's infected, right?'

Dace froze so quickly that an ill-advised giggle rose in my throat and had to be smothered. I stepped around him. Someone had to examine the apprentice and I was already contaminated, Sannet's blood merrily speckling the front of my shirt and mingling with the drops of my own from my ear. Besides, we needed to keep Sannet alive at least long enough to ask him where he'd gotten his amulet.

'Don't get any closer to him,' Brix said, which was *something*, coming from the woman who didn't even want to stop long enough to wash out a cut. 'Gray, don't. We –'

'We don't have time. We can fight about this later.' I crossed the floor to the doctor. She was using her little finger to clear bloody foam from the corners of Sannet's mouth. As I watched, it shed tiny pieces of grit that looked like violet sand and I knew that if I picked the grit up and looked at it closely enough, it would be made of tiny obelisk-shaped crystals, like the ones inside the amulets.

She glanced up at me. 'Are you here to help, or to finish what you started with his eyes?'

'To help, I hope.' I knelt. 'He's got a necklace on – even if you're right that the plague spreads through blood and spittle, we think that the necklaces are making it worse. It may be what's making him attack random strangers.'

'You said that magic accelerates the sickness, right? The last necklace we saw had a spell written on it. Or on the skin next to it, actually.' Brix sat on her heels beside me. She had followed me. Of course she had. She leaned forwards, eyeing Sannet's shirt. 'We should see if it's the same this time.'

'If you can tell me anything about what's happening,' Tynan said, 'start now.'

'Amulets like this have amplified the toxicity of spells I've done near them,' I said.

'They have?' Brix looked at me, startled. 'You didn't say anything.'

'I didn't know *why* it was happening.' I unlaced Sannet's shirt. The amulet was there, twin to the one we'd found in Jaliseth's cellar, a slender vial of black fluid with a purple spark spinning at its centre. Just like with the dead Roy, the pewter legs set into the case of this one had spread out and embedded themselves in Sannet's chest, hooked through like some kind of obscene piercing. A neatly written spiral of runes encircled the vial, this time readable as a static sequence like the one that kept my earring in place. They were glowing.

'It's the same, Gray.' Brix sounded calm, but she was breathing quickly. 'That's the same Ranaran prayer as last time.'

The flesh-seeking spell that had been curled around the amulet back in Varriel was also here, scratched across the casing, crisscrossed with another, difficult-to-read set of characters. The flesh-seeker wasn't glowing. Yet.

I fought the desire to jump backwards. 'We should clear the room.'

Tynan looked up at me. 'Why?'

'This could kill him,' I said. 'Or the rest of us, unless I can find a way to snuff this spell. We've seen this happen in Varriel. Get the other people out of here, please.' I glanced over my shoulder at the wall of horrified spectators.

'He's right. That amulet is very dangerous; we've seen one explode.' Dace hovered on the balls of his feet. He glanced at the librarian. 'Get everyone out of this room,' he barked. 'Now.'

The librarian immediately began hustling the others out the door, like a bewildered hen with chicks. Dace remained, watching us, fingers twitching.

'You could always leave, too,' Brix said.

'Some of us have ethical principles,' he said, without looking at her or me. 'Doctor, is there any way to save this man, or find out where he acquired that plague amulet?'

'I'll do my best, of course. But I'm not sure I can get it off him without clipping the skin.'

'*Don't touch it,*' Dace snapped. 'Touching the last one was what *made* it explode.'

'Fine, I won't.' The doctor rocked back on her heels, her face drawn and pale. 'Why "plague amulet"? Temples says the plague is caused by spirits of ill-health, "plague ghosts". It's why we have the incense burners.' Tynan reached inside her shirt and brought out an amulet on a braided leather cord. It was a cheap tin version of Sannet's, dark, inactive – and legless, thank the gods. 'I don't know where Sannet got his, but Thane gave me this one weeks ago, insisted it was protective. It hasn't hurt me yet. It might be the reason I've been able to move through so many sickrooms without getting ill myself.'

'Take it off,' Brix said. 'It isn't safe.'

Tynan did, slipping it into her pocket. She shook her head. 'My training and experience have been that plagues are caused by bad water or bad air, like any other sickness, not by ghosts or necklaces. Help me understand.'

'Look at this.' I pointed with my little finger at the tiny, haphazard spiral of lit runes on Sannet's amulet. 'I think someone is doing this on purpose – spreading the amulets like . . . like seeds. The bodies we saw in Varriel had crystals growing in their blood. The amulet we smashed there had a similar crystal inside. If the crystals are what's amplifying the toxicity, it would make sense that they're sickening people. And in an alley just off the Godstown square we saw something.' I hesitated. 'A human corpse, I would have said, sewn together, manipulated with necromancy, except the thing wasn't dead. Does any of this sound familiar to you?'

She glanced up quickly. '*Sewn?*'

'I know it sounds mad,' I said. 'But I promise—'

'Not as mad as some things I've seen in this city during the last few weeks.' Tynan straightened Sannet's neck, which seemed to ease his wet, gasping breaths. 'Help me get him to the infirmary. Since we can't get it off of him, it ought to be enough to place him in isolation, right? Or will the explosion go through walls?'

I shook my head, unable to keep from remembering the easy way the magic had cut through the Roys back in Varriel. 'But it could kill you.'

'That's a risk doctors always take.' It was only when Tynan gave me one last, appraising look that it occurred to me to wonder exactly what she'd been testifying about at the trial. Medical evidence about Moyra's death, presumably. 'Tonight my priority has to be keeping Sannet alive, but in the morning, Master Gray, you and I are going to talk.'

Valera and the other Guildies still hadn't reached the Guildhouse by the time the librarian insisted that the doors be barred for the night. Dace, drawn and pale, only agreed after insisting that he be allowed to sit up and keep watch, so they could be let in the moment they turned up.

'*If* they're still alive,' Brix muttered.

Tynan said she'd sleep in the infirmary just off the kitchen, near Sannet, in case he stopped breathing during the night. The only beds the librarian had to offer Brix and me were a couple of cots in an empty dormitory upstairs. Nobody, of course, wanted to be near us, blood-spattered as we still were.

The dormitory was dusty and didn't have a lamp, but it was quiet and we were alone. I pulled off my filthy shirt and my boots and stretched out on my creaky, inadequate bed. I tried not to imagine how it felt to struggle for air with an amulet hooked into your skin.

Brix pushed her cot sideways until it was touching mine and lay down. I concentrated on the evenness of her breath, as if it could blot out the strangled, pulpy mess in the infirmary.

'Gray.' Brix's hand slipped into my pocket and drew out the ward-stones, clinking them together like a pair of dice.

'We going to have that fight now?' I said, taking the stones.

'Only if you insist.' Her tone was light, but she wasn't smiling. 'You saw something on Sannet's amulet.'

'Runes. Not hidden, the way they were on the amulet we found at Jaliseth's.' I squeezed my eyes shut, then open again. *Stay awake.* I needed to, at least until we could talk this out. 'It was an incantation, or actually just . . . a piece of an incantation. Whoever scribed it would probably have the other half of the spell written on or near them.'

'But that's magic, complicated magic.' Brix sounded doubtful. 'Who's doing magic in Genereth besides Guild wizards? And you, I mean.'

'Nobody that I can think of. Temples uses incantations, but usually a very small and unshielded set. It's mostly Ranaran here, from what everyone has been saying, and I can't imagine the blind priestesses inventing a spell like this, mixing . . .' It took too long for my mind to supply the words I wanted. The idea slipped away from me like a wriggling fish, dropping back into the void growing inside my head. Little saints, I was tired. And my ear stung where the gash from Sannet's fork had formed a fragile scab. I had scrubbed my skin nearly raw when we'd finished in the sick room, but I still didn't feel clean. I rubbed my eyes with the heel of my hand. 'It's probably someone unofficial like me. I can't be that unique.'

She rolled her eyes. 'Yes, I'm certain there are dozens of men with handmade bodies running around the city. I take it you're going to tell Tynan and Dace all this.'

I shrugged. The evidence was there for anyone to see. All they had to do was pay attention.

'And when were you going to tell *me*?'

The breath in my lungs went icy, jagged. I didn't move and neither did she, but a new distance opened between us. 'Tell you about what?'

'Whatever it is that you've been hiding from me. I know it isn't just the crystals. Gods, Gray, I'm not stupid.'

I rolled over to face her. 'I don't *know* anything, remember? You weren't wrong about that. I saw a woman when I did the divining in Varriel. She looked like she was dead, laying in a coffin, but she spoke. She said her name was Moyra, and she said she was *kept*. That's all.'

'Kept?'

'Your guess is as good as mine. I don't understand any of this.' I couldn't read Brix's face in the darkness. 'I thought that it was just something to do with the history of Jaliseth's amulet, a magical echo, some other person who had died because of it. I didn't think Moyra was really speaking to me. Even after she started showing up in my dreams—'

Brix's silhouette was rigid, unmoving. 'You still should have told me. Since when do we keep secrets from each other?'

'Since we got to Genereth, apparently,' I said. 'Or are we only allowed to talk about it when they're my secrets? When were you going to tell me about your family? We're together for a year and you never mention that they exist, and then I'm not supposed to wonder? What in the hells are you afraid of that you can't tell me? Or is it telling *them* about *me* that's the problem?'

No. Wrong. I forced myself to stay where I was. If I sat up, the ugliness inside me would boil over. My knuckles ached, gripped around the wardstones, but I couldn't let go. If I did, the flimsy ties holding me together might break.

She didn't pull away. The quiet crawled by, and all I could hear was my own heart and her breath. The knife's-edge words were still balanced there between us, dangerous. But she didn't pull away.

'You should know me better than that,' she said, at last.

I knew I should.

'I wanted to come here because I thought we could find a way to stop this plague,' I said, when I could trust my own voice. 'But I hate this place. I don't understand anything, and . . .' I licked my lips. 'I'm afraid, Brix.'

Her lips brushed at the sweat caught in my hairline. She shifted sideways, coming to rest in the crook of my arm. 'Me too.'

Neither of us apologised. But she held me, and I held her, until the velvet web of fatigue and comfort covered us both.

She was dead.

Moyra.

Dead, but this time she wasn't in the tank. She was still dripping with that dark fluid, though, her hair plastered to the sides of her face, watching me. She was sitting on a cup-shaped white stone structure that looked like a font.

'It *is* a font,' she said.

I couldn't think of anything more interesting to say than: 'I'm dreaming.'

I was standing in a room with a grey marble floor, inlaid with intricate silver crescent patterns that probably cost more than most entire houses. There must have been stained glass windows some-where, too, throwing pieces of jewelled light on the stones and metal at my feet. That, and the font, meant this was some god's sanctuary, or at least the mental equivalent.

'Not exactly,' Moyra said, a bit rueful. 'Bringing you here was the best I could do. You've had something on you, before, some magic that kept me from being able to speak to you clearly. But today you're not using them.'

No. The wardstones.

'Shit.' Had I activated the stones before I fell asleep? I'd had them in my hands. Had I pronounced the runes? I couldn't have dropped them. I pressed the heels of my hands to my temples, trying to silence the panic chewing its way into my guts. Gods knew why I was dreaming about Moyra, but it was only a matter of time before the dream changed, became the one where someone stabbed me or burned me, became the one where I fought. 'I've got to wake up.'

Moyra looked at me, almost pityingly.

'No, it *is* a dream,' I insisted. 'Divining doesn't work that way. You're not really talking to me, and I'm not really here, and if I think hard enough there's a way to wake myself up, there's—'

Moyra pointed at the floor. The silver inlay beneath my feet bloomed with purple light. The crescent pattern I was standing on was, on closer inspection, a moon made of sigils of a type that I had never seen before. They had a shape similar to the script at the top of the buildings out on the Genereth streets. An uneasy flash of doubt passed over me. If I was dreaming, why would I imagine myself in a room full of runes that I couldn't read?

'Because you're not,' Moyra said. 'You do need to learn the pattern on the floor, though.'

'Gods, I'm a fool,' I whispered. 'It's not divination at all, is it? The first time was, but this – *you're* doing this, aren't you?'

'Sorry.' Moyra sounded not at all sorry. I suppose if I was somewhat dead I wouldn't be all that worried about my guests' comfort either. 'I had to warn them somehow, and you were the only one that I could reach.' She pointed to my chest.

Jaern's amulet hung there just as it did in real life, black and silent. I touched it. 'Are you saying that this is how I'm able to speak to you? Why would that be?'

'I don't know,' Moyra said. 'But that amulet is connected to the one I wear, somehow, and I know that your amulet has got her worried.'

'Who?' I sat down. My head throbbed, which also argued for some kind of long-distance communication.

'You *know* who,' Moyra said, with the slow precision that people usually reserve for someone who has asked a particularly dim question. 'Look, she watches us. If I say her name, she'll hear me. You can help us – you can stop it – but you have to work harder than this. Think. You've seen her scribework. You've seen her eclipse people, haven't you?'

'Just–' I lifted a hand. 'Let me catch up. Are you alive or not? Can we sort that out before we go on?'

This seemed to bother her. 'Does that matter?'

'Well, my next question will be somewhat different if you're speaking to me from the afterworld,' I said.

She hunched one shoulder and stared at the floor. I waited, and tried to decide what colour her hair was under the goop. Black, I thought, although it was difficult to be sure. She was in her early twenties – maybe just twenty, now that I looked at her. Her face had the kind of sharp-boned edges that meant hunger, and hard work without a lot of sleep. She wore some kind of simple, straight garment. A nightgown, maybe, or a . . . I frowned, rifling in my mind for the word. What did women call that thing?

'Chemise,' Moyra said, without looking up.

'Gods, quit listening to me think,' I said. 'It isn't fair. I could have been thinking insulting things.'

She smiled. 'But you weren't, were you? Don't worry, I can't do it all the time, but we are more or less sharing minds right now.' She paused. 'And I don't know how much longer I can keep talking to you, so we should hurry. Why do you keep asking if I'm dead?'

'When I divined for you, you didn't seem to have a heartbeat,' I said. 'I thought you were a piece of history, a victim who had died from the amulet before Jaliseth got it.'

'Not a victim, not like that. I'm here because my beloved . . .' She looked down at her feet. 'He couldn't let me go. The Guild could have helped me, you know. They could have stopped it.'

'They could have done a ley-breaker,' I said. 'They should have. I'm sorry.'

'I haven't had a heartbeat for months. But I'm not exactly dead. I'm kept. In . . .' She waggled a hand in the air, her turn to search for a word.

'Stasis,' I said.

Her eyebrows lifted.

I shook my head. 'No, I can't hear your thoughts, I've just lived with a grandfather who never finishes his sentences. You're Tirnaal, then? They're the only people I've ever heard of being able to survive stasis. Or enter it. I didn't know it stopped hearts, though.'

'I'm not sure it does, for everybody.' She pushed a strand of dripping hair back out of her face, hooking it behind one ear. 'It's funny. Being Tirnaal meant the Guild wouldn't take me. And now I'm the one trying to keep them alive.'

'The Guild thinks you're dead, buried somewhere near Ranara-temple. They had your murderer on trial yesterday, albeit posthumously.' I hesitated, but there was no delicate way to ask such a question. 'Who was the living person, in the vision I had back in Varriel? The one with a heartbeat who wrecked my spell and broke my memory?'

'You *saw* her? She saw you? I didn't know that.' Moyra frowned. 'When she takes people they usually don't remember. I was hoping that you wouldn't remember – that she'd assume you didn't know. We're out of time. She'll be sending for you.'

The room around me *thinned*, like a piece of cloth stretched too far. The dream, or vision, or whatever it was, shifted under both of us. 'Who saw me?' I said.

'They're coming.' Moyra stood. 'Now. You understand me? She's afraid, and she's sending them to hurt you.'

'*Who?*' The sharp, wicked tang of smoke tickled my nostrils.

No.

I got to my feet, but the floor was buckling. When I looked down, my arms were covered in sigils that I hadn't written. For a vision, this was ending in a sickeningly familiar way. Moyra walked towards me, tense, as if each step was a struggle, leaving damp black footprints on the grey floor. Somewhere behind me, stained glass shattered.

'What do you mean, "she's" sending them?' I tried to wipe out the magic on my skin, but it was attached to me. It was already smouldering. *I* was already smouldering. 'Answer me, Moyra, if you want me to help you. Who is coming?'

'You must wake up,' Moyra said, simply. She lifted her hand, and I saw the delicate ring of black stitches around her wrist, the gleam of steel at her fingertips. 'The dead are here.'

She reached for me, and I burned.

NINE

I woke up. The bed was on fire.

The flame spell was still in my mouth, hot, bitter, jagged, and I brought my teeth down on it with such force that they squeaked. I had to keep my jaw shut, couldn't even scream as I leaped out of the cot, snatched the smoking blankets and the straw-stuffed tick mattress and threw them to the floor.

In another few seconds I had stomped the tiny flames out and stood trembling in the dark, panting and trying not to puke magic on to the scorched remnants of the blankets.

Shit. Shit shit shit—

It was out. The fire was out. It had been small, just a spark, barely enough to cause damage. Brix hadn't even awakened. She was curled up on her side in her cot, undisturbed by my nightmare, the spell I had spewed, the death that had come within inches of us.

The sigils I had pronounced in my magic-addled sleep were still lit along my bare arm like malevolent jewellery, glowing red curves dancing against my flesh and bone. I put a hand over my mouth and tried, unsuccessfully, to slow my breathing.

I had ash between my fingers. The stink of it crawled into my nostrils.

Just a spark. Just the beginning of the spell cupped in my hand, just a nightmare. That was all it took. And Brix—

I had to get away from her before I hurt her. I twisted on my heel. I was in the hall before I even realised I had opened the door.

Incense braziers stood smoking beneath each window in the hall-way, throwing a haze of spices into the air. The damn building was too big. There were too many shadows in every corner, writhing in weird patterns as the moonlight seeped in through the basket-woven shutters. I still had enough fear pumping through my veins that I could have sworn I saw some of them move. I plunged blindly down the hall anyway.

I needed water, something to rinse the taste of ruined magic out of my mouth. What I found was the dining hall. It was empty, and nobody had scrubbed the brown, sticky place where Sannet had fallen. I was panting and the air in that room had not improved, the potent tang of old shrimp mingled with magic and blood. I tried to walk past the stain, across the floor towards what I judged was the kitchen. I made it three steps before I went to my knees, gagging.

They're coming.

The dead.

I knew I should tell someone. I should find Dace and try to make him do something, but what? I tried to picture myself explaining – *I had a dream in which a dead woman told me something bad is going to hap-pen but not how to stop it, and then I nearly burned my partner alive* – and gagged again.

A dark smudge detached itself from the wall at the far end of the room, near the infirmary door. 'Are you ill?' it said.

I breathed deep through my nose, trying to cut through the nau-sea. 'No. Go away, Tynan.'

The doctor ignored me and crossed the room to a square masonry shape in the corner that I had thought was some kind of oven. It must have been a cistern, because she dipped a clay cup into it, and then brought it to me, full of water. She stood there without comment while I sat on the floor and drank. I tried to decide exactly how much trouble I was in.

'I don't have the plague,' I said, when I could talk.

'I can see that.'

I got to my hands and knees, and then, slowly, to my feet. 'Do you just skulk around at night, then?'

'Yes,' she said. 'I'm the one who made the decision to let you in the Guildhouse. I have some responsibility for you.'

'That's a comfort.' I picked up the cup and made my way over to the cistern. She followed and waited, again at her ease, a comfortable cat outside a familiar mouse hole.

I drank until my stomach was bloated and sore and I had purged the taste of ashes. I wiped my mouth with my wrist, aware I was still breathing too hard.

'How long has this been happening?' she said.

I dipped a handful of water and splashed my face. The jitters in my fingers wouldn't calm down. I clenched my hand into a fist. 'Nothing's happening. I just—'

'I could help you, you know.'

Help for a man who shouldn't exist – from a stretched-thin doctor in a dying city? The offer almost sounded like mockery, but in the flickering light of the braziers I couldn't discern anything on her face beyond a sort of cool politeness. 'I don't know what you're talking about,' I said.

'Being haunt-minded,' she said, with that soft precision that I was beginning to dislike. I turned away from the cistern and considered vomiting again, but she kept talking, without moving. 'Usually it's because you've seen too much. Soldiers get it, but doctors do, too. I've seen it in people whose spouses are too ready with their fists.' She paused. 'And, since this plague started, in survivors. You're hardly the first.'

She wasn't going to leave me alone until I said something. Besides, a coal of profoundly uncomfortable hope was flickering in my chest. What if Tynan actually could help?

'I have nightmares,' I said, before I could talk myself out of it. I'd gone from feeling overheated to damp and clammy with sweat.

'Nightmares.' There wasn't judgement in the word. It wasn't *only nightmares?* or *you think a few bad dreams amount to a significant problem, when a whole city is dying?* She sounded, perhaps, a little bored.

They make me dangerous. I couldn't get myself to say it. 'If we're going to talk about this, can we at least go someplace with fresh air?'

Tynan grimaced. 'There's not much privacy in a Guildhouse. Outside of the infirmary, I haven't got the authority to use so much as a cupboard and I don't want to ask for it. The ranking officer here is a man who, until two weeks ago, was never in charge of anything bigger than a scriptorium. That "test" I did at the door . . .' She paused. 'It's nothing. I think the duke knows it's nothing – foaming powder, a bit of theatre that he and the Roys are trying to pass off as some kind of protection to keep the city from panicking. I figured it out weeks ago, but I haven't told anyone. The people in this building are near enough to breaking without that . . . and without whatever it is you are.' She crossed her arms and beckoned me with an inclined head. 'We can sit in here. If it helps, I'm often up at night and I can promise you, they're all asleep. Nobody will disturb us.'

'If you say so,' I said. 'I don't suppose we could open a window? It still stinks like that damn cremation spell.'

She had started to sit at the closest table, but paused at the word *cremation*, her nose wrinkling with disgust. 'Is that what it was? Gerrick – our librarian – told me he'd never seen an incantation like it, seemed inclined to think it wasn't a real spell at all, just a lucky mistake.'

I rolled my eyes. 'Yes, a precisely calibrated, blood-orientated mistake that neither blew up in the caster's face nor caused useless effects.' I pointed at the char circling the room in a pattern that used to be pink flowers, near the ceiling. 'Ash, and it found the oxblood in the paint they used on the roses, but it didn't set the room on fire. So it was a cremation spell, but I'm not surprised Gerrick's never seen one. They're not common.'

She considered this, then settled on to her bench, resting her elbows on the table. 'You're not a Guild wizard, then.'

I displayed my bare wrist. 'Rather obviously.' Come to think of it, I was still shirtless. The back of my neck heated. 'Sorry about—' I waved a hand at myself.

Tynan leaned her chin on one hand. 'It's only a body, and a doctor can't afford to be fussy about bodies, Master Gray.'

'Just Gray.' There was a window a few steps away from the cistern, with a brazier burning beneath it. I threw the latch and opened the shutter, letting in a blessed gulp of cool air and a puffy cloud of insects. The night outside didn't exactly smell sweet, but at least the odours were the kind that you could identify – dirt, sewage, cooking fires.

By contrast, the Guildhouse smothered and confused me. There was that odour of disease, under the incense, and chemicals. I turned back to Tynan. This didn't feel right. But then, with so much latent fear still pumping through my body, it was unlikely that anything would have felt right to me. Tynan was looking at me expectantly. I shoved my indecision aside and sat across from her.

'So,' she said. 'Shall we begin, just-Gray? What happened?'

I still couldn't find the words to begin speaking for several moments. I picked at a spot of candle grease on the table. 'Does that matter?'

'If it's the reason you're really here, yes,' she said. 'It does.'

'I'm here because the Guild asked me to investigate a plague.'

'You know that isn't what I meant,' she said, and there was something different about her voice. The shape of the sounds had changed, accented the way Sannet's had been. Maybe she was stressed, reverting to old speech patterns. She folded her hands on the table. They were capable, calloused, prominent veins twisting across the thickly mus- cled wrists and knuckles. For the first time I wondered how old she was. Older than me, certainly, but she could have been anywhere from my mother's age to my grandmother's. 'We both know,' she said, 'what you really are.'

They're coming.

I blinked, trying to clear my head of the lingering grip of my nightmare. *Focus, Gray.* 'According to the Guildlords, I'm a criminal, if that's what you're implying,' I said. 'Nonstandard incantations and running with an escaped slave were the main charges, I believe. There were others.'

Tynan searched my eyes for a long time. I was betting that Dace hadn't told her much, and I wasn't going to admit to Jaern's crimes. My skin might have carried the words to call the dead, but that didn't make me a necromancer.

'You're suffering,' she said, with a note of surprise.

I winced. It hardly seemed correct to dignify what I was doing with such a strong name. Not when there were people hacking their lungs up. Not with Sannet sleeping in the next room, ruined mind, ruined eye and all.

'A year ago I lived through something I shouldn't have. Did things that I didn't want to. I have nightmares.' I hunched my shoulders, feeling exposed in a way that had nothing to do with not having a shirt. Jaern's amulet shone against my chest like a velvet-dark piece of night sky, ostentatious. 'That's all. I should be able to find a way to sort it out, but I haven't. It's not suffering. It's just . . . a problem.'

There. Now she was going to tell me there wasn't anything she could do for me after all, or click her tongue and advise me to drink clear soups and avoid wine, or tell me to take up knitting.

Instead, she stood and rifled around in her trousers' pocket. She brought out something that fit in her hand and sat back down. She planted it on the table in front of me.

'That,' she said, and now the accent was gone, her voice once again matter-of-fact. 'A mouthful before bed. It'll prevent the dreams, and it'll calm you during the day.'

It was a squat, thick glass bottle of some dark fluid. If I was sup-posed to take a mouthful every night, this bottle would last me maybe a week. I didn't touch it. 'Drin?'

'Indeed.' Her eyes narrowed. 'I'm surprised you know it. Mostly it's only used in Genereth and you're an outsider.'

'I know very little,' I said. 'The amulets have drin inside, probably as part of an alchemical compound. Any idea why that might be?'

'Off the top of my head?' Tynan didn't take her eyes off me. 'Drin is a narcotic, a sedative made in the wall chapels from old funeral honey. In high enough doses, it's damn near a paralytic. It seems to help ease the plague symptoms and slow its progression. Maybe it was meant as part of a charm.'

My stomach turned. '*Funeral* honey?'

'Heathen.' Tynan gave an unexpected grin. 'Ranara-temple keeps beehives all over the city and harvests the honey for ritual mead and for funeral use – it's a Generethi tradition to coat the dead in honey, so that their trip to the next life will be sweet. Each funeral gets its own jar of honey, but most families can't afford the whole jar so they put a ceremonial smear of honey on the corpse and sell the rest to the drinlords. Consecrated honey is supposed to make a better syrup, because the Lady of Shadows has blessed your journey towards the Lord of the Afterlands.'

'This sort of thing is *why* I'm a heathen,' I said. 'Where did you get the drin?'

'I bought it, of course,' she said. 'From a drinlord stall near Deadchurch. It's moderately illegal not to buy it at Temples, but it was half-price and there's an emergency in the city. Are you this suspicious of everyone, or just doctors?'

My earlobe was burning – Dace was moving around in the building and the regulator earring was reminding me, with every nauseating tug, that the Examiner General had me on a leash. If the wardstones had really stopped working, I'd have to involve him. 'Of everyone,' I said, rubbing at my ear. 'What's Deadchurch?'

'One of the wall chapels. Tirnaal territory.' Tynan went silent, for long enough that I thought she might leave, and take her drin with her. When she did speak again, her voice was measured, careful. 'The Examiner General came and spoke to me for a long time after most people had gone to bed. He says you can help solve this thing, end the plague. If he's right, the Tirnaal need to ask for your help.'

I went cold. 'What's a Tirnaal doctor doing working for the Guild? Guild doctors are at least journeyman wizards. Tirnaal are against associating with wizards. Something about blasphemy, isn't it?'

'I'm not Tirnaal,' she said. 'I just care very much about someone who is. It's to the clans' advantage to have a friend in the Guild-houses, to ensure that the more predatory wizards can be avoided or neutralised. The point is, there's a plague now. It's possible you won't throw them to the dogs the way the rest of the city would.'

'I thought the Tirnaal families ruled half of Genereth,' I said. 'What do you need me for?'

She smiled, without humour. 'They run their streets and make their medicine as long as the rest of the city feels like letting them. Have you ever seen a city when it decides that the people it tolerates as conveniences are getting too successful? When it's frightened, and needs someone to blame? Have you ever seen what happens then?'

'You mean the riot,' I said. 'The law is supposed to prevent that kind of vigilante "justice".'

'I mean a purge.' Her eyes stayed locked on mine. 'The law is sup-posed to prevent random wizards kidnapping Tirnaal children and selling them as Guildhouse slaves, but that still happens. The city is ready to boil over, Gray. The Tirnaal aren't getting sick as fast as the others, and the rumours are beginning. Some of them say they're hoarding a secret cure, that they're the ones selling plague amulets, that they've made some dark bargain with the gods. About two hundred Tirnaal were rounded up a week ago, arrested for "spreading disease". Mothers, babies, even. If they don't die in the Temples sick pens, they'll be executed as panic grows – unless we can prove how the plague works and exonerate them. The Examiner tells me that you have the wits and the instincts to do this, and more to the point, Brix seems to trust you. But Brix doesn't know how bad this nightmare business has gotten for you, does she?' Tynan pushed the bottle closer to me, with a dull scrape of glass against wood. 'Take it.'

I took it. I had no intention of swallowing the damn stuff, no mat-ter how seductive I found the prospect of not having to feel anything for a few hours. But if the Guildhouse had a laboratory, it was possible that I could talk Dace into letting me do some alchemical tests. Hells, maybe Brix and Tynan could even tell us how to get into Deadchurch, see if they could help us find out who had been buying drin lately. There were plenty of reasons to *possess* the drin. But I wasn't going to drink it. That would mean admitting I was at the end.

The wardstones weren't foolproof. Getting rid of the nightmares was my only chance now, the only way I could have something approaching a normal life. If I took the drin and even that didn't work—

'You're not still wearing the plague amulet that Thane gave you, are you?' I said, because I had to say something. 'It's too dangerous, even if you think it protects you against the plague.'

'So you say,' she said. 'But I notice you're still wearing yours.'

'It's not the same,' I said. 'Mine is older, and . . . I think it connects me with someone. There's a woman in my dreams, a Tirnaal woman. I think she's—'

A long, gurgling scream cut through my words. It came from upstairs, towards the front of the building where the dormitories were.

Brix. No.

The dead are here.

We ran.

TEN

It wasn't a fire; the darkness still puddled like ink in the hallways, pressing around us. And the big front door was barred when we reached the foot of the staircase, so nobody had broken in. Dace was already two steps up the stairs, crouched like a wary animal. 'It came from upstairs,' he said, pausing on one foot. 'Nobody but you has gone up or down. I've been on watch.'

'Brix.' My blood sang with panic. Moyra had tried to tell me, and I'd wasted time whining to Tynan about my problems. I started past Dace, but he put a hand on my chest.

'Together,' he said, quietly. 'You go nowhere without me.'

'An accident, or . . .' Tynan's voice died.

'Maybe rioters. Burglars. It doesn't matter.' Dace pointed back towards the kitchen. 'Sannet is pivotal to this investigation. Go to the infirmary and protect him, doctor, unless it becomes unsafe, in which case you're to get out into the street and fetch the Royal Police.'

Tynan turned without a word and jogged back into the darkness.

Dace glanced at me, seemed to make up his mind and tossed me a pencil. We sprinted up the stairs.

The shadows breathed menace as Dace and I reached the landing at the top of the stairs and turned towards the bedrooms. The building had fallen into silence. Brix stood in the hallway, eyes wide.

Relief hit me so hard that my knees went loose and wobbly. 'Brix, thank the gods.'

'You don't believe in gods.' She looked from me to Dace. 'What's going on? Who was screaming?'

'Quiet.' Dace stepped forwards until he was between Brix and me and the rest of the hallway. Opposite the dormitories a line of tall windows punctuated the wall, equipped with wicker shutters that closed tight against mosquitoes. Two of the shutters had been hacked to bits, the warm darkness of the night outside swallowing the dim light from the low-burning braziers. A moth fluttered through the opening. One shutter remained, throwing sinuous curves and shadows across the floor, shadows that almost had a shape I recognised.

Dace paused, head cocked sideways, listening.

He was using the wrong sense. My nose had long since gone numb to the all-encompassing incense, but there was something else on the air here, a penetrating metallic scent that reminded me of being ten years old, learning my sigils: alchemical paint, and in quantity. Dace eased his way to the dormitory door just ahead of us.

He lifted the latch and pushed the door open with his foot, flattening himself quickly against the wall as he did so. I followed his lead and kept myself in front of Brix. Nothing, however, charged out and attacked us. The room beyond the door was pitch-black and silent.

I whispered the illumination spell written under the skin around my left wrist and felt it flare gently to life. Dace's breath hissed out, and I knew, in my gut, that I was appalling him. However much he was forced to trust me in a pinch, if we survived this, he'd never let me and my rune-written skin go free. Then Brix took my hand, and walked with me as I carried my light into the dark.

This room was a dormitory with six beds, three on each wall, and clearly lived in – clothes were hung on hooks and draped across the beds; blankets were rumpled over the sleeping forms of the occupants. Against the wall, discarded pairs of shoes lay empty, wrinkled and comfortable. It all looked homey and normal, except for the sigils.

In the middle of the floor a spiral had been written in large, smeared red characters. It had, I fancied, been active until a few minutes ago, which didn't make much sense. It wasn't the kind of thing you'd use inside a room. This was the type of incantation that ships' magicians used on becalmed vessels, a desperate gambit to manipulate the wind. And the air was wrong – stale, used-up.

The whole room felt wrong. I was so distracted by trying to figure out how the spiral worked that it took me nearly ten seconds to realise what was bothering me. There were six sleeping people, but no movement. There wasn't so much as the sound of breathing.

'Gray,' Brix said.

She had let go of my hand and was standing at the foot of one of the beds. When I swung the light towards her, I saw it: a blue, suffocated face, barely recognisable as one of the apprentices from earlier.

'It's all of them,' she whispered. 'They're dead.'

The dead are here.

'That's why they were moving air currents.' The words almost wouldn't leave my mouth, difficult to push past the hideous realisation. 'They were stealing breath.' I moved quickly to the middle of the red spiral and scraped my foot across it, smearing a long streak through the sigils with my heel.

'We've got to check the other rooms,' Dace said. 'And Brix should go downstairs, get Tynan and get out of the building. The bastards who did this could still be here.'

'No,' I said, almost involuntarily. 'Brix isn't going anywhere, not by herself, not with suffocation spells being flung hither and thither. We need to be smarter than that.'

'We need help,' Dace insisted. 'And official witnesses. These people were murdered with magic. If this ends up being a wizards' duel, the last thing we need is the possibility of collateral damage.' He bypassed me and turned to Brix. 'Madam, *please*. I have a duty to make sure you don't die in my custody.'

Brix pulled away from me.

'Stop it.' I scrambled to stand between her and the hallway. 'No!'

'Gray, you're not thinking. Listen.' She took my face between her two hands. Her fingertips dug into the muscles of my jaw. 'The killer would have had to pass us to go down the main staircase, right? So if they're still inside they have to be in the bedrooms, and I can get down the stairs without them seeing me. Dace is right: we need help.' She paused. 'And you know that if I'm here you'll be holding back, thinking about that girl who caught a paralysis spell. You have to let me go.'

Moyra.

'You can't go.' I knew she was right, but that didn't make this easier. 'Not alone. Brix, not you, I can't–' My voice broke.

'You won't.' She kissed me once, hard, and my heart rose to meet her. 'I'll find you.'

'Keep yourself alive,' I said.

She grinned. 'Keep the bastards pinned down, whoever they are. I'll be back.'

And just like that she was gone, into the dark.

The second room had already been hit.

Dace and I found the source of the scream as soon as we stepped inside: Gerrick the librarian, slumped in a smear of dark blood on the floor. He must have awakened and caught the murderer in action, because this suffocation spiral, scrawled on the plaster wall, was even more hastily written.

The five other dead people in the room were in their beds. At least two spells had been loosed in here: the suffocation, paint still wet – and something else, which had caved the librarian's chest in. His ruined ribcage gleamed faintly orange, luminous with magic residue.

'Bonewarp,' Dace said, his voice a mix of fascination and horror. 'I've never seen one in the field.' *The field*, as though he and I were on the same side.

'I have,' I said. 'Bonewarp is dangerous, reckless. It's one of the spells that can bounce, so it can double back at you if you're not careful, twist your own joints. It would have been a risk, using it in here.'

He glanced at me again, with that calculating, shrewd look that I was beginning to hate. 'Any idea who would be sophisticated enough to throw one?'

'No.' Even through my growing fear, my mouth filled with the sharp taste of resentment. 'There isn't an Unguild murderers' meeting where we introduce ourselves, unfortunately.' I looked down at the pencil he'd finally entrusted me with, trying to decide what kind of spell would possibly be useful against enemies who stole breath and shattered bone. I pushed one sleeve up. 'Hold the light over here for a second.'

He did, watching with narrowed eyes as I scribed on my forearm. 'That's—'

'If you say "illegal",' I said brightly, 'I'm going to hit you right in the mouth. Either let me help, or let me go.'

'Fine. Wreck the spiral, please.' Dace cast rapidly under his breath as he moved back towards the door. He was quick, focused, and all at once the kind of hunting Guild enforcer that I had dreaded my entire life. A spell written on his arm lit scarlet and flowed down to his curled fingers.

Shacklebright.

He'd had the thing scribed in advance, which meant that he had anticipated using it that night. Which meant, unless he had known the building would be attacked, that he'd been prepared to use it on me.

You are an abomination, though, aren't you?

It shouldn't have hurt.

I smeared the sigils into nothingness and followed Dace, my own frustration rising steadily with my heartbeat. This whole thing was wrong. Whoever had written the suffocation spirals wasn't sophisticated, they were angry, brimming with hate. These people had been slaughtered, their breath snuffed out – *apprentices*, mind, *librarians*. Who could hate a *librarian*?

We stepped into the hallway at the same time that the murderers did.

There were at least three, standing beside the still-swinging door of the next dormitory. They weren't Guild wizards – no robes, and no licence sigils. Dace was two steps ahead of me when he let the shacklebright spell go. It caught the wizard on the left, a woman with brown hair dappled throughout with pale streaks. The spell crackled across her body and broke into sparks as she fell, bound.

One of the others spun, chanting as he did so. I grabbed Dace's elbow as I threw myself to the floor, yanking him down with me.

The spell whizzed over our heads in a hot pulse of orange light that would have neatly asphyxiated us, had it impacted properly. A windthrift spell, as I lived and, for the moment, breathed. These pricks had a real affection for suffocating people.

The floor was glowing.

'Dace,' I said, alarmed. I hadn't seen any spells scribed on the floorboards, and the wizards hadn't had the time to kneel and write anything while I'd been watching them. I pointed at the inexplicable orange spiral, but by the time Dace turned his head the sigils had faded out, leaving nothing behind but shifting shadows.

Dace grunted, then pronounced a nice little slipknives spell and sent it hissing across the floor towards them. He had, evidently, been more worried about intruders than I had thought. The one who had thrown the last incantation yelped when it bit him, the blades of magic hopping up from the floor and slicing into his hands.

Still, slipknives against windthrift wasn't a smart choice. Maiming vs. killing. There was also the fact that I could only see two wizards now – the third must have ducked back into the dormitory. Dace was going to lose if I didn't cast.

I spoke, feeling each sigil as it lit in a string down my arm. I pointed and watched the web of red light shoot itself across the floor towards the boots of the invader. It curled itself around him, leafing out like vines smothering a tree. When he tried to chant, I sent the vines shooting into his open mouth.

Dace stared up at me. 'What are you doing?'

The spell was called leafgrip, but it wasn't easy to keep control of, and I couldn't afford to waste my attention. I pointed with my chin towards the door. 'The other one.'

Dace got to his feet – stupidly, because it slowed down his casting. Before he could get even a few syllables of his next spell off, the dormitory door banged open, belching a nest of spiky blue shafts of light.

'Look out!' I shouted – stupidly, because it made me shift my attention.

My leafgrip spell snapped, and the man I'd been holding shuffled backwards. A row of blue spikes cracked upwards through the floor until one impaled Dace through the arm and held him, suspended in the air, wriggling and gasping for breath. The rest of the spell grew towards me, like living crystal. I couldn't even see the person who had cast it, beyond a very tall silhouette in the doorway.

A shaft of blue darted sideways and brushed against my pointing hand. The magic was freezing cold and sticky, like touching ice with wet fingers. I couldn't pull away from it. At least I wasn't bleeding.

I threw myself backwards, tugging against the spell, stretching until I could get my free hand around the base of the closest brazier. Pain shot up my arm and the roast-meat stink of burned skin sizzled into the air as I flung the lit brazier at the silhouette.

The brazier hit the wizard's legs and feet with a clang, scattering glowing coals. It must have broken their concentration, because the spell shattered, releasing both me and Dace to thud to the ground. I fell face-first. The mass of tiny blisters on my palm split against the floorboards with a pulse of black, nauseating, all-encompassing pain.

Dace wasn't making a sound. I'd have to draw the enemies' attention. Spiders it was, then.

I pushed myself up to my full height and stepped sideways until I was standing over Dace, who was not moving. I pointed at a spot on the ceiling above the cursing person who was trying to dance away from the smoking coals and chanted as quickly as I could. Runes sprang alight along the backs of my fingers, and a swarm of glowing yellow arachnids whirred down from the ceiling.

Just the look of the spell is enough to make most people back up, but I'm fond of the action: when the spiders get to you, they bite. The numbing effect that follows isn't quite paralysis; think of it more like getting pins and needles in your entire body, all at once.

It seemed to disconcert the silhouette, which screamed and leaped out of the doorway and into the hallway, revealing itself to be a rangy young man with a copper ring in his nose. He was slapping frantically at the ten thousand yellow spiderlings swarming towards his face.

This was a tricky moment, because I'd had to let the leafgrip die and Dace wasn't maintaining the shacklebright anymore. The other two were going to try something. I had to hope that the one I had wrapped in spiders was the most dangerous. Maybe I could get him between me and his allies.

I curled my fingers towards myself. The spiders clutched the man with the nose ring and dragged him forwards. The others were chanting something, but I couldn't make out what. He advanced, step by unwilling step, his heels leaving dents in the soft pine floorboards.

'Let me go.' He struggled, which was a bad choice. The spiders have barbed legs. Struggling makes their grip go tighter. 'Let me go, stinking Guild pig!'

'Stinking *freelance* pig,' I said, lifting one finger. The web of spiders tightened even further, and he cried out.

He was about six feet from me when he realised how the spell was working and stopped resisting. Because I'd been pulling, he flew towards me at speed, one hand out as he pronounced a set of sigils. They lit across his collarbone, visible at the neck of his shirt.

A matching set lit along my jaw.

I hadn't known that spell was there, and barely had time to shout the last few syllables of the runes written under my skin, grabbing control before it surged into existence. The magic snapped my head back and my arm into extension, elbow locked, bones a rigid line. The spell boomed along it, a pulse of force narrowed down to a thin, knife-like projectile bursting from my forefinger.

My magic met his, as our outstretched fingers brushed each other. *CRACK.*

The air around me shimmered and broke in a wave of sound. When I could see again I was on my back, staring up at the ceiling, and everything had gone silent except for a weird, high buzzing noise.

Dace was up before me, bleeding, pulling me back on to my feet and yelling. I couldn't hear him over the whistling tone in my ears. I shook him off, reeling, trying to find the enemy.

They were gone. So was a large portion of the windows.

I staggered over to the hole in the shutters where a tall window leading to the balcony had been. One of the attackers was crumpled where the spell had flung him against the railing, his neck bent at an unnatural angle, eyes staring. This wasn't the one I wanted; this one was in his forties, and looked more like a cattle drover than a wizard. I leaned out, but the dark courtyard below showed no sign of the other two.

I needed to find the tall man with the pierced nose and make him tell me how he had cast that spell. The runes under my skin were odd, archaic. Pronouncing them was like speaking in a dialect you weren't born to, and even a simple incantation like the shacklebright I carried was different than the one that Dace had used. Jaern's magic was just like the false god himself – mean, glittering, full of pain. Nobody else should have been walking around with that particular ancient set of runes in their repertoire.

'Gray!' Dace's voice finally penetrated the buzz in my ears.

I turned and picked my way back inside. 'They could still be here. There could be others.' My voice sounded strange and muffled. 'We need to search the rest of the building, now.'

'Gray, the bodies.' Dace grabbed me by one shoulder. His other arm hung, bloodied and limp, by his side. 'They went downstairs!'

I frowned at him, trying to decide whether I had hit my head when I fell, or whether he had hit his. The *bodies* went downstairs?

Dace leaned in and shouted at me as if I had gone deaf, which I suppose in a way I had.

'*They're necromancers.* They raised the bodies and sent them downstairs. We have to get to Brix and Tynan, now.'

The stairs took too long to descend, but at least they gave me twenty seconds or so to plan. Dace was running behind me, shouting something that didn't matter – a rebuke, maybe, or instructions. I lost track of him when I hit the deeper murk of the landing.

A woman's scream tore through the air, and I sprinted towards the dining room.

'Gray!' Brix held a fireplace poker in one hand, her back to the kitchen door and her other arm in front of a drooping form that I recognised as Tynan.

When I burst in, five lifeless, pallid corpses were moving towards the women in a loose half-circle. A short distance behind them stood the killer with the copper ring in his nose. He twisted towards me as I began incanting.

The technical name for the reanimated dead is marulaches. Creating them is a trick mastered by few, even necromancers. It takes an unusual amount of concentration, an iron tolerance for pain and a handy dead body that isn't too far decayed to be useful. Even then, marulaches can't be left to perform tasks without a master, especially if that task is, say, anything other than bludgeoning someone to death. I needed to remove both the marulaches and their master, and I was no longer interested in being subtle.

The toxicity chewed into my gut as the sigils around my navel lit. I swallowed past it and threw shacklebright at the wizard. The spell licked at my own hand, caressing the already-blistered skin, sending fresh gouts of pain through me. Still, the sudden fear on his face was glorious.

He threw himself to one side, hands out, sweeping his spell and the marulaches around in front of him. They came in a group, puppets with tangled strings, a row of already-dead shields. They managed to block most of my spell, transforming into a shambling mess, knotted together with magic.

I pulled on the shacklebright. The knot collapsed on to Nosering, who had conjured it in the first place.

With him pinned down for at least a few seconds, I sprinted towards Brix and Tynan, strands of red lightning trailing out behind me.

Tynan was pitched sideways, all her weight on one leg, staring at me like I might be responsible for the corpses. I should have said something encouraging, but I still had magic coiled around both arms and didn't trust myself to talk much. I had to maintain a spell that was binding six writhing bodies, five of which couldn't feel pain.

Brix was breathing hard, her eyes searching the room behind me. There were tight lines around her mouth.

Dread spiked in my gut. 'Brix?'

She nodded, but coughed, and spat. It wasn't blood, though. Instead, puffs of pink light burst from her lips.

'I'm all right,' she said, but she wasn't. The determination shone in her voice like a sword. 'There's another bedroom on this floor, and we got Sannet and a few of the others safely outside before those things chased us in here. Tynan fell. I don't think she can walk by herself. Where's Dace?'

It was a good question. He hadn't followed me into the room. Of course, he could have simply gone straight out the front door, but that didn't seem likely. No matter how much he annoyed me, I didn't think the Examiner was the type to forsake his duty in order to save his own skin.

But I didn't have time to hope that Dace would show up and help. The marulaches were eerily silent, except for a meaty pop now and then when one of them broke its own bone trying to escape the spell. There was nothing from Nosering, but in a moment he'd figure out that he could order the marulaches to pull in the same direction as he was and overwhelm me. If I lost control, gods forbid, the wizard could cast. If he could run five marulaches, he was both skilled and ruthless. We needed to end this, now.

I glanced at the kitchen door.

'It's locked,' Brix said. 'I would have gone through it otherwise. Can you open it?'

I shook my head. I couldn't write a breaker without letting my concentration slip. Scribing with all five of the undead trying to kick me to death didn't sound like a good idea. Besides, upstairs Nosering had allies, at least one of which could have still been alive. We needed to get out before they arrived.

'There's no exit from the kitchen, anyway. We're trapped.' Tynan's eyes rolled back towards the bundle of corpses. 'My friends. Gods, they're my *friends* – that's Gerrick.'

My stomach twisted as I recognised the marulach she was talking about. It still had ink stains on its fingers. 'All right, listen,' I said, as confidently as I could. 'Both of you are going to walk past the marulaches and outside, while I hold them.'

'We'll be too slow for that. I'll have to help Tynan.' Brix's knuckles were white where they gripped the poker. She kept the tip pointing at the marulaches. 'The wizard is still under there. He's not dead, is he?'

He most certainly was not. The spell jangled like a tin bell when his heartbeat throbbed against it, and the resistance of his warm muscles felt different than the leaden cold of the dead. He was alive, and he was angry.

Angry. I'd lay down any amount of money that he was the one who'd suffocated everybody on the top floor.

'He's trying to get free, at the moment.' The words slipped around as I spoke them, drunken. 'And it's taking all my attention to keep him silenced.'

'What happens if he's unconscious?' Brix eased herself out from under Tynan's arm, propping her carefully against the wall.

'The marulaches start wandering around randomly instead of obeying his orders,' I said. 'Why are you talking instead of leaving?'

Brix moved towards the ball of marulaches, holding the poker in front of her like a fencer, snatching up a knife off a table as she went.

'Brix,' I said.

'Hold him,' she said, without glancing back at me.

There wasn't time to argue. The marulaches were pulverising themselves, but one had wriggled its head and shoulders loose from the spell and flailed its arms in her direction. Even if it didn't have working joints it could still do a lot of damage if it got free. I poured my mind into the magic, reached out with a tendril of red lightning and roped the marulach back into bondage.

Ribbons of hurt arced down my back and twitched my muscles into one large, interconnected cramp. The lightning net tightened. Nosering tried to shriek – the spell prevented it, but the scream echoed in my head, repeating like a gong. At least he wasn't having a better night than I was.

Brix darted around the back of the ball of flesh, poker raised.

Thwack.

'Gods! Stop!' Thick, putrid pain burst over me as the iron bounced off the bands of scarlet lightning and crunched into a corpse's arm. I tasted copper. 'That wasn't him.'

'Damn,' she said quietly, circling the mass of bodies. 'I can't see him.'

Then just run. Get away. I couldn't say it though, couldn't waste the breath or the words. I could barely pay attention to where she was as she moved in slow sidesteps, knife and poker ready to jab in at Nosering if he showed himself. It would have been useful to have another wizard there. Where in the hells was Dace?

'*Behind you,*' Tynan shouted.

Something dark moved in the doorway that led towards the staircase. I turned my head in time to see the other wizard, the one with the pale streaks in her brown hair. She leaned forwards into the spell as the magic spun off her fingertips.

The white globe of blades hissed towards me, fast, and clipped me across the shins as I twisted sideways, too slow to avoid it altogether. A sharp knife can cut you before you feel it, but not slipknives. The feel – icy, brilliant, thin – is the entire point of the spell. The cuts sang to life on my skin, and I stumbled.

The red light wrapped around my arms flickered.

No, hang on!

142

I grabbed for the wobbling shacklebright spell with my mind as the slipknives circled me like a snarling dog. Hot blood trickled down to my bare feet. It was only a matter of time before the incantation cut me again, and if Streaks was smart, she'd send it to slice higher next time. My balls cringed upwards at the mere thought.

The slipknives nipped in and caught my kneecap. I yelped, and nearly lost the spell for the second time.

Tynan muttered something. She lurched forwards and half-fell towards the nearest table, which still held a scattering of plates and cutlery. I couldn't spare enough attention to tell what she was doing until a carved wooden cup sailed through the air and came within inches of striking Streaks' head.

Two plates and a salt cellar followed, with the salt cellar actually making contact. Streaks fell back a couple of steps, and the slipknives followed, giving me a moment's respite. I made a mental note to thank Tynan, if we lived through this.

Brix sprinted across the room, poker held low like a pike. Streaks brought the slipknives spell around and shot it towards Brix.

But Brix was nothing if not quick on her feet. She leaped nimbly and snapped the poker down across Streaks' forearm. The wizard stumbled back with a gagging cry, clutching her ruined arm to her. Her spell didn't die, though – the white-hot ball of knives whizzed towards Brix, who never took her eyes off her opponent. Streaks crouched, then surged to her feet, twitching the spell towards her.

She was met with a quick crack of the poker across her knees. Streaks went down, howling, and the slipknives finally fell dark.

Before I had time for relief, another marulach twisted its head and shoulders away from my spell. I tried to loop the magic back around it, and couldn't.

Acid rose in my throat. Shacklebright goes poisonous quickly, especially without shielding runes. I didn't have much time before I lost my vision to the fine-grained ache knitting itself across the back of my eyes. Once that happened, odds were I wouldn't be able to find my way out of that room.

'Brix.' It took everything I had left to get the word out. She looked at me, and her face changed from triumphant to afraid. I followed the direction of her eyes and saw the thick welts on my arms, under the lines of magic. 'You need to go.' My voice shook in my own ears. 'Take Tynan. Go.'

Brix crossed the floor to where the doctor was leaning against the table. She slipped Tynan's arm around her shoulders and glanced at me. 'Follow us. You stay alive and you follow us, do you hear me?'

'I hear,' I said. 'Will you go?'

Brix half-carried Tynan towards the foyer. I waited until I saw them reach the exit and disappear. Then, intolerably slowly, without letting up on the spell, I began to move towards the foyer myself.

'Gray!' Someone was yelling my name from across the room in the most annoying fashion possible. It was Dace, of course. Or perhaps, given my spell-shot state, an accurate hallucination of him. He ran to me. 'I got the rest of the apprentices out. They're safe. Brix and Tynan and the others. We have to get out of here. Come on, Gray.'

The sound spiralled around my head as he said it: *Coooooooome on, Grraaaaaaaaaaaaaaaaaaaaaay.*

It twitched into the passages of my ear canals, boiling through my skull and into my sinuses. My eyesight spiralled, too, and replicated on itself until it looked like there were seven or eight copies of the man, each staring at me with something close to terror.

The marulaches went still. There was only one body moving now, twanging against the magic threaded through me. The necromancer was almost free.

'Can't,' I said. 'Can't let go. Stop talking.' The shacklebright spell painted a bright line of agony in my brain. Keeping my hold on it was like clinging to the sharp side of a knife with lacerated fingers. I tried to take a step and stumbled.

Dace caught me, one hand on my bare shoulder.

The runes written under my skin rose against his palm.

I squinted, but his horrified expression seemed to indicate that I wasn't imagining things. Even through the haze of pain, I had enough wit to be interested. This had, so far, only happened with Brix. Pillow talk aside, my working theory was that Jaern's spells responded to her because she was Tirnaal. If they were also responding to Dace—

I blinked. 'Well, *hells*.'

Dace's jaw set. 'If I carry you, can you hold the spell?'

I tried to nod, but ended up slumping against him. He grappled with me for a moment, cursing in a low, steady baritone, his hands slippery with liquid I eventually identified as blood. I had forgotten, in the eternity since we'd been upstairs, that he was injured.

Grip the knife. Hold the spell.

I felt, rather than saw, Nosering crawl out from underneath his pile of corpses. They weren't moving anymore, but I still couldn't focus the spell just on him. The minute I moved the shackles off the marulaches, he could send them towards us. Nosering paused when he got to his feet, pawing through his pockets. He withdrew something that looked like the vial that Tynan had handed me earlier, the one that was still in my pocket. The necromancer gulped his drin and then threw the bottle away, stalking towards us with more speed than anyone as spell-shot as he must have been should have been able to achieve.

'Kaylor,' Dace breathed. 'How . . .'

'Dace.' Nosering's voice grated over the syllables of the Examiner General's name like gravel. 'It's good that you're here to see this.' His dull eyes fixed on me. 'Now give me that amulet, pig. The lady has need of it.'

Dace finally managed to sling one of my arms across his shoulders, grasping my wrist with his good hand and dragging me backwards across the flagstones. Nosering was speaking, familiar syllables on the dead air. I glanced at my forearm, and saw the red sigils waking up.

Don't let go.

'Dace.' I tried to get my feet under me and failed, spectacularly. 'He's casting, go, drop me, go—'

'Shut up.' Dace's grip tightened on me. 'Shut up and hold them, we have to protect the people outside.'

'Help me, then,' I said.

'How? I can't scribe anything with my hand like this, I can't—'

Don't. Let. Go.

'Permission,' I said. I wanted to add *quick, before he burns us*, but you can't hurry someone into giving you themselves, not even to avoid being incinerated.

'Damn you.' Dace panted. 'Do it.'

I snuffed the shacklebright just as Dace pulled me into the foyer of the Guildhouse. My vision splintered like a broken mirror, but I finished pronouncing the flame spell on my forearm before the necromancer could.

A sheet of fire burst from my outstretched hand and poured into the dining hall, building a wall of heat and death between us and Nosering and Streaks – unless she'd crawled off somewhere. Dace grunted as I let the toxicity of the spell flow from me to him, where his hands touched my bare skin.

The marulaches lit like shambling torches. I lost track of the necromancer as the flames caught the walls.

And then the Tirnaal wizard and I were outside, in the dank city air.

ELEVEN

There were survivors.

Dace and I stumbled towards them as the fire took the building behind us, our steps maddeningly slow. I was still spell-shot enough that the people ahead were just a confused jumble of flickering shapes against the darkness.

'You asked for *permission*,' Dace muttered, beside me. He sounded bewildered, almost peevish.

'People who aren't Guild pricks often do.' I lurched against him.

'But how in the hells does it work? You can't tell me that you knew that pulse spell upstairs was written on your jaw. You *did* know that the sheet fire spell was on your arm. Nothing about you makes sense.'

'A bit rich, coming from an Examiner General who's somehow Tirnaal.' The poison of Jaern's magic slithered through my veins, hot, hurting. I barely managed to keep my wits about me enough to ensure that I wasn't touching Dace's skin, grasping the smooth black fabric of his shirt instead. If I let him take any more of the toxicity, he'd go down. 'How did you manage to get through your Guild induction without them finding out?'

His shoulders stiffened under my arm. 'You don't know anything about me,' he said, harshly. 'About my life and what I am.'

We reached the knot of people grouped around the well. Brix was still supporting Tynan. In the eerie firelight her face looked drawn, pained, but she had been giving orders to the apprentices about some burden they carried, someone . . .

Sannet.

'He's alive,' I said, surprised.

'Ten out of thirty people in the Guildhouse are alive.' If it hadn't been for the iron control she was exerting over her voice, I would have said that Tynan was near to panic. 'Only ten. And the fire's spreading. We've got to decide what to do next.'

'The Roys will be here soon.' Dace dumped me unceremoniously down to sit on the ground, blood pattering from his fingertips down to the cobblestones. 'They'll help us, they'll . . .' He swayed briefly on his feet. '*Saints*, this hurts.'

'Put your head between your knees,' I said. 'It helps. Why will the Roys be here? Tynan didn't go get them.'

He bent at the waist and gestured with his good hand back towards the fire. 'There's a burning building. People will notice. Some neighbour will send for the fire brigade, at least.'

'It's going to be merry havoc when they do get here,' Tynan muttered. 'They'll want to slap us into the filthy sick pens they've got set up in Godstown. It was difficult enough before all this to convince them to let the wizards maintain their own quarantine.'

'We shouldn't be here when the Roys arrive.' The toxicity pounding inside my skull, the raw, blistered flesh on my hand and the choking fumes were making everything fuzzy and difficult. I had to concentrate on each word to make sure it wouldn't catch on my teeth on the way out of my mouth. 'Listen.' *Concentrate.* 'The Guildhouse was sacked, by someone Dace recognised.' I yanked my eyes around to focus on him. 'Right?'

'I'm not sure.' He supported the elbow of his injured arm with his other hand. 'The wizard who made the marulaches looked like Gali Kaylor, a wizard who was put out of the Guildhouse for fraternising with Temples acolytes. I met him a few times during the investigation into Moyra Behrel, but it's not as though I knew him well.'

'He knew you,' I said.

A grim smile flickered across his face. 'A lot of wizards know me. A lot of criminals get to know their local police, too. It doesn't mean we're friends.'

'Sit down, Examiner,' Tynan said. 'Before you fall.'

Dace sat down exactly where he was, his knees folding a shade too rapidly. I was running out of time.

'Look, this whole business keeps coming back to drin. It's in the amulets, this Kaylor or whoever he was drank it, Moyra—' I stopped, and cleared my throat. This wasn't the moment to admit to Dace that I'd been seeing visions with a dead woman up to her chin in the stuff. 'The point is that someone's got to be buying it in quantity, right? Gallons, maybe.'

'That would be illegal for anyone outside Temples,' Tynan said, and now that strange accent was back, the one that resembled Sannet's, curling through her words like an alien bit of lace.

'But profitable.' Brix frowned. 'Moving that much drin around the city . . . the Roys would have to know about it, wouldn't they? They're probably being given a cut of the drinlords' take to keep them quiet. And if the rogue wizards who attacked us tonight are involved with the scheme then the Roys aren't likely to investigate the attack very hard. In fact, tossing us into the Godstown sick pens would solve a lot of their problems.'

'We can't just disappear.' Dace looked at me. Was I supposed to have a plan? 'Valera and the others will try to find us here. We should leave some sort of signal for them.'

'Little gods, *no*.' I surged upwards against my aching joints and narrowly found my balance. I wasn't sure I could actually take steps, but at least I was on my feet. 'That would endanger us and them, assuming Valera and the others are even alive. Shortly this courtyard will be a box, with fire on three sides and one way out. Throw in some Roys on horses and . . .' I swallowed down my nausea. It didn't help. 'We have to leave, now, and hide. Where can we go?'

'Easy.' Brix put a hand on my chest. 'It's going to be all right.'

'Everyone keeps saying that and they're wrong.' I was babbling, half-foolish with fear, and I knew it. I couldn't stop. 'It's not going to be all right. When has it ever been all right for us, unless one of us forced it to be?'

Looking down at her, I realised how crazy I must sound. How crazy I must have sounded for months now, casting spells in my sleep, going into panics because of a scent or a phrase. The dreams, the hallucinations, the boundless fear . . . maybe this was just more of it. Maybe she would tell me to shut up. Maybe I really was crazy.

'Brix,' I said, uncertain.

Her hand didn't move. Her fingertips felt cold but real, and centring. 'We'll find somewhere to lay low. Won't be easy, but–'

She believed me. Something wound tight inside me released. 'Where could we lay low?'

Brix hesitated, glancing over her shoulder at Dace. 'We could make for Deadchurch. Ask for sanctuary with the aunts.'

'Your aunts,' I said.

She shook her head. 'Not like that. It's a title, not a blood relationship. They're the leaders of my mother's clan. They'll know my name.'

'No.' Dace's breath was coming fast. 'The original plan was one thing, going with the authority of the Guild and the police behind us to ask for cooperation. Going like this, wearing a Guild sigil, bleeding–' He ground his teeth. 'They'll kill the wizards, Brix. You know they will.'

'They won't. They'll listen to me.' She shot me a look. 'I promise they will, Gray. They have to. They owe me that much.'

That was one hell of a cryptic statement, but there was no time to analyse it. Brix's possibly problematic relatives wouldn't matter all that much if we couldn't make it through the night. I forced myself into practicality. 'How far is it?'

Brix's shoulders relaxed. 'Two, maybe three hours of walking, since everybody is hurt.'

'Not everybody,' Tynan said. 'Some of them are just spell-shot, or scared. They're going to have to help move the others.' She reached behind her and planted her hands on the low wall around the well, then used it and her good leg to lever herself upwards, panting. 'Help the Examiner and get the apprentices on their feet.'

The apprentices were mostly intact, albeit staring, shivering and about as coherent as you would expect from a bunch of eighteen-year-olds who had just seen their friends and teachers killed. They were simple enough to boss into carrying Sannet, who was still unconscious. Once I had them in a loose group, I moved to help Dace stand.

He jerked his elbow away from me. 'I don't need your help.'

'You're a shitty liar,' I said. 'And I'm damned if I'm going to let you bleed to death. Get up.'

'Gods.' He laughed, but it sounded faintly hysterical. 'It's not in your self-interest to keep me from bleeding to death. Do you not realise that? Why . . .?'

'I'm an idiot. Come on, up.' I pulled him to his feet. I *was* an idiot, but there had been too much death that night. I glanced at Brix, who was half-carrying Tynan.

'Right.' Brix gave one long, shuddering exhale. 'Well, follow me.'

The night echoed with the distant sounds of breaking glass, raucous voices and the odd, tooth-gritting scream. Evidently the riot – or at least the fear of it – had moved outside Godstown. Orange light flick-ered against the low-slung clouds, as though patches all over the city were burning. It was no wonder that nobody had come to investigate the Guildhouse.

Genereth in the dark didn't make any more sense than it did during the day. Brix kept halting every few streets to confer with Tynan in some Tirnaal dialect that I didn't understand. I gathered that getting to the wall chapels without wading into the fringes of the riot wasn't a straightforward proposition.

A thin mist had rolled in off the water, carrying with it the iron-heavy tang of the riverbed mud. Brix and Tynan led us through the black, snaky streets slowly. The apprentices walked next, all in a bunch, taking turns trundling Sannet along like a bag of oats. Two of them were still crying, soft and constant, with a rhythm like the sea. The edges of the cobblestones cut into my bare feet, and my blistered hand was a mass of jabbing aches that I nevertheless had to use to keep Dace upright.

We were strung out, slow-moving, vulnerable. A couple of the apprentices kept stopping every moment that someone else wasn't herding them along, staring and stunned. The mist clung to us like a shroud. Nobody should have been out on a night like that, but I kept thinking I saw shimmers and glimpses of movement.

'The mist off the river.' Dace was leaning on me now, without even trying to pretend he didn't need the help. 'The air currents make it move, curl around on itself. A lot of people think they see things in it. I used to—' He blinked. 'We've got to keep moving.'

We turned into a wider avenue, its sides lined with dark, tight-shut buildings, fronted with empty stalls that in normal hours were probably used to sell vegetables and cheese and cloth. A loose knot of people, some of them carrying torches, were moving from stall to stall.

'Turn around,' Brix said, ahead of me. 'Now.'

The looters started towards us at a loose amble.

'Too late,' Tynan muttered.

There were only five or six young men, but they weren't hurt and we were – and three of them were holding heavy sticks. Dace drew away from me and managed to lock his knees and keep from falling. I took the hint and stepped out in front of Brix and Tynan.

'Evening, gents,' I said.

'Someone take your shirt?' The looter who spoke was a tall man, broad-shouldered and rangy. He shifted his torch from one hand to the other, his eyes flicking between me and the apprentices, frowning a little when he saw their robes. 'Wizards? What are you, a slave?'

'If you'll just return to whatever it is you were doing,' I said, 'we'll be on our way. I'm sure none of us have seen anything illegal. Just some locals, conducting legitimate business, at night, in plague-infested streets.'

'What if I think you ought to donate a little something to our cause, slave?' He spread his arms wide, swaggering. 'Like a toll for passing a guardhouse.'

'I'm not a slave,' I said. 'I don't think you'd like to discover what I am.'

'Well, you're for hells-sure no wizard.' He advanced towards me – but slowly, which meant he wasn't certain.

'I'm Unguild. One of the bad kind.' Laypeople had almost as many horrifying legends about unlicensed wizards as the Guild did. Maybe I wouldn't have to actually throw a spell. Maybe intimidation would be enough. I allowed myself the smile that I almost never use – Jaern's death's-head grin, the one that makes most people back away. 'Would you like me to prove it?'

The looter didn't move, but his friends did, falling into a sloppy knot behind him. Some of his easy confidence had left him. 'You can't hurt us. The Guild –'

'Isn't here,' I said, and had to ignore the way it made the rest of my group flinch. Without taking my attention off him, I waved a hand back towards Brix and the others. 'Get going, you lot.'

The looter eyed me uncertainly, crouched, ready to spring towards me.

Off to the left, in the deeper shadows along the buildings, a flutter of sound came whispering through the mist. It wasn't footsteps, exactly – it was softer than that, a weird sort of pattering. It almost sounded like wet feet on the cobbles, but it didn't seem likely that anybody but me would be foolish enough to be stumbling around Genereth barefoot. The looter swung his torch towards the sound.

A dark shape loomed into the light and then out again, as rapidly as a fish darting through water. I caught a flash of movement to the right, and this time I saw the shape's hand, and the glint of steel at the fingertips.

'What did you do?' The whites of the looter's eyes showed bright against the darkness. He backed in exactly the wrong direction. 'What is that thing?'

'Don't.' I didn't have the time to make him believe me. 'Don't, it'll–'

The thing lunged out of the mist, long arms wrapping around the looter with an embrace that was many-jointed, too flexible. Threadwork criss-crossed its wrists and elbows – the stitched creature from Godstown.

Wrong, Corcoran.

Fear shot through my body like liquor.

Not the one from Godstown.

This one had teeth.

'Help!' The looter struggled in the creature's grasp, flailing powerlessly. This creature was taller than the one we had seen before, grappling for the looter's hands and wrists with languid ease. Whatever the thing was, it was strong. 'Wizard, help!'

I drew breath to incant, but the thing's head whipped backwards, jaws yawning wide, steel needles gleaming. Before I could get more than a half-dozen syllables out of my mouth, the teeth snapped shut on the looter's throat. He went limp.

'Go!' I spun on my heel. 'Brix! Get them out of here, *now!*'

The apprentices, burdened as they were with Sannet, were still faster than Brix, who was dragging Tynan as she hobbled along on one foot. Dace, his ruined arm tucked against his abdomen, was frozen, staring into the mist around us.

'Four,' he said.

I skidded to a stop beside him, turning and trying to see what he was looking at. 'Why are we counting instead of running?'

He didn't move, and now I could see them: dark shapes hulking in the fog, surrounding us like a pack of wild dogs. 'I see four,' he said, with delirious calm. 'How many do you count?'

'Shit.' I turned back towards the dead man on the pavement and tried to think past the heavy lump of pain between my eyes. Either the looters and their attackers had disappeared into the roiling banks of mist, or my vision was still deteriorating. I could hear them, though. The screams and slaps of flesh on flesh sounded curiously flat against the wet air. It was impossible to pinpoint their direction. I couldn't cast, not into that soup, not without seeing what I'd be killing.

Dace lifted his good hand, but lurched sideways, barely catching himself before he hit the ground. I grabbed his arm and got under it. 'Now *run*.'

He tried. It was still not much better than a jog-hop as we pursued the others. When we caught up to them they had reached the head of the avenue, where it was bisected by a cross street.

'Don't stop,' I said, as Dace and I drew near. 'If they're anything like marulaches, they're slow and they don't think for themselves. Our only chance is to keep moving, be unpredictable.'

'What are they?' Brix sounded almost ready to sob. 'Gods, what in the hells—' She coughed then, long, damp and hacking. Spumes of pink light burst from her lips.

A shape emerged from the mist, over Brix's shoulder. The hand snaked towards her, pale-fleshed, braceleted with thread.

'Move!' I dove forwards and shoved the hand up and away from her. *'Move now!'*

The creature fell backwards and we all broke, dragging our wounded away from the gangly shadows in the fog. Nobody could reach an all-out run, not even the apprentices. To their credit, they didn't try to drop Sannet, although that may have been because they weren't thinking clearly.

It took several minutes of blind panic and doggedly pushing forwards under Dace's weight to realise what the stitched things were doing. The minute anyone would slow or break from the main group, they'd appear, brandishing their needle-teeth and their metal fingertips. They'd swipe and claw, but . . .

. . . they never actually touched anyone.

Marulaches don't think.

These weren't marulaches, though. They were fast. They were almost using tactics. I watched as one loomed in an alleyway in time to force an apprentice back towards the group. We were running in a bunch, like sheep.

'Sheep*dogs*,' I said, aloud. 'We're being driven.'

'What?' Dace was pale against the night, clammy with sweat, breathing hard.

'They're herding us.' I shifted, smears of his blood cooling on my arm. 'Where would they be herding us?'

Dace looked like he was having difficulty keeping his eyes open. 'Box,' he mumbled.

The apprentices were too grieved to focus and use combat magic safely, even if they were far enough along in their training to know the spells. Dace was hurt. Tynan was hurt. Brix was sick. We needed to make a stand, keep these things from completing whatever sort of rudimentary plan they had . . . and I was the only one who could possibly do it.

'Brix,' I shouted. 'We've got to stop. They're—'

But she had already stopped, facing a blank masonry wall. Dace and I nearly ran into her as she let Tynan slip to the ground and turned around, jaw set grimly.

'There's nowhere else to go,' she said. 'This is one of the notches in the wall beneath the old guard towers. We're trapped, unless we run towards Temples.'

Box.

'Get behind me,' I said. 'All of you.'

I turned as the gentle pattering filled the air and watched the shadows appear in the mist, one by one. The stitched things arranged themselves in a loose semi-circle and terror enveloped me like a cloak of ice. My mind buzzed through calculations.

I counted six of them, not four. Each one was unique in disturbing ways. They didn't all have teeth, for example, and some of them seemed to have extra fingers. One was missing an arm, like a coat without a sleeve.

Think, Gray. Find a way out.

Marulaches run with necromantic magic and glow orange. The stitched things weren't glowing, which probably meant that however they were being controlled, it wasn't with necromancy. They weren't advancing, they were just . . . holding us in one place.

Sheepdogs imply a shepherd.

Something else was coming. Something worse.

'Gray.' Brix was only twelve inches or so behind me, but against the blood singing in and out of my ears her voice sounded miles away. Distant. Thin. I couldn't make myself turn towards her, my eyes fixed on the things that should have been dead, but weren't.

Running hadn't worked. I could fight, but I was already exhausted and half-sick with toxicity. I had to decide on a spell that could handle six – saints, *six* – of these things that didn't seem to feel pain. I didn't have to win. I just had to knock the things down long enough for Brix and everybody else to backtrack.

157

Think.

If they were alive, there was a chance that they could communicate. Maybe I could bargain, or at least stall for time. You know, with things that looked like their heads had been sewn to their necks.

This is insane.

Still, there was nothing else left to try. I moved forwards, careful to stay well out of reach of the nearest creature. 'Can you hear me?'

I knew, as soon as the words were out, that they couldn't. Their ribs expanded and contracted – they were breathing – but they didn't react to my voice at all. I frowned, inching closer. They weren't dead, but they weren't exactly alive, either. It was as though someone had scooped the will and personality out of bodies before altering them. What eyes I could see weren't focused on anything, staring straight ahead with pupils blown out so wide that I couldn't see what colour their irises were at all. They were weirdly mindless, blank, almost like yavad addicts, or . . .

Mindblown. They look mindblown.

It all made sudden, crashing sense. The stitched things were the remains of people whose minds and memories had been cracked with magic, hollow things with no personality left in them. They were living bodies that could be manipulated by whatever monster was out there with a spool of black thread. It was worse than slavery. It was worse than death.

'Gods,' I whispered, appalled.

The thing in front of me looked at me. 'She wants you.'

I had only a split second to realise how drastically I had miscalculated before its arm shot out, too long, with too many elbows. Its metal-tipped fingers closed on my forearm. It was warm.

'You will come to her.' The thing spoke in a grating, inhuman whisper, susurrating like grit across stone. I saw something silvery gleam, where its shirt flapped loosely against its breastbone. Its fingers tightened.

'Brix, run!' I threw myself backwards against its grip. It didn't budge.

Slowly, inexorably the thing began to drag me towards it. Its lips parted, revealing rows of steel teeth. I was close enough to see the amulet with its legs sunk deep into the thing's chest now, to smell the overpowering honey-sweet stink of it. 'You will come to her.'

'Get away from him!'

I caught a lungful of her scent and knew Brix was beside me. Pure, clarifying fear filled my body, and time seemed to slow. I watched as she lifted the knife she had taken off the table back in the Guildhouse dining room and, neatly, like a tailor, slit the stitches on the creature's wrist.

They unravelled.

I stumbled back, the hand still clutching my forearm until I slapped it away from me, frantic. The creature went to pieces, the seams in its body yawning apart as it crumpled and fell where it stood. Instead of guts it spilled light, a snake of violet that broke from its empty body and shot upwards into the sky.

The other creatures paused, turning towards the light. For that split second, they were ignoring us.

Nobody had to speak. Before I could really think, Brix was hustling Tynan sideways along the wall, followed by the sobbing apprentices. I was shoving Dace forwards before I realised I had grabbed him. I risked one quick glance over my shoulder. Behind us, the things had gathered around their fallen comrade like vultures over carrion. Then they broke, shambling clumsily away.

The trap spell. No.

'Go . . .' I meant to shout it, but I didn't have the breath. I was practically carrying Dace, straining forwards, when the explosion thudded through the air.

The shock wave caught us all and threw us to the cobblestones. I yanked myself and Dace back up, counting the people around me.

Nobody was dead, but everybody was too slow. I looked back one more time.

'*Go!*'

Four of the stitched things had escaped the blast, too.

Vomit boiled in my throat. People. That's what the things were. Somebody was making the creatures out of *people*. Somebody was stealing the personalities of the living, and then cutting and changing and—

It doesn't matter right now. Keep going.

I drove myself forwards over the cobblestones on feet that felt like blocks of ice. Brix was coughing steadily now, a hack that sent blasts of pink illumination flaring around her face.

No.

The word pounded in my head even though I knew I was wrong.

No, this isn't going to happen. I won't let it.

And then Brix halted.

We weren't even in front of a house. Beside us loomed the carved black door of what looked like a large, three-storey chapel, if someone had been whimsical enough to embed a chapel in a city wall and board over the windows. Without hesitating, Brix charged up to the door and pounded on it with her fist. 'Open up! We need help!'

A slot in the wall above the door opened. The business end of a crossbow pointed out.

'Go away,' said a male voice. 'Looters all say they need help. Yell for the Roys.'

'My name is Brix Rivest,' Brix said. 'Daughter of Magdala Rivest, granddaughter of Faya Rivest, and these people are under my protection. If you want me to leave you're going to have to bloody well kill me, so *open the gods-damned door* before I kick it in!'

Sluggishly, unbelievably, the door opened. An old man with blue sigils inked on his cheeks above his beard stood there holding a lantern.

We were inside before he had time to do more than gape at us, open-mouthed.

'Rivest,' he said, as Dace and I hurtled past him. 'I never thought I'd see the day we'd hear that name again, I–'

'Shut the door.' I stumbled and nearly dropped the Examiner. 'We have people who need a doctor.'

'Who–' he began.

Brix had propped Tynan against the wall. She whirled around to face the gatekeeper. 'Shut the door!' With each word, pink glimmered around her mouth. 'They're still out there, you fool!'

He fumbled towards it. Brix watched while the heavy, walnut door swung shut. She stayed on her feet, swaying gently, until the locks ground home, and the giant, heavy bar settled into its hooks. Her eyes found me.

And then, slowly, without a sound, she fell.

TWELVE

She was alive. I spent the first five minutes assuring myself of that, while the room went to the hells around us.

Brix had collapsed in some sort of foyer. Everyone seemed to be panicking, drawing back against the carvings on the stone walls, hustling towards some exit behind us. They must have been speaking, but all I heard was the clattering thud of my own heart.

'Stop it, Gray,' Brix said, and coughed again, pieces of pink light bursting from her lips as though she was a lamp, glittering through the dimness, catching themselves on my shoulders and hands and hair.

I did not stop what I was doing, which was scribing sigils above her collarbone with the grease pencil that Dace had given me back at the Guildhouse a world ago, before I'd thrown so many foolish, dangerous spells.

'Tynan says magic makes it worse,' I said. 'If it's a spell I can break the ley. I can get it off of you. I just—'

'Gray.'

'Fuck,' I said. 'Fuck.'

'*Gray.*' She wrapped one hand around my fingers. This made it difficult to keep scribing, so I had to look her in the eyes, had to see the pain there, had to admit this was really happening.

The room around us had emptied out, except for Dace, who was slumped against the wall, half-conscious. Even Tynan had been carried out when the Tirnaal gatekeepers had run from the plague, talking fast in a Tirna dialect that I didn't understand. Logically, we only had a few minutes before they came back, and I needed to know my next move. I still couldn't move. My wits, when I needed them the most, had fled.

Brix touched my chin. Her cool fingertips against my skin woke me up, made me realise what I had to do. She was the one spitting light; she shouldn't have been the one doing the comforting.

'I know you don't think it will help.' For a wonder I got my voice to be steady, although I could tell by watching her face that she was not deceived, not yet. 'But just let me try. At least then we'll know. At least let me prove myself wrong.'

'I'm the one sick, and you're shouting at me,' she said.

'I'm not shouting,' I said, and then realised that maybe I was. I lowered my voice. 'Please, Brix. You can be angry with me about it later, and I'll sit silent and let you.'

'Silent? You?' She smiled, but it was groggy, twitchy with suppressed pain. 'Can I get that in writing?' Her words triggered a spasm, and more stained-glass bits of light. She grasped the fabric of her shirt, holding the collar open. I kissed the base of her throat briefly, then started counting the sigils I'd already written. One was smeared beyond usefulness. I licked my thumb, wiped it out and replaced it.

'And if the ley-breaker doesn't fix it?' Brix's voice vibrated through her chest, under my hand. 'If I can't vouch for you when the Tirnaal return to deal with us, Gray, they'll . . . dispose of all the wizards. Even the apprentices that they know aren't infected. Even you. You don't understand how much they hate magic, how harmful they think it is.' She hesitated. 'Promise me something.'

I had finished scribing the characters, but a note in her voice made me wait to pronounce them.

'Of course,' I said. 'Anything.'

'No, I mean it.' Her eyes stayed fixed on mine. 'Promise you won't do anything stupid, not even to keep me alive. You won't hurt yourself, or other people. *Promise*. Now.'

The words lay heavy on my tongue. They had a taste, like dust and blood and metal, and I could feel the dark well of fear yawning inside me, deeper than it had ever been. I didn't have the guts to keep this sort of promise. Wanting something to be true wasn't the same as not lying when you said it, and I knew that deep in the marrow, where my magic crawled.

But—

'I promise,' I said. 'I promise you, Brix.'

And she let out her breath, with relief this time. She relaxed against the stone, and I finally pronounced my sigils.

The incantation I'd scribed on her lit and then crumbled, sigils fading away to nothing. The ley-breaker swept through the room, cold, taking with it the ability for *any* magic in the area to work for the next couple of hours. Toxicity rocketed up my spine, clawing through me like a knife. I heard Dace gasp when the wave struck him.

Brix looked up at me, eyes glazed with pain, and coughed. Pink light bloomed around her, as though she were burning from the inside.

It didn't work.

I couldn't bring myself to actually say the words. Magic was all I had, the only value I brought to this situation. If magic couldn't help—

No.

'Wait. Gray.' Dace was fumbling in his pocket as he crossed the floor, wobbling on his feet. Was he going to offer me another useless pencil? 'Here.' He held out a bottle, half-full of some dark liquid.

I recognised the flask he'd been drinking from after the riot. 'Brandy? Yavad?'

He hesitated, then pushed the bottle into Brix's hand. 'Drin. It'll at least ease pain.'

'What in the hells are you doing with a bottle of drin?' I said.

'Does it matter?' He slid down to one knee. 'It's Brix's decision, but we don't have unlimited time before they come back, do you understand that? Would you just—'

Footsteps echoed against stone behind us, punctuating a clatter of voices. The Tirnaal were returning, and it sounded like they were already arguing.

'They're coming.' Brix sat up with a lurch, gasping for breath around that horrible wet, gurgling cough. 'I have to be able to talk.' She took the stopper off Dace's bottle and put it to her lips.

'Three swallows,' he said. 'No more, not until tomorrow.'

She gulped it down and then shoved the bottle back into his hand. For a few seconds I thought that this gambit, too, had failed. Then, slowly, her pupils widened out as her breath eased. A flush of bright colour travelled over her cheekbones.

'Oh.' She braced one hand against the floor. 'That's . . . strong.'

'What is it doing?' I leaned forwards, glancing at Dace. 'What did you do?'

He wasn't looking at me. Neither was Brix, her eyes focused on something behind me.

'Aunt,' she said.

I turned. A group of Tirnaal stood as far back from us as they could get and still be in the room. Two of them were swinging bronze censers, overwhelming the room with smoke that reeked of cinnamon and frankincense. A handsome woman with a broad nose, iron-grey hair, and heavy bracelets of blue runes inked around each wrist appeared to be in charge, regarding us through the fumes.

'The doorkeeper says you identified yourself as Brix Rivest,' she said. 'And that you claimed clan protection for these spelldogs.'

'That's right. Gray, if you'd just . . .' Brix plucked at the laces of her shirt with one hand. I put one arm behind her shoulders and helped her to hold the neck of her shirt open, displaying her tattoos – rows of tiny, intricate runes layered below the delicate lines of her collarbones.

The aunt stalked forwards and peered down at Brix's ink. Her face changed almost instantly. 'Holy moonlight.' She crouched, reaching forwards to cup Brix's jaw in her hand. 'It *is* you. Mother of the moon, Magdala's girl, come back to us. We thought you were dead.' Her gaze flicked to me. 'And this is?'

'Corcoran Gray,' Brix said, steadily. 'My friend.'

My partner. The shape of the missing words ached. She was keeping me alive – she was keeping all of us alive – and I knew that, but it wasn't simple, sitting there with the ache and keeping my face flat and unmoving.

The aunt held my eyes for a moment longer, calculating. Finally, she sighed. 'Whoever you are. Get her up off that cold floor, and come with me.'

It wasn't exactly an infirmary that they led us to. I carried Brix up a flight of stairs and through a narrow door. The room we entered was round like the moon and cluttered with a comfortable spattering of rugs, cushions, tables and tapestries. The walls were covered in time-scarred carvings, icons of the gods interspersed with religious scenes where the Lady of Shadows presided over the lives of her people. The floor dipped in the middle, a half-circle indentation that had probably once been a reflecting pool for the statue of Ranara that still smiled atop a pillar there. The goddess was of weathered brown stone and looked unusually human, stripped of the silver coating that would have originally made her resplendent.

'If we're in Temples,' I said, 'I am not dressed appropriately.'

'Heretic,' Brix said, nestled against my bare chest. 'We're not in Temples. Put me down, and I'll explain.'

The apprentices were huddled in one corner, milling around the place where they'd dropped Sannet. Tynan was leaning against the wall, barking instructions. She began talking rapidly to the aunt as soon as we came in, gesticulating towards Dace. I strode to the nearest cluster of cushions, kicked them into a rough heap and knelt to place Brix on them.

The aunt cleared her throat. 'If you could all give me your attention?'

I did not, until Brix gave me a scowl. I sighed, and turned to face where the aunt stood, one arm supporting Tynan. Tynan was giving whispered instructions to an apprentice, who was crouched bandaging Dace's wounds. The Examiner himself sat hunched on the floor, his eyes fixed on the woman who was speaking:

'We might as well be direct, since this is an emergency situation in more ways than one. My name is Aoine. Tynan has told me what happened at the Guildhouse.' She gave Tynan's shoulders a squeeze. The doctor looked like she might pass out at any time, but managed to plant a distracted kiss on Aoine's cheek.

'*Oh*,' Brix said, under her breath.

I straightened, startled. So the doctor had a Tirnaal wife. I wished I knew whether that meant she was likely to speak for us. The apprentices were one thing: Tynan knew them, felt responsible for them. But Dace and I were just spelldogs she'd met a day ago, and Brix was . . . coughing. It was possible that Tynan would decide to simply protect her own.

'I've brought you to the council chamber because it has incense burners,' Aoine continued. 'And good locks. The streets are dangerous enough that I won't be able to get a message to the rest of the clans until dawn – that's about six hours away. I won't know our next move until I can consult with the other aunts. I suggest you sleep if you can; we'll find a way to get you some food. Wizards are advised that magic is not done inside Deadchurch. This used to be

167

Ranara-temple, after all, and the goddess does not allow magic there.'

Bullshit. I managed to keep from muttering it out loud. What did people think Ranaran priestesses used, when they sold luck coins or made fertility charms? Why did people think the priestesses went blind, if not because of the unshielded magic eating away at their eyes? The blindness was half the reason why the goddess was known as the Lady of Shadows, after all: for every bit of light, there had to be a commensurate measure of darkness.

Aoine's gaze fell on me and lingered longer than was comfortable. 'We'll be back as soon as we can. But we cannot risk letting you expose any more of our people to plague or magic. Tynan, if you're ready.' She turned. Two of the Tirnaal, young men with tattoos crawling up their necks, positioned themselves under Tynan's arms and lifted her, carrying her out of the room while Aoine followed.

The big double door closed. A moment later the locks ground home. I was left alone with the semi-delirious Examiner General of the Mages' Guild, a pack of apprentices quickly sobbing themselves into silence, and my dying partner.

And the goddess, of course.

I sat down beside Brix, put my back to the statue and tried, resolutely, to ignore it.

'Not Temples,' I said. 'Where are we, then?'

'Deadchurch.' Brix's eyes kept flickering shut, then popping open again. 'A wall chapel. There are thirteen, all nicknamed for the district that they used to serve – Saltchurch, Thieveschurch, like that. Deadchurch served the cemetery. The chapels were supposed to be a divine defence for Genereth.'

'Ah, that's much clearer,' I said. 'Everybody puts creepily-named Temples at the extreme edge of town, to make it take as long as possible to walk there.'

Her lips twitched. 'I do know what you're doing. I will wake up again, even if you let me sleep.'

I tried, but I couldn't force a smile. 'I'm sorry. I just—' I looked over at Sannet. He was the colour of old porridge, too miserable even to writhe. He looked like he could die at any moment.

Brix studied me. 'The ancestors built the wall chapels,' she said, hoarse, after a moment. 'As a point of Generethi civic pride. The idea was that the dukes would use the walls to defend us against enemies, and the chapels would get the gods to defend us against hurricanes and the river flooding.'

'Did it work?' I said.

'No. They built Godstown, didn't they?' Her eyelids drifted downwards. 'Temples abandoned the wall chapels eight hundred years ago. We took them.'

She was tired, and in pain, and I should have let it go. I should have been reassuring. But: 'Rivest,' I said.

'I was going to tell you,' she whispered. 'They knew my mother. I promise I was going to tell you, but . . .' She blinked, slow, almost stoned. 'I have to sleep, Gray, I'm so tired, and this drin is making me feel . . . I have to . . .'

My throat felt tight, but I managed to keep my voice light. 'Sleep. I'll wake you up if I get bored.'

Her eyes dropped shut.

'Brix,' I said, because I couldn't help myself, and because I was afraid.

She didn't answer, but her hand found mine and held it.

Hours passed while I didn't sleep, too numb to think much, surrounded by slumbering people. It was still dark outside the windows when I roused myself and sat up with a start, lifting my back and shoulders away from the base of the statue I had been leaning against.

She wants you. To get you, she'll take them.

She'll take all of them.

I had been awake, but I was hearing Moyra's voice again. That must have meant I was on the edge of slipping down into a doze, into the place where I couldn't control my magic and nothing made sense.

I took deep breaths and forced myself to look around the room. I was sitting an arm's length from where Brix lay, my hand cupped over Jaern's amulet where it hung, heavy against my breastbone. The rest of the room was quiet, filled with the great, billowing clouds of incense from the bronze censer that was suspended from the goddess' clasped hands. The apprentices were all sleeping in a pile. Dace, the last time I looked at him, had his eyes closed.

And Brix–

I leaned towards her, but her chest was still rising and falling with gentle regularity.

'How is she?' Dace sat cross-legged against the wall some ten feet from me, the bones of his face sharp-edged where they pressed up against his skin. The bandage that the Tirnaal had applied seemed to be fretting him, but at least it wasn't showing stains yet – maybe they'd managed to stop the bleeding.

'I don't want to talk to you, Dace.' I couldn't afford to lose the time. Not to something as asinine as a Guild enforcer's pity. I had to think. *She'll take them.* Maybe it didn't mean anything. Maybe it had never meant anything. Maybe Moyra was just a hallucination, a piece of my fears that I'd managed to weave into the tapestry of my nightmares.

'Did you sleep?' he said, ignoring me.

'No.' The wardstones were still in my pocket, clunking against the vial of drin that Tynan had given me. But I couldn't sleep, not in that room full of people. Not until I could be sure that the stones would work, keep Moyra and the rest of it out of my head long enough to rest. I had to grind my way through the dizziness of my own fatigue and start sorting out what I knew: the plague amulets kept people alive, at least temporarily. If I could figure out how they worked, I might be able to use Jaern's amulet to help Brix. Conversely, I might be able to figure out the plague amulets if I could analyse Jaern's – the dead god had used the amulet to keep from feeling the pain of his own spells, and at least once had used it as a weapon. Where would Jaern have scribed the spell to activate it? My thumb slid over the metal and glass, smooth and unblemished, warm from contact with my flesh. I thought about magic, and bones, and . . . *skin*.

She wants you.

There really was only one location that made sense, wasn't there?

'Do you want help, then?' Dace sounded testy, with an undercurrent of real anxiety. He was almost shuddering with nerves. 'With Brix. There's only a couple of doses left in that bottle. You can't depend on drin-sellers for charity, you know. And breaking the ley didn't work.'

'Thanks for reminding me.' I dropped the amulet, frustrated. The activation spell was probably written somewhere on my body, waiting to be called to life. If I could figure out which sigils the false god had used, I could activate his amulet. Even if any healing it did for Brix was temporary, it would at least gain us a little time. I could get Brix to Temples, with their secretive ecclesiastical incantations, and force them to help her. But none of the techniques I had used to learn other spells under my skin applied here – I had seen Jaern use the amulet to absorb the toxicity of his own spells, but he had been clothed at the time. I wasn't even certain what type of incantation I was looking for. Whatever called up the amulet was something I had no point of reference for, magic that I had no idea how to go about unravelling. 'And I have some drin, so you can keep your charity.'

'That isn't what I meant.' His voice was abrupt, like the slap of stones dropped down a well. 'Breaking the ley didn't work for me, either.'

I looked up. Ley-breakers were so illegal that I'd never heard a Guildie admit to doing one. 'What?'

'I think it's because the centre of the magic that's causing all this is elsewhere – not on the victims. If it was centred on the amulets, they should be fragile, fatigued by the spell. They're not.' He hesitated, then pushed forwards. 'When Thane got sick I broke the ley for him, even though it was wrong. He was still spitting light when he had to come back here to Genereth for the trial. He never could stop thinking about the dead woman.'

'She had a name,' I said. 'Moyra.' And then I saw her, standing beside Dace. She was dripping black fluid that was now all too familiar: drin.

She's taken one of them, the vision of Moyra said. *She wants your skin. She's here.*

I blinked, hard. The vision didn't leave.

Help us, Moyra insisted. *It hurts. You can help us.*

I squeezed my eyes shut, spikes of panic jabbing through me. This *had* to be a hallucination, brought on by too much magic and not enough sleep. I couldn't start dreaming while I was awake. I couldn't. There would be nothing left of me.

When I looked again, Moyra was gone. I let my breath out, light-headed.

Dace was glaring at me. 'You're not listening to me.'

Irrational anger pulsed through me. I hadn't wanted any of this – hadn't asked to wear a handmade body, or to see gods-damned ghosts with my waking eyes. I wasn't going to sit and be scolded by a hypocrite.

'I was listening,' I said. 'You were talking about Thane. I take it he's the one who killed Moyra, which means what? That you and he were both officers, running around the province snooping into the love-lives of Guildmates? Enforcing all those gods-damned regulations right down to the last bump in the parchment, even if it meant that someone died?'

His face hardened. 'Don't talk like you know anything about it. You're no innocent.'

'And when Thane pushed the Guildie, what's his name – Kaylor – the poor idiot tried to run away with his paramour.' Chasing this felt better than the quicksand of fatigue, better than not being able to trust my own senses. This was a puzzle, a straight line to follow. 'They get caught, yes? He panics, throws spells, and Thane kills her. Right in front of her lover – and with paralysis, no less, so she dies of suffocation because nobody can bring themselves to flout the regulation and break the ley. And then Kaylor breaks into the Guildhouse and kills every wizard there – suffocates them, in fact. Where did he learn necromancy? I thought your precious regulations prevented that sort of thing.'

'We're not talking about that,' Dace said.

I opened my eyes wide at him. 'Maybe *you* aren't.'

He'd gone rigid, one hand clenched into a fist so tight that his knuckles blanched under the strain. 'You don't know anything about it.'

He was wrong, of course. I did know something now, one of those shiny pieces of knowledge that slips into place as sweetly as a key in a lock: Dace wasn't well, and it wasn't just the blood loss. He was trembling, shivering like a man with ague.

'Drin,' I said, softly, 'or plague, Dace?'

His eyes, that ambiguous colour like lake water, flickered. 'If I thought I had the plague I would tell you. Guild regulations–'

'Are solidly against all of this,' I interrupted. 'Are you telling me that the Guildlords would be pleased that their Examiner General has been going about his duties three parts blasted on drin? Not to mention the other – which still doesn't make sense to me, by the way.

Tirnaal think magic is a dirty sin, and after throwing spells like you did last night, a Tirnaal should be ghostly.'

'I am not three parts blasted.' His face had gone rigid. 'Drin doesn't work like that. In higher doses it kills pain and eases breathing, which is why I thought it would help Brix. In small amounts it mitigates the effects of magic toxicity. Takes the edge off, makes it so I don't lose the solidity of my body and go transparent – ghostly, you call it. I'm not an addict. I only take it so I can practise. Otherwise I'm like any other wizard.'

'Not like any other wizard,' I said. 'The Guild won't even let Tirnaal learn their sigils. You know that, Examiner. You enforce that.'

He stared at the floor, jaw working. 'Don't tell them about me. Please.'

Was he asking me to lie to the Guild, or the clan? It didn't matter. I wanted this conversation to be over before one of the others woke up. 'Fine.'

Dace frowned. 'Fine – that's all you have to say?'

I threw up my hands. 'You don't want me to tell the aunts or the Guild that you're a drin-licker Tirnaal wizard, so I *won't*. What did you expect me to do, blackmail you?'

He went a deep shade of scarlet.

'Hells,' I said, startled. 'That's really what you think of me.'

'I don't know what to think of you,' he said hoarsely, though gods knew what he had to be upset about. His good hand was toying with his earring, reminding me what our real relationship was. 'There's the reports from last year – thirty deaths–'

'Thirty-*two*,' I said, through my teeth.

'What?'

'Thirty-*two*.' I heard my voice getting louder, but I couldn't stop it. 'There were thirty-*two* deaths, you prick, and I saw them, so your precious reports got that wrong, too. I never heard all the names, but I know all the faces. If I had been a little faster–' I stood, and moved across the floor until I was as far from him as I could get, facing one of the stone carvings on the wall. 'I didn't kill them.' My damn voice was trembling, too, and I didn't even have a drin addiction to blame it on. 'But I saw them die, and there were thirty-two. Get it right, next time.'

The wall carvings were icons of the gods, shown in their traditional poses. Just to my left was an image of Jaern, but I wasn't going to look at that, not now. I kept my eyes on the one in front of me: the Queen of the Eclipse in granite, doling out healing and fertility charms to a throng of worshippers. Ranara had bare feet, a dull, smirking face and surprisingly intricately carved clothes. I began counting the jewels on her necklace, waiting for my heartbeat to slow down.

'I'm sorry,' Dace said. And then, quietly: 'What really happened?'

I knew the words weren't easy for him to say. I knew I should say something in return, if only to ensure that he remained an ally. I touched the goddess' shoulder with one thumb and followed the line of her arm. The stone was cold, and covered in a thin layer of soot and grit. My thumb left a clean track, showing where once upon a time the granite had been painted lavender.

'I told you. I died last year.' My own voice surprised me, too deep, as though someone else was speaking. 'So did a lot of other people. I'm not vain enough to think I got my second chance because I deserved it, but I thought maybe there was a point to my survival. Something I was supposed to do, some purpose I was supposed to fulfil. But lately . . .' I looked up from the deity that I'd freed from her coating of dirt. 'I had to stop Jaern. That's what happened. That's all that happened. I had to stop him, and now I have to live with it.'

I glanced towards the carving of Jaern, grinning out from the wall. It must have been old, because it was an accurate carving, capturing the dead god's grace and malice. Even the face was right. It looked like him – looked like me.

'The Guild wouldn't have charged you with the deaths if they were truly due to this necromancer, or whatever he was,' Dace said. 'Regardless of the individual Guildmasters' desires, the tribunals are regulated by the Charter, not by custom. Why didn't you just tell the council all of this?'

'Why don't you just tell them that you're Tirnaal? That's not in the Charter either, and yet here we are.' My hand was still on the carving. All that was left to clean of the goddess was the charm in her hand. I did, and then froze, staring. 'Dace.'

'Not all of us are like that,' he said.

That wasn't the argument I wanted to have just at that moment. 'Can you stand? Come look at this.'

He grunted, but got to his feet and made his way to stand beside me. 'What?' His eyes fell on the chunk of stone I had just burnished to brightness. He sucked in his breath.

'Is that what I think it is?' I pointed to the tiny, shining piece of metal that the sculpted goddess held in her outstretched hands. It had been touched, at some point, with silver gilding, and a piece of onyx had been fitted into the granite. It looked like one of the plague amulets in miniature, a piece of doll's alchemy. And, circling the image of the goddess, was a series of characters. A prayer.

'This doesn't make sense.' Dace seemed to have forgotten all about me, reaching out to touch the carving. 'Deadchurch is hundreds of years old. The dukes stripped all the gilding and jewels out of the wall chapels three generations ago. These icons haven't mattered in a long time. The plague amulets only appeared three months ago. So why would ancient carvings show Ranara holding one?' His finger-tips lingered on the prayer.

'What does it say?' I said. 'I don't read Tirnaal.'

'Nothing. It means *accept our sorrow*. It's a kind of penitent's prayer, a renouncing of magic use. I believe Ranaran novices use it to bind themselves down to service. Why would this matter?'

176

She's taken one of them.

'No.' I jerked backwards, away from the carving, as though that would change what Moyra had told me. 'It's not possible.'

Dace faced me, too close, awash in the scent of his sweat and blood. 'What's not?'

I crossed the floor, almost running. I needed to hear Brix's voice. I needed her to tell me that what I was thinking was ridiculous, that these things couldn't happen twice in one lifetime. People didn't lose themselves to the divine. Goddesses didn't intervene in the affairs of normal folk.

I knelt beside her. 'Brix.' Her eyes moved under her eyelids, but otherwise she didn't stir. '*Brix.*'

'Gray.' Dace wasn't going to give up. Why had I expected him to? He wasn't my friend. He was my jailer. The earring gleaming beside his jaw proved that.

I sank back on to my haunches. Brix was close enough to touch, but I couldn't remember the last time I had felt so totally alone. I reached for her hand.

And, miraculously, she moved. 'Hey.' She opened her eyes, focused on me, then frowned. 'What in the hells is wrong?'

'Everything.' *Breathe. Tell her the truth.* 'But I need you to be awake for this.' I gathered myself and addressed Dace. 'You told me that I was the most dangerous thing you'd ever seen. You were right. *I am.* You want to know why I was in Varriel, trying to buy wardstones in the first place? I wanted silencing stones. I have nightmares, and I talk in my sleep.'

It took him a moment to understand. His face tightened. 'Gods.'

'I sincerely hope this does not involve the gods,' I muttered.

'I knew this already, if you've forgotten.' Brix's voice was rough with exhaustion. 'Is that why you woke me up?'

'They've changed,' I said. 'When Jaliseth had me divine for the origins of her amulet, I saw a dead woman. Moyra, the same Moyra who died here in Genereth. Last night, she warned me of the attack on the Guildhouse. Tonight I've seen her here, in Deadchurch, warning that somebody is hunting me. That they're *here*.'

'What?' Her fingers gripped mine. 'How? The street doors have been locked since we got here.'

'We need to leave,' I said. 'Before we endanger everyone else.'

The locks ground in the big double door. It swung open, revealing an old man that I recognised as the doorkeeper. It couldn't be morning yet, could it? I glanced at the windows. The inky black outside was lightening to silver.

'You.' He pointed at me. 'The aunts of Deadchurch are ready to speak to you.'

Our time was up.

THIRTEEN

The aunts of Deadchurch did not appear to be quite the wizard-killing threat that Dace had led me to expect. Except for the glimpses of blue tattoo-work at the edge of a sleeve or a neckline, the six might have been the sort of sturdy village women I'd spent my life being scolded by. They wore loose shirts and trousers in browns and greys, their jewellery the only concession to rank. Each of them had a fistful of heavy silver rings studded with chunks of raw amethyst or turquoise. Other jewels glinted in earlobes and noses, on anklets and, in Aoine's case, on a pair of heavy silver bracelets. They strode into the room, selected cushions and sat down.

'Brix and I—' I began, and was immediately silenced with a wave of rune-written hands.

'First,' said Aoine, 'hospitality.'

Three young men entered, carrying trays. Behind the food came Tynan on a litter, having acquired a heavy splint on her leg overnight. The bearers carried her over to the aunts and eased her down on to a cushion. The young men distributed trays to everyone, including the apprentices who were just now sluggishly waking up.

Brix sat up as one of the young men placed a tray on the floor. It held three clay cups of some gold, steaming liquid that smelled like wine and spices. She picked one up and inhaled its scent while I tried to hold what I hoped was a non-threatening smile. Dace sat down, just behind me, and took the cup that Brix handed him without saying anything. His face had gone blank.

'Spiced mead.' Brix pointed at her cup. 'Want one?'

'I'd rather be able to warn people about the possibility of impending destruction,' I said.

'They'll start questioning us in a minute,' Brix said, out of the corner of her mouth. She still looked like she felt awful, with a low, constant clearing of her throat even as she lifted her cup to her lips and sipped the honey-wine. 'But they won't listen to you if you insult them, so take a cup, Gray.'

I took one.

Aoine seated herself in the middle of the group of aunts. 'Tynan has convinced us that there's no need for the youths to remain. They can be taken downstairs and fed.' She waited, warming her hands on the side of the cup, until the young men had gathered up the stumbling apprentices and herded them out of the room, leaving just Dace, Brix, me and the unconscious Sannet to face our interrogators.

Dace was unusually silent and still. I took a gulp of my mead and burned my tongue, acid sweetness mingling with a heavy tang of cinnamon, like drinking incense. Daylight poured through the windows and blushed, rosy, against the walls. Somewhere out there was whoever had sent the stitched things to retrieve me, still hunting. Time was running away from us.

'Thanks for the mead,' I said, because nobody was saying anything. 'Should I just call all of you "auntie"?'

'Aunt.' Aoine looked up from her cup. 'Not "auntie". I don't think you quite understand how serious this is.'

'Brix is sick,' I said, evenly. 'I am deathly serious.'

Aoine swirled the mead in her cup, setting the specks of ground spices whirling. 'Indeed?'

'Indeed,' Brix said. 'And unless one of you has a cure for the plague that you're not mentioning, we're short on time, so perhaps we could skip the part where we impress Gray with the gravity of the situation. I know you have questions, but I have a few too. What's going on?'

'Maybe you can tell me that.' Aoine put down her cup. 'Genereth has had the plague for months. The Royal Police have been overbearing. Monsters chase a long-lost daughter of the clan to my door, accompanied by wizards of all things –'

'Are you going to cast them out?' Brix said.

'No. The spelldogs are under your protection.' She glanced towards Brix. 'Your mother was known to us, to me especially. However, your friend's profession is . . .'

'Perverse?' Brix suggested, dangerously helpful. 'Immoral?'

'I was going to say unfortunate.' Aoine's smile had gone brittle, like cooling glass. 'But at the moment, it might be useful.' She finally looked at me. 'Tirnaal don't believe in using magic to manipulate nature. It's pure hubris, thinking you know better than the gods. Right now, however . . .' Aoine paused, delicately.

It never failed. People who loathed magic in others still found themselves able to get past their objections when they had a use for it. I crossed my arms over my chest and wished I had a shirt. 'You have something you want me and my unfortunate profession to do, I take it.'

Aoine flushed. 'Two hundred Tirnaal have been thrown into the sick pens at Temples. We haven't been getting sick as rapidly as anyone else in Genereth, so there's all sorts of rumours flying.' Her fingers tightened on her cup of mead. 'They're saying that we're hoarding a cure, hiding a cache of amulets and selling them at marked-up prices, all sorts of mad nonsense. We need you to look at the young man –' She glanced quickly at Tynan for confirmation.

'Sannet,' Tynan said. 'You said, back at the Guildhouse, that his amulet was what was causing his sickness. If we can prove that the amulets are what first triggered the plague and find their source, we can prove that the Tirnaal are innocent. We need you to help us question him and find out where he got the amulet.'

I shrugged. 'I'd suggest waking him up and asking, as a first step.'

'That won't work. Tynan says he's not in his right mind. We need specific answers, and we need them now. The news of the fire at the Guildhouse is all over Genereth this morning. There's some saying the fire was the work of the families. The Roys are rounding up Tirnaal on the street.' It was one of the other aunts, this one a woman with two salt-and-pepper braids and a skinning knife sheathed at her belt. She adjusted the hilt so it was tilted more comfortably across her lap. 'Don't try to be coy. We know that you spelldogs can do things like this. If you're not helping us, you're helping *them*.'

My mind flooded with purple light, with the soft pattering of feet on stone, with a grating, steel-toothed voice.

You will come to her.

'No.' The word was out even before I knew it was in my mouth. 'Do your own sinning.'

Aoine rose and stepped around the tray of teacups. 'You don't understand. We're not wizards. We don't know how to read the runes. Get Sannet to tell us what he knows about where the amulets come from. He managed to find one *somewhere*. Maybe he can tell us something about how they work. That's all anybody is asking.'

'*You* don't understand.' I pointed at Sannet. 'I assume that you can torture him as effectively as anybody, so there's only one thing that you could need me for. You want me to crack him, steal his memories for you.'

'We can talk about this,' Brix said, extending a hand.

'I'm not going to invade another person like that.' I met her eyes. 'I can't.'

Aoine's upper lip curled in disgust. 'Don't you care about what happens to Brix's people? Hundreds of Tirnaal are on the edge of being turned into godsbones, sacrifices to avert the plague. The city has been accusing us of *causing* the plague because we're not dying as rapidly as they'd like us to, and you want to stick at asking a few questions?'

'Ah yes, Brix's people.' I was on my feet, aware that I was doing something incredibly foolish. 'You've all really been there for her all these years, haven't you? Wore yourselves out hunting for her and Anka after they were taken. Ironclad loyalty you've all displayed.'

'Gray,' Brix said, warningly.

I took a step backwards, but I didn't take my attention off Aoine, who had gone rather pale. 'You want me to break a man because you're afraid, and you think this will buy you some safety. I'm telling you that if I do what you want, use magic to force my way into his head, it'll ruin his mind. Wreck him, make him an un-person. It's like killing someone – it's murder, just the same as slitting his throat would be.'

'Sannet is dying,' Tynan said, and holy saints, the false accent was back, annoying as a flea. 'He may never regain consciousness. It's not the same thing as cracking a healthy person. I understand your having moral reservations, but this is an extraordinary circumstance.'

It took me a couple of seconds to be certain that I had heard correctly. 'Are you actually recommending that I harm your patient? You've worked in a Guildhouse; you know what being mindblown is like. I thought Healers took an oath.'

She had the grace to look uncomfortable. 'He's not going to wake up. The knowledge in his head could actually help the living. You have to try.'

'People are dying,' Aoine said. '*Brix* is dying.' Behind her, the door opened and closed. A young woman entered, almost jogging, and came to whisper in Aoine's ear. Her expression changed, going rigid with dread. She advanced towards me. 'There, you see? The Roys are here. They're on the street outside the doors with a Guildlord, asking to see me. What am I to tell them?'

'Guildlord,' said Dace. 'What Guildlord? Is it Valera Trist?'

'I have no idea. She must have forgotten to introduce herself while she was threatening to have the lot of us arrested.' Aoine's eyes glinted. 'Either do this for us, Corcoran Gray, or explain to me why I shouldn't hand you and the other wizards over to them.'

'No. Maybe there's another way,' Brix said, but then she began to cough. Light broke around her like pieces of the dawn. I crouched beside her, watching with increasing panic as her lips went blue. The fit went on for a full sixty seconds before she was able to drag air into her lungs with huge, desperate, gulping breaths. Her eyes fixed on me. 'You promised.'

I hadn't forgotten. But the aunts were right: if they were depending on Sannet to become lucid and answer questions, the two hundred Tirnaal in the sick pens would die, the plague would spread until it burned itself out, and Brix would burn out with it. The spells in my head and the sigils under my skin were all I had to offer. What if there *wasn't* another way?

Killer. Poison. Necromancer.

I hadn't forgotten any of it.

I rose and crossed the floor to Sannet.

The apprentice who had attacked me a scant twelve hours ago was stretched on his back, on a hastily assembled pallet of cushions. A soft pink glow haloed his lips. At least that weird blue sheen wasn't so prominent on his neck now. I squatted next to him, wishing I had some idea what I was going to do.

Think, Gray.

I could do it, scribe a spell on Sannet's forehead, plunder his memories. It would work, in ideal circumstances. But it was also possible that all I would do was speed up his death. I might never get the answers we needed.

There had to be a way to make sense of this whole problem without breaking his mind. I wasn't going to empty Sannet the way the stitched things had been emptied.

Think.

Magical trinkets were usually not that complicated. They couldn't be, since they had to hold the entirety of a spell. Even if you did make something big enough, really intricate spells stressed objects so much that they broke after a couple of uses. Thus, whatever spell was on the amulet had to be simple, small, like the wardstones in my pocket or the ring in my ear.

I opened Sannet's shirt. The amulet glittered, the pewter and glass still held tight against his skin like a parasite, the black liquid inside shimmering around the pulsing purple spark at its heart. I felt for his wrist. His heartbeat throbbed in time with the spark. Not only was it attached to him because it was touching him, the *magic* was tied to him.

His sleeve had fallen back towards his elbow when I took his pulse. On his forearm were three irregular, brown-black circles. I turned his hand over, studying the fingers.

It was there, the black rim around the base of the nails, the first symptom of advanced magic poisoning.

'What are you doing?' Aoine had moved up behind me while I wasn't watching and now was staring down at me. 'How long does it take to do one interrogation spell?'

'Half an hour.' I shifted my weight back on to my heels. 'This changes things.'

'What does?' Aoine crossed her arms, a quick, angry motion. 'This isn't helpful.'

'Is it helpful to know that he doesn't have a real plague?' Silence descended again, broken only by Tynan's low, startled exclamation. 'This isn't a normal sickness. The crystals, the symptoms . . .' I gathered my thoughts. I had to be convincing. 'I've seen lesions like the ones on his arms before, and the dark nails confirm it. He's got magic poisoning. I think everyone who's sick has magic poisoning.'

'Are you trying to tell me he's spell-shot?' Tynan's voice dripped with derision. 'From one spell in the last two months? That's ridiculous.'

'No. You can sleep off being spell-shot. Magic poisoning happens when you're spell-shot and then you keep taking toxicity past the point your body can stand. The Guild has a lot of regulations about how frequently you can perform certain incantations to avoid it. Poisoning is rare because it hurts so much that people pass out and quit incanting. Sannet thought magic was going to bring the "plague ghosts" down, but he also thought that magic would keep him alive.' I pointed at the lesions on his arm. 'I don't know how he managed to keep going, but that's what happened to him – or at least part of it. It's almost like he couldn't feel what he was doing to himself.' I paused.

I lose time. I find cuts and scrapes I don't remember getting.

It worked. The process would have been slower with Jaliseth, since she didn't pronounce the spells she carved. But the theory worked.

Aoine grimaced. 'And the spell on the amulet, the one he thought would save him?'

I brushed my fingertips across the metal, where I could see the clumsy runes carved. They weren't part of the static sequence or the flesh-seeker. These were the runes that I hadn't had time to analyse back at the Guildhouse, the ones that were only part of an incantation.

She'll take them.

'It should be nothing,' I said slowly, feeling my way. 'It's cleromancy, a kind of communication, or divination. There's no reason for it to offer any kind of protection.' I could tell that, but Sannet should have been able to tell, even as an apprentice. I laid out the spirals for various spells in my head, counted the runes and compared them with the ones that were on the stopper. Nothing quite fit. 'It's almost like the kind of thing you'd see on a djinn's vial.'

The answer snapped into place as I said it. If this was part of an incantation from a djinn's vial, this wasn't a way for Sannet to talk to anybody. I had seen a spell like this before. It wasn't communication, it was transport.

'Stop touching it.' Tynan leaned forwards. 'Stop!'

I laid my hand flat on the amulet and pronounced the runes. When I ran out of the ones that were scribed, I pronounced the ones that *should* have been next.

They lit, where they were written under the skin across my breastbone.

The plague amulet blazed with purple light. Sannet's eye snapped open, and he made a strangled, pained sound. The spell in the vial beat against my palm like a heart. I bent, and watched as the brown lesions on his arm shrank and then faded. One by one, the rest of the symptoms – the stained fingernails, the blue tinge to his throat, even the pink around his mouth – coalesced into a violet orb, hovering over the back of my hand. I twisted my fingers one way and then the other, fascinated, while the orb moved.

There it was, all the poison this boy had been playing with, at my disposal. The runes over my heart burned, each character cutting into me, a wash of agony so complete that it almost made me numb.

'What in the hells are you doing?' Tynan was staring at me like I was a viper in her bed.

'Answering your questions,' I whispered. 'There's your plague that's not a plague, doctor.'

'Help,' Sannet croaked. 'Please.'

If this worked the way I thought it did, I could simply let the toxicity slip into the amulet. The poison should remain contained, at least long enough for me to figure out how to dispose of it. If it didn't—

'Stop it,' Tynan hissed. 'You're playing with things you don't understand. Stop it now. This whole business was a mistake. Bringing you here like this –'

I bit into the side of my cheek and concentrated on the pressure and the taste of blood. It gave me enough focus to feel with my mind for the smooth-edged opening at the middle of the spell. I found it and, with great care, manipulated the orb of poison inside.

The amulet went dark. I grunted, and let the spell end. And then, with a musical tinkle of glass, the amulet in my hand cracked and fell apart, nothing but a handful of glass shards and twisted, magic-fatigued bits of metal. The drin leaked out on to my fingers, sludgy and warm, like blood. I dropped the mess and looked with disgust at my hand.

Everyone else was looking at me, even Sannet with his single eye.

'Sorry about the eye,' I said, wiping my sticky fingers on my trousers. 'Where did you get your amulet?'

'Who are you?' Sannet struggled up on to an elbow. 'Where am I?'

'Corcoran Gray, blasphemous criminal. You and I had a fight. You're in Deadchurch.' I watched him. 'Don't you remember?'

'You – no. I don't. I remember you talking to me, but I don't remember why.' He lifted one hand towards his face, touching his bandage gingerly. 'I had a vision. While I was at prayer. I thought I saw the goddess, dreamed her, maybe, but she told me about you, and your name was . . .' He frowned. 'Jaern. Are you an acolyte?'

Dread spread in my belly like an oil slick.

'That isn't my name,' I said, as calmly as I could. Nobody in Genereth should have known about Jaern. 'You often talk to the goddess in your dreams?'

'I was praying at the temple. My friends had just died, I wanted to speed their souls to the afterlands.' He swallowed. 'I knew they died because they did spells. I knew it was only a matter of time before I died, too. And the priestess seemed to know, somehow, and she gave me a blessed amulet. It worked. I was safe, for a long time. And then I . . . started to forget things. Little things, at first, and then hours . . . days . . .' Something flickered across his face. If he hadn't been covered in blood and muck, it would have looked like awe. 'I dreamed about Ranara, and she comforted me.'

'That doesn't make sense,' I said. 'Even if she exists, the Lady of Shadows isn't interested in doing anything for people. None of the gods are. Maybe the priestess was tricking you. Maybe Kaylor managed to put together a cult in his search for revenge. Maybe—'

'Get away from him,' Tynan said, low, dangerous.

Maybe meeting a god was more common than I had thought.

I turned. She was watching me.

'You're a doctor.' I couldn't keep from making the connections, even though they were ridiculous. I couldn't stop talking. 'A wizard-trained doctor. You've worked in a Guildhouse for long enough to know the signs of magic poisoning. Why did you want me to break his mind? Were you trying to keep him quiet?'

We're all exhausted. Sometimes I've been so tired I can hardly remember what I've been doing.

'You kept Thane's amulet,' I said. 'I told you to take it off, but you kept it, didn't you?'

Slowly, unbelievably, Tynan stood. On a broken leg. 'Shut your mouth.' The plague amulet around her neck – Thane's amulet – swung as she moved. 'You've spewed your filthy blasphemies long enough.'

'Why does your accent keep changing?' I rose, my stomach knotting. With her weight on a shattered leg, Tynan should have been shrieking in pain. Instead, she took a step towards me. 'Who are you?'

'You know who I am.' Tynan, or whoever she was, crossed the distance rapidly, albeit awkwardly, clunking her splinted leg behind her. She was nose-to-nose with me now. 'You might deceive these others, but never me.' She grinned. Pink light curled around the inside of her mouth. 'I helped you build this body, my lord. I remember well enough how to take you out of it.'

'Tynan!' Aoine stepped forwards. 'What's wrong? What are you doing?'

Without hesitating for even a second, Tynan twisted, lightning-fast, and snapped the flat of her hand into Aoine's throat. The aunt went down, choking, and Tynan lunged at me. I only just managed to catch her wrist before her clawing fingers could grasp my amulet. She was strong, much stronger than an injured woman should have been. She smiled, that same dreamy, sweet smile from the statue behind me, even as she drove my hands backwards, even as the room exploded into action. Brix crossed the floor and leaped on to Tynan's back, pressing her forearm across Tynan's neck.

Tynan didn't seem to notice her, eyes never leaving Jaern's amulet. 'Give it to me. It's mine. That skin is mine.'

'Ranara.' I should have asked how: how I could be talking to a deity, how she was able to inhabit a doctor, how she had been able to inhabit Sannet and Jaliseth and start a plague. Instead, I said: 'Why?'

'Magic is a sin.' Tynan grabbed Brix's hair with her free hand and twisted her sideways to the floor. Then she leaned into me, finger-tips brushing my chest. A bone in her wrist snapped under my hand.

And Tynan's amulet whirred and clicked, legs unfolding from the case and reaching for me.

'No!' Movement flickered at the edge of my vision. I turned in time to see Dace spring towards us. He grasped Tynan's plague amulet and yanked, snapping the leather cord. He twisted and threw it, legs wriggling in the air. 'The censer,' he shouted. 'It might boil off the drin and stop the trap spell.'

Brix, who had just scrambled back to her feet, caught the amulet by the cord in one outstretched hand. She turned and dumped it into the bucket of smoking coals the statue held. For one long second nothing happened and we all stared at each other.

Then the amulet cracked, and, with a hiss, dumped its contents on to the coals in a puff of honey-scented steam.

The purple light in Tynan's mouth flickered and went out.

She wobbled on her feet. 'What—'

Then she began to scream.

I spent the next ten minutes standing very still while the aunt with braids held her skinning knife to my throat. Aoine and the rest of them swarmed around Tynan, who was sobbing with pain. Everybody was yelling in Tirna, and nobody seemed to remember – or maybe nobody cared – that I couldn't understand a word. Eventually Aoine gave a terse command and the aunt released me. I made my way back to Brix, who was still on her feet. Dace hovered beside her, watchful.

'What are they saying?' I said.

'They are discussing what to do with you, and all the choices are bad.' Brix's face was lined with pain and worry. 'They're saying what just happened isn't possible.'

'That I healed Sannet or that Tynan was possessed by a goddess?' I said.

'Either. Both.' She glanced at me. 'Was it the amulets?'

'I can't find another commonality between them,' I said. 'I don't think it was Ranara-worship. Sannet seems like he was religious, but Jaliseth has always preferred Farran and Tynan talked like she thought the whole thing was superstition.'

'Jaliseth?' Brix frowned. 'You think she was . . .'

'Possessed,' I said. 'Yes. At least until she took the amulet off. I know I have odd friends, but believe it or not most of them do not have secret death-trap cellars full of dead people. Jaliseth said she had been losing stretches of time, remember?'

'Then that means that you're vulnerable.' Dace's eyes wandered to where Jaern's amulet hung around my neck. 'Unless you're saying that yours is different, somehow.'

'It didn't react when I pronounced the incantation for Sannet's.' But that wasn't why I didn't want to take it off. I couldn't, not until I knew what the goddess, or whoever she was, wanted it for. 'I don't know exactly how Jaern made it work, but it doesn't use the same mechanism as the others.'

'Jaern?' His eyebrows twitched together. 'You mean the necromancer posing as Jaern.'

'If you want to think of him that way. The point is that I know how the plague amulets work now. If we can find another one, it's possible that we could use it to remove Brix's infection. Poisoning.' Sweat burned my eyes and I scrubbed my sleeve across my face. 'Both, I mean.'

'Both?' Brix grimaced. 'How can it be both?'

'The little crystals,' I said. 'We know they spread person-to-person, and that they make you sick. I think the amulets start the crystal bloom in a given place, and then magic use accelerates it.' I drew a deep breath. 'Which is why we need to get Brix to Temples. Sannet said that he got his amulet there.'

'What?' Dace stepped backwards, appalled. 'Are you hearing yourself? These are the pieces of alchemical jewellery that have been killing people, remember? If the amulet really came from Temples, that means that Kaylor and his pack of revolutionaries were involved with the priestesses. The whole thing must be some kind of giant power play on the part of Temples, revenge for Moyra's death. Temples has always wanted the Guild out of Genereth, and so have the Tirnaal families. They're exterminating us.' He shook his head. 'We're not going to play around with theories. We have to shut the whole thing down. This is a matter for the law. We need Valera, the police and as many Guildmates as we can find.'

'We?' Brix's eyes narrowed.

Dace flushed, but he didn't back down. 'It's your decision which side you want to be on. I don't recommend you side with Temples.'

He glanced at the door. 'We need to go, now, before the aunts remember to alert the doorkeepers.'

'The aunts and the priestesses aren't our main problem,' I said. 'The goddess is, and we have no idea where she's located.'

He twitched his shoulders, annoyed. 'Yes, I heard you say that. What evidence do we have that a deity is involved, beyond a sick woman's delirious statement? I thought you didn't believe in goddesses?'

And here I had thought that Dace did. '*Someone* has been sewing bodies together with thread. If the tailor wants to call herself Ranara—'

Brix elbowed me in the ribs, hard.

Aoine had broken away from the group and was striding towards us. She was still massaging her neck where Tynan had struck her, voice cracking. 'Tynan can't even talk, she's in so much pain. What did you do?'

'I didn't do anything.' In spite of myself, I backed up a step. Aoine looked capable of taking my throat out with her bare hands. 'It was the amulet she was wearing, the one she got from Thane. Gods know where Thane got it. Probably from illicit potion traders in Varriel, like my friend Jaliseth did.'

Aoine was studying me, eyes narrowed. 'Explain.'

As though *I* was the one who had put her on the floor. I had told Tynan not to wear the amulet. If anyone had listened to me, I could have kept them safe. My chest felt tight, frustration buzzing through me. *Now* they wanted me to explain, now that it was too late?

'All right. I'm still not certain of anything, but all right.' I glanced at Brix. She looked exhausted, like she might puke or start coughing again any second. I needed to get her out of this place and to Temples, whatever Dace said. I wasn't going to lose anyone else. 'At first I thought Sannet's amulet was like a seerstone. For communication. The priestesses have made similar things before in Temples, insisted that it helps your prayers reach Ranara in the starlight lands. Seerstones are incredibly dangerous to use, so it would make sense that you'd die quicker with one around your neck. But it didn't make sense that it could make you better at first.'

'Tynan said the amulets were superstition,' Aoine said, frowning. 'Harmless.'

'But I saw one explode in Varriel,' I said. 'Not harmless. Not Guild-made, either. Dace only dragged us here in the first place because the Guild had no idea where the amulets were coming from. They're the ones who have been dying.'

'Don't get distracted.' Brix's breath was hard-fought, scraping in and out of her lungs. 'You said the amulets made people better at first. You talked like one could make me better.'

'One made Jaliseth better, at least temporarily, and it kept Sannet alive.' I hesitated, then ploughed forwards. 'I think the amulets store and move magic toxicity. At first, the amulet pulls poison from the wearer and the reservoir in the amulet will store it. With Jaliseth, it was the toxicity that came from working with magic on the stones. But storing the poison is only half the incantation. If a caster completes the spell, I think it removes the sickness permanently, seals the poison into the amulet, like a cork.' I wished I was more certain about that part. 'Otherwise the poison builds up and spills back out, concentrated, and they die, transferring poison – via the crystals that form in their blood – to others in the process. The spell works by moving magical toxicity, directing it at people, like shooting an arrow.'

'And you knew how to activate the rest of a spell that isn't scribed,' Dace said.

I tapped a thumb on my own breastbone, hoping he'd seen enough of the business with Sannet to understand what I was telling him. 'I recognised the first half of the incantation. The other half *is* scribed, just somewhere difficult to see.'

'It's a war. Or . . . a hunt.' Aoine's face relaxed in comprehension. 'That's why it seemed to only strike wizards at first. The plague spells see to it that they can't recover from magic use. That's why it's also spread to people who use cheap charms and black-market spells, prophylactics . . . and it explains why the Tirnaal have been slower to get sick, because for us, magic is a sin.'

'But why?' Brix burst out. 'Why would anyone do such a thing? Kill so many people?'

'Presumably they hate either the Guild or magic itself.' I looked at Aoine. 'Maybe they even think magic is a sin, to be purged from the earth.'

'You're forgetting.' Aoine's hands clenched into fists. 'There is another way that magic users can recover. The Guild and the Roys know perfectly well that using us will save their own skins. The Tirnaal are not likely to start a war if it will cost hundreds of our own people their lives, *wizard*.'

'Everyone who starts a war is willing to sacrifice hundreds of lives, *aunt*.' This was taking too long. Every heartbeat that went past was another moment I could never get back, another instant that I could have been getting Brix to healing. 'If you have a better explanation of how the amulets work, correct me. Otherwise, I've done what you asked, and I want to get Brix to Temples.' I stopped, nauseated by a pulse of heat and pain from my earlobe. I turned hurriedly, but I couldn't see him. The room was full of unhappy Tirnaal, overturned tea trays and the haze of smoke from the incense burner, but no Examiner. 'Where is Dace?'

'The Guildlord. She's still outside.' Aoine went ashy. 'But the door-keepers will stop him, they won't let him—'

Brix moved towards the door, and I followed.

'Wait!' Aoine's hand closed on my arm.

I turned. 'There's no time. We both know how Valera will scapegoat the people in Deadchurch, but Dace either doesn't believe that or he doesn't care. He's an accomplished wizard, but he's bound by the Charter.' I let my teeth show. 'I'm not. So let me stop him.'

Aoine looked up at me for a moment longer, searching my eyes. 'Stop him, then. Get him away from here.' She released me. 'Hurt him, if you have to, but keep that poison away from my people.'

The stink of magic already hung heavy in the air when Brix and I burst into the foyer. A pair of Tirnaal doorkeepers lay twitching on the floor, the rancid green light of a tetany spell encompassing them. Dace crouched beside the door, fiddling with the locks.

The locking mechanism was surprisingly elaborate – I hadn't paid much attention to it when we had come tumbling through the door the night before, but now I saw that it was no simple bar and hooks. Instead, a set of metal collars held the bar in place, with two padlocks dangling from them. Dace was in the process of forcing these locks, scribing a breaker – the ironbiter breaker I had taught him – in a circle around each lock. When Brix and I came sprinting into the room, he straightened, pencil still between his fingers. For a second he almost looked relieved to see us. Then he saw my face.

There are times when talking is appropriate, like when you're trying to distract your enemy, or when there's a chance of resolving something with words instead of actions. Other times, though–

Dace turned slowly to face me, hands held low and ready. 'Don't do this.'

I didn't talk. I ran at him, chanting, the magic hot between my teeth – Jaern's magic, the burden of wickedness I could never shed, poison, gorgeous, cruel.

The runes crackled to life across the back of my shoulders. It wasn't tetany, or a simple binding spell; this was a brilliant, malicious combination of both. The toxicity hit me like a load of ice, crushing my body downwards even as my fingertips touched Dace's face. A blast of black light left my hand and the spell whose name I didn't know inserted itself between his teeth, forcing his jaws apart, holding him in one place. He twisted, to no avail. He hung, body and voice trapped within the humming, skin-close prison of the magic. He looked at me with a pitiful mixture of shock, anger and betrayal.

Brix dashed towards us, leaping over the prone doorkeepers, who were just now groaning and starting to come out of Dace's tetany spell.

Dace tried to talk, but all that emerged was a garbled sound. He looked even more chagrined.

'Yes,' I said. 'You can't speak clearly. I'm sorry about that, but it's the whole point of this spell.' I held on to the magic with trembling muscles. 'Have you got it, Brix?'

'Almost.' Brix was beside Dace, taking the pencil from between his fingers. We needed to get the regulator off of him. Once the earring wasn't touching him any longer he couldn't incapacitate me with the thing, even if he managed to free himself from my spell. 'What do I scribe?'

I recited the runes carefully as the poison of my own spell seeped back at me, and Brix wrote a quick half-circle incantation on Dace's jaw around the earring. In another moment she had pronounced them and was fiddling with his earlobe.

'Hurry,' I said, in spite of myself, the sick pain pounding behind my eyes. 'Hurry.'

The earring opened at last with a tiny click, and Brix held it up briefly before slipping it into her pocket. She glanced at the door. 'Valera will probably still be outside, but there's a back way.' She inclined her head towards Dace. 'What are we going to do about him?'

In truth, I had hoped that the spell would knock him out. I knew from experience that it was exquisitely painful, and sometimes shock and intensity of pain will make people lose consciousness. But Dace was still doggedly awake, in visible agony.

'Get moving,' I said. 'I'll follow.'

Brix lingered for just a heartbeat more before slipping through a door to the left of the big entrance. I approached Dace and looked into his eyes.

'I'm sorry,' I said. 'I didn't have a choice. You weren't going to let us go to Temples, not before you broke up the entire operation with Valera. Kaylor and whoever he's recruited to help him will fight you to their last breath, Dace. They hate you. They'll wreck everything before they let you get a dram of good out of it. But I need their amulets to still be working, at least for a little longer. I can't let Brix die.'

His eyes were fixed on me. He couldn't speak, but that didn't matter. I knew what he'd say.

Liar. Criminal. Killer.

Maybe he wouldn't be wrong.

I tightened my grip on the spell and pushed it, just a bit more. His back arced, his entire body in spasm, throat working with smothered cries. Still I had to hold my grip on the incantation, watching his eyes, waiting for the moment when they rolled back in his head.

He went limp, slumped inside the shell of magic, and finally I could let go. He hit the ground like a sack of grain.

I stood over him, wondering whether the sickness slithering in my gut was entirely the result of the spell.

'I am sorry,' I repeated, as though it would do any good. He had been right not to promise me freedom, right not to trust me. Every fear he'd had about me had come true. Every fear I'd had about *myself* had come true. I hesitated, but there was no other option. Locking me up was the only way to keep everyone else safe.

'I'll come back,' I said.

Then I jogged after Brix.

FOURTEEN

Emerging from Deadchurch was like being reborn, albeit we were birthed into a very narrow space between the chapel and the undertaker's house next door. We picked our way through a ditch that served as the dump for the wastewater of both buildings. The morning light slanted into the gap between the roofs and fell on my shoulders, heavy and hot and sweet. Brix only wobbled a bit on her feet.

'We're not just going to go traipsing out into the street, are we?' Brix's breath came in laboured snatches. 'Valera might still be there.'

'We're not going to go into the street at all if there's an alternative.' I dug around in my pocket, pushing past the wardstones until my fingertips brushed the bottle of drin. 'Before we go anywhere, you need to dose again. Three swallows, Dace said.'

She absorbed the fact of the bottle in my hand with admirable composure. It wasn't until she met my eyes that I realised she was angry with me. 'Where did you get it?'

Brix doesn't know how bad it's gotten for you, does she?

That had been a mistake. 'From Tynan. She said it might quiet my dreams – while she was in her right mind, back at the Guildhouse, so I don't think it's tainted.' Guilt flooded me like a taste. 'I know. I should have told you.'

'Yes.' Her voice was quiet, which meant she was very angry, indeed.

She did take the bottle, though. 'Was this because I didn't tell you about my family?'

'No.' I pushed past her, certain that I didn't want to be having this conversation. I rubbed at the back of my neck. 'I wish I had a shirt.'

Brix made an irritated noise and unscrewed the stopper, before sniffing at the drin. 'It smells all right.' Before I could reply she tossed off half the bottle's contents, grimaced and shoved the bottle back into my hands. 'I still hate the taste, though. You carry it. You're the one who's going to take it tonight.'

'Like the hells,' I said. 'Unless we can get every trace of this gods-damned toxicity off you—'

'Which we apparently will, if we get moving in time to reach Ranara-temple ahead of Dace and Valera.' She shouldered past me. 'Come on.'

In the daylight, the street in front of Deadchurch looked more normal, with vendors warily trying to open their shops. Valera was planted in front of Deadchurch's front door, with her hands on her hips and four Royal Police standing around behind her, looking ill-at-ease. As Brix and I slipped out from between the buildings, Valera strode up to the door and hammered on it.

'*Now*,' Brix murmured, and hustled me around the corner and out of sight before the Guildlord and her friends had time to turn and look behind them.

We continued like that all the way back to Godstown, dodging from shadow to shadow, a reckless enough path that I wondered whether Brix was a little stoned. At one point she had me hide next to a refuse heap while she rifled through some poor fool's laundry line. She returned with a hooded overshirt made of loose-spun brown wool. I pulled it over my head and immediately began to itch.

Brix looked me up and down. 'Better.'

'Good, then let's go.'

She caught my arm as I tried to move past her. 'No.'

'Let me go,' I said. 'You've only got a couple of days left, according to Dace. We don't have time to –'

'Stop it.' Her fingers tightened into my arm. 'You want to know, so I'm telling you. My mother, Magdala Rivest, was a Deadchurch aunt before she died: a fighter, an important politician. Any respect the Deadchurch family gives me is because of her, and when she died I thought our clan would look after us forever. But when Anka and I were taken –' She paused and licked her lips. 'At least you've known, for your whole life, that your grandfather wanted you. I don't know if my clan even tried to get us back. Even now . . . the way they treat you, the way they treat everyone who's outside the family . . .' She shook her head. 'I couldn't – I didn't know how to talk about it. It seemed pointless as long as we were up at the cabin. I wasn't ever going to come back here. It wasn't ever going to matter.'

I pulled away. 'It's your own business.'

'But I should have told you.' Her muscles were taut. 'You know I should have. You've been angry with me about this since we got to Genereth. Why can't you admit it?'

'I'm not –' I caught myself before I could lie. 'I'm just a *friend*, though, isn't that right? So what right do I have to be angry, after all?'

'That isn't fair.' Colour drained out of her face, leaving stark shadows under her eyes. 'You know it isn't fair. You know why I said –'

'I know what I *am*,' I said, hoarse. 'Stuck inside this skin, spewing poison, hurting people –'

'Shut your damn mouth.' She stared into my eyes, jaw set. 'You have no idea what it's like to live with you, so don't pretend you do. I'm not a coward. Quit protecting me from you.'

Coward.

'Very well.' My heart rattled in my chest, hard, hurting. 'We've been together a year, Brix, and you never mentioned these people, not once. We don't hide things from each other, not as long as we're sharing a bed. Gods, you share my *life*. You should have told me.

You should have claimed me. And I should have told you about Moyra sooner, and about the drin, and I should have known what to do, and we never should have come to Genereth in the first place – and exactly where does admitting all of this get us? Can we just move?'

She started walking again. 'This has got to stop. You can't just decide to avoid it.'

'It seems like we should deal with your damn cough before we attempt to repair my conversational style.' My feet hurt, and my hand throbbed where my blisters had burst. The streets were three-quarters empty, even at the hour of the day when everyone should have been either shopping for that day's meals or heading to work.

'Corcoran.' Her hands clenched. 'You can't–'

'I *can*,' I said, between my teeth. '*Don't.*'

She stalked along in silence for a while before exhaling, frustration floating off of her like smoke. 'All right, how are we going to get into the temple? If Tynan really was possessed by the goddess, won't Ranara know what we look like?'

I had been trying not to think about that. The walls of Godstown loomed just ahead of us, pale stone rising above the roofs of the shops and houses, the same clean colour as fresh-scrubbed sand along the sea.

'First, we don't know that it was the goddess,' I said. 'We only know that someone thinks it makes sense to claim to be Ranara. It could be that Kaylor thought it gave his quest for revenge a gloss of grandeur. Secondly, even if we grant that a goddess is somehow real and the one who's possessing folk, we don't know that she'd be located in her temple.'

'We don't?' Brix moved ahead of me. 'Are you sure?'

We had reached the wall, and just ahead of us stood the gateway to Godstown. It was a potential chokepoint, but as we drew closer it looked quiet and safe enough. Scuffs of something dark marred the pale stones of the arch – mud, maybe.

'I have limited experience with goddesses,' I said. 'But we've never been to Ranara-temple, so none of the priestesses know what we look like. They can't read minds. If we're fast enough—' I paused before we went through the archway. Maybe laying out the odds wasn't really what she was asking me to do. 'Brix, if you don't want to do this—'

She shook her head. 'We need to get one of those amulets, since Jaern's won't work. Nothing else has managed to do more than slow this thing down. We're out of time, whether you want us to be or not.' She looked me up and down. 'I do wish you weren't quite so distinctive-looking.'

'If I had anything to scribe with, I could run an illusion spell. It would make me sick and I wouldn't be able to talk, but I could make myself look different. As it is—' I pulled my hood up over my hair.

She wrinkled her nose. 'I suppose that will have to do.' She strode through the arch and led us back into Godstown.

Once again the sheer enormity of the place took my breath. The temples were the largest places of worship I had ever seen, walls of creamy stone glowing in the tawny morning light. The roofs rose in a series of domes, blood red with white and gold scrollwork around the edges, flashing like a platinum necklace set with rubies.

In contrast, sad clumps of coughing people huddled on the cobblestones beneath the shadow of the domes. Several Roys with crossbows seemed to be pushing them towards a low door set into the side of Ranara-temple. Beside me, I heard Brix draw in a hitching breath before she started off across the plaza.

A smoking, burned-out cart leaned drunkenly against the steps of the central dais. The statue of the goddess there gleamed, smiling determinedly at nothing. The cobblestones were spattered with more dark stains – mud, blood, ash. As we drew closer, the directions the Roys were shouting at the sick became clearer:

Stay in line. Your turn will come soon enough. This is all just a precaution. There are many doors into Ranara-temple.

There *were* many doors into Ranara-temple. Brix and I chose the largest, a giant bronze set of doors. A small group of healthy-looking people were taking turns moving towards the half-open door. A large, silver-plated statue of Ranara dominated the arch above the door, seated on the crescent moon and beaming down at the people below. To enter the temple, you had to walk between her prettily pointed toes, like sheep being herded into a narrower and narrower chute.

No. I couldn't think like that, couldn't give in to the tension crawling through my muscles. We needed a plague amulet. This was going to work. It had to work.

Brix eyed me as we joined the group of petitioners at the feet of the goddess. 'Anything wrong?'

'No.' Even if there was, we didn't have a lot of options. The Roys were right there. Breaking from the crowd when we were this close to the entrance would be suspicious.

Beside the gigantic, open bronze doors of Ranara-temple was a young woman in a cream-coloured priestess' robe. The people in line each approached the priestess, presented an offering and stated their business. She, in turn, listened and then split them into groups. Some she let pass into the temple, others she sent away with advice. The woman ahead of us was carrying a pair of pigeons. She confided, in a whisper that carried back to Brix and me, that she and her husband had been trying for a baby. The priestess wrung the heads off the birds, tossing the bodies into a wide, gilded trough at the foot of the goddess before she performed a blessing, one hand on the woman's belly.

'If nothing has happened in three months, come back,' the priestess said, while the woman blushed. I wondered a little what the priestess would do if the woman did come back. Say that the pigeons were an inadequate sacrifice?

But the priestess was looking at Brix and me now, with eyes beginning to dim with milky cataracts, fingering the crescent-moon necklace that dangled from her neck. It was tin, its surface chased with tiny, intricate curlicues of runes – prayers, most likely.

'You come to seek the Moonmother's blessings?' The priestess' half-blind eyes travelled across us, probably searching for an offering.

'Healing,' Brix said. 'I'm ill, and we heard that Ranara can heal people who've caught the sickness.'

'Necklaces,' I said. What was I supposed to use as a sacrifice? 'We heard that there were necklaces that worked to gain the goddess' favour.'

'And your offering?' the priestess said, when Brix and I kept standing there, awkward.

'We were hoping there was another way to enter the temple,' Brix said. 'Times are hard, and–'

'No. The goddess doesn't grant anything to those who don't work for it. All must give.' The priestess' smile went hard. 'A beggar might offer the goddess only a single copper coin when the king might offer an entire city, but everyone who seeks the Moonmother's blessing must offer sorrow and sacrifice.'

Out of the corner of my eye, I saw a pack of helmeted Roys start to cross the plaza, towards the crowd of the sick. A figure in a blue robe walked ahead of them.

Valera. No.

Brix scowled. 'But that's not how it's supposed to work. If we don't have anything, we can't give you anything.'

'Here.' I dug the wardstones out of my pocket and held them out to the priestess, hoping that either her poor vision or the state of her magical education would keep her from knowing that the wardstones wouldn't work to silence anybody but me. They were art, after all, and beautiful in their own right – maybe they would end by gracing some reverend mother's bookshelf.

She took the stones and rolled them through her fingers, brushing her skin across the textures.

'Gray,' Brix whispered, appalled. 'What—'

'We can get other stones,' I said.

'They'll do.' The priestess gave a short, sharp nod. 'Come inside.'

We passed from the warm light and the scrutiny into the cool dimness inside the temple. To my surprise, the priestess followed through the open half of the great double door and pulled it closed behind us.

'Why are you shutting us in?' I said.

The priestess seemed briefly disorientated. When she spoke, her voice wavered, hoarse. 'The doors have to be shut for morning prayer. Follow me.'

The inside of the temple was as impressive as the outside, but in a different way. I had, for some reason, expected to step directly into a majestic sanctuary, all columns and soaring tapestries, or perhaps to see the stained-glass windows from my visions of Moyra. Instead, the priestess led us through a confusing series of plain, plaster-walled hallways that reminded me of nothing so much as the rabbit warren of tunnels in your average jail. We passed a few other women in Ranaran garb, with sleeves pinned back and practical canvas aprons tied over their robes. Some of them were smeared with rusty stains. All of them ignored us.

After several dizzying minutes we reached an open metal door set into the stone walls. Just inside, several incense braziers stood beside a table littered with apothecary's tools. Beyond stretched the largest room I'd ever seen. It was not a dungeon.

Pillars soared away from us, reaching towards the cobalt-coloured ceiling. Lances of sunlight shone through myriad small windows, punctuated by gilt stars. The constellations wheeled across the expanse of the underside of the dome and centred around one glorious, stained-glass full moon. It was like stepping from day into the deep quiet of a starlit night.

The floor was huge and hexagonal, broken only by a spiral staircase to our right that crawled upwards and, in front of it, something cylindrical and white. A ring of dark human shapes stood against the six sides of the walls – crypts, I guessed, with life-sized statues in front of them representing the dead. The floor was grey marble with pale metal inlays in swirling patterns that reflected the light. The beauty of the sanctuary was marred somewhat by rows of pallets lining the floor. On most of the beds unconscious people lay coughing, tended by a lone, robed healing sister.

'People from the sick pens,' the priestess said, which didn't explain why nobody seemed to be doing any treatment. The Ranaran priestesses I had known elsewhere had been sensible, hardworking women. I couldn't imagine them ignoring the sick this way. 'The amulets are over there. We'll need to do the prayers to retrieve one.'

I looked in the direction the priestess was pointing, and my heart stuttered. The white thing in front of the stairs was a marble font, blooming like a lily under the flat roof of a side chapel. It almost seemed to glow, lit up by another moon window – this one depicting the sharp crescent of a partial eclipse. After a moment I saw that the illusion was helped along by a pair of tall silver mirrors that stood beside the font, whose faces could be manipulated to keep the light focused. Above the font, suspended over the floor by a metal pole, was what looked like a skeleton that had been dipped in silver – godsbones, the remains of ancient human sacrifice.

I recognised this place. In my dreams or nightmares or visions or whatever they had been, I had seen Moyra perch on that font.

The priestess took off walking at such a pace that Brix and I had to jog to catch up with her.

The claw-footed font was as tall as the lower border of my ribcage. It wasn't full of water, though. Instead, a silvery pool of what seemed to be liquid metal reflected us all back.

'Quicksilver?' Brix leaned towards the font, her brow furrowing.

The priestess was rolling up one sleeve. 'No, it's vuthine. Some people call it moonmetal.' The priestess plunged her arm, naked to the elbow, into the font. Her muscles worked as she groped around beneath the thick, silvery surface, lips moving in what I assumed was prayer. Then, slowly, she pulled out a necklace.

A crescent moon, dangling from a piece of leather.

It was a simple Ranaran charm. Wearable prayer. A worthless piece of tin.

'There you are.' The priestess extended it towards us, almost smug. 'Full of blessings of Ranara.'

'But that's not—' Brix bit down on the words, but not before I heard the spike of frustration and dread in her voice.

'We're interested in the other necklaces,' I said. 'We've got friends that got them here. Is there something else we have to do? Somewhere else we should go?'

'Other necklaces?' The priestess' arm dropped to her side. She smiled again. 'Are you saying that an Eclipse Moon isn't good enough? For someone like you, Corcoran Gray?'

No.

They knew who I was. We were trapped, and I couldn't think of anything but Moyra, on her back in a tank of dark liquid. I couldn't stop myself from imagining Brix in a tank like that.

And you know how that dream ends, don't you? With you, burning everyone you care about.

No. I wasn't going to burn anyone, no matter how bad this got. I had to force myself to think clearly. Except for the one robed and veiled healing sister still moving around the tables full of instruments and incense, everyone else in the room seemed to be unconscious on the floor. We still had a chance to run, if I could keep the priestess from calling for help.

I reached up and pushed the itchy, miserable hood back. If I had to face this, I was at least going to face it as myself. 'Who are you?' I said. 'Who are you really?'

The priestess didn't move. Just to our left, the healing sister straightened and removed her veil.

Gali Kaylor stepped forwards, steel ring glinting under his nose. 'Shut,' he said, precisely, 'your dirty mouth, wizard.'

Brix went pale, but didn't move. 'Gray?'

'I don't know,' I said, trying unsuccessfully to watch both of them at once. 'He was in the fire. I don't understand how he's not dead.'

'Aye,' Kaylor said. 'You and those Guild pigs would have liked that, wouldn't you?'

The priestess folded her arms. 'I wonder if we can dispense with the farce. I've given you plenty of chances to admit to your real name. I'll grant you that I wasn't using this vessel the last time you saw me, but you used to be quicker than this.'

What had Sannet said? *She told me about you, and your name.*

Oh gods, no.

I swallowed, and reached for the memory of the dead god.

'Nobody enjoys a prize if they get it too easily,' I said, with his inflection. Jaern had been 900 years old, living longer than any man had a right to by keeping his soul separated from his body. The person inhabiting the priestess knew Jaern's face, which only made sense if they were as ancient as he had been.

Brix glanced at me, startled. I took a couple of steps, enough to put myself between her and the priestess. The goddess. Whoever it was. 'All this flitting from body to body seems a little elaborate.'

Her eyes snapped with anger. 'I *tried* to speak with you directly, though I don't know why I bothered. You've violated every agreement we had. You bound me to this temple. You forced me to use my children as vessels. Do you know how many of them had to die for me? Did you think I wouldn't recognise my own work when you showed up at the Guildhouse?' She stared at me. A blue-green sheen covered her neck, almost to her jawline, like her flesh had been turned to copper and left to tarnish. 'No. I suppose you did that on purpose, didn't you? Was it a challenge? An insult, to present yourself as some sort of road conjurer? If you wanted to speak to my real face, all you had to do was play honestly. What do you want?'

My real face. My stomach lurched, but I made myself give Jaern's mocking smile. 'I'm here now – what better honesty do you desire?' How in the hells was I going to get Brix out of there? Kaylor was watching our every move with grim, focused hate. Any second they were going to try to kill us. 'I want you to heal Brix and let her go. Why, what do *you* want?'

'Stop stalling.' The priestess pointed at my chest. 'If you're willing to bring that into my temple, we both know it means you want something more than one woman's life. I won't ask you again: what are you really doing here?'

She meant Jaern's amulet, glittering against my breastbone. I didn't think anyone could use it without the spell I must have been carrying somewhere under my skin – but then again, she had that spell. She had *me.* I shifted my weight on to my toes, heart clattering in my ears. 'This conversation is boring me,' I said, but I knew I was running out of time. 'Remove your plague from my servant, and then we can discuss this like civilised folk.'

'It can't be,' the priestess said, staring at me. 'Back at the Guild-house you told the doctor that you lived through something you shouldn't have. I thought you were acting, playing haunt-minded to test me, but – it can't–'

Game's up. Time for the last move.

'Jaern is dead.' It was a relief to speak in my own voice again. 'I'm nobody – just an unlucky road conjurer who faced the Lord of Secrets and watched him die.' Brix fell into a crouch with her back to me as Kaylor approached. There was no way out; we would have to fight. I pronounced the runes that circled my knees. 'I don't like death, or killing. There's no point. But if you don't let us go –'

The priestess watched the sheet lightning spell gather in my hands. Her smile didn't drop.

'No,' she said.

I barely heard her pronounce the spell before the riptide of magic hit me. The air in the room shifted, thickened, and the priestess – no, *Ranara*, the goddess herself – glowed like the sun. The current swept me off my feet and rushed me backwards, smashing me into the wall between two windows with a crunch that knocked the breath from me.

'No!' Brix's voice rose above the sound of blows. 'Let him go!'

If I could get the rest of my spell off, I could give Brix a chance to get out of the room. I hung there, feet dangling above the floor, struggling to inhale against the panic and the weight of the magic crushing me into the stone. *I can't see.* Where was Brix? The air around me was heavy, like water. *I can't breathe.* I clawed at my throat.

'Brix,' I said, but all I could see was the priestess, her hands pulsing with blinding white light. She watched me choke with odd, gentle pity.

'So you killed Jaern,' she said. 'You must be very clever.' One of her fingers straightened slightly, and I could take one gasping inhalation, and then another. I'd lost my spell; my hands were empty. She wouldn't give me time or breath for another one.

'Please. My partner. Let–'

She flicked her wrist sideways, and my arms snapped outwards. I cried out, unable to help myself as my joints all cracked simultaneously. Agony shot through my limbs, sizzling to the tips of my fingers. 'Bonewarp. You've likely heard of it, but I doubt you've seen my own version. I was the first to think of it, you know. Capturing the arthritis that bothered my children and using it to punish backsliders.' Her lips curved. I wondered why I had ever thought that look on her idol's face meant mercy. 'There's nothing I wouldn't do for my children.'

She twitched her wrists again, and knives entered my joints. I couldn't see. I couldn't even scream. Hot wires of pain pulled my bones apart, shoulders and wrists and elbows, hips and ankles. I didn't have enough breath, didn't have any thoughts, had nothing but the hurt and the fear and the dreadful, terrible knowledge that I had failed.

You've lost.

You've lost her.

When the suffering eased – ever so slightly – and I could think again, I realised I was babbling, repeating myself in a low moan.

'Please, just let her go, I'll do whatever you want, please ...' I caught myself, but it didn't matter.

'Yes,' Ranara said, and holy saints, she almost sounded kind, standing there and holding the agony over me, hovering, waiting like a crow to pick out my eyes. 'I know you will.'

'What do you want from me?' I said. 'Why are you killing them? The wizards—'

'I want Jaern's spells. I want his amulet.' Her eyes widened. 'And I haven't killed anyone who didn't deserve it. You know it, in your own stolen bones. Magic done by mortals is a sin, especially magic as the Guild does it. I tried to tell them, didn't I? As long as they kept their dirty fingers out of the business of the gods, the plague couldn't touch them. Magic releases all sorts of pain and poison in the world. And then the pain has to go somewhere, doesn't it, Corcoran Gray? Who do you think has been catching it, all these centuries?'

She twisted her wrist, and I twitched with a new wave of torture.

Vomit rose in my throat. 'Please, I'm not going to fight you. You don't have to—'

'You're learning a lesson,' she said. 'Pay attention. This is your chance to repent, and help me rid my children of the magical taint forever. You resisted me before. You hurt Kaylor. We had a terrible business pulling his pain into amulets. Used up three vessels keeping him alive. But I made him a promise, you understand, and I kept it.'

'Used up,' I said. 'I don't understand.'

She laughed. 'A vessel is just a body. Just a person who doesn't deserve the life pulsing in their veins. Now, you're clever. Think about it. You can't destroy pain, can you?'

'You can only move it.' I stopped, understanding, sick to my core, revolted in a way I had never been before. 'No. They're people, not reservoirs. People like Moyra, and . . .' I shook my head. 'No. *No.*'

'They all say no, at first.' Ranara lifted her hands.

And then I heard a quiet, matter-of-fact voice chanting on the other side of the parchment window cover. I recognised the spell: it was a breaker, a sloppy one.

Dace.

The metal window gratings on either side of me exploded into the room towards Ranara. She flung her hands up to protect her face and I soared sideways, choking. I probably would have cracked my head on a pillar if a hand hadn't snaked through the window and grabbed my ankle, pulling me downwards and outside.

We hit the ground together, rolling over and over in the muck of an alley garbage-heap. I had just enough time to register where I was before Dace yanked me to my feet and shouted:

'Run, now!'

FIFTEEN

I don't know how long we ran before my wits and breath came back to me. Dace led me through a dense maze of alleyways, ignoring me every time I tried to get him to stop, until I finally dug my heels in and fell headlong. He grabbed me by the collar and dragged me, one-handed, into a doorway, where he pushed me down to sit on the threshold.

'We've got to go back,' I said, when I could talk. 'They have Brix, they—'

'Can't kill her as long as they want you,' he snapped. 'We can't let them have *you*, idiot. There's something about you and your damn amulet that she needs. She said as much. We have to think.'

My joints still weren't working right, and I kept choking at odd moments, but I was regaining the ability to think in a straight line. 'How are you here?'

'You're not the only one who can divine.' He wiped sweat out of his eyes. 'I knew you were going to Ranara-temple. As soon as your spell faded, I followed you. I made a spiral in the alley.'

'And where's Valera?'

He didn't move, blocking my path should I decide to stand up. 'Why don't you tell me exactly what happened before we start worrying about Valera?'

'I got my arse kicked.' My wrists felt like the bones were sliding

214

around, loose. The low fire of lingering magic twitched in my flesh. What good was it, if the spells couldn't save us when I needed them? What good was I? 'I didn't even get a spell off. Ranara has Brix. Let me go.'

'Ranara,' Dace said. 'You're still seriously insisting that the goddess—'

'I don't care whether she's a goddess.' I thudded the back of my head gently against the doorframe. 'Why is it that you pious believers find it so difficult to accept that a deity might actually be doing things? She could be a necromancer like Jaern was, or an alchemist, it doesn't matter. I have to get Brix out of there.'

'You can't,' Dace said, with flat certainty. 'Not without a plan. If you go back in there and lose, not only will Kaylor and his goddess and this group of fanatics kill every magic user in the provinces, but they'll have no reason not to kill Brix.'

I struggled for calm. 'You don't understand what you're asking me to do.'

'I'm asking you to save thousands of lives,' he said. 'To save the practice of magic itself. What do you think Brix herself would say?'

A wire in my head snapped, and I surged up to stand on ankles that grated like stone on stone. '*Shut up!* This whole thing is your fault. We never would have been here in the first place if it wasn't for you. Ranara never would have come for us.'

He stepped backwards, white-faced, silent. Abruptly, I remembered the initials scabbed into his skin, the incantations swirling under *my* skin. This was my fault. I'd made the deal with him, after all. I was the one who carried death with me, the one who dragged Brix to Temples. I was going to be the one to get my partner killed.

'Dace.' My voice sounded gravelly and full of panic even in my own ears. '*Please.* You don't have to come with me, you don't have to help, you can wait in Godstown and arrest me the minute Brix and

I come out of that temple and I will sit and let you. But you have to let me go back.'

Dace waited, one hand clenched into a fist. Slowly, I realised he was waiting to be attacked.

'I'm not going to hurt you,' I said.

'Gods.' He let out his breath. 'Let's think, before we kill each other. It took ten minutes after you left me at Deadchurch for the spell to finish. When I let them in, Valera and the Roys were too busy rounding up the Deadchurch family to listen to me when I said you were on the way to Ranara-temple. We could try to find them.'

'Valera did hear you, apparently,' I said. 'She was outside the temple when Brix and I got there. You think she would work with us against Ranara?'

He shook his head. 'She won't believe that a goddess is sitting in Godstown manufacturing stitched monstrosities, no. But she might help us arrest a necromancer.'

It was too thin. Ranara had handily defeated me. Damaging or even destroying Ranara's 'vessel' wouldn't do anything to stop the goddess herself. And Valera would what . . . *arrest* her?

'Valera will get her head kicked in,' I said. 'Ranara – whoever she is – doesn't play around.'

'So your theory is that you and I should go running up to the front door by ourselves with no plan and no help?' He glanced up at the sun. 'It's been maybe an hour. We'll have to find another way in, figure out what we're dealing with. Can you walk?'

I could, barely. 'Are we going back towards Godstown?'

'No.' Dace set off at a rapid pace, threading down alleyways, avoiding the main streets. 'Stop talking. I'm trying to get us somewhere safe. You can argue with me there.'

'What safe place?' I said.

'Hells, do you ever listen? I told you to shut up, for once.' Dace fell into step beside me, cradling his injured arm. I tried not to think about my unstable joints, and shut up.

The sun had strengthened into punishing heat, with clouds of mosquitoes swirling through the river-damp air. Sweat collected on my skin and stayed there, soaking through my clothes and dripping down my spine. The cobblestones were warm, hot in places, and as the shaky panic and Ranara's spell began to wear off, I started to feel the ache in my toes, exacerbated where the knuckles had loosened and then tightened again.

After about an hour, Dace paused. Perspiration shone along his neck and jaw, and there was another dark place on his bandage.

'You're bleeding again,' I said.

It broke whatever internal focus had been distracting him. 'It doesn't matter. I'm all right.'

He wasn't. 'You're not going to save the Guild if you bleed to death, Examiner.'

'I'm not going to bleed to death,' he said. 'I'm going to die because I'm running with an unlicensed wizard, about to do something incredibly illegal.'

We had stopped in the shadow of a building that had once been an expensive stone house. Now it wasn't much more than a crumbling façade, shedding long strips of whitewash. The ground-floor windows were boarded up, with a series of plain-spoken murals executed on the boards in bright colours. I squinted. They were *very* plain-spoken murals.

'You brought us to a brothel,' I said. 'Doesn't seem like your style, I admit, but I wouldn't call it *incredibly* illegal.'

'That's not what I was talking about. I just need a minute to think.' Dace was looking past the building, which formed part of the city wall that curved down towards the river. The brothel stood on the outskirts of a market that hunkered precariously on the riverbank, backed up to the broken-down docks. The stalls seemed to be selling penny buns, second-hand clothes, firewood, wilted flowers, all cheap, ordinary goods. But judging by the wealth on display among the merchants, the market's real wares were probably much more expensive – and illegal. The flower woman in particular seemed to be doing well for herself, with heavy gold bracelets on each wrist and an impressive pair of bodyguards yawning beside her. While Dace thought, I watched no fewer than six furtive people buy flowers. I expected them to cross to the brothel, but they made their way out of the square again as quickly as they could. She wasn't a pimp.

'She's selling drin,' I said.

'She's at least someone who will help us if we can pay her.' Dace swallowed. 'Ranara has to be stopped. If you're right, she's killed a lot of my friends. She wants to kill Brix – hells, she wants to kill magic itself.' His eyes had gone hard, like green river ice. 'You're carrying magic she either wants or is afraid of. So the first step is to look into what's under your skin.'

'You think I haven't tried?' I said. 'Brix's touch makes the runes visible, but only for a split second, and never predictably enough to write anything down. I'm a competent wizard, Dace. Acarius is a brilliant wizard. We've tried every divining spiral invented, and none of them reveal the spells I carry.'

'Not *every* divining spiral,' Dace said.

He moved before I had a chance to ask what in the hells that was supposed to mean. We crossed the square under the silent attention of everyone there.

'They can see your Guild sigil,' I whispered. 'They'll remember you.'

Dace didn't turn his head. 'They already know who I am, and they'd remember us anyway.'

The flower woman was weaving a bouquet together with quick fingers as we approached. When we got closer I saw that the bracelets weren't her only piece of jewellery. An emerald stud winked in one nostril, and she wore two silver rings in each ear, each with a tiny gold honeybee charm dangling from them.

'Never thought you'd deign to come back,' the flower woman said, without raising her attention from her work. 'What's the occasion, got yourself a boy at last, Dace? Or a girl? Or anything?'

'That's even less your business than it was the last time I saw you,' Dace said. He was smiling, but when he spoke both bodyguards straightened and began paying attention.

'Then I'm not sure why you're here.' The woman held out her completed bouquet. 'Did you want to buy some flowers? I'd make you a bargain.'

The bunch of daisies bulged where a vial of drin was wrapped up in the stems. Dace didn't flinch, and he didn't look at the flowers. I wondered how long it had taken him to learn to stand still while being jabbed.

'I'm here to bargain. I want access to the spiral in the old chapel for a couple of hours. I have an unlicensed wizard.' Dace pointed at me without looking at me. 'He can do things that my vows forbid. Don't you have a debtor that you want to find and squeeze, or some money that you want warded, or an enemy that you'd like cursed? Or anything?'

She snorted. 'You want me to sell you a sin for the price of a spell? You used to know better than that.' She put the flowers down and wiped the sweat from under her chin, and I saw the blue runic tattoos that curled up the sides of her fingers.

'What would it take?' I said.

She looked at me for the first time, her gaze sweeping from the top of my silver head, down to my bare feet, and back up again. 'Have money of your own, do you, dear? I can pay you better than this one does, if you want a job.'

Heat spread up the back of my ears. I revised my earlier conclusion: she *was* a pimp. After all, nothing forced drinlords to limit themselves to one illicit business at a time.

'Stop this,' Dace said, quietly. 'I already know the family has been doing a good business lately, right? Temples has been buying more drin than usual?'

Her eyes flicked to him. 'Now how would you be knowing that? Who's been talking to you?'

'Nobody. At least, nobody that would count to you. Someone is using Ranara-temple as cover to enact an alchemical plot and they need drin as a reagent.' His gaze didn't waver. 'So they're supplying you with more ingredients for drinmaking, and they're buying up all your extra stock, aren't they?'

'A lot of extra,' I said, mindful of Moyra in her drin-filled coffin. 'Gallons, I'd think.'

The woman turned her attention back to the flowers, fingers busy. 'It's none of our business why Temples wants to buy our drin. It's perfectly legal for us to sell to them. We've been making money – legal money – hand over fist. Even you should be pleased with that. Arguments between the Guild and Temples–'

'Listen!' Dace slapped the flowers down on to the stand. Both bodyguards surged closer, but Dace never looked at them. 'Wizards are being murdered. I know you don't care about that, but there are two hundred Tirnaal that are about to be blamed for it, Thieves-church family among them. It's a full moon. If they're going to sacrifice us, they'll do it tonight. We don't have time for you to punish me. Are you going to let me use the spiral or are you going to let all of them die?'

'Us?' the woman said, harshly. 'Since when have you been concerned about the fate of the Tirnaal? Since when have you cared about anything besides your dirty magic?'

Dace's jaw tightened. 'The fact that instead of leading an arrest sweep I am standing here talking to you ought to count for something.'

'It buys you two hours upstairs,' she said, 'and I don't envy you the hangover you'll get from the thing. After the time's up, you're not my responsibility anymore, understand? Only two hours.'

'We'll be gone in one,' Dace muttered, and turned on his heel.

'Don't you have anything to say?'

Dace halted mid-step, his entire body rigid. 'I don't think so.'

'You want to use the spiral or not?'

Dace didn't turn, staring straight ahead. It took him a full thirty seconds to speak. 'Thank you.'

The bodyguards relaxed, and the flower woman went back to weaving daisy stems. But Dace didn't move again until I touched his elbow.

The tiny upstairs room in the brothel was even hotter than the street, and the stench of the river hung heavy in the close, damp air. Dace shut the door behind us and looked around in revulsion. It was a stone-walled square, with crumbling plaster, one tiny slit of a window and a sad pile of empty bottles in one corner. The floor was the only interesting part: it was stone, and the centre of it was taken up with a large, intricately carved rune spiral.

'It used to be a Jaern-temple, but leave it to us to ignore magic as long as there's money to be made on vice.' He kicked at the bottles, viciously. 'This used to be a secret library. Now it's where the Thieves-church aunts fill bottles for drin addicts.' The dark spot on his bandage was bigger. 'Do you have anything to scribe with?'

Us. I cleared my throat. 'Are we not going to talk about what just happened?'

He wasn't looking at me. 'I'm not sure why we would.'

'Family can be difficult.' I reached for his wrist. 'You're going to drip blood on the spiral if we don't fix your bandage. Let me see that.'

'Family?' He gave a quick, bitter burst of laughter, but he didn't resist as I took his arm and untied the bandage. 'They're nothing. A drin gang that had no compunction about using their children as runners, all while insisting we were so much better than the filthy spell-spitters.' He glanced at the spiral on the floor. 'When the chapels were built, this is where the Jaernic priests did interrogations for the governor of the old prison – that's why they called it Thieves-church. This spiral makes secret things evident.'

'It's a giant extraction spell?' I grimaced. 'So you could strip information out of anyone's mind, anytime you want?'

He shook his head. 'Not extraction. Closer to divination, although it's not precisely that, either; it's something older. It doesn't crack minds. It interrogates bodies, even dead bodies. It reveals secret things on a person or on what they carry – bruises, the tracks of poison, snags of thread . . .'

Hidden spells. He didn't need to say it. 'And it's stuck here, mouldering unused at the top of a Tirnaal brothel?'

'It's a sin,' he said, sing-song, clearly quoting someone. 'As far as the clan is concerned, it's lost knowledge. They're too superstitious to destroy it, but they won't allow anyone to study or use it, either. I only figured it out because it was my job to scrub this damn floor and I couldn't stop thinking about it, hanging around pubs and listening to drunk apprentices talk, trying to put the pronunciations together . . .'

'A lot of work, self-teaching,' I said.

'Not self-taught. Nothing so grand. *Untaught.* Presumptuous. Dangerous.' He winced as the bandage came away from his wound. 'When I was fifteen there was a murder, a girl, one of our own. We all suspected one of the men who visited the brothel, but of course there wasn't evidence. And I knew . . .' He was staring down at my hands as I worked, eyes glazed and unseeing. 'I *knew* the spell would do it. I knew I could take enough drin to keep from going ghostly.

222

So I had some of the others lure him here, and I used the spiral to get the proof. Her blood was under his fingernails.'

'And that was enough for the police?' I said.

'What makes you think the clan bothered with police?' He met my eyes. 'The murderer was found hanged with a "confession" note pinned to his chest. The innocent man the Roys had arrested went free. And as thanks, my clan put me outside the city walls with nothing but my clothes and a knife. I went upriver and apprenticed myself to the first wizard I could find and I swore I would never come back to this gods-forsaken pit, and yet here we are. Can you hurry?'

I bit down on the inside of my cheek, unsettled. I needed to focus on the bandage I was trying to amend. Dace's wound still looked nasty, but it had scabbed over, except for one place near the wrist that was oozing bright new blood. I repositioned the bandage so clean fabric was against the wound and began rewinding it.

'You could have gone to the other clans,' I said, wrapping as fast as I could. 'Brix's clan would have taken you in, wouldn't they?'

'They might have been kinder, but they still would have told me that what I wanted – that what I *am* – was impossible. That Tirnaal don't become wizards, that I shouldn't exist.' He winced as the fabric tightened, but kept his voice steady. 'I've never been interested in . . . in the kind of relationship you have with Brix. Men, women, none of it appeals to me. My work is my life, like a spouse, and they disowned me for it. These people aren't my *family*. They never were.' He paused. 'Why do you care?'

It was a good question; one I hadn't answered for myself until he asked it.

'You didn't have to help me, back at the temple,' I said. 'You're still helping me. It . . . matters.'

He blinked, and pulled his newly bandaged arm away from me. When he spoke again, the words came quickly, as though he was running. 'The Deadchurch aunts made me empty my pockets, and I only managed to keep back one blue pencil. I nearly used that up divining for you at Temples.' He took the mashed stub of a sky-coloured grease pencil from his pocket. 'The spiral only works if your name is scribed into it.'

So we were done talking, then.

'Better than nothing.' I took the pencil, crouched and studied the carved floor. The sigils were old-fashioned and unfamiliar, but you could work out the logic: this was, essentially, a very focused, very powerful form of physical divination. Along one edge was a blank, smooth run of stone. I wrote my name on it, carefully. Now all I had to do was the scribing to tie it into the rest of the spiral.

The whisper of my fear was still there as I worked, always snapping at me from behind, reminding me that Brix was with people who could kill and think they were doing holy work. Brix was ill, and alone, and I had to get back to her and explain that I had been a fool. I had to tell her it *didn't matter* – her name, her family, none of it – as long as she was all right, as long as I could be with her.

'You still have drin?' Dace squatted beside me.

'Why?' I pulled the half-empty vial from my pocket and held it out to him. 'Do you need some?'

'Not as badly as you do.' He pushed the bottle towards me, impatient. 'One swallow won't hook you. It will steady your hands enough to finish the scribing.'

I flushed. 'I'm all right.'

'You're not. And every minute we spend sitting here arguing about it is a minute that Kaylor and his friends could be hurting Brix. Take the drin. I of all people am not about to judge you for it.' One corner of his mouth twitched upwards. 'I won't even call you a drin-licker.'

'Nobody can even tell me what the stuff is made of,' I mumbled.

'Funeral honey.' He shrugged. 'Mixed with powdered minerals from deposits in the swamps to the south. The minerals are called saintstears. They're processed alchemically with poppy sap. There are about sixteen steps to the refinement process. Do you need more, or can we get on with it?'

'Hells, fine, yes.' It still took me a long time to unscrew the stopper. The possibilities were many-faceted and myriad: *what if it makes you foolish? What if it makes you someone you're not? What if you never feel anything again? What if it doesn't work?*

What if you'll always be broken?

One swallow. That was all I was going to take.

The drin was warm and sweet and thick and it went down much easier than I'd thought. I closed my mouth and swallowed again, waiting for the calm that everyone promised me and feeling nothing but delirious dread. I focused on the bottle in my hands. On the inside of the stopper were a lot of scratches, half-illegible under a slick of dark liquid. A lot of . . . precisely positioned scratches. Like a sigil. I frowned, and brought it closer to my face. Was it glowing?

'Dace,' I said. 'We've got a problem.'

Dace took the vial and the stopper, jaw working. 'A location beacon. I never asked where you got this, did I?'

'Tynan gave it to me back at the Guildhouse.' And I was an idiot, to have only been suspicious about its contents, and not the bottle itself. 'Look, if we leave the stopper here, they'll have to investigate, search the house. It would buy some time. We could move.'

'This is the only revelator spiral there is, to my knowledge,' he said. 'And I am out of both paint and criminal connections to beg for help. I don't want to do this either, but there is no other way. We just have to hurry the hells up.' He took the vial, put it to his own lips and drained it. His pupils dilated as I watched. 'Now.'

He was right. I'd almost used up the stub of pencil that was all we had to scribe with. He had barely stopped bleeding. We were backed into a corner. I forced my breath out, willing myself to focus, and finished the scribing.

The drin wasn't sitting well in my stomach. He moved behind me while I checked the sigils one more time. When I put my hands on the runes, it felt like I was pushing through deep water. The drug must have been starting to take effect.

I sat back on my heels. 'Gods, I feel drunk. I won't−' I coughed, but it didn't help. I wasn't going to be able to pronounce the spell. I was supposed to be the one driving this incantation, but I couldn't. Maybe that wasn't accidental. 'Dace,' I said.

In high enough doses it's damn near a paralytic.

'I'm not going to hurt you.' His smile was perhaps meant to be reassuring, but his teeth shone darkly, coated with drin. Mine probably looked the same. I licked them, and wondered how long it would take to get the taste out of my mouth.

I tried to shake my head, and couldn't. His hands clamped on to my shoulders, guiding me carefully towards the floor. The smell of pigment and dust floated around me. In another few seconds he had me on my back on the spiral.

His concerned face appeared above me. He was fitting his hands, even the injured one, to the sigils. 'I am sorry. We have to know what we can use against Ranara, what she can use against us. You're the resource she wants, not just the amulet.' His eyes met mine, upside-down. 'I promise not to take more than I have to.'

SIXTEEN

For a long time there was nothing but me, stuck inside my galling, thistle-lined skin. Sigils crawled over my body like insects as the divining drew them out, one by one. When the magic eased enough for me to hear and see again, Dace was muttering the names of the revealed spells under his breath with horrified recognition.

Shacklebright, flamespike, illusion, huntseye —

It hurt, and I couldn't even gasp for breath.

Leafgrip, deathmarch, fleshbind, holy hells, no, here's eversleep, ruewrack —

'They're not my spells,' I said.

There was a silence, and for a moment I thought I was slipping back down into the blank darkness of the divining. Then he spoke, no longer near me. 'Yes. You kept saying that.'

I tried to move and discovered that I could, albeit with muscles so screamingly stiff that they made me clumsy. I sat up, and nearly fell backwards again.

'Easy.' Dace stood against the wall, palms still blue with paint. 'That must have hurt. Don't rush.'

'We don't have any time for me not to rush.' But my wits were still spinning, thrumming with the hideous sensation of exposure. Even Brix didn't know every spell I carried. Even she hadn't had to sift through my nightmares. I hadn't wanted Dace to know my body that well, hadn't wanted to hear the aversion in his voice. 'I need to get back to my partner. Did you see the activation spell for the amulets, or not? Could you recreate it if you had to?'

'Gray, please,' he said, softly.

Familiar dismay twisted inside me, disappointment so intense that it was almost grief. I had thought I knew who he was. I thought—

'Oh, shit, don't.' My throat burned. I sounded weak, even to myself. I got to my hands and knees, and then my feet. 'Don't try to talk to me about it, don't try to be kind, just—'

'I thought maybe, if you proved yourself to the Guild—' Dace looked half-sick, staring at me with the horrified fascination that most people reserve for executions. 'I don't know what to do. The *death* you're carrying.'

'I know. Stop it. Stop trying to make it easier.' I had just started to like the idiot. 'You didn't have to trick me, *take* from me like this. You could have asked me.'

'I'm sorry.' He meant it. That was the worst part.

I exhaled, recovering myself with difficulty. 'Look, I've never expected you to let me go. But you gave me your word about Brix. You promised.'

Dace moved to the divining spiral and began smearing the sole of his boot across my name. I waited for him to acknowledge what I had said, confirm that he'd keep his word, but he didn't. He worked in silence, grinding the blue pigment into the stone until every piece of the characters was gone, every bit of evidence that I was ever there.

'Did you get the incantation?' I said. 'Or was it just the ones you were listing?'

'You have a very potent, very old-fashioned ley-breaker written around one of your legs, knee to ankle.' He sounded almost like a student, spitting back a response to an examination.

I shook my head. 'I did a normal ley-breaker on Brix in Deadchurch, and you did one on Thane in Varriel. They didn't work, so that's not it.'

'There was also one above your heart that I didn't understand. It looked incomplete, like a piece of a larger spell.' He still wasn't looking at me. 'It didn't make any sense to me, but then you've done several incantations that I would have said wouldn't work. Find me something to write with and I'll write it out for you – maybe you'll recognise it.'

I moved to the narrow slit of window and stared down at the marketplace. Where could we find something to write with? Surely even illicit markets sold ink?

The street had gone quiet as the day passed into late afternoon, the punishing heat of the sun driving everyone into the shade. Several of the shops had closed, but a group of people stood beside the shuttered flower stall, talking with the drinlord.

As I watched, she gestured to the brothel, and the man she was speaking to turned to look up at it. I recognised him, even before the afternoon sun caught the ring in his nose.

'Dace,' I said.

'What?' He shouldered in beside me. Whatever else you could say about the Examiner, he wasn't stupid. It only took him a few seconds to take in the situation below and move away from the window. He dropped the empty bottle of drin, with its location-beacon sigil, in the middle of the blue smear on the floor. 'Come on.'

The brothel's shape mimicked that of the Deadchurch chapel, but a lot of wooden partitions had been put up. Instead of the rooms flowing in orderly sequence, doorways and tiny staircases seemed to sprout randomly, like mushrooms. Dace led me through the tangle, muttering curses under his breath.

We passed three people in the hallways, two women and a man. They had an unnerving, glazed look to them, as though they'd just rolled out of bed. Their reddened eyes found us, then slid away, as though we were pieces of furniture. Dace didn't slow down.

'Drin,' he said, shortly. 'A lot of it. They won't remember us.'

Eventually we hit a long staircase that spiralled down into a dimness that proved, when we reached it, to be the kitchen. An elderly woman with a set of sigils tattooed on her chin was napping, sitting up, in a rocking chair beside the hearth. Accompanied by her snores, Dace moved quietly across the floor, to the door that opened on to what was presumably an alley. He pushed it open a crack and waited for several seconds before nodding to me. 'It's clear.'

The alley outside was even worse than you'd expect an alley in a slum to be. Dace grabbed my wrist and plunged into the darkening heart of the city. After twenty minutes he let go of me and stopped, leaning against the side of a house, panting, wiping the hand that had touched me against his trousers.

'There's a tunnel,' he said. 'Access to the cellars of Ranara-temple, where the legitimate drin gets delivered. If Kaylor followed us to Thieveschurch and managed to intimidate the aunts into letting him into the houses—' He grimaced. 'He'll be chasing us. I wonder if he'll think to divine for my Guild licence sigil.'

'Probably,' I said, watching as the runes that his grasp had triggered faded on my wrist. It wasn't fair how quickly they disappeared. If only they had lingered long enough to memorize I could have used *him* for a change, figured out precisely which death I was carrying with just a touch. I wouldn't have had to walk around like this, turned inside out, raw, exposed.

He paused at a corner and peered around it. The street beyond was one of the avenues leading down towards Godstown, but the rivers of dusk gathering along it were deep and broad. Only a few of the houses had braziers burning in front of them. Many didn't even have candlelight showing at the windows. 'Do you have any idea what we're going to do once we're inside Ranara-temple?'

'Not we. You don't have to come with me.' I didn't anticipate how difficult it would be to say the words. I wasn't relishing the idea of facing Ranara again, alone.

'I told you that I'd ensure Brix's freedom. You think I'd go back on my promise?' I couldn't read his face very well in that light, couldn't tell whether the emotion I saw flickering across it was anger or hurt. He stood stiffly for a moment, then snorted. 'Bastard.'

Relief flowed through me. I laughed, shakily. 'Prick.'

'Well, if that's settled, perhaps you can fill me in on your plan.' He turned down an alley and halted. A man, heavily cloaked and hooded, sat beside a pair of broad cellar doors with a wineskin, singing to himself. Slumped against the other side was another drunk, who must have been passed out.

Dace went directly to the singing man. Clumsily, one-handed, he unlaced the neck of his shirt and pushed the fabric to one side. There, on his shoulder, was a twisty blob of old, dark tattoo-work that might have been a stylised honeybee. 'Open the tunnel, please.'

The man stopped singing and got to his feet. Standing, he was head and shoulders above Dace, but he didn't lift his hood. I supposed it made sense for sentries guarding smuggling tunnels to want their faces covered. 'You're slow.'

'Hurry up and open the doors then,' Dace said, impatient. 'Since when does a Thieveschurch sentry keep carriers talking on the street?'

'This street is private.' The sentry pushed the hood back, and I went cold. A copper ring glinted in his nose. 'Good for dealing with fools who believe they're the only ones who can think ahead.'

'Kaylor,' I said. Suddenly, the lack of movement from the other sentry made sense. The man wasn't drunk, or passed out. He was dead.

Dace dropped into a defensive crouch. 'Murderer.'

'Hypocrite,' spat Kaylor. He had decent clothes on under the torn and stained robe, which must have been dark blue at one point – the mark of a full wizard, his last tie to what he had been before he was cast out. More to the point, he wore a Temples amulet on a cheap leather cord, which swung as he shifted his weight, measuring us.

Smiling, saints help us. 'You wouldn't let Moyra train as a wizard, but you'll run straight to the Tirnaal drinmother when it suits you?'

'You're angry at the wrong person.' Dace's fingers twitched. 'I've only been the Examiner General for a month. I'm not the one who threw the spell that killed Moyra Behrel, or the one who kept her from joining the Guild. Some of us have been working to change those policies, from the inside—'

'To benefit yourself!' Kaylor lifted a hand and began to pronounce a spell. Sigils lit, deep blue, in a collar around his neck, and a jagged spike of fear shot through my chest.

Softheart.

Beloved of rapists and assassins, the spell would put its objects into a compliant torpor from which they would never wake. Softheart curdled more of a person's wits every minute that it ran until they were mindblown and blank. I had seen it reduce grown people to the mental equivalent of toddlers. It was illegal sixteen different ways, and there was no chance that Kaylor had learned it from the Guild. This would be something Ranara had taught him, which meant it would probably be worse – the same way the goddess' version of bonewarp had pulled joints out of place, instead of just inflaming them.

Dace didn't have anything scribed. I had options, but most of them would fill me with so much toxicity that I'd be useless for hours. We weren't going to be able to defeat him in a straight duel, not when I couldn't predict what he'd cast, not with the weight of Ranara's training behind him. I kept my own hands down and gambled.

'You're making a mistake,' I said. 'I know Moyra's why you've been killing the Guildies, why you needed them to suffocate and suffer the way she did. I know what Ranara promised you, but she's not going to give it to you. She's already using Moyra up. She's not going to bring her back.'

Kaylor halted as though I'd slapped him, the spell still eight syllables short. 'You don't know anything about it.' His hand clenched. 'This Guild dog just admitted that they murdered her. I was there, at the trial. They saw to it that nobody paid. Well, they're going to pay now. I'm going to give you to the goddess and she's going to judge you.'

Something clicked in my head. 'Ranara said to bring us in alive, did she?'

He took a breath and started chanting again, hurriedly. If he couldn't kill me, I had a chance. I leaped towards him, caught his hand in one of mine, and grabbed his throat with the other, forcing him backwards. Kaylor tried to speak. I tightened my fingers around his windpipe. He opened and shut his mouth, squirming between my hips and chest and the brick wall.

Kaylor gagged out one more syllable of the spell. Beside me, Dace spat at the collar of paint Kaylor wore before grinding his sleeve against the glob of saliva. The spell died.

'I'll kill you.' Kaylor bucked against me. 'I'll kill you!'

This was getting tiresome. 'No, you're going to listen. The Guild arrested me in Varriel and pressed me into service finding out where these amulets' – I thumped my elbow against his amulet, and he winced – 'have been coming from. Dace is certain that they're being used to spread the plague and I think that they're letting Ranara seize control of people's minds. We're both right, aren't we?'

Kaylor was still wriggling, but I was angry, and Brix was running out of time.

'When I was still upriver I used one of the amulets to divine,' I said. 'And I saw Moyra, in a coffin or tank full of drin. She asked me for help, so I came to Genereth to help her. They have my partner in Ranara-temple, you fool, and they have the woman you've been killing people for. Moyra's not dead, she's *kept*. Ranara is keeping her.'

Kaylor went still.

'The coffins.' His voice box buzzed against my palm. He sounded pitifully bewildered. 'How did you ... you couldn't know about them.' He lifted his chin. 'You're lying! You and the Guild dog are trying to trick me! Moyra and the others will live again, as soon as the Moonmother cleanses the city, as soon as the life wizards have stolen is returned.'

'Gray.' Dace glanced down the street towards Godstown, as though it didn't all just look like confused flickers of light and shadow from here. 'He's not going to change his mind. We've got to decide what to do with him.'

I shifted my grip, moving my left hand from the rogue wizard's throat to cover his mouth. Breath puffed from his nose on to my fingers, panicky, heartbeat hammering through his ribs. He thought I was going to kill him.

I ran through the hideous spells that Dace had seen under my skin and dismissed most of them as impractical or too permanent or outright murderous. 'Just let me think. There has to be another way to do this.'

'To handle this one?' Dace glanced from my captive to me. 'I don't think you're considering all the possibilities. There's the eversleep spell. It takes a long time to scribe one, but you're already carrying it. If ever it was justified, just for long enough to get him to the police—'

'No.' A sick taste flooded my mouth. 'I won't do that.' Eversleep would allow me to manipulate Kaylor's actions, control his will – at least until the overwhelming toxicity of the thing made me useless. But it meant forcing myself into his mind, invading another person. It wasn't permanent, so it was a step above softheart, but only just.

Dace studied me for a moment. 'This is someone who was bent on murdering you just seconds ago. You saw what he did at the Guild-house, and you have the means to punish him. Are you actually arguing that it wouldn't be ethical?'

'It's necromancy,' I said. 'I won't cast it on a living person.'

'Indeed, necromancy is generally better suited to the dead,' Dace said.

'This isn't a joke.' I turned my head so I could see Dace better. 'If I do that, if I just take someone's mind like that, I'm no better than Jaern. I won't—'

Kaylor snagged one of my ankles with his toe. I stumbled backwards, flailing, as he began to chant.

Dace had wiped out Kaylor's softheart spell decisively, but he must have had something else scribed under his clothes. He yawned, and a cloud of red fireflies burst from his mouth and swarmed around my head, fluttering against my nose and eyes.

I couldn't open my mouth to cast, or they'd go down my throat. I scrambled backwards in a vain attempt to get away from them.

Dace was chanting. I couldn't see him, but the voice was coming from my left. Kaylor would have to spend a good portion of his concentration on running the fireflies that were disabling me, which meant he'd have to attack Dace physically.

The fireflies started to settle on my skin, their tiny feet kissing like pinpricks of flame, leaving itching blisters. I covered my face with both hands and tried, frantically, to listen for Kaylor. If I could run at him, maybe I could knock him down, give Dace a chance to do something. Maybe I could—

But I didn't hear Kaylor move, or chant. Instead there was a quick patter of light footsteps, a strangled cry and a gurgle.

The spell around my face dissolved. I stood panting in the dusk, trying to reorientate myself, peering through swollen eyelids. Dace stood with his hands down, staring at Kaylor, who was crouched against the wall. Kaylor was making a series of muffled moans. He pressed his hands to his mouth, smearing something dark.

It took me longer than it should have to recognise the woman who stood over him, knife in hand. It was the moment when she reached out to give Kaylor an irritated slap across the back of the skull that did it for me – the tattoos on her wrists showed up even in the twilight.

'Aunt,' I said.

Aoine nodded at me. 'Wizard. Got yourself in a bit of trouble, I see.'

There were several questions I would have liked to ask, but the blisters on my face made it difficult to hold my eyes open, let alone speak clearly. Besides, there were more looming forms in the shadows that I thought belonged to other Tirnaal. What were they doing here?

'What did you do?' Dace looked like he wanted to step towards Aoine, but he didn't move. 'Cut his tongue out? We need to question him.'

'I meant to quiet him, not kill him.' Aoine wiped her knife on Kaylor's shirt. 'He's still got his tongue. He's just going to find it difficult to speak clearly enough to cast for a while. It only takes a nick on the tip.' Grim satisfaction thrummed in her voice. 'Some Tirnaal do know how to silence a wizard.'

Dace ignored the dig. 'Why in the hells are you here? How did you even know where we were?'

'We didn't.' Aoine turned towards him. 'You brought the law down on Deadchurch, and half of us were hauled away to Temples. The Guildlord and the Roys took as many of us as they could catch before we scattered. All the families know about the Thieveschurch tunnels.' The looming shapes in the dark were clearer now, men and women, all of them carrying weapons – sticks, knives, one girl with an axe. Aoine's face was taut with worry. 'They took Tynan, broken leg and all. I'm not going to lose her. I'm not going to lose any of them. We're here to bring them home.' Aoine glanced over her shoulder and gestured to somebody behind her. 'Come and convince this one to speak.' Two Tirnaal came and took hold of Kaylor.

He was staring at me, blood running down his chin. 'I'll still kill you,' he said, thickly. 'I'm not going to tell you a damn thing.'

Aoine looked at him, unimpressed, grabbed his ear, and twisted.

He screamed and thrashed. When she stopped twisting, he slumped there silent.

'Ready to answer my questions?' Aoine said, her face inches from Kaylor's. 'I can make it a lot worse, spelldog. What's the simplest way to reach the hostages? Where are they being kept inside Ranara-temple?'

He glowered at her. 'The goddess will punish you.'

'Aoine.' I stumbled forwards, trying desperately to think of a way to appeal to her. I sounded thick-tongued myself, and I didn't even have the excuse of a nick from a Tirnaal blade. 'Please. We need your help. They have Brix. We have to get into Ranara-temple.'

'They have *everybody*, wizard. They came hunting you, and they found us.' She jerked a thumb towards me. 'Get this one tied up, too, and get him back to the chapel. We'll deal with all of this once we've got the hostages safe.'

'No,' I said. 'Wait. I know you don't like wizards, but I'm not asking you to give me anything, not asking you to trust me, I'm just asking you to let me help. You won't get the captive Tirnaal free alone. You don't know what you're up against in there. Let me—'

'No,' Aoine said, sharply. 'You're running with this Guild spelldog. To me, that looks like you're on the same side. Tie him.'

Two men approached me, wary, rope stretched between their hands as though I were a bird they were trying to net. I stepped backwards. 'Think better of this. I can't let you take me, but I don't want to hurt Brix's family.'

'Then you shouldn't have desecrated our home,' Aoine said. 'You shouldn't have hauled Brix into a place where she could be taken captive. There are too many lives at stake, wizard. I'm not going to risk them for you.'

'Aunt.' Dace stepped between us. 'Gray is right. There's unsanctioned magic being practised in Ranara-temple, more than you can handle. You can, of course, kill us, but when this is all over you'll have to deal with another Guild investigation, more arrests, more trouble.' Desperation glowed in his eyes. 'Or you could let us help you, and I will use my position as the Examiner General to ensure that the families aren't brought before the law.'

'I'm not going to kill you,' Aoine said. 'You're just going to sit quiet while we retrieve our people, and then the aunts will decide what's to be done.'

'Those tunnels are the only way into Ranara-temple apart from the main doors, and you know it.' Dace leaned forwards. 'Leaving us on the street like this isn't any better than cutting our throats. It just looks prettier. I'm offering you aid, *official* aid. Why not take it?'

'The Guild lies. They've always been ready to sacrifice Tirnaal to protect their own skin. Tynan says that magic use is the whole reason why this disease is spreading, and you can't offer anything else.' Aoine made a short, angry gesture. 'Why would I want to be stuck with you behind me in the tunnel? I don't know what you want from me, spelldog, I—'

It just looks prettier.

Of course.

'Wait,' I said. 'I can get Dace and me into the temple. If you'll let us go.'

'I won't have you with us, endangering my people with spells,' Aoine said. 'We're getting our people out with knifework, not with magic and meddling with nature.'

'I don't need to be with you,' I said. 'Dace and I don't need to enter the tunnel. The Deadchurch family can do what they want, and we won't interfere, but you've got to let us go.' They both stopped staring each other down and turned their attention to me.

'What?' Aoine said.

Dace's eyes narrowed. 'How?'

I took a deep breath, and told them.

SEVENTEEN

Illusion is both easier and more difficult than you'd think. It's easier because it involves painting a picture in other people's minds, and most people pay so little attention to their surroundings that they'll agree with almost anything you put in front of them. It's difficult because running illusion feels like you've swallowed nails, and it's slippery. There was nothing to scribe with, but Dace had seen Jaern's illusion incantation written under my skin. I had to use that, trust its elegance and hope that we could be quick. By the time I finished, what felt like a ball of spikes had blossomed in my gut and was merrily gnawing at my insides.

'How do I look?' Dace turned in a slow circle. He looked exactly like Kaylor, except that he wasn't bleeding. He didn't remotely sound like Kaylor, though. We'd have to find a way to make sure he didn't have to talk much – difficult, since I couldn't talk at all without ruining the spell.

'He's lovely. Very convincing.' Aoine settled her cloak around her shoulders. Her group of Tirnaal, about thirty of them, stood silently behind her. Two were holding the bound and gagged Kaylor by the elbows. Aoine was insisting on bringing him along to help them navigate the tunnel and find the Tirnaal prisoners, an idea I thought was appallingly risky. 'Now, listen: the two of you are going to Godstown and to Ranara-temple, approaching through the supplicant door. That's the one they've been using to move sick Tirnaal. Right?'

I nodded. I wasn't thrilled with the idea of Aoine and the rest of the Tirnaal prancing through the temple. Once they found the hostages, there was bound to be some sort of confrontation. I had to hope the sheer numbers would give us some advantage.

'The Deadchurch family and I will move in through the tunnels.' Aoine swam one hand forwards through the humid air like a fish. 'We'll come out in Ranara-temple's cellars and work our way upwards until we find the hostages in the main sanctuary, by which point you two will have managed to incapacitate the door guards for us and we'll be able to exit. Right?'

Dace glanced at me. My frustration must have shown on my face. I had tried to tell Aoine that incapacitating the door guards – who were, as nearly as I could tell, just a couple of priestesses – might not do any good. 'We will try,' Dace said. 'But you might be caught in a more significant fight than that, aunt.'

'Fight,' Aoine said. 'You keep saying that. Apart from getting a few acolytes to stand aside, I don't understand what you're so afraid of. There's thirty of us. What's there to fight in Ranara-temple?'

'Monsters. Like the things that chased us to the doors of Deadchurch. Made by the person behind the plague and the deaths. And, unless I miss my guess, the person encouraging the Roys to take hostages for sacrifice.' Dace paused, considering. 'The same person who hurt Tynan.'

Aoine's face changed, going rigid with anger. 'Then it's time to stop talking.'

I crossed my wrists behind me and glanced backwards as Dace took hold of my sleeves.

'I'm ready,' he said. For a second the magic thinned and I could see through the placid version of Kaylor's face to Dace's real expression beneath it. He was ready, but he was afraid.

The Examiner General took hold of me, and together we plunged into the dark.

We reached the Godstown square just as the great witchlight braziers in front of the houses of the gods were being lit. Candle-bearing acolytes touched fire to the coloured powder in the braziers and it burst into giant representations of birds, flowers and trees. Ranara's, of course, was a large, silvery crescent moon. If you watched it for long enough, it would shimmer into the profile of a smiling woman and then back again. The huge door that Brix and I had entered earlier was closed.

We slowed just past the Moonmother's statue. I tried to push through my low, constant headache and orientate myself under the multicoloured light. Dace didn't look like he felt any better than I did. At least his bleeding seemed to have stopped.

'The supplicant's door.' He pointed. 'Over there. There's a light burning.' Indeed, a small witchlight glimmered over an elaborately carved side door, with a gape-mouthed gargoyle leering at passers-by. Presumably the light meant it was unlocked.

We crossed the square at a sedate and hopefully inconspicuous walk and strolled along the temple wall, where people had scratched prayers and luck charms into the soot stains that marred the cream-coloured stone. There were a lot of beggars still out. One sat cross-legged not far from the door. The beggar didn't bother with the monotonous pleading that some used; he sat silently with head bowed. He seemed to sense Dace and me as we drew near, though, turning slightly towards us and stretching out two cupped palms.

Dace halted. The beggar's fingers were tipped in steel.

'I found him,' Dace said, with admirable self-control.

The beggar stood, and without speaking, shuffled to the door. It put its hand into the gargoyle's mouth. There was a click. Even before the door swung open, the thing was shuffling back to its position.

A priestess was waiting for us – a different woman than the one who had led Brix and me into the sanctuary. I began to wonder how many of them there were, and whether they knew who or what they were serving. I kept myself slack-jawed and staring, the way I would be if Kaylor's softheart spell had taken hold.

'He was more trouble than I expected.' Dace sounded calm, but his grip on my wrists was hard enough to hurt. 'I'm supposed to put him with the other one.'

'I had no orders to that effect.' The priestess paused in the act of shutting the door behind us.

'He's fair mindblown,' Dace said. 'Like a baby. If we don't put him in a bed with restraints, he'll wander off into a corner somewhere or fall down the stairs. It's just long enough for me to make my report, and those are *my* orders. If you want to go and tell them that you left me standing here—'

But the priestess was already shaking her head with the annoyed acquiescence of someone who has too much responsibility and not enough power. 'No, no. Take him down to the sick pen then – straight, then second left, then down. But it wouldn't hurt for the Elder Sisters to coordinate a bit. Just because the night chapel doesn't have any patients, we always get told things last.' She stood aside and swung the door open, looking past us into the dim square. 'He and the other spelldog must have split up, then. You let the others know to watch for him?'

Dace didn't let me stop moving, his distracted irritation matching hers. 'Of course. I'm not incompetent.' He pushed me forwards a little harder than I had expected. Pain clanged through my skull, sparking across my vision in little nauseating bright-coloured arcs. Hells, that was going to be distracting.

I must have tensed up, because as soon as we were out of sight and earshot of the priestess Dace let go of me. 'All right?'

The spell was hard to hold. I relaxed my grip enough to speak.

'Yes. I just need a minute.' I put out a hand to brush the stone wall, taking slim comfort in the solidity of it. The tunnels were even worse at night, empty and still, lit only by a hanging oil lamp every fifty feet or so. 'She said second left.' But when I tried to move in that direction my stomach clenched and I had to stop, panting, and wait for the burning agony to subside.

Dace made an impatient sound. 'Let me help, you daft idiot.'

It took a moment before I could think past the pain enough to realise what he was offering. 'No.' I shook my head, as slow trails of agony traced the inside curves of my skull. 'I can't let you do that. This—'

—*hurts too much.* I couldn't get the words out.

'I know what I'm doing. This is me giving permission.' He hesitated. 'Or asking for it, if you prefer.'

I still couldn't speak, but I nodded. His fingers brushed mine.

The reduction of suffering was so sudden and so sharp that it knocked my knees loose and I slumped against the wall. He was breathing hard, jaw clenched. He still looked like Kaylor, though. The spell had held.

'You . . . you didn't have to . . .' I said, uncertain. At this rate he'd be ghostly soon and pass out, be vulnerable to capture. 'Why did you do that?' It was a bad way to say what I meant, which was *thank you.*

He shook his head. 'Come on. We don't have much time.'

'You don't have any drin.'

'I know I don't.' He paused, maybe realising that it was a bad way to say what he meant. 'You could have used that eversleep spell, ethics be damned. You could have walked in here with Kaylor, and it wouldn't have hurt you like this. I didn't expect . . .' He swallowed. 'Let me make up for my mistakes in my own way, Gray.'

There wasn't any more to say after that. Keeping the spell running meant the toxicity would build up again quickly. All I could do was tighten my grip on the illusion and move as fast as I could.

We reached our destination about the same time my jaw started to cramp. The rank, unmistakable odour of the sick pens hovered around the door. Dace hesitated, then pushed it open.

Most of my attention was focused on ignoring the pain, but I still had enough to feel a sinking despair when we stepped into the room. Its vaulted ceilings stretched, cavernous, into blackness. Three oil lamps struggled to make a frail puddle of light in the area near the door. A single healing sister appeared to be on duty. Her grey hair was pulled into a messy braid and a shawl was knotted over her shoulders, muffling her from her elbows to her chin. She sat at a table near another lamp, grinding something in a mortar and pestle, the scrawny muscles of her forearms standing out as she leaned into her task.

Dace shut the door behind us and locked it with one hand. He was holding my wrists again with the other. The healing sister, seated at the table, barely glanced up. Her pestle didn't stop its throbbing scratch of stone on stone. 'Another patient?'

'He needs a bed,' Dace said. 'I'm supposed to put him with the Tirnaal woman who was brought in earlier.'

The healing sister stopped grinding, squinted at Dace and frowned. Alarm jumped through me. If she found an inconsistency in the illusion she might manage to break it, and then we would be done for. I brought my concentration to bear on the magic and a sharp streak of agony shot up my windpipe, so intense it forced a grunt from between my lips.

'*Tonight*, if possible.' Dace's fingers on my wrists had loosened, ready in case the sister tried to raise an alarm and we both needed to contain her. 'I have other things I'm supposed to be doing.'

The healing sister climbed wearily to her feet. 'Come on, then, bring him this way.' She picked up the lamp on the table, a clay bowl with one side pinched into a spout, its wick burning with a pallid, depressed flame.

Dace and I followed her as she moved into the dark, deceptively quiet ward. At first I thought I was looking at rows of the dead, stretched on pallets on the floor. Then I heard the noise: gurgles, coughs and the low, constant rasp of breath rising from people that huddled against the flagstones. We pushed further into the room, through the stifling odour of bodies and unchanged bedding. Out of the corner of my eye I saw one woman, motionless, the folded blanket under her head crusted with dried blood.

The thorns in my belly churned, slow, unending. Heavy, aching starbursts kept skittering across my vision as the poison built, my spell warring with the perceptions of everyone watching me.

All I had to do was keep control of the spell long enough for Dace to get rid of the healing sister. If I could just hang on. If I could just get to Brix.

We reached a row of white curtains stretched across the room, dangling from rings set into the ceiling. The sister pushed the curtain open and held it, waiting for us to enter. On the other side stood about six beds, proper beds, made of solid wood.

Two of the patients slept, breathing with unnatural deepness, bound to their bedframes with leather straps. I recognised a couple of the apprentices that we had believed dead in the Guildhouse fire. They were blistered and smeared with soot, but they looked very much alive. The air was dense with the heady, queasy stench of drin.

The third captive was Brix. She saw me, and I knew, abruptly, that I had made a mistake.

'No!' Brix's tormented, keening shriek tore through the air. 'What did you do to him?' Brix tried to sit up, but the leather cuffs holding her wrists and ankles held firm. 'No! No!'

The sound hit me like a headsman's axe. The poison in my blood spiked, ripping into my fraying concentration, pushing, pushing–

'Gods,' muttered the healing sister. 'Can't you do a spell on her, too? She's been nothing but trouble since they brought her in.'

Shards of agony jabbed themselves into my eye sockets, in the spaces between my knuckles, in the cage of my breath. The spell was slipping away from me, I couldn't hold it, I couldn't—

'Once I get him taken care of,' Dace said, too loud, too hearty. 'You can get back to what you were doing before. I'll manage this.'

The illusion snapped and went cold, the link between us melting in my grasp. I stumbled away from him, dizzy with anguish, bile rising in my throat. He tried to cast and garbled the words, wrapped in the residue of the bad spell, while the healing sister stood with her mouth opening and shutting, like she was trying to decide whether to scream for help.

Then she went still, her eyes rolling back into her head.

Can't win this one with magic. Stay on your feet.

I spun on my heel and slapped the lamp out of the priestess' grasp. It tumbled to the floor and smashed, plunging us into darkness.

I jumped backwards and held myself ready, tense, fighting my heaving stomach. The difficulty would be finding the healing sister in the dark. She'd make for the door, or for whatever alarm system they had in place, and then I could trip her. I waited, listening.

'Corcoran.' Brix's shaky voice cut through the darkness. 'She's got something sharp.'

When the sister told me to sit down on the floor and put my hands on my head, I obeyed. When she told Dace to go back to the desk at the top of the sanctuary and fetch another lamp, he did. I sat with the dregs of ruined magic still roiling my blood and tried not to vomit.

When Dace returned the light was shuddering in his grasp. My broken concentration had spoiled the magic for him, too. He set the light on a shelf that jutted from the stone wall and looked down at his own trembling hand. The fingertips had gone transparent. 'What do you want me to do, Gray?'

'I'm the one giving orders, not him,' said the healing sister, with

Ranara's voice. She was still holding a slender tool to Brix's throat – a surgical knife, I thought. 'Fortunately for you all, I want our pretty fellow intact.' She glanced at Dace. 'You're an interesting complication, however. I hadn't realised you were Tirnaal.'

I dragged my attention away from the knife. By now I was almost expecting the blue-green shimmer climbing out of the sister's collar and towards her jaw.

'Ranara?' I said, the word grating across my sore throat.

'So you *can* be taught.' The healing sister smiled. 'You can't get away from me, wizard, not in Genereth. I can't see so far in other cities, even when people are wearing the amulets. But here, with my vessels around me –' She clucked her tongue gently. 'It really was foolish. You're going to sit quietly while the spelldog ties you up, understand?'

This was maddening. Not only could I not see a way out, but I was going to die with my hands clasped on top of my head, like a dolt, and Brix was going to have to watch.

'I understand,' I said, although I absolutely didn't. Presumably Ranara was using her 'vessels' by running some sort of intensified eversleep spell – that much made sense. The amulets were obviously where the runes were scribed; but how was she able to get the magic to take hold without pronouncing them? My mind crawled back through the last two weeks, putting pieces together. 'How many of them? How many people have you used this way? You used Jaliseth, didn't you, to spread the plague upriver? There's no Ranara-temple in Varriel, but there's a big Guildhouse. She had the tools to fashion more amulets, used her customers to get them on the streets. Gods, you were even building a stitched thing in her cellar. If she hadn't taken the amulet off –'

'Kaylor posed as a potion man and sold her the amulet. He's been a busy fellow. Not his fault that I didn't think to build hooks into the amulets until after we had the lapidary.'

'And the explosions?' I said, desperately. *Think, Gray. Find a way out.* 'Why wreck your vessels? Did you just get tired of them?'

She looked at Dace. 'Gag him now. I'm *tired* of his chatter.'

Dace went to a table against the wall, heaped with bandage linen, and picked up a handful, helpless. I knew he wanted me to tell him what to do, to find some way to keep Brix alive without sacrificing ourselves. But time galloped past and I couldn't think of anything but Brix's pulse, jumping beside the shining death of that scalpel.

Dace had to tie me, and I had to sit still while he did.

The restraints were simple and effective: a wad of linen stuffed in my mouth, and thin rawhide cord to bind my wrists behind me. He helped me up on to my knees.

'That's far enough,' the sister said. 'He can watch from there. Spelldog, go back to the table and bring me the jug on it.'

Grimacing with distaste, Dace pawed one-handed through the mess spread on the little work desk – loose piles of clean and dirty cloth, stacked bowls and cups, bottles and wineskins. He came up with a corked clay jug and a tiny metal cup.

'Pour a measure,' Ranara said. When he did, the cloying smell of drin caught my nostrils.

He stood there for a moment, looking at the dark liquid.

'Give it to me,' Ranara said, impatient.

Dace lifted his head. 'What for?'

'Brix is going to drink it before we go upstairs, to make her symptoms better and to make her more compliant.' Ranara's fingers tightened into the meat of Brix's shoulder. 'Aren't you, my dear? Don't you want to feel better?'

Brix shook her head, mouth shut.

Ranara leaned in until her face was an inch from Brix's. 'If you don't,' she said, with iron, implacable goodwill, 'I'll kill him, and I won't kill him quickly. I don't need him in his wits, just breathing for the next few hours. Some kings think they're a terror if their torturer can manage to draw out a prisoner's death for a day, but oh, child –' she grinned '– I can keep him dying for so much longer than that.'

'Why are you doing this?' Brix said, miserably.

Ranara blinked. 'You're Tirnaal. That means you're mine. All the Tirnaal are mine. I promised to heal you – and free them – and I will. At least the good ones. I'm going to let you sit up, then you're going to drink this medicine. And then you're coming upstairs with me, where the rest of them are, so you can be cleansed. Do you understand?'

Brix wasn't looking at me. She was somewhere in her own head, I thought, watching me bleed. 'I understand,' she said. 'Just don't hurt him. I'll do what you say.'

'How nice.' The sister flicked the buckle on the wrist restraints. Brix sat up.

No. It came out as a muffled grunt against my gag. I shook my head, frantic.

'Stop making those noises.' Ranara didn't take her eyes off Brix, holding out her free hand towards Dace. 'Give me the drin, spelldog.'

'I don't think so,' Dace said.

Ranara turned on him, but the healing sister had joints that had probably spent years scrubbing floors and lifting hundreds of the sick. It was a less than ideal body if you needed to beat a Guild enforcer for speed. By the time she realised what he was doing, Dace had already swallowed the measure of drin and begun to chant.

'No!' Ranara lunged at him, scalpel slashing low.

He stepped back neatly, without so much as breaking his incantation. But the runes came to life on *my* skin, along my left shin, one of the spells he'd seen back in Thieveschurch. I hurriedly got to my feet, put my head down and launched myself at Ranara just as Dace finished the spell.

The ley-breaker took hold just as my shoulder made contact with Ranara's knees. Cartilage crunched, and she tumbled back against Brix's bed. My breath froze in the air as the magic in the room went cold and then, inch by inch, died.

The blue-green collar around the healing sister's neck faded.

'Worked.' Dace sounded astonished. 'The antique spell *worked*.'

Brix punched the sister, who pinwheeled backwards and went down. Brix leaned forwards and unbuckled her ankle restraints while the sister tried, groggily, to get to her hands and knees. Brix swung herself off the bed and on to the sister's back, forcing her face down against the floor. Then, for the first time, she looked at me. 'Get me the bottle. The one Dace poured out the medicine from.' She inclined her head towards Dace. 'He's in no shape for it.'

I crossed the floor, though I wasn't sure exactly how I was going to carry the drin when my hands were still tied behind me and going numb. Dace had stumbled against the wall, clutching the jug with one hand. I had to back up to him and feel around until I could grasp the jug's handle, then move much more slowly than I wanted to in order to carry it without dropping it.

I brought the drin to Brix, who grabbed it and rolled the groaning sister over. She pried the sister's teeth apart with careful force and drizzled a couple of measures of drin into her mouth. After that, it was a matter of waiting for the woman to go limp against the floor.

'Gray.' Dace was staring at his hands. He was transparent to the elbows now. He took a step towards me. 'I need . . . the toxicity . . . gods, I knew your spells were worse than normal incantations, but this . . .'

I grunted again, frantic.

Brix was still breathing hard when she got to me, but she was solid, thank all the gods. Her fingertips ran across my face, skirting where Kaylor's spell had blistered me. Her touch trailed down my arms, to the white lines on my wrists where the bindings were. 'Did anybody do anything else to you?' Her eyes locked on mine. 'Are you still yourself?'

I nodded.

She yanked the linen out of my mouth and I choked as the cloth came away.

'I'm sorry,' I gasped. 'I mean, you don't want me to say sorry, but—'

'Oh, thank the gods,' she said. 'Hold still and let me get you out of this, and then we can figure out what's wrong with Dace.'

'He used one of Jaern's spells.' My voice sounded far away from me. 'Under my skin. It poisoned him, even more than his own magic would. Little saints, Brix, *my* skin, *my* spells, I hate this, I—'

'Shut up, love.' She took me by my aching wrists and dragged me over to the table, searching until she found a scalpel. She slit the cords and I worked to smother the great, ugly guilt inside me.

'The Deadchurch folk,' I said. 'They're upstairs, your family—'

'Stop calling them that.' She met my eyes. 'The Deadchurch Tirnaal knew my mother. They're my clan. But *you're* my family. You and Anka. That's it, that's all I have. Is it enough?'

My eyes blurred. 'Brix, you almost – I'm *sorry*, Brix, gods I'm so sorry—'

'*Stop.*' She took my face between her hands, quiet, fierce. Her thumbs pressed against my cheekbones. 'You're going to stop that, now.'

'Did they hurt you?' I finally had enough feeling in my fingertips to touch her neck.

'No.' She kissed me, first my wrist and then my mouth. 'They weren't interested in hurting me. It's worse than that. They want – *she* wants – servants. Children, bound to her forever. She wants to own us, Gray. All of us, all the Tirnaal.' She turned. 'Now come on. We're helpless as long as we stay within the range of that ley-breaker. Rouse Dace.'

The Examiner General had sunk down into a crouch against the wall. He was staring straight ahead; his pupils were blown out so wide that they had almost entirely obscured his irises. He'd pulled the toxicity of Jaern's magic down on himself, on top of his injured arm and the revelator spell from earlier. There had to be limits to how much drin you could swallow without knocking yourself out completely, and Dace was probably right on the edge of suffering from magic poisoning. I had only the vaguest idea of how that would affect a Tirnaal, but I didn't imagine it would be better than what had happened to Sannet.

'Gray, hurry,' Brix said.

I grabbed his shoulder, but he only flopped under my hand. 'Dace.' I shook him again, and this time he lifted his head, staring dully in my direction. 'Come on, you have work to do.'

'Can't . . .' he mumbled. 'Hurts.'

'Yes, you can,' I said. 'You've got to. If ever there was a time for wizard police, I would think a necromancer, mass kidnapping and subversion of the actual Royal Police would be it.'

'The Examiner General,' Dace said, managing to mangle every syllable, 'is not police. He ensures the safe practice of magic through compliance with the Royal Charter in order to preserve the integrity of . . .' He lurched forwards, his face coming to rest against my shoulder. '. . . of the throne and the . . .'

'Stand up, then, not-wizard-police.' I grabbed a fold of the flesh under Dace's arm between my thumb and forefinger and twisted.

He gasped and flinched away from me, but his eyes lost some of their glazed look and found Brix and me, confusion overtaking his initial panic. 'What happened?'

'I pinched you,' I said. 'Sorry. Sober now?'

'No,' he said, fluttering transparent fingers at me. 'But not quite high enough, either.'

'Too bad. Up you get.' I hauled him up to his feet, where he stood swaying while I fetched him the container of drin. 'We have to go, now. The Deadchurch clan won't survive confronting the—' I hesitated.

'Goddess.' Brix grimaced as the word passed her lips. 'We might as well say it. What are they doing here?'

'Trying to rescue the hostages.' My throat still felt raw. 'I told them it was a bad idea. Come on, it's possible Ranara is mostly paying attention to us. We might be able to give the Tirnaal time, if nothing else.'

'Fuck.' Dace tipped the jug of drin upwards and drank several long swallows before letting it thud down on the workbench. His transparency flickered away, at least for the moment, but he still didn't seem steady. He rifled through the mess of bandages and tools and came up with a piece of chalk. 'Let's go.'

We stepped out from the curtains and into the dark ward that stretched in front of us, dank and clammy and layered with shadows and sorrow. The guttering half-light of the lamps revealed the sick in their motionless ranks, staring at nothing as we passed them. There was no sound except the laboured breathing of dozens of people, gasps fluttering in the air like moths. Brix's hand found mine.

We had almost reached the pool of light from the oil lamps when the first patient stood up.

EIGHTEEN

'You can't win.'

Our opponent was an elderly man, his nightshirt hanging down to just above his skinny knees, skin gleaming greenish-blue at his throat. A cheap tin pendant pulsed on his chest, drin leaking from the stopper and forming a sticky wet place on his linen. He staggered towards us, his hands out, fingers splayed like claws. 'You can't.'

'Shit,' I said.

'He's slow.' Brix shoved me towards the door. 'We can run. Go. Fast. Now.'

The old man halted, his head turning as we ran towards the exit. A person in a bed nearer to the door began to thrash.

The old man collapsed behind us as the new host sprang to its feet in front of us.

No, her, *not it,* my brain insisted, taking in the pregnant young woman who lurched around to stare at us. She was bleeding from her nose, with dried yellow mucus crusted around her mouth. *She's still human. I . . . hope.*

'What do you think you're going to do?' she croaked, in an amused, even tone. 'Find me? Kill me? I'm a goddess. We don't die.' The pregnant woman took a couple of painful steps towards us before stumbling and leaning hard against the bed. 'Besides,' she said, her gaze following us as we sprinted the last few feet to the door, 'what are you going to kill? These innocents?' She tapped her own chest. 'They feel it, you know. I'll leave them when there's no use left in them, and then they'll be able to feel everything you've done to them.'

'It's locked,' Dace panted.

I had already discovered that, fumbling with the latch with fingers that were still half-numb.

'They'll know you're the one who decided to hurt them,' Ranara said, with the dying woman's voice. 'That's all you do, with your poison spells. Hurt people. Tempt them. Manipulate nature. It's disgusting. You know it as well as I do. You know what you are.'

Brix pushed my hands to one side and threw the bolts back.

'I heal my children,' Ranara insisted. 'I protect them from people like you. They love me.'

The door swung open. We burst through, and shut it behind us.

Something thumped against the door with a wet, heavy *thwack*.

'How can we keep this shut?' I looked frantically around the hallway, but there was no way to wedge the door.

'We've got to free that woman,' Brix said, panting. 'We can't let that *thing* keep taking control of people.'

'We've got to be quick and hope that Ranara drops this host,' I said. 'She'll try to take someone who's ahead of us, get between us and the way out.'

We had jogged to the first turning when I heard the door swing open behind us. Then there was nothing but speed and fear and the long sameness of the passageways. We ran silent, listening for the dragging shuffle of footsteps behind us, and my wits ground wearily at the problem: how was Ranara doing this? More importantly, why?

Necromancers survived long ages by uncoupling their souls from their bodies. They gained other bodies by murder or by craft. If Ranara had been the one to help Jaern make his body, she should have been able to make herself one. But she hadn't, instead taking control of other people's bodies with amulets – why live second-hand, controlling and killing people from afar? Why couldn't the goddess leave her temple?

Eventually the hallway widened and we came to a broad set of double doors. They were heavily bound in bronze, the kind of thing you'd put on an exterior wall – or, if it was on an interior wall, on a room you didn't want anyone meddling with. The latch turned smoothly and silently under my hand as I pushed the door open a crack, praying for a rush of outside air.

Instead, I got a rush of incense.

The sanctuary embraced us as we entered, rank with the scent of bodies and candle wax. Two shafts of light poured through the eclipse window, bounced off the mirrors flanking the font and fell on the shining godsbones. The room was empty, dark except for the mirrors and the bright contents of the white font, the reflected illumination barely extending to reveal the shadowy effigies on the crypts that lined the walls.

Nobody was there. The pallets that had covered the floor were gone, along with the bodies of the sick. The smell lingered.

'Where are they?' Brix whispered. 'What have they done with all the Tirnaal?'

'Maybe Aoine and the Tirnaal have already been here,' I said, uncertainly. 'Maybe they've already freed the hostages.' But even as I said it, I knew it was wrong. The hostages weren't just scapegoats. Ranara had wanted to *own* the Tirnaal. Surely she wouldn't have allowed Aoine and the others to just traipse in here and quietly haul the hostages away?

'There could be another exit – something leading to the gardens, or to a back street. Or something else like the drin tunnels.' Dace stepped sideways, frowning at the effigies. 'Maybe one of these is a false front.'

The effigies looked exactly as unpromising as they had before: statues of departed faithful carved in some dark blue substance. It almost looked like wax, impractical as that seemed; given the heat in that room, you'd have thought it would go tacky. Still, blue stone wasn't easy to find in chunks this large, and I had rarely seen such detail in stone carving. The statue nearest to me had a mole above one eyebrow and delicately rendered fingernails. She even seemed to have strands of hair. It didn't seem like the kind of thing you'd put in front of a hidden door.

Brix coughed again, light spewing around her head like a terrible halo. 'I don't like it.' She drew in a long, wheezing breath. 'They were all sicker than me. You couldn't move them out of here so quickly.'

Taking our chances with possessed pregnant women in the hallway abruptly seemed less fraught than advancing into that warm, manufactured starlight. I turned towards Brix and the exit.

In the shadows, across the room, one of the statues took a step away from the wall.

'Oh hells,' I said. 'This is getting tiresome.'

'Back,' Dace said, retreating deeper into the room himself, eyes on the statue. 'Don't let them touch you.'

'There's another one.' Brix's hand reached for mine as we watched a second statue peel away from its niche. This one was a young man, and he was between us and the door. Dace, Brix and I moved further into the sanctuary in a knot, our backs to each other, and watched as, one by one, the statues *all* walked towards us. There were about a dozen of them, although I didn't take the time to count. They didn't shuffle, but they didn't exactly move like humans would have, sliding across the floor with an uncanny grace. Their eyes stayed shut. They had us surrounded.

'Tell me this is some kind of standard Temples trick,' I said, glancing at Brix. 'Tell me that it's something I would know all about if I was better at picking a god and worshipping them.'

'I've never even heard of anything like this.' Brix's eyes flicked from statue to statue. 'Are they like the stitched things?'

'No,' I said. The stitched things had been recognisably human. These didn't even seem to have proper skin. 'I don't know how this is happening.'

The statues advanced until they were six feet from us and stopped, their arms dangling loose by their sides, eyes shut. We were backed up, our heels against the silver flourishes that covered the floor around the font. They weren't quite spells, but I still didn't want to step on them.

Brix tensed, ready. 'We can't let them hold us here.'

The statues' wax-sealed eyelids flicked open, making a sound like a low, tearing purr.

'What the hells are they?' Brix jerked backwards against me.

The statues' eye sockets held nothing but low-burning orange flames. As I watched, they grinned, showing long, carnivorous white incisors set in pink gums.

'I don't think they're wax,' I said.

Brix was staring at the teeth.

'Of course they're not wax.' Dace spoke with a slow cadence, like he was thinking very hard about not slurring his words. I wondered, briefly, exactly how much drin he'd consumed to stay upright, and how long it would be before he went down again. 'Witchclay. Cursed. Very illegal.'

'Oh, well, as long as we've got its *legal* status sorted,' I said. 'Curses aren't real, Dace.'

'You think gods aren't real either,' he said, 'and look where that's gotten you. Witchclay is a torture device. You touch someone with a lump of it, it bonds to their flesh, and you control where the clay touches.' He glanced at me. 'That's why it's illegal.'

'Enough!' snapped Brix. 'Gods save me from hearing *two* wizards hold forth about every damn horrible thing under the sun or moon instead of doing anything.' She grabbed a lit candelabra, drew back her arm and thrust it at the closest statue, hard. It struck the statue square in the face.

The clay shattered, cracks spiderwebbing upwards from the carefully carved chin, sheets of broken blue clay flaking off.

Underneath was . . . skin. Human skin, criss-crossed with black thread.

'Oh gods.' Brix's voice climbed with alarm. The candelabra clattered to the floor. 'Gods, Gray—'

The statue's mouth opened wider, needle-teeth lengthening, dripping venom.

'Get down,' I said, extending my arms. 'Both of you, get down!'

The statue lunged, and I cast.

Brix and Dace threw themselves to the ground. Runes lit down the outside of my thigh, uncomfortably hot against my clothes. The spell manifested as a fan of orange spikes at the tips of my fingers. I watched the pulse leave my hand and widen into a horizontal sheet of orange light.

The wave of force hit the room with a loud, flat WHUP.

The statues all staggered. Several of them fell. I had only a moment to feel satisfied by this before the spell struck the hexagonal stone walls and bounced, orange light flashing across the inlays on the floor.

Oh no.

Every force spell would, theoretically, produce a counter-force, but I had never used this one in an enclosed area before. My own wicked spell hummed back towards me. The statues were climbing to their feet again, those sharp teeth gleaming in the false moonlight. Being hit like that should have slowed them down. It should have hurt them. I couldn't stop watching.

No.

'Get down!' Brix shrieked, raking her fingernails across the bare top of my foot with a clarifying burst of pain. 'Get—'

My knees let go. I fell.

The force hit the statues a second time, and they shattered, spraying chunks of witchclay around the room. Bits rained down on me and I imagined it burrowing through my hair, seeking flesh, and rushed to brush it off, frantic.

Brix cried out and scrambled back to her feet, shaking pieces of clay off her body.

'It's all right,' Dace said, still sounding drunk and amiable, pushing himself first to his knees, and then up on to his feet. 'It's volatile, probably not active after hardening, it's—'

From somewhere off to my left, a low, grating moan started, and then went on, building to a keening wail. Another joined it, then another. I stood. The statues were now incomplete, skin showing where the clay had been knocked off. They didn't seem able to move well without the clay, and no wonder: the flesh beneath was raw, angry, covered in scars shaped like runes, scabs, and rows of neat, black stitches. One had the clay sheared off its mouth and chin, teeth set into the jawbone with narrow copper collars, fitted like studs, leaking venom where the bone had cracked.

'Are they . . . alive?' Brix sounded like she was on the edge of vomiting.

I didn't see how anybody could be alive in that condition – not held together with wire and brackets and wax. These were even further gone than the stitched things we'd seen before, a hideous mix of necromancy and alchemy.

'We've got to get away from them.' It was true, despite the nagging, horrible feeling I had that they weren't our enemies, any more than the sick old man and the stumbling pregnant woman had been. This was, somehow, more of Ranara's 'healing' work.

We couldn't get to the door. Five statues were struggling back to their feet, with enough clay clinging to their rotting bodies to stumble towards us.

'The . . .' Dace pointed, irritated. Maybe he couldn't remember the word *stairs*. He was on his feet but seemed only about half-lucid. We moved across the floor as quickly as we could, which wasn't very quick considering that Dace was struggling to stay upright. The spiral staircase curled up to the soaring ceiling, a wrought-iron helix leading to a trap door.

'Up,' I said. 'Up, for the gods' sake, *up*; if it takes us to the roof at least we'll be outside.'

Brix started climbing, disappearing into the shadows above me. I pushed Dace up next, trying to keep my attention split between the statues, which were laboriously changing course towards us, and him. Dace stumbled, his bandage dark with blood. He cursed softly, in Tirnaal.

'Up you go,' I said.

He went up a few stairs almost on his hands and knees, feeling his way forwards, then stopped, panting. His hands were leaving scarlet smears on the metal stairs.

'You have to keep going,' I said. 'I know you're spell-shot, but—'

'I'm bleeding.' He looked at me, a silhouette with blurry edges, the whole of him slipping towards transparency. 'I'm dying, I think. I just don't want to die in here, Gray, I don't . . .'

'You won't,' I said. 'I promise. But you have to go up the stairs.'

He dragged himself up towards Brix's outstretched, encouraging hands. I turned my body sideways and followed, and tried to choose another spell from under my skin.

Shacklebright, flamespike, nausea, huntseye—

I didn't think nausea would do much to stop the things that were pursuing us. Shacklebright would keep me stuck on the stairs. Flamespike, then. I pronounced the runes.

They hissed, orange and agonising on the soft inner surface of my left upper arm. I pointed at the floor at the base of the stairs and a pillar of fire first licked around my fingers and then burst upwards from the marble, heat and black smoke roaring between us and the broken statues.

'Gray.' Brix shoved the trapdoor upwards and it flopped open with a bang. 'Move!'

Cool air poured over us. Brix's foot was disappearing through the trapdoor as I turned. Dace and I followed, eager for the clean, cold outside. From above came the measured cadence of women chanting.

Below, the fire snapped, wax boiled and slowly, unbearably, the smoke rose.

NINETEEN

The trapdoor opened on to a narrow walkway leading around the edge of Ranara-temple, sensibly lined with waist-high wrought-iron railings. Above us was a small metal roof, just enough to keep rain off the trapdoor and a short run of the walkway. To our left loomed the giant red dome that covered the inside of the sanctuary, all painted metal. Ahead of us was another dome, this one presumably over one of the hospital rooms. Between the two domes was a wide, flat expanse of white stone covered by an openwork canopy made of dark, curling metal filigree, barely visible against the black sky and the stars and the huge yellow disc of the moon.

It took me a heartbeat to sort the things on the flat area into categories. The people were simple enough – some ten or fifteen priestesses in their white robes moved around the edges of a crowd that stood grouped around a low stone altar platform. The Deadchurch Tirnaal milled about, mingling with the two hundred-odd hostages, and, in the middle of them, Aoine crouched beside a huddled, splinted form that I recognised as Tynan. They were holding hands. So the Tirnaal had, as I'd feared, been tricked or overwhelmed by some intervention of the goddess. But I had not been expecting the silvery helmets of the confused, cowed-looking Royal Police, or the blue robes of a very frightened-looking Valera Trist.

On the platform stood a red-haired priestess and, impossibly, Gali Kaylor, free, the blood dried on his chin. As we crept forwards, he turned towards Valera.

'Murderers first,' he said, his words still thick.

'As you say.' The priestess, her hand glowing white, gestured to Valera. The spell caught the Guildlord and pulled her to the platform. The priestess pushed up her sleeves. 'Shall we begin?'

Beside her was a circle of stone that I couldn't identify. I would have called it a font, similar to the one that we'd left downstairs, except it was too short – it almost looked like the mouth of a well. On either side of it were a pair of pewter-framed mirrors taller than a man, each of their oval faces angled to catch the moonlight and point it downwards, into the well. This had to be the eclipse window, the source for the light caught and refracted in the godsbones skeleton in the sanctuary below.

'Start?' Brix whispered. 'Murderers first? What is she talking about? Ranara said she wanted the Tirnaal for *servants* . . . she called them her children. What's happening?'

'Presumably this is more of my neglected religious education.' I glanced backwards. 'Dace?'

The Examiner General was draped against the railing, one arm wound through its loops and crenellations as if he was afraid that he might pitch over the edge. Parts of him kept flickering in and out of transparency. 'Sacrifice,' he said. 'That's why the priestesses are here, at a guess – the Tirnaal hostages are here to make new godsbones. Sacrifice to end the plague, the way it was done in the old days – not pigeons, people.'

Servants. Sacrifices. Maybe to the goddess it was the same thing.

The moon loomed above us, full-bellied, spilling so much light across the rooftop that it threw noon-dark shadows. The shadows felt odd, though, like they were pointing the wrong way. Which I supposed was to be expected – sunlight would have hit the walls and filigree from a different angle, thrown the shadows in another direction.

I glanced downwards, where the shadows rippled and moved against the white stone, and I saw it: the same sort of pattern there had been back at the Guildhouse.

'It's a spell,' I said. 'The *shadow*. Gods, it makes a *spell*.'

The priestess moved then, pointing at Valera and then watching calmly while Kaylor dragged the struggling wizard around to stand beside the well.

'My children.' The priestess turned her face up towards the moon. The flesh of her throat shimmered like an aquamarine. 'Your city is soaked in death. I've heard your cries.' She paused. When nobody responded, she continued, louder. 'I bring you healing.'

Valera's dogged voice carried through the heavy, hot night air. 'Oh, so you're going to heal them, are you? The way you healed the others, the ones who disappeared?'

'Be silent,' Kaylor hissed. 'I won't let you ruin this now.'

'Bring the offering!' crowed the priestess.

'No!' Valera scrabbled at Kaylor with what seemed to be bound hands. 'This is wrong!'

'Accept our sorrow!' Kaylor said, grabbing Valera's hair. He dropped something over her head – something that sparkled in the moonlight like a piece of the night sky itself.

I sprinted forwards, too late. I had only gone a few steps when Kaylor shoved Valera forwards until they were both standing beside the 'well', the shadows from the filigree cascading over them.

The priestess turned towards them, smiling. 'I accept your sorrow.'

And then she cut Kaylor's throat.

For a moment he kept his feet, while his blood spattered downwards and Valera screamed. Then he tumbled into a heap and the priestess started chanting. Around Valera something purple began to glow.

The moment my toes touched the shadow-runes, the sound and action of the spell hit me like a wall of honey, slowing me down, vibrating deep and sweetly in my body. Magic is supposed to hurt, but this didn't. This had all of the seductive intoxication of any really complex incantation with none of the pain, and it caught me like a hook.

'Ranara.' My own voice struck my ears as blurred, too deep, too slow. 'Stop.'

'I thought you'd be here.' She looked up, calmly. 'You'll be privileged to see the cleansing of the city.' She flicked her knife towards Valera, who was covered in Kaylor's blood.

'I won't . . . let you . . .' I tried to move, but my body was made of lead, swimming in the magic. I wanted to stay where I was and fall into the music and the beauty and the glorious, ever-shifting light and dark around me.

The crowd of hostages swayed as one, almost falling asleep on their feet.

'Wait,' someone said, in the accent that had crept out of the mouths of everyone that the goddess had taken. 'Just wait. Sleep.'

I could. Wait, and rest, and sink further into the numb almost-calmness that at least wasn't the fear. I was so tired. Gods, I had been tired for so long. I wanted to stop. My eyes dropped shut.

Gray!

Excruciatingly slowly I opened my eyes, turned my head and saw Brix running towards me, her hand outstretched. The crowd was half-enveloped in white light, as though they'd stumbled into a glowing spider's web.

Gray, move!

I glanced down and saw the silver-white tendrils of the spell climbing my own legs. They'd nearly reached my hips. I pushed forwards, and the lovely façade of the spell sloughed off. The colours shredded into stark flashes of light that turned my stomach.

266

The warmth built into heat, then into torment so sharp that I cried out.

Brix had reached the crowd of hostages, and was barrelling between them like a sheepdog among lambs. 'Get out of here! Run, now!'

The dazed crowd shifted, then began to move.

The expression of flat sweetness on the priestess' face twitched into boiling rage. 'Stay still!'

Everybody froze.

Get them off the roof. Get yourself off the roof. I couldn't get the words out. I took another step. It was like shoving through snares of sharp wire. I couldn't see Brix or Dace, couldn't take my eyes off the goddess long enough to look for them. 'Stop . . . hurting . . .'

'Wizards *should* hurt,' Ranara said, eyes wide, indignant. 'They think they have the right to meddle with magic, spread poison, stick their dirty fingers anywhere they please. The Tirnaal are mine. They've always been mine. And they'll live long after the rest of this polluted city is scrubbed off the face of the earth.'

Valera's body arced, eyes rolling back in her head. Ranara was doing something near her mouth, manipulating a bottle.

Drin spilled down Valera's chin and chest and the amulet around her neck flared with light. In the smears of Kaylor's blood covering the Guildlord, crystals began to grow, forming so rapidly that it was difficult to see, encasing her until she looked like a giant piece of ice.

'She's still alive,' Ranara said brightly. The amulet around the priestess' neck pulsed, steady as a drumbeat against her verdigris-green flesh. 'That's the wonderful thing.' She put one hand on the crystal, then turned to the rest of the scattered crowd and raised her free hand, light cupped in the palm. 'Be healed.'

Everyone drew in a collective breath. I had expected the spell, if that's what this was, to jump from the priestess' hand towards the crowd, but the opposite happened: the pink light gathered on the mouths and noses of the dying Tirnaal, then shot towards Ranara, like lightning streaking from the earth back up to a thunderstorm.

Coughs stilled. Faces twisted with agony calmed. Brix snapped up to stand straight, her hands at her throat, light enveloping her body. Even twenty feet away, I heard her give a sobbing, incredulous gasp. Dace, who had just now reached Brix, reached out with his injured arm.

Ranara grunted. I saw every bone in her skeleton as the lightning flashed through her and then into the crystal beside her – the rock that had, at one point, been Valera Trist. It had turned a deep, velvety purple, glowing from within with a low, pulsing light.

'Gods,' I said, appalled. 'She *is* alive, isn't she? You're stealing her life, doling it out to others that you made sick, calling it healing—' Anger shot through me, more anger than I had known was in my body. 'You've killed people. You dragged your so-called "children" up here, made the abominations in the sanctuary below, for what? To show off in a flashy rooftop ceremony? To bind a few hundred people to your cult?'

'You think you know everything, don't you?' The magic around my legs contracted, closing like the jaws of a trap. She grinned. 'The magic here makes everything stronger – healing, judgement, pain. The people on this roof are the only ones who'll survive tonight, wizard. You should be thankful that you were chosen.'

The light in the crystal beside her concentrated, as though it was collecting illumination from somewhere beneath.

'No,' I said, and cast.

The spells on my skin came to roaring life, and not just the one that I had chosen to pronounce – *all* of them lit up, pressing sharp against my skin, multicoloured. The one I'd called was the same I'd used downstairs. It surged out of my fingertips and sent everyone sprawling, except Ranara. The goddess braced her feet and put her arms out against the blast, protecting the crystal behind her.

The magic hit with the sick crack of a blunt instrument meeting flesh and I saw both of her wrists snap into unnatural angles.

The goddess didn't fall. She turned her dead eyes on me.

'So,' she said.

The spell-shadows under my feet throbbed with a dark blue light, humming with power. Wherever the shadow fell across my skin, my spells rose to meet it. I could finally see, in detail, exactly what death I carried. Jaern had been wicked, and suffering, but nobody could say he hadn't been an artist. I couldn't move. Behind me, everyone sprawled on the ground, still.

Dead?

No, I couldn't think like that.

'Why?' I blurted. The pillar of amethyst light behind her was growing stronger, shooting upwards into the sky. 'What in the hells do you want? Power? Revenge? You say the Tirnaal are your children, but they were sick because of you. Everyone in this city who has died, died because of you. Why hurt them?'

'If they're sick, it's because they sinned,' she said. 'Fooled around with luck charms, or prophylactic spells; a divination spell here, meddling with the incantations inked on to them there. The Tirnaal were never meant to use magic themselves. That's not why I made them. This isn't some petty mage lord's ploy to control a city. This is a judgement, and a rescue. I will make my children clean again.'

She started to chant. I tensed, but it was only an illumination spell: a tongue of flickering white fire that she sent to hover behind me. Perhaps she meant to blind me, or to light me up better for an attack. Either way, the spell I was ensnared in kept me from turning to look at it. I was going to have to cast again, tormented and half-blind as I was, and it was going to have to be something strong enough to silence her.

I could throw flamespike, hope to catch her robes on fire. But that would kill the priestess in whose body she was riding. I could throw shacklebright, but without being able to feel the pain, it wouldn't hold her.

The goddess' gaze drifted down towards my feet, and my heart dropped.

The set of shadow runes I was standing in was changing, altering their shape as the light moved. As I stared, the spell that had been binding me died and new set of runes came to life, blazing white as though they'd captured the moonlight itself. The magic woke beneath my skin, thrumming with exquisite pain and all-encompassing, brilliant fury, crawling upwards towards my amulet – Jaern's amulet.

The priestess fell, wailing, clutching her ruined wrists to her chest. Something seared my breastbone, like a hot coal. I clawed at my chest.

The priestess was screaming, screaming . . .

Greenish-blue taint climbed my neck. It was hot, and sickeningly fast. The world around me went wavy, muffled as though I'd plunged into black, deep, boiling water. From far away someone was shouting. Still the priestess, I thought, her voice shrill with panic:

Stop her, stop her before she takes him, he'll kill everyone, stop—

TWENTY

It was quiet, and dim.

As the magic took me, I sank back into the ease and the blur, the empty feeling of warmth and light and colour. I was vaguely aware of the existence of other people – of the screams, and the running – but only in the way that you can sometimes know, in a dream, that you're dreaming. Mostly I just saw the goddess, young, slender, dead-eyed – cold.

'Moyra,' I said, surprised.

'No,' she said, gently, 'although I am using her face.' She seemed to be walking beside me as I made my way across the roof. When she reached out to hold my hand, her fingers scraped against my flesh, freezing and hard. I had barely noted the sensation when I lost it again, buried in an avalanche of comfort. The touch could have been mistaken for affection if you didn't know the taste of the real thing. 'It seems fitting, since it was her lucky chance that hooked you.'

I blinked. 'Hooked me? My amulet doesn't have legs.'

She kept her grasp on me as we moved, leading me forwards across the slick roof tiles. We glided like dancers. 'It was Moyra's luck, I suppose, you stumbling upon the amulet tied to her life when you were divining, but when she kept being able to reach you – no doubt because of Jaern's amulet – well, I couldn't just let you run wild, could I? I thought you were Jaern. I had to take you. I had to take the people with you. Do you think I couldn't hear Moyra call you?'

We had reached the stairs that led downwards off the roof, into the warm, close dark of the sanctuary. From a distance, as though I was watching someone else, I realised that I didn't want to go down.

'Why . . .' Moving was like trying to stand waist-deep in a fast river. I was on the brink of drowning.

'Come now,' Ranara said. 'Down you go. We don't have time to dawdle.'

I was forgetting something. Or someone. A name flickered at the edge of my mind and I turned my head back towards the still-reeling knot of people, just for a moment. There was a name in the crowd that I needed to remember. There was—

'No,' Ranara said, and my head snapped back around without my willing it to. A blazing ball of agony burst inside my skull. I tried to scream and couldn't.

'You're making me forget,' I said.

I could almost see the face in my mind, could almost remember. *Freckles, I can never count them.* Whoever it was flickered just outside my consciousness, just out of reach, a face and hands and a voice. I needed to remember. I needed—

'Don't talk such foolishness.' Ranara's touch was stiff, inexorable. 'You're dying.'

She was dead.

I choked. Ranara turned me around, lifted my arm and took aim at the lead tiles of the roof above the trapdoor.

You divined for her and she was dead.

'You know how it ends,' her voice rasped, in my ear.

You're dead.

'This is how it *always* ends.'

It wasn't until I felt the vibrations in my throat that I realised I was incanting.

Flamespike. The spell meant impact and heat. The roof was made of metal. It would melt and fall and block the only way down, trap the crowd on the roof.

Brix.

'No!' I brought all my concentration to bear and managed to strangle the unfinished magic. The knife of pain came lancing back, sharp at the root of my tongue, blinding, choking. When it left I was stumbling down the steps into the dark. My tongue was still intact – for the moment – but my mouth was full of blood.

'Stubborn,' Ranara hissed. I couldn't see her anymore, but then again I was fairly certain she had never really been there in the first place. It still felt like someone was shoving me down the steps from behind. I made it to the bottom of the stairs, to the tangled heap on the floor in front of me where smoke curled off unfamiliar shapes. When the spent-candle scent struck my nostrils I realised what they were. Vomit sprayed across the marble as Ranara made me step across the pile of ruined, burned statues.

'Disgusting,' the goddess said, with prim disapproval. 'You'll have to come and clean that up, afterwards.'

'After what?' I struggled to find the strength that had allowed me to cut off the spell on the roof, but it wasn't there. I couldn't even raise my own hand to wipe the sick off my mouth. The goddess' iron will pushed me across the floor to the font, surrounded by runes that gleamed in the light that came streaming in through the stained glass. The mirrors on either side of the font seemed to be catching purple light from above us, directing it down into holes in the floor at the base of the font. Ranara moved me forwards and I watched as my hand plunged into the liquid metal. 'What are you doing to me?'

'I would have taken care of you, like all my children,' Ranara said, as she made my fingers grope on the other side of the bright vuthine. The metal pressed against my flesh, heavy and cool while the rest of me sweltered in the dark. 'All you had to do was obey me, fear me, stop interfering in knowledge that belongs to me.'

My fingertips finally brushed a lever, grasped it and pulled. One of the empty crypt panels on the wall behind me shifted, stone grinding against stone, dust puffing out. Ranara twisted me around on my heel, my arm still dripping, and marched me across the floor, leaving a trail of skittering, metallic drops on the wax-spattered black floor.

'I don't know how you were raised,' she said, coldly, in my ear, as she forced me through the door that had been behind the panel. 'Perhaps you were permitted to disobey your parents. But I cannot allow disrespect.'

The steps behind the panel sloped with gut-dropping steepness as I went down into the darkness beneath the floor of the sanctuary. Behind me, the panel slid back into place. 'My mother prayed to you,' I said. 'She sacrificed to you. She still died.'

'Lucky she didn't see you grow up,' she said. 'You think she'd be happy knowing you're doing magic even the spelldogs call forbidden? You're so ruined that even those blasphemers know you should be silenced.'

At the bottom of the stairs, the darkness spread out around me, full of moving air currents and scents I didn't understand. There was the yeasty, almost alcoholic smell of drin on the air, but it was mingled with dusty herbs and the sweet creep of rot.

'Hypocrite.' I knew it was foolish even while I was saying it, but I couldn't help myself. 'You do magic. You're no goddess. You're a leech, using magic to steal life and health from people. You don't keep your promises, you—'

The pain tore through me again. This time, she let me scream.

When I had to stop for breath, she made me move again, whispering sweetly in my ears, 'Have I made my point?'

'Yes.' I panted, but I still couldn't fill my lungs enough. 'Can I cast an illumination spell, or are you going to walk me around in the dark?'

'This bitter attitude of yours is unfortunate,' Ranara said. 'You act like I'm doing this for my own amusement. Of course you can cast an illumination spell. I want you to be able to see me.'

To *see* her? As I muttered the spell and felt the toxicity scratch its way inside my skull, I wondered exactly what I'd be seeing. The only one I had seen raise the dead was Kaylor, and she'd cut his throat on the roof. Ranara was no necromancer. If she wasn't a goddess either, what did that leave?

A pewter filigree of spells spread across the floor under my feet, scintillating with pieces of multicoloured light, incantations that at first seemed impossible. There were so many, writ so large. Logically it should have been layers of magic, several incantations that inter-locked and worked together. But this looked like a single spell, larger and more complex than anything I had ever seen. It should have been unmanageable for a single caster.

I passed through the archway and into another room, this one with low, vaulted ceilings that would have been at home in a wine cellar. In a puddle of light to one side stood a stone table, grooved to allow liquid to drain and holding a row of shining surgical tools. In front of me a trio of mirrors ringed a human-sized amethyst, like the one on the roof that encased Valera.

Godsbones.

I flinched, but once the thought had taken hold there was no stopping the realisation. I was looking at a human skeleton, every inch of the bone crusted with crystals. They couldn't have been attached to the bone with craft. They had grown there, like they had on the corpse in Jaliseth's cellar, crowding in clusters in the secret places between ribs and knuckles, spiking over the flat ster-num and shoulder blades, turning the skeleton into one giant, glittering stone.

'The spell – does it have to be moonlight?' I said. 'The trigger, I mean. Why put your light-sensitive spell in the cellar? Why the mirrors?'

'This is the problem with your kind,' Ranara said. 'Always trying to take the divine to pieces, understand it, as though it's a trade like making boots or wagon wheels. When will you understand that I don't do magic? I do alchemy, and miracles.'

Bullshit. I managed to keep myself from saying it out loud – any more disrespect and I thought the goddess would detach my tongue from my jaw – but only barely. This was no miracle, no overflowing of divinity. This was a spell, some hideous and complicated mode of capturing and storing magic toxicity in the crystals. She had filled up another crystal – poor Valera – on the roof. *The cleansing of this city,* the goddess had said. Did that mean that the incantation was ... reversible? Did she intend to sicken everyone?

I looked around as best as I could without being able to move my head. The rest of the chambers weren't filled with casks of wine. Blue witchlight flames burned on high-set lamps, inadequate bulwarks against the smothery, living darkness, illuminating notches in the walls and rows of rectangular shapes.

'Coffins,' I said.

'No, not coffins.' Ranara seemed a little distracted. 'Coffins are for the dead. None of these are dead. Well, almost none. We should fix the mirrors.'

I swallowed as she walked me forwards, struggling past the overwhelming sense of her presence, the pressure of her in my skin and sinews. I had to keep thinking, had to keep my mind working as *me*, or I'd lose myself altogether. 'You still haven't told me what you want me for. It can't just be mirrors.'

'You'll see in good time,' Ranara said.

'And how am I hearing you?' I said. 'I know you weren't really there on the roof – that was some sort of illusion to make me walk along without resisting. But it feels like I'm hearing you speak with my ears. Is that an illusion, too?'

'Of sorts,' Ranara said, and now it looked like she was standing beside me again, wearing Moyra's face. 'It's not the same thing that wizards do, if that's what you're asking. I don't tell lies when I send visions. I always use real people, people who have given themselves or who have been given to my service.'

'And did Moyra give herself, or was she taken?' I couldn't make my arm lift to gesture at the coffins, but I could sort of nod. 'Did you take all of them? Which one is hers?'

'They're nothing,' Ranara said, and jerked me towards the nearest row of coffins, or tanks, or boxes, or whatever in the hells they were. 'Look, Corcoran Gray. Learn something.'

The first coffins I passed seemed oldest, constructed of wood and smeared with tar to make them waterproof. Those had nearly rotted away, their contents nothing more than black sludge. It took a little wandering to reach the stone coffin with Moyra in it.

She lay just under the surface of the drin, on her back, crusted in a delicate layer of amethysts. The amulet glowed red against her sternum, but that wasn't what startled me. Her face was distorted, tongue protruding between blue lips, the face of someone who had died of paralysis, strangling in the free air.

Her eyes were open. They were staring at me, begging for help.

'You see?' Ranara was the one speaking, but Moyra's lips moved, her voice creaking out. 'You see why I have to do it? Why I have to stop it? As long as magic is being practised, as long as wizards are running free, nobody will ever be safe. This is what magic does. It makes people broken, like her . . . like you. You see?'

'*You* did this,' I said. 'Not magic. Magic hurt her, but it could have helped her, too. The right ley-breaker—'

'Don't blaspheme.' Ranara marched me back to the laboratory at the heart of the vaults, where the air seethed with a mixture of acrid scents from the reagents on the workbenches. Tucked in a niche to one side stood an idol that I hadn't seen earlier: a life-sized, cedar-coloured rendition of a woman coated in something like amber, kept on its feet by a complicated system of bronze latticework.

Only as I drew closer I saw it wasn't made of cedar wood. Inside the half-inch gold shell was a desiccated, mummified corpse.

Taut leather covered prominent bones, and was in turn covered by a simple white priestess' robe and whatever the golden substance was. The face had been well-preserved, down to the mindless, sugary, familiar smile frozen on the lips.

'You,' I said.

'Me.'

This time, I wasn't surprised when the eyes opened and the goddess regarded me.

She wasn't using Moyra's voice anymore, but I could still feel the pressure of her in my muscles. Nor could I exactly tell how she was speaking – the words came vibrating through the darkness, as though whispered by hundreds of voices. I thought uneasily about the coffins, and *kept* people, and wax.

Ranara stepped forwards. The bronze frame around her body moved with her, bending and straightening where it was bolted to her joints. At her waist it widened into a splay of limbs. They touched the floor in a circle like a court lady's crinoline skirt, the runes etched into their surface glowing with low, red light. It was a brilliant bit of runesmithing, eight-legged, much more stable than a human skeleton. I couldn't keep from watching it as she moved, as delicate as a spider. She lifted one hand.

Her fingers clicked. When they touched my chin, they were sticky.

'Honey,' I said. The smell of it was all around me.

'You wear your hair differently than Jaern did,' Ranara said, in her hundred voices, twitching my face side to side.

'You're covered in crystallised honey,' I repeated.

Her eyes, when they met mine, were violet – not just the iris. The rich colour spread from corner to corner. 'As it happens, honey is the simplest way to mummify a body in a damp riverside city. I needed to live long enough to care for my children. Jaern was supposed to ensure that for me, but when he decided he didn't want to pay his debts, he cursed me to remain here, in the temple, forever.' She lifted her withered hands, and I saw, cut into each palm, a small but perfectly rendered pair of rune spirals, the strongest set of binding sigils I'd ever seen. 'So I took . . . measures.'

Measures. A hell of a way to say *mummified myself alive.* My stomach flopped over on itself.

'Gods,' I whispered.

'We were that. He collected secrets, and I . . . fixed people. Made them better. Made them correct. I'm not a necromancer. I'm a surgeon. Or I was.' She looked down at her own hands. It was a long, creaking process. Six or seven small, bronze joints along the back of her neck and arms had to bend to allow her to tilt her head and flex her wrists. 'He was interested in everything, of course, insistent that the body we built – this body, your body – be as perfect as possible. It took a long time to find all the pieces. I was very proud of it. Of course now my work is less . . . elegant.'

'The stitched things,' I said. 'They were mindblown people, and you made them.'

'When their minds were gone,' she said, calmly, 'there was no sense in wasting the bodies.'

'The Roy, back in Varriel,' I said. 'The explosion? Was *he* mindblown?'

'I had to secure my children.' The goddess stared at me. 'I needed empty servants in each town, watching, killing when necessary. What was I supposed to do, allow some petty policemen to interfere with my plan? Wait until his personality ebbed? I had to hurry the process along, change him while he was still alive. And then when I felt you, when the lapidary disappeared, cheated me out of my service, when I *saw* you, with Jaern's lying face—' Fascinated, I watched as the mummy ground her teeth. I couldn't see them, but they squeaked like rusted hinges. 'I don't like triggering the trap spells. They're for emergencies. But I confess that I wanted to kill the people with you. Punish you, force you to come to the temple. I knew Jaern wouldn't let *himself* die.' She paused, and although her expression didn't change I could feel her hatred on the air, as heavy as the toll of the great temple bells. 'Jaern was more subtle than I knew, and waited to place the magic on my skin until I was deep in meditation. I wanted . . . I wanted to make him face me. I knew if I had what he carried that I could rid the world of magic so much sooner. And this body is *mine*. I made it.' She touched a lock of my hair with fingers that flaked sweet, crystallised honey down on to my shoulder. 'I still say it was fine work. I can't do such fine work anymore, not with my hands like this. You saw.'

My gorge rose, but the pieces were finally coming together in my head. 'Ranaran priestesses use unshielded incantations . . . you weren't meditating when Jaern hexed you. You were stoned, using drin to keep from feeling the toxicity.'

Agony grasped my throat and squeezed the very roots of my tongue. When it left I was on my hands and knees on the floor at her feet, gurgling, spitting blood. As I watched, tiny crystals began to sprout in the scarlet puddle. 'Jaern *did* die.' I coughed. 'And you're going to die, too, no matter how many people you hurt.'

'Your friends won't find the way down.' The bronze framework around the body shuddered as she bent her head to look at me. 'You're the one who's going to die here, Corcoran Gray.'

Through the haze of pain, I finally had enough wit to be afraid. Brix and Dace could be trying to find a way to come after me. They'd walk into this mess and see me and think I was free, and be trapped.

If the spell overwhelmed me again . . . if I couldn't keep my wits about me and figure out how to disarm Ranara . . .

'I'm sorry.' The lie tasted foul, like choking down dust, like smiling while you suffocated. I told it anyway as the goddess set me back on my feet. 'Forgive me.'

'Yes. It's time for you to repent.' Ranara was, I thought, trying to display an emotion on her face. She had to have other feelings besides that drugged, flat sweetness. But the empty smile was all there was, the face held immobile. 'You see, Jaern was supposed to help me perfect my children. He was very clever, like you're clever, and had a way with incantations, the way you do. I couldn't do the magic myself.'

'Why not?' I wasn't in full control of my eyes, but I didn't think I could be imagining the runes that glowed up and down the bronze frame surrounding her, or the ones throbbing at the foot of the giant crystal. Someone had to be controlling them. It seemed unlikely that a lot of other people had been coming in and out of this crypt.

'It's a sin,' she said, surprised. 'He, of course, was an abomination, so it didn't matter if he sinned. I would have dealt with him, afterwards – but first I needed him to help me to protect my children. First I had to make my children strong.'

The iron grip of her will on my body marched me across the floor to where the crystal-coated skeleton stood, its spine still arched in a rictus of pain, open-jawed skull howling towards the ceiling.

Ranara's hundred voices echoed, full of satisfaction. 'It took me a long time and a lot of experiments to figure out how to do it, but then – so long ago now – they brought me a boy for healing. He was transparent, and I knew that, at last, I had my solution. He'd worked in the mines digging for lapis pigment, and they had found a nest of saintstears crystals. He'd handled them for quite a long time before anyone knew there was something wrong.'

My head twisted to look the crystal-crusted skull in its empty eyes. 'The crystals made him magic-immune?' I said. 'Crystals like these?'

'They absorb magic toxicity, but they also change your blood over time. With repeated exposure they'll infect you. He didn't feel the pain of magic. It still killed him, in the end – it always will, as you're discovering. A nasty death.' She sighed, with hundreds of throats. It sounded like the wind moving through branches. 'It took several generations of experimentation before my children stopped dying from the crystal graft. More before the mutations took hold. Do you have any idea how many nasty deaths have been required to grant my children this sort of peace? So much work, guiding them, watching them suffer and lose themselves, becoming ghosts – do you think I'm going to let someone like you spoil it all?'

So this was how Brix's people had begun. There was no djinn fore-bearer back in the mists of time. The Tirnaal magic immunity was nothing more than an alchemical trick, after all – a giant sigil hacked into the stone floor, a crystal that could change and mutate a bloodline, a goddess building herself the perfect family.

'But you're hurting people,' I said. 'All of them. Moyra, the others in the coffins—'

Ranara managed to widen her eyes. They creaked. 'Moyra was dallying with a wizard and that sin killed her. Yet when the priestesses brought her here to be embalmed I forgave her. Kept her alive to help power all of this.' Ranara lifted one hand in what was no doubt supposed to be a sweeping gesture towards the sigil and the skeleton, bronze joints whizzing and popping. 'And then, her humble sacrifice brought Kaylor to the temple to ask for my help bringing the others in his Guildhouse to justice, and together we made them suffer. He gave me his sorrow to build the sacrifice. You'll give me yours to cleanse the city. Everything happens for a reason.'

'So what was that business upstairs for?' I said. 'If you were already torturing Moyra and all the people like her, if you already had a plan to end the use of magic, then why kidnap all those people?'

I flexed one hand and discovered, with a jab of surprise, that I could move that little piece of my body, but none of the rest of it. Maybe there was a chance, after all. Surely even this gigantic incantation had to be controlled by the caster the same way any spell did. If that was the case, then Ranara would lose some of her control if she lost her concentration.

'The people needed to be healed. The moon needed to be caught. And you needed to be brought to the rooftop where I could perform the proper incantation on you. Enough talk. It's time.' She moved me across the floor until I was facing one of the great mirrors.

It looked like glass and silver, but felt like ice under my fingertips. Once tipped in the correct direction, it gathered all of the moonlight pouring in through the holes at the centre of the ceiling and focused it on to the crystal-studded skeleton. The crystal caught the light and refracted it, doubling and changing, rippling across the runes carved into the floor, rivulets of violet spreading out and shining in the darkness. They still looked incomplete, odd, pieces of something like an echo or an amplification.

'There,' I said. 'The mirrors are changed, though why you needed me for that—'

Ranara remained where she had been during my ill-fated spurt of rebellion, the pretty toes of her shoes touching the spatter of blood I'd left on the floor.

'Movement has a cost for me,' she said. 'You know that magic wears out metal, or your kind would have covered themselves in rune armour by now. Every time I use these spells to move, I hasten the day that I won't be able to move at all. I needed vessels to spread the cleansing, like Jaliseth, or Sannet, or Tynan – or willing servants, like Kaylor. But you, of course, are special.' She was still grinning.

'You carry Jaern's spells. You carry the amulet he made with my craft. Now I need wait no longer.'

The crystal-studded skeleton towered above me on its silver-covered base. As Ranara pushed me closer, I saw that under the tarnish the metal was covered in layer after layer of sigils. The work was brilliant, old-fashioned, beautiful; magic in the same style spiralled up and down my forearms and behind my ears and in the innermost places of me. My hands moved without my volition to touch the silver base, just beside the godsbones' crystal-studded heels. 'Jaern built this for you?'

'I gave him a perfect body and an amulet so he never had to feel pain while he cast,' she said. 'He promised me the power to protect my children. I will have my due.'

It wasn't the bargain that didn't make sense. I could readily believe that Jaern, who had lied with the same easy confidence that he flirted, would promise anything and everything in order to get what he wanted. The part that bothered me was that Jaern would make *this* spell. If I read it correctly, the godsbones carried a hugely expanded version of the transport spell written on the amulets. If the amulets killed people by releasing their stored toxicity via the crystals, this was meant to unleash poison on an unimaginable scale.

The spell on the floor would amplify the ruin and blast a wave of death across the city – maybe further, if Ranara had learned to channel the energy in the godsbones the way she channelled moonlight. *Thousands* would perish, in agony, without even knowing why. We wouldn't just lose Genereth. We'd lose everyone.

'I still don't understand.' There had to be a way to stop this, to take myself out of play. 'It's not a complete incantation. There's no direction to it. If you use the spiral to amplify the toxicity, there's no reason why it shouldn't destroy the Tirnaal as well as everyone else. Hells, there's no reason it shouldn't kill you.'

284

'You're the key, fool,' she said. 'Jaern built this for me, but he didn't want me to use it. By the time we made our bargain, I already knew magic would eat the world like canker. I knew I would need to defend my children. But I didn't reckon on Jaern's duplicity.'

If she had met the Lord of Secrets, known him and trusted him to keep his word, I wasn't the only fool in the room. I focused on the runes in front of me. 'So he put a chunk of the spell under his own skin and kept you here?'

'He wanted to use it for himself,' Ranara said. 'This skeleton – it's a sink for magic toxicity, connected to the amulet I built him. For centuries, he used it to cast without paying the price of his spells – his ambitious, huge spells. For centuries, toxicity has been collecting here, along with what I remove from my followers and priestesses. Over time I needed more skeletons, more bodies . . . I can't heal without their sacrifice.' From the darkness and the coffins and the crypts, the whispers rose again. 'Just as I can't repair the world without yours.' For the first time her smile changed, her lips parting to show her teeth. They were made of pointed, sharp steel. 'Now.'

Vibrations rose in my own throat. I tried to resist it with everything I had, keep the magic unsaid, keep the spiral from being completed. It wasn't enough. I listened to my own deep voice chant, and watched the runes around the godsbones come alive, snaking out around me, lighting up channels in the floor that reached to the very edges of the room. The sigils lit above my heart. In front of me, the skeleton glowed, heat pouring off its decorated bones.

I could feel everything – the reservoir of poison I was standing on, the flickering agony in each of the poor bastards in their coffins. I threw all my consciousness against the thorny nest of torment that was Ranara's will. I managed, barely, to keep my mouth shut, but not to keep myself from making noise. A growling, inhuman wail rose from my throat.

'Stop that! Obey me!' Ranara pitched me forwards, grinding my nose into the metal and stone I knelt on. 'I'll cut out your tongue with your own teeth and still make you say what I want. I'll ruin you, Corcoran Gray. Now *open your filthy mouth.*'

My jaw ached. I tasted bile. And slowly, inexorably, my voice began to sound.

Smash.

The room dimmed. The moonlight throbbing through the runes under my hands went out. Someone had broken a mirror.

'Let him go,' Brix said, in the dark.

TWENTY-ONE

Several things happened at once. My body leaped to its feet, twisting me around on the platform with speed that made me shriek. Ranara's metal framework burst into clacking movement, hauling her back into the dark among the coffins. The agonised whispers from the crypt covered everything in an overwhelming blanket of ocean-crash sound, making it impossible to tell where she was.

And I realised I was momentarily in control of my own mouth. 'Brix, she's got me, you've got to knock me down, you've—'

Ranara took me.

'—*you're trying to ruin everything, you thieving little traitor,*' the goddess hissed, with my mouth. '*What are you trying to prevent? You think this farce of a relationship was ever going to work out? I – urg—*' I wrested enough control of my muscles to cut off the spewing words. Not a sound from Brix, thank the gods.

Ranara pried my jaw open again. '*Magic is wrong. I can see that now. I know I have to submit myself to the Moonmother. You would, too, if you weren't a traitor to your own kind.*'

Ranara pronounced the illumination spell written around my left wrist and I watched, helpless, as the ball of white fire shot across the room to hover in front of another mirror, one that had been tucked in a corner. The runes beneath me lit up again, albeit fainter.

That answered my question: it didn't have to be moonlight, but the runes weren't as stable this way.

'You could be happy too, if you'd admit that we were never meant to be together. It's unnatural, a Tirnaal and a wizard. You have to be realistic. Sometimes we all have to make sacrifices.'

To my left one dark shape flitted through the shadows, then another. Was it Brix *and* Dace, then?

There was no time to be certain. Now I was facing the crystal again, on my knees and close enough that the moisture of my breath condensed on the godsbones, or the martyr, or all that remained of the poor boy who had only wanted to stop feeling the poison before it killed him.

Smash. A second mirror shattered, and the runes went dark again.

Ranara shrieked, enraged. She twisted me towards the broken mirror, punching the illumination spell bigger, the poison of it whizzing through my muscles and bones. She sent my light flying to the ceiling, revealing Brix as she sprinted from one mirror towards another and Dace making his way towards the surgical table. They both halted, staring.

All around us, silent, stood a ring of people so soaked in drin, so crusted with newborn crystals, that it took me several seconds to realise that they *were* people. Ranara had raised her family from the coffins where she kept them.

'It doesn't matter if you break every mirror,' Ranara said, in the whispered voices of the coffin-people. *'I'll still—'*

'You will not!' Brix smashed the mirror she stood next to and then walked towards me, purposefully. Now that she was closer, I could see what she'd used to knock the mirrors out of commission, a long thing that at first I thought was some kind of metal pipe. It was silvery, knobbed at one end. Brix smashed the mirror closest to me – the one pointed down at the runes, and then stood in front of me, staring me in the eyes.

'Let him go,' Brix said. 'I don't care what you are. He's *mine*. You don't get to take him.'

I gurgled, struggling for any sort of control of my own voice. To my left, two drin-covered bodies fell into breathless heaps on the floor as Ranara abandoned controlling them to hang on to me. The goddess was strong. Holy saints, she was strong.

Brix was close enough now for me to see the freckles along her jaw, even in that pale, fickle magic-light.

'*How are you planning to make me let him go?*' My hands reached out and fastened on to Brix's shoulders. '*You can't hurt me by attacking him. You'll just be hurting him, making it so that if I ever do let him go, he'll be in even more dreadful shape than he currently is.*' I grinned. '*You can't win.*'

I couldn't do this. I couldn't stop her by myself. I gathered all the will I had left, pushed it up into the ringing agony that sat where I used to have thoughts. I shoved the words into my mouth. They tasted like blood. 'Skin,' I whispered, through my rigid jaw.

Brix stared at me for a moment longer, then reached forwards and grabbed Jaern's amulet.

'*No!*' Ranara lunged with my body.

Brix was too quick. She pulled, breaking the chain, and sent the amulet skimming across the floor like a beetle towards Dace, shouting as she did, 'SKIN!'

He dropped to his knees and caught it, chalk in hand, writing so quickly on the floor that his fingers blurred – scribing the same incantation that was written above my heart, the same one that was allowing Ranara to control me.

My arm snapped out straight and pointed at Dace. The chant bubbled in my throat.

You know how this ends.

The goddess' attention must have been scattered, split between watching Brix, directing all the people she'd called out of their torpor and controlling my tongue and arm. Feeling tingled back into my feet and legs.

It doesn't have to end the way it always does. It doesn't have to burn.

I hooked one toe behind my opposite ankle, and pulled.

Ranara realised what I had done a split second before my jaw cracked against the stone floor and thrust my arms forwards, knives of force ripping through my bones as I caught myself. Someone screamed. After a few seconds I realised it was me.

But Dace was chanting, and I had stopped the spell with a half-dozen syllables left.

The room went dark. The spell around me flexed – tore – and broke.

I lay face down on the floor, panting, wondering whether I'd managed to break my wrists. It took Brix a few moments, groping in the dark, to reach me and turn me over. 'Gray?' Her fingers found my hands, and then felt their way up to my face. 'Is it you? Have I got you back?' I kissed her fingertips and heard her long, shaky exhale. 'Gods, you *are* back.'

'For the moment.' I forced myself to sit up, every muscle shrieking, the air catching in my lungs like fire. The room wasn't all the way dark – the distant witchlights among the rows of coffins and a few of the runes on the floor were still softly lit.

'Shit, the . . . the not-goddess.' I twisted back towards the laboratory. In the bad light I couldn't see more than a short distance, but I should have been able to pick the red glow of Ranara's runesmithed exoskeleton out of the dark. 'Where did she go?'

Dace ran towards us, the lower half of his body flickering in and out of visibility. 'Did it work? Did it free him?'

'I think so.' Brix was still regarding me doubtfully.

'I don't even know how you're standing up,' I said to Dace, getting to my own shaky feet. 'You were dying, remember?'

'Ranara healed all the Tirnaal on the roof – she didn't expect that to include me, I'll wager – and Brix helped me. Also, I'm still very high.' He didn't waste more than a glance on me before turning to scan the dark around us. 'We couldn't tell where the mirrors were directing light in the sanctuary upstairs – it looked like they were just shining into the grates at the base of the font. Would have been a problem finding you if you hadn't thought to drip moonmetal across the floor. Where do you think she went?'

'I don't know.' With the shattered mirrors, the light was no longer the purple column that had been pouring down from the roof. Instead the only illumination in the room was caught in the runes and the witchlights between the coffins. But staying in one spot meant risking the goddess finding a way to take back control of me. I took a deep breath and pointed. 'That way. I hope.'

We moved towards the surgery table in a nervous bunch. In the crypts beyond, one witchlight after another winked out. I listened for the noise of Ranara's framework, but I couldn't hear anything over the tormented whispers, moans and cries of the people waking up in their tanks.

There was also, of course, the people *out* of the tanks. They wandered through the room like a flock of starlings wheeling through the sky, bunching and scattering all around us. Hands grasped at us out of the dark.

'Where is the damn goddess?' Dace muttered, batting away a set of reaching fingers.

'Surgeon – alchemist, maybe – not goddess.' I was reeling on my feet, unable to get my thoughts to run in a coherent groove. 'She's a . . . she cuts and changes, she made things . . . I don't know how to get away from these . . . these things . . .'

'People.' Brix grimly shouldered aside a body that could have been a child. 'They were people, once.' We were being driven now, by the simple, overwhelming pressure of other bodies.

'If they're alive, there's something wrong with them.' Dace shoved an arm away from him. 'Are they mindblown? Is that why they're acting this way?'

'Not yet.' I swallowed. It didn't help; having someone else wield my voice made owning it again exquisitely painful, as though I'd swallowed sand. 'They rot in the coffins and afterwards, when their personality and will and spirit are all the way gone, then Ranara . . . she . . . remakes the flesh.'

Brix looked at me, horrified. 'You mean this is where the stitched things came from?'

'Yes,' I said.

'No.' Dace planted his feet. 'Enough. This atrocity has to end.' With that, he pushed up his sleeve to scribe an illegal incantation.

I held back one set of gentle, grasping tank folk so he could work. Then another. Then I couldn't keep track, surrounded by the claustrophobic press of cold, crystal-rimed bodies.

'Hold them,' Dace said. 'Just for a minute.'

I glanced at his arm. Illumination is generally what people use to light up an area, and for good reason: it's not very toxic, albeit not very bright. What Dace had written was dawnbreak, toxic as the hells and bright as noon. It seared into existence against the ceiling above his head, stabbing into dark-accustomed eyes and giving us a sweeping view of the crypt.

Ranara stood directly in front of us.

The light flared, and Ranara's bronze-articulated arm shot out and clipped Brix across the face, knocking her backwards. At the same time, her other arm reached out and grabbed me by the throat, lifting me off my feet.

'Did you think I would surrender now?' Ranara drove me backwards, charging away from the light. Whatever cost there was to her movement, she was angry enough to pay it. I struggled pointlessly against the immovable bronze limbs, blood thudding in my head, lungs shrieking for air as I slammed into the godsbones. I had one second to feel the rock against my back – and realise that it was warm – before the skeleton's hard, stone-studded arms locked around me.

The moonlight coming through the mirrors may have been flickering and dying, but Dace's dawnbreak spell was alive. The runes burned with it, radiating heat like coals. The magic hummed, vibrating through the crystal, sounding in my own blood and bones and teeth. Ranara chanted with practised, elegant ease, her scruples about doing magic apparently forgotten. The spell on the floor spun with light and colour, beautiful, flickering with raw power, spilling towards the great violet stone . . . and me. The goddess had almost finished when something moved behind her.

It was Brix, blood streaming from her nose.

Ranara must have seen my eyes focusing on something over her shoulder, because she began the slow, lumbering process of turning her rotting, unwieldly framework around.

'Mistake,' I said.

Brix raised the thing she'd used to break the mirrors. With a giddy sense that I was hallucinating, I recognised it: it was one of the femurs from the godsbones in the sanctuary above. It must have been heavy; Brix grunted as she lifted it, the muscles in her arms and shoulders bunching.

Ranara cut off the chant, her lips drawn back in a snarl. She moved to hit Brix again, but not quickly enough. Brix bobbed, weaving sideways, and twisted from the hips. The silver femur swung through an arc like a hammer and caught Ranara's elbow with a sickening crack, driving it in the wrong direction. I expected the club to bounce off the bronze, but instead a snapping noise echoed through the chamber, as though Brix had brought an axe down on rotten lake ice.

She'd delivered a direct blow to the line of runes. I watched as the deformed line of the spell flickered and went dark.

'You don't get to hit me,' Brix growled. '*Ever.*'

Ranara picked up a different spider-limb and brought it around. 'I'm the mother of the Tirnaal. Your protector. Your *goddess*. I only want what's best for you.'

'You're not my mother.' Brix was somewhere behind the goddess, weaving in and out of the shadows and in and out between Ranara's limbs. 'You hurt people. You're a monster.'

'Stop it!' Ranara tried and failed to spin rapidly enough to keep up with Brix. The silver bone clanged off the knee of one of the spider legs. The runesmithing went dark and the fatigued metal crunched, the delicate interplay of the joint buckling. 'What do you think you're achieving?'

Brix was, evidently, done talking. This time the silver bone bounced off not part of the framework, but the meat of Ranara's honey-coated arm.

The gold shell cracked, crumbling just like the wax that had shattered around the poor, sewn-together bastards upstairs. Where the air touched Ranara's skin it shrivelled from a rich, dark brown to black, desiccating before my eyes, chunks of flesh sloughing off glistening bone.

Brix swung again. The tip of a leg went spinning off into the darkness, and now the goddess listed dangerously sideways.

'You think you can win?' the goddess said, with her many voices echoing from the tank people that were shuffling towards us. 'I'm a *goddess*. Even if you kill me, you can't stop me. You can't stop destiny. I *made* you, and all of my children like you. To die at your hands would be . . .' With a series of disgusting crackles, Ranara tilted her head to one side, as though solving a puzzle. 'Fitting. That's what it would be, fitting. And so—'

With that, Ranara turned back to me, reaching out both of her ruined arms, the honey flaking off in sheets. Her leathery fingers brushed my cheek, her steel fingernails carving a long gash down the side of my face, splattering hot blood against the godsbones crystal behind me. As quickly as water running downhill, the crystal caught the toxicity in my blood and replicated, growing across my face, pressing in around me, crackling, pushing – I was being buried alive inside the rock.

She resumed the chant in that grating, whispery voice. The runes at the base of the godsbones lit, one by one.

Breathe. I could, but barely, the hard edges of the crystals crowding around my mouth and nostrils, shoving at me. I couldn't feel anything but the stone, and Ranara's cold, rune-carved hands.

Her hands.

I gulped air and pronounced the spell, Jaern's binding spell, with rock stabbing at the corners of my lips. The runes written on Ranara's palms lit, for probably the first time in several centuries. Toxicity from Jaern's magic and from the crystal behind me crawled up my spine.

'No!' Ranara recoiled as if I had burned her – which I suppose, in a way, I had. 'Stop!'

I didn't stop, pushing the spell even as the magic cut into my gut like razors. All the pain and horror of ten thousand incantations pulsed under my skin, all the stolen magic from generations of wizards, all the pain that had made generations of Tirnaal.

His pain, I thought. Jaern's pain. I had never wanted it, but now the agony was a weapon, and something dark in me rejoiced to wield it. I smiled with my teeth against the stone.

'You'll never survive without me.' Heavily, clumsily, Ranara wheeled around to where Brix was lurking in the dark. Brix was limping, but she was smiling.

'We've done for you,' Brix said. 'Haven't we?'

'You're nothing!' Ranara tried and failed to take a step towards Brix. 'You think any of you matter without my blessings? You think that anyone will care what happens to you if you're just the same as any other grovelling, snivelling person, afraid of magic, afraid of sacrifice? Make him stop!' Ranara shrieked, lunging towards Brix.

'No,' Brix said, and struck the goddess across the face.

The honey around Ranara's jaw and chin shattered. The runes on her palms blazed as the last of the magic written on the bronze framework, one sigil at a time, shuddered for a moment and then went dark. The goddess fell away from the frame, dropping to crouch on the floor.

Long, thin cracks shivered up her legs and great chunks of crystallised honey crashed to the floor. She twisted, turning towards me. Even then, even with pieces of her feet shredding against the stone floor, she was smiling.

She managed to take three steps towards me before the air and the decay reached her joints. One foot broke off at the ankle, then the other, and she collapsed, hard, to her hands and knees.

'I don't understand.' She dragged herself forwards, shedding fingers, speaking in her own hollow, dead voice. 'I would have ended it. I would have cleansed the world.'

Her hands were gone now, and she was pulling herself forwards with one elbow. She had reached my feet when Brix caught up with her and brought the femur down across the back of the goddess' hairless head. The last of the honey-shell cracked and peeled away, and the room went silent.

Brix looked up at me, panting. 'You all right?'

'I'm fine,' I lied, muffled by the brittle stone that still clutched me. 'I'm going to pass out soon, but I'm fine. You?'

'I'm alive, and not coughing pink light.' Brix scanned the crystal. 'How do we get you out of there?'

Something was happening to the tank folk. I had halfway expected them to fall when Ranara did, poor half-alive creatures, kept where they were by the force of their injuries and illness and prevented from dying by Ranara's magic. And indeed, some of them did fall. Others, though, burst into wails, stumbling forwards with the growing horror of freedom on their faces.

Dace jogged over to us, still half-transparent from the daybreak spell, his face drawn with tension. 'We've got to get him out. Ranara's dead, but the spell running through this godsbones thing wasn't hers.'

'It was Gray's?' Brix said, with alarm. 'Gray, stop it! Snuff the spell?'

'I'm not running this.' I tried to spit and my tongue only brushed rock. It tasted oddly sweet. 'It's an amplification spell – it makes everything stronger. If it touches the godsbones–'

'You pronounced it,' she said. '*Un*pronounce it!'

'Ranara pronounced it with my mouth.' I closed my eyes and groped for the pieces of the spell that Ranara had made me recite. 'It should be snuffed now that she's dead.'

'It's carved into the rock,' Dace said. 'I think you're part of it.'

White light seeped slowly through the spiral of runes cut into the floor, moving towards me in an inexorable progression, like water flowing through a series of complicated irrigation ditches. The tank folk scattered when the light came near their feet, as though they were afraid of it, as though it hurt. I stared at the light and concentrated. It slowed, as runes slung across my ribs prickled with life and the pain corkscrewed up my spine. The rock pressed in tighter around me.

My skin. My cursed, rune-written *skin*. That was what was keeping the spell active.

'Dace,' I said, 'Brix, I want you to get out of here. Take whoever you can. I can hold it for a while.'

'You think I'm giving up?' Brix said. 'You think I'm going to lose you again?'

'It's Jaern's spell,' I said. 'And Ranara's, and mine. It's all tangled up. We're sharing the spell, just like you and I have shared spells before, Brix. It's three of us working at the same time – the other two feel like they're pushing the magic even though they're dead, and I'm holding it back. I don't know how to stop this. I don't know how to ruin a spell that's written in stone and driven by two dead gods. You've got to live, Brix. You've got to go.'

Her jaw hardened. 'I'm not leaving you. There's a way out. There's got to be a way out. It might be Jaern's spell, but it's your skin. It has to be you. Nobody else can stop this, so *think*, damn you.'

'Maybe if the magic running through it wasn't activated when it shattered,' Dace muttered. 'Maybe if you were unconscious. Maybe –'

'I'm the only thing holding it back at the moment, so don't hit me until we have no other choice, all right?' I said.

'There's a centre to the incantation somewhere under your feet,' Dace said. 'You have to admit that much.'

'I don't have to admit anything,' I snapped. 'The Guild thinks that all spells are the same, but they're not. I've seen spells centred in different rooms than their action, I . . .' My words dried up.

'What is it?' Brix crept closer to me. The moonlight was also creeping closer, lapping at Dace's heels. 'What are you thinking?'

I wasn't thinking. I was teetering on the edge of pure, claustrophobic panic. The crystals pressing into my skin would soon begin to pierce my flesh, feed off my blood. I'd fuse to the skeleton, another sacrifice to the goddess who was quickly becoming a pile of dust at my feet.

I fought for speech. 'The spell isn't centred on the floor.'

Behind Dace one of the tank people staggered towards something on the floor that I couldn't see. I couldn't turn my head. The figure bent down and picked it up just as I recognised its staring, strangled face. The crystals covered my nose.

It hurt, Moyra said. *Just like this, it hurt. They could have saved me. They could have stopped it. You have to stop it. You're the only one still controlling the spell. It has to be you.*

298

I reached for her with the spell, feeling for her mind, familiar from my dreams.

The amulet. Jaern's amulet.

I couldn't say it, couldn't breathe, couldn't move.

I had wondered whether suffocating would be like drowning, but, as I held my last breath, it wasn't. The magic closed around me like the sea, crushing, immense, with none of the numbing cold of deep water. This was all hot pain and the unbearable, eternal pressure of my heart.

Snap.

Something struck the stone shell around me, but I couldn't let go. The magic was still there even as I fell away from myself, even as my lungs ached and tried to burst in my chest. The incantation burned in my mind like a jagged spike of fire, the magic that only I could reach now.

Snap.

My heart strained like a wild thing against my breastbone.

Snap.

Something shoved up against my fingers. *The amulet.* All three pieces of the amplification spell came together – amulet, spiral and me.

I spent the last air in my lungs on an incantation, my tongue swelling as grit formed inside my lips. I whispered, and the ley-breaker twined around my bones blazed with anguish, each rune imprinting itself on my nerves like a brand. I got almost to the end of it before I ran out of breath and there was nothing but the crystals trying to crawl down my throat.

CRACK.

The stone around my face broke, and I could see Dace, clutching a heavy jug from the alchemy workbenches. He had been hammering it against the crystals. He crammed his fingers in the hole and broke off chunks until my mouth was clear. The white light on the floor lapped at my toes.

I inhaled. The last three syllables rolled off my tongue like a prayer.

The amplification spiral caught the spell and Jaern's ley-breaker tore through the room – tore through *me*, every twisting character I carried alight with searing agony. The shrapnel of each broken spell lodged under my skin and I couldn't scream.

But the magic stopped.

First the moonlight swept backwards, unwinding like a spring. Then it just broke, shivering into pieces like the shards of a broken mirror. The light within the crystals around me ebbed, heat dropping away, and I became aware, slowly, that I was sobbing.

Moyra lay on the inlaid stone not three feet from me, obviously very dead. She wasn't staring anymore – whatever magic had given her the strength to stagger across the floor had allowed her to die at peace. Her eyes were shut, her mouth smiling gently.

We had done it. The magic was retreating, and as it did, the crystals were dying. Moyra had put the amulet into my hand. Dace had kept me breathing.

And Brix had –

'Little saints,' I croaked, my swollen lips making the words come out thick and blurred together. 'Brix, you defeated a goddess. With a stick.'

'She was not a goddess.' Brix took the amulet out of my hand, panting. 'No more. No false gods. No sacrifices. No perfect family.' She threw it to the floor and brought her foot down on it, hard. The amulet broke under her heel and a huge, throbbing pulse of energy blasted outwards. Brix sprawled back, Dace fell and the tank folk dropped like wheat before the scythe.

Shattered crystal tinkled to the ground around us, dull, dead. I thudded to the floor beside a mound of debris. It took me a minute to recognise what it contained.

Once, there had been a goddess in Genereth. Now there was only a pile of old bones.

When we stepped back through the secret door and into the sanctuary, the Tirnaal from the roof were dispersing out through the big double doors to the Godstown square. The priestesses were piling the 'wax statues' to one side of the big room, and clean, early daylight poured through the tall stained-glass windows. One of the priestesses screamed when she saw us appear in the hole in the wall. I couldn't really blame her. We were magic-drunk, covered in blood and – in Dace's case – transparent to the hips.

For me the pain of the toxicity had gone from being pressing to being so overwhelming it was almost interesting, a kind of fog that I floated on. I watched as the priestesses ran towards us, and wondered if the halos around them were hallucinations or something the sunlight in the room was actually doing.

It soon became apparent that most of the priestesses didn't have a clear memory of what had happened the previous night. A few of them didn't have a clear memory of anything much but arriving at the Genereth temple as novices; it appeared that the amnesiac effect of Ranara's manipulation was in full effect. It was surprisingly simple to convince them that we weren't a danger. Then again, I was having difficulty remaining upright; perhaps I didn't look threatening.

'You three?' A half-familiar voice echoed across the sanctuary, penetrating even the haze settling in around my wits. It reminded me of something.

. . . *storks?*

I squinted. Valera Trist was sitting on the floor near the door, with a few other people from the roof who seemed to be wounded. As I watched, she rose and wobbled her way over to Dace.

'Examiner!' Valera had a bandage around her head and one around her wrist. To her credit, she mostly pretended not to notice that half of him was ghostly. She stuck out her uninjured hand. 'It's good to see you alive.'

'You too.' Dace took her hand, warily. 'How much do you remember about last night?'

'Other than the Roys working like the hells to break me out of a giant crystal? Enough.' Valera grimaced and gestured towards his transparent feet. 'Some of it is ... not our most pressing business. But the rest ...' She paused. 'Before you can be returned to duty I need to know what happened. The council needs to know what happened. I'm taking you into custody now, along with the other two. There will have to be a trial.'

'Neyar's pups.' Brix's hands clenched. 'You just don't give up, do you? A wizard – a Guild wizard – was made half-mad with grief, then used by an alchemist who collected people and rebuilt them. With *thread*. You can go down those bloody steps and see her lab.' She pointed at the passage we'd just emerged from and glanced at me. 'Gray? Aren't you going to say anything?'

'No.' The burden of all the toxicity I'd been pushing past during the battle was getting heavier, crushing me downwards. My knees buckled. I sat down, hard. 'Arrest me already.'

'Little saints, Master Gray,' Valera whispered. 'You *are* a mess.'

And then, to everybody's chagrin, I put my head down on the stone and passed out.

TWENTY-TWO

The nightmares were waiting for me, of course, flitting between light and heat and hazy, tangled dreams full of stone and darkness. But my dream-self only died a couple of times, and both I and the spells on my arms kept quiet. The world, in brief glimpses when I swam up to it, seemed unreal and full of pain. At least there was no fire.

When I finally opened my eyes I was alive, clothed and in bed. A good bed, in fact, with sheets and a blanket. I sat up and then had to hold very still, head spinning.

'Easy. Don't rush or you might faint again.' Dace sat across the room on a straight-backed wooden chair, shuffling through a folio full of loose parchment.

'Again?' I squinted. Except for a scab on his lower lip and a healing bruise below one eye, he looked every inch the Examiner General, down to scrubbed skin and clean black clothes. That probably meant that he had gone back to his role as my prosecutor. Which meant that him sitting and reading at my bedside made no sense. 'Am I hallucinating?'

'Possibly,' he said, without looking up from his papers. 'The Examiner is playing nursemaid to the outlaw. It does have the tang of the ridiculous.'

The room came into focus: stone walls, plaster ceiling, wood floor. The only furniture was a bed, a chair and a three-legged stool. A very solid-looking door blocked my exit and a green prison circle was scribed on the floor around the bed. I studied it. It would not be simple to break.

A jail, then.

'Nice circle,' I said. 'You're learning.'

'Thanks.' Dace still didn't move. 'I strive to not have to be corrected twice.'

'Where's Brix?' No response. 'Answer me, Dace. Tell me what's going on. You owe me that much.'

He gathered his papers into a pile, crossed one booted ankle over his knee and regarded me. 'I owe you?'

My throat seized up. I should have expected this, but I hadn't. 'Then I'm just . . . asking.' I ran my hands through my sticky, tangled hair. 'As a friend. I know it's the last time I can do that.'

He exhaled. 'We're still in Genereth. In the duke's guard tower. The militia has been kind enough to house our criminal since the Guildhouse was burned down during the riots. I argued for this cell instead of one in the dungeon so you wouldn't die before trial. You've been delirious for about a week. Brix's been with you. She is not being held, and stepped out to get something to eat. I expect she'll be back soon.' He paused. 'Her freedom papers were formalised three days ago.'

'And Jaliseth?'

'Was pretty well cleared when Ranara admitted to using the amulet to control her. I've already written the order for her to be released.'

'Thank you,' I said.

His attention was back on his papers. 'You've kept your part of the agreement; I had to honour that and keep mine.'

Reflecting on my unstained honour didn't make the prospect of facing trial and execution any more pleasant. 'So do you haul me to Varriel?'

'You were judged to be a flight risk. The council are coming here, since the plague seems to have more or less ceased.' Dace stood and walked to the window – which was really just a plate-sized hole in the wall cross-hatched with bars. 'The last two Guildlords are expected to arrive tonight.'

Fleeing seemed unlikely, given that I wasn't sure I could stand up. I swung my feet over the edge of the bed and put them against the floor. I felt like an old man, weak and tottery, coated with sweat and grime as though I had awakened from a long fever. 'I suppose everything starts tomorrow, then.'

'Indeed.' Dace stared steadfastly at a narrow section of sky outside.

'So I'll stand trial in Genereth,' I said, both to shake some of the terror off the words and because I wanted to puncture his calm. He had nearly died beside me a few days ago. He could at least look at me. 'Good. Perfect. Hell of a place to hang.'

The tips of his ears went red. 'It would be inappropriate for me to speculate on what your sentence will be.'

'It's not speculation. The Guild never would have believed it if I had gone to them claiming to have killed one god – but two?' I shook my head. 'It makes much more sense to believe that Corcoran Gray is a particularly noxious and dangerous unlicensed wizard, guilty of causing numerous deaths. Best to dispose of him.'

He glared at me for a moment. 'You're *going* to stand trial.'

'I know,' I said. 'And I'll be found guilty, and–'

'You're going to *try not to be* found guilty, damn you. You'll mount a proper defence, and respect the judges, and control your mouth for once. You're not going to get to court and do' – he waved a hand at me – '*this*. Understand?'

I straightened. 'What in the hells have you got to be angry about? I'm the one who has to stand there before the Guildlords–'

'Sit,' he interrupted. 'We give you a chair. It's a civilised process.'

'—*sit* there, stuck up for everyone to see like some kind of specimen, with the task of proving to people who hate me why I shouldn't be hanged. Don't act like I shouldn't be upset by this, Examiner.'

He stared at me for a moment longer, jaw working. I think he would have said something else, but at that moment the door swung open to reveal, behind a jailer in a chain shirt, Brix. She was carefully balancing a wooden bowl full of something that smelled like porridge. When she saw me, her face lit up. 'You're awake!' She rushed in, pausing only to step carefully over the rune circle.

'I'll be going.' But Dace halted just outside the still-open door, glancing back at me. 'I'm the one who has to examine you tomorrow, Gray. I advise you to tell the truth.' He paused. 'Or maybe I'm . . . asking you to.'

Then he was gone, the door shut, and the locks ground home.

'Here.' Brix shoved the bowl into my hands. It was broth and grain of some kind; millet, maybe. It was yellow. 'It's been difficult feeding you while you were delirious. You've gotten skinny. How are you feeling?'

'Like someone scooped my guts out.' I set the bowl carefully on the three-legged stool that stood beside the bed. I was hungry, but the thought of eating was vaguely repulsive. Brix had spent the last week forcing food down me and probably doing even more disagreeable offices. That wasn't something anyone should have to do in the first year of a relationship. Carrying news of my conviction and death to Acarius – that wasn't something anyone should ever have to do. 'Listen, I'm going to lose. At trial.' I had to get the words out. 'You've got your papers. You don't have to stay and watch it happen. It's all right. I'm all right, I'm . . .'

She took my hand. The words died in my mouth.

Her touch was warm and strong. Our fingers slipped against each other smoothly, fitting together as though they had been carved out of a single piece of wood. I ran my thumb across her knuckles, then bent and pressed my lips to her palm. Her other hand came to rest in my hair.

'Sorry,' I said, after a moment. 'That was stupid of me, wasn't it?'

'Yes,' Brix said.

When the morning of my trial dawned, a pair of Guildies in journeymen's robes appeared to shepherd Brix and me to the court. I had imagined that the tribunal would be held in either an impressive judgement hall or a dank interrogation cell, but they led us to a dusty meeting room with a table and a few chairs – and another flawless prison circle, keyed to me. My fate was apparently just another administrative detail. It was a bit insulting.

Five Guildlords sat behind the table, resplendent in their embroidery. To one side of the table sat Dace and Valera. On the other Tynan was propped in an armchair, with a blanket over her knees. Aoine sat beside her. Both women were deep in intense conversation, and they looked exhausted and vaguely annoyed. As my guards, Brix and I walked in, they went silent.

Looking at Tynan, the feel of having the goddess in my wits and muscles came rushing back. 'Are you all right?' I blurted. 'Did she hurt you? Did *I* hurt you?'

'I don't think I'm allowed to speak to you, yet,' Tynan said. But her hands and wrists weren't bandaged, so maybe she'd been healed during the ceremony on the roof.

'Sit.' One of the Guildies waved Brix to a chair beside Aoine and then shoved me towards a three-legged stool that had been placed in the middle of the prison circle. I sighed, but there was nothing else to do. I stepped into the restraint.

Everybody was staring at me. It was the most uncomfortable room I had ever been in, including prison. I sat.

'This tribunal will come to order,' said the Guildlord at the head of the table. I recognised her from Varriel. She had tight-curled red hair cropped close to her skull, fully eight inches of embroidery on her sleeves and a disconcertingly astute gaze. She was presumably the judge. 'The Guildlords and representatives of the Mages' Guild are here to determine whether violations of the Royal Charter have occurred, and to mete out punishment for any violations thus uncovered.' She turned towards Dace. 'Examiner?'

Dace rose, clutching his folio. 'The prisoner's name is Corcoran Gray. It is likely that you all have heard at least something about him, given the scandal that surrounded the former Examiner General's disgrace and trial last year, the disaster at Cor Daddan and the bounty that the Guild has, in the past, offered for his capture. The accusations against the prisoner are . . .' He glanced at me. '. . . numerous. The council have a full list available to them; I will note only the most serious and recent.' He looked down at his papers, cleared his throat and read: 'Unlawful divination. Illegal incantations including force, flamespike and several spells that the Guild currently does not have classification for. Purchase of illegal alchemical goods. Brawling.'

'I *brawled*?' I said, unable to help myself.

'The prisoner will remain silent until given leave to speak.' Any trace of friendship that had ever been in Dace's expression had vanished. 'He is also charged with reckless casting, endangerment and interfering with a Guild officer in the performance of his duty. Then there is the matter of the deaths.'

'Murders,' Valera said. 'There are a lot of dead Guildmates and apprentices, my lords. They didn't die of old age.'

'There are dead Tirnaal as well.' Aoine sounded tired, but dangerous. 'It's time the Guild recognises that our deaths matter, too. We've been dying, imprisoned and blamed since the plague started. Now you say the plague was caused by magic gone wrong. So who is going to repay the families for this injustice? Temples? The Guild?'

'Gray didn't kill any Tirnaal,' Brix said. 'He didn't kill any wizards, either. I was there. I saw.'

The judge rose briefly to her feet, leaning over the table. 'The witnesses will keep quiet until questioned, or be removed.'

A seething, resentful silence followed. Dace spoke into it with care. 'Of the deaths that occurred during the course of this investigation, a significant portion were caused by the plague, misadventure, or the actions of the late Unguild wizard, Gali Kaylor. It is the remaining deaths that the council must examine: the ones leading to the corpses found in the vaults beneath Ranara-temple, and the deaths last year at Cor Daddan. It is possible that murder has indeed been committed by the prisoner, but that has not been determined.'

The judge nodded. 'Begin questioning.'

I looked at Brix, but she was watching Dace. The Examiner General put his folio on the judge's table and walked with measured steps to the edge of my prison circle. 'Tell us your name, please.'

'Gray.' He waited, and I sighed. '*Corcoran* Gray. I haven't got a longer name than that, my parentage is muddled.'

'Did you understand the charges?'

'Yes.'

He didn't lift his eyes from his papers. 'Do you dispute any of them?'

That question actually took some thought. My muscles ached, stiff from lack of activity. My wits felt stiff too, creaky, as though I wasn't catching everything that was going on. It was true that I'd cast illegal spells. The council had Dace's testimony to that effect, and presumably Jaliseth's. It seemed like a waste of time to establish as much. And why were they letting Brix stay with me? Why were Aoine and Tynan here?

'I didn't kill anyone,' I said. 'And I don't think I brawled. In general, I try to run before I fight.'

'So you don't deny that you made illegal alchemical purchases?' Dace said.

I frowned. 'No. You know why I had to.'

An expression I couldn't quite identify flickered across his face. 'And you don't deny that you used unsanctioned incantations?'

'No. You were there. You saw me use unsanctioned incantations.' I tilted my head to one side. 'At least once, you handed me the grease pencil to do it with.'

'Testimony from witnesses of the disaster at Cor Daddan has established that thirty' – Dace glanced at me – 'excuse me, thirty-*two* people died. Those deaths have been attributed variously to Keir Esras and his corrupt Guild faction, to Corcoran Gray and to a necromancer who called himself by the name of the god Jaern.' He paused. 'The council has no doubt compared the prisoner's appearance with his description from our records. I assure you there is no imposture happening, neither is an illusion spell running. I myself have witnessed the prisoner undergoing a ley-breaker that would have stripped out illusion spells, and when the prisoner was first arrested I conducted extensive divining to confirm his identity.'

'Examiner, I'm not sure I understand what you're proposing,' the judge said.

'The prisoner told me he died last year,' Dace said, 'in the process of disabling the necromancer who he claims was responsible for most of the deaths. Through a necromantic process, the prisoner's soul was transferred to the necromancer's body. That necromancer had placed certain spells under the skin of the body. Last year witness statements to the same effect were discounted as being improbable. Now, however–'

Valera snorted. 'You believed his . . . his ghost story?'

'No,' Dace's eyes flicked to me. 'With the court's permission–'

He wasn't asking the court, I realised, startled. He was asking *me*. I lowered my chin, the smallest assent I could manage.

'—I believed *this*.' With that, Dace began to chant.

The illumination spell around my left wrist came alight, searing. I moved to cover it with my other hand, as though that would prevent the council from noticing the magic.

'Stop it,' I said, as light spilled between my fingers. 'Stop!'

Dace snuffed the spell then, but the damage was done. The council was staring at me, open-mouthed. They all knew what I was carrying. I was exposed.

Dace wasn't even looking at me. 'I submit to the council that the prisoner's account of the events at Cor Daddan and the witness accounts are consistent. When combined with the evidence of the prisoner's skin it is logical to conclude that the necromancer Jaern was the one responsible for the deaths, and the prisoner was, at most, a bystander.'

'Agreed.' The judge sounded a little shaken. 'But there's still the Generethi deaths.'

'Indeed.' Dace turned. 'You have several more spells under your skin where they cannot be detected. Isn't that right?'

I advise you to tell the truth.

'Shit,' I said. I had trusted the bastard.

Dace advanced towards me. 'Actually, this is a yes or no question.'

I stared up at the man who had made me a divining focus, who was cracking me open for everyone to see. For one instant I wanted to hit him, right in his smug, half-smiling mouth. 'Yes.'

'Dangerous spells,' Dace said. 'To my own knowledge, flamespike, huntseye—'

'Yes, yes.' I stood, not that it would do any good. I needed to be on my feet, not perched on a stool. 'We all get the point, Examiner. I've got a damn arsenal of spells under my skin, spells you can't take away from me. I'm dangerous. I'm an abomination. What in the hells are we delaying my sentence for?'

Dace raised one finger. 'This brings us to current events. When I handed you the grease pencil, what were we doing?'

The council looked as confused as I felt. This was an odd line of questioning, even given the notoriously esoteric nature of Guild tribunals. I frowned. 'Running up the stairs of the Guildhouse to confront Kaylor. If you recall, he had just suffocated more than a dozen people with windthrift incantations.' Surely Dace had already told the Guildlords his version of what had occurred, from the moment he met me until I had managed to snuff Ranara's spell.

'All those people,' Valera said. 'I still can't believe it. Guild regulations . . . the wizards who died should have been protected more effectively.'

'As you say.' Dace's voice was icy. 'It's a shame that we were separated during the riot in Godstown. If you had been there, no doubt you would have known of a Charter-sanctioned incantation that would have allowed us to anticipate the future enough to prevent the attack. I confess I did not.'

Valera had the decency to blush, all over her birdlike face.

'The prisoner will describe the confrontation in the upstairs hall of the Guildhouse,' Dace said. 'Including the exact spells used.'

'Kaylor and two of his friends threw spells at us,' I said. 'Windthrift, and two others that I didn't recognise.'

'And you cast a spell. Multiple spells, actually.' Dace glanced at the sheaf of papers he'd put down. 'Not incantations I'm familiar with. They were illegal, were they not? Carried under your skin.'

'Yes.' I shifted my weight from one foot to the other, but I couldn't find a position that wasn't uncomfortable. 'I threw a spell I call leafgrip and another that involves spiders. I don't know the name of it. It hurts, so I don't do it unless I have to.'

'You say that you "run before fighting", but in this instance you apparently did not even attempt to flee.' Dace looked up at me mildly. 'That seems like an untruth. Can you explain?'

'I couldn't run.' A spurt of anger started in my chest. 'You know I couldn't run.' I was unlicensed. Any magic I did was technically illegal. There was no point to this dance, unless Dace was trying to help his career by pinning me thoroughly to the wall.

'The prisoner will please assume,' Dace said, coldly, 'that even if I could somehow discern his internal logic, if I am asking questions now it's because the court has no such ability. Explain why you couldn't run.'

'Because,' I snapped, 'the Examiner General was throwing slow, useless *legal* spells and ended up half-dead on the floor. I didn't want him to die.'

'Why not?'

I blinked. 'What?'

'Why keep me alive?' Dace hadn't taken his eyes off me. 'I am, at best, a difficulty to you. With me dead you could have roamed about Genereth on your own recognisance, made your own bargains if necessary. You could have gotten your cure from Ranara-temple and gone home. Why stand and fight when you were outnumbered?'

The air was too warm and there were too many people watching. I couldn't decide what to say. Everything that came to mind sounded absurd. Why try to keep Dace alive? *Because he needed help.* That was self-evident. *Because he's my friend.* That would do Dace no favours, and anyway I wasn't sure it was true.

'Like I said, Gray doesn't kill people. He doesn't leave them to die.' Brix spoke without moving, arms crossed over her chest, scowling at the entire tribunal – including me. 'Not even when it would simplify things.'

'Thank you, Mistress Rivest.' Dace didn't look at her. 'Your testimony will be recorded. I'll note, however, that the question was posed to –'

'Because it had to be me,' I interrupted, before anyone could remember their threat to remove Brix if she spoke. 'I have spells under my skin that can hurt people, but I also have spells that can help. They were all I had to hand at the Guildhouse. There was no time to scribe. And at Ranara-temple I had no other choice. I knew what I was carry-ing, thanks to you. I'm not a saint, but what kind of demon would I have to be to sit there and let the city die when I had the solution under my skin?' I paused, but the words had already come out of my mouth. Not a saint, but not an abomination, either. 'It was just a piece of work that had to be done,' I said, slowly. 'And I did it because I was the only one who *could* do it. That's the answer. There isn't anything more to say.'

'Nonsense.' Valera shot to her feet. 'You had plenty of self-interested reasons to preserve the Examiner's life. You needed medicine for your partner.'

'Which he could have gotten himself, once I had delivered him to Genereth and he became aware of the existence of a "cure" at Temples.' Dace spread his hands. 'While it may be technically pos-sible that a man who risked his own life to defend the life of his jailer would then somehow change enough in the span of a few hours to fill the vaults of Ranara-temple's catacombs with scores of victims, some of whom had been dead for months—'

'Very well.' The judge cleared her throat. 'The prisoner will not be charged with the Temples deaths, or those in Cor Daddan. You've made your point, Examiner.'

'I haven't, actually.' Deliberately, Dace turned his back on me. 'The council is, of course, familiar with the Charter. It is everything that our current practice of magic is built on and the basis of the position that the Guild enjoys, balanced between the rival powers of the throne and Temples. The Charter is our guide, our security, and unless our understanding of it changes' – he paused – 'it's what will kill the Guild.'

The judge's eyebrows went up. 'What are you suggesting, Examiner? I know your record too well to believe that you're asking us to aban-don the Charter.'

'If you are,' Valera said, 'this tribunal will have to reconvene to examine you.'

'A fact I am aware of.' Dace sounded remarkably calm for someone skating on the edge of being stripped of his rank and the vocation that he loved. 'I'm asking the council to hold in mind our future. The council and the Guildlords have many policies that aren't directly referenced in the Charter. For example, it's common knowledge that Tirnaal do not become wizards, but this is a custom, not a Charter requirement.'

Aoine cleared her throat. 'All of this finally brings us to the reason that Tynan and I are here. According to her own testimony before the Tirnaal Sisterhood, Corcoran Gray is the partner of Brix Rivest, which makes him a member of the Deadchurch clan and thus Tirnaal. That means that *we* have jurisdiction over his actions, not the Guild. If he's been found innocent of murder, then it's not the Guild's business what happens to him next.'

Her own testimony? I lifted my head, startled. Tynan was smiling at me. More to the point, so was Brix.

'Partner?' Valera crossed her arms. 'Since when do Tirnaal marry wizards?'

'Well.' Aoine reached across and took Tynan's hand, sandwiching it between her own tattooed palms. 'Since at least twenty-five years ago. Always assuming they can find a wizard who deserves it.'

'This is nonsense,' said one of the council members, a gruff man with a red moustache who hadn't spoken until now. 'He's not Tirnaal – not by blood. I'm not even certain that this Rivest woman is Tirnaal. We've just heard testimony that the prisoner has spent a lot of time doing intricate magic, and the Examiner's notes show that Rivest cast a spell to remove his regulator earring. Tirnaal are not suited to practice.'

Aoine raised an eyebrow. 'Is that what the Guild thinks? That we don't engage in your wilful manipulation of nature because we're not any good at it? Has it ever occurred to you that we don't choose to participate in something that leads to so much suffering?'

The male wizard lifted his chin. 'Perhaps it would have been more accurate to say that Tirnaal don't generally attain the magical competence necessary for licensure.'

'And yet,' Dace said, dryly, 'despite both positions, I am Tirnaal.'

The entire room let out its breath with a *whoosh*.

'This is going too far.' The judge's voice hummed with disbelief. 'We can all tell that you have a desire to spare the prisoner, Examiner. We can all appreciate that you feel you are under some sort of an obligation to this ... person, with the manufactured skin. But to step into what is an obvious lie about your heritage—'

She halted, as Dace awkwardly began to shed his clothes – first belt and tunic, and then his shirt. He turned, allowing everyone in the courtroom to study a slender back covered in a litany of dark, runic tattoos. Brix had runes across her collarbones and a single line down her spine, which I had assumed to be more or less standard, but Dace's ink sat on him like a burden, thick as a cloud of flies, curling around the edges of his shoulder blades and extending down towards his kidneys.

The silence quickly built from uncomfortable to excruciating, while both the wizards and the Tirnaal stared.

'Not a lie,' Dace said.

'You should go transparent,' the judge said. 'When you cast.'

'I take measures to aid my recovery,' Dace said, precisely. 'I practise within the Charter, keep my vows and uphold Guild law.' He shrugged back into his shirt. 'There is no law against Tirnaal practising. There is only custom. Tirnaal custom, and Guild custom.'

The council – except Valera, who was steadfastly regarding her shoes – seemed too shocked to respond. Watching her, I thought I saw a faint tinge of red creeping along her cheekbones and wondered whether Dace had coordinated this with her. After all, without our intervention she would be nothing but a set of crystal godsbones on a rooftop.

At last the judge with the moustache spoke, looking a bit like he'd just discovered a spider in his soup. 'Why didn't you tell the Guild this when you entered your apprenticeship?'

'Was it relevant?' Dace said. 'Whatever your opinions of my morality, I think most of you will admit I am magically competent. The Charter says nothing about a wizard's heritage as a qualification for licence. For that matter, the Charter doesn't give permission for the enslavement of anyone in the service of magic, despite which the Guild has, in years past, declined to intervene when rogue enslavers kidnapped Tirnaal children for sale to wizards.' He looked directly at Brix. 'It will do so no longer. The licensing restriction for Tirnaal isn't law. Neither is the ignoring of enslaver activity. Both are a matter of bad custom.' He paused. 'And I am proof bad custom can be altered.'

The judge's nostrils twitched. 'What are you asking the council to do? Extend the robe to every bit of riff-raff that comes asking?'

'The council already has.' Everyone looked at me as though they were annoyed by the interruption, which seemed unfair considering that this was supposed to be *my* tribunal. 'Listen, I'm as Unguild as they come, but when the Charter was written there was no such thing. Wizards had to be brought in from unlawful practice and granted sigils when they swore to uphold the limits and methods of magical practice that the Charter outlined.' I glanced at Dace. 'That's where all this is going, isn't it? Proving I acted in emergency circumstances, that I can perform to Guild standards . . .'

'You're saying the Guild should offer licence to you?' Valera sounded, for a wonder, a little subdued. 'On the strength of your service at Ranara-temple, you mean?'

'Dace is saying that,' I said. 'Aoine is saying you should let me go because I'm Tirnaal by . . . marriage, I think. I'm apparently not even supposed to be talking.'

'This investigation has demonstrated rather conclusively that Gray has knowledge that the Guild does not,' Dace said. 'Knowledge that the Guild cannot afford to ignore, since significant threats from necromancers and alchemists seem to be becoming more common. With the destabilising of Ranara-temple it's possible that the balance of power will become skewed. We could, gods forbid, return to magical war.' He gestured to me. 'Gray can save lives. His skin alone could provide material for several months of study, none of it actually forbidden, all of it possible to integrate under the Charter if the council wills it.'

'Why not just say it? The Guild needs Gray. You won't survive without him.' Brix spoke with some relish. 'How uncomfortable that must be for you all.'

This was going too quickly. All at once I could imagine a long life stretching out ahead of me, full of spell-work for Tirnaal aunts that would always think of me as dirty for doing it. Conversely I could spend my days balancing Guild regulations and an endless parade of the kinds of problems that regulations don't solve. Both possibilities seemed fraught, stifling. 'Look,' I said, 'I appreciate everyone trying to claim me, but—'

'Gray,' Dace interrupted. 'You are dangerous and important enough that the council only has two options: license you, or execute you.' Something close to a smile hovered around his mouth. 'So sit down until you find out which they choose.'

I looked at Brix. For the first time in weeks, the worry lines in her forehead had gone smooth. She caught my eye and, ever so gently, shook her head.

I sat down.

It took the council three hours to decide not to execute me, and the rest of the afternoon and evening to determine exactly what rank I was to have and to tattoo my wrist accordingly. The new sigil was still seeping silver ink and sore when they let us go the next day, into the damp cool of a Generethi morning. The Guild had agreed to pay for our transport back to Varriel, if we chose.

Dace walked us to the docks, which were still relatively empty. The plague had died around Genereth, but a lot of clean-up remained to be done. He led us to the boat that he had commissioned and then stood with us. Brix stared at the river. I stared down at my tattoo.

'I don't know how I feel about this,' I said. 'Being . . . respectable.'

'Alas,' Dace said. 'Respectable was the best I could do.'

I flushed. It wasn't that I didn't know what he had done for me. It was that I had no idea what to do now. Just because I had a sigil on my wrist didn't mean that my future was simple.

He waited for a moment and then, when I didn't speak, turned to Brix. 'What are your plans? You're coming back upriver anyway – you could stay in Varriel, practise at the Grand Guildhouse, keep working with me to improve the Guild from the inside.' He gestured towards the red domes behind him. 'Or you could both stay here, I suppose. The Deadchurch aunts would adopt Gray.'

Brix's face was turned up to the sunrise, where the pale, fading moon and the rising sun were still in the sky together. 'I think it's time we went home. We're two weeks late. My sister will be worried. Even Gray's grandfather might have noticed we're gone.'

I shrugged. 'Respectable folk do get to live where they choose, don't they?'

'They do. In that case –' Dace dug in his pocket and dropped a pair of round, cool stones into my hand. They were, impossibly, ward-stones keyed to my name – Jaliseth's stones, the same pieces that I had traded to the priestess to get Brix into the temple. 'Found them at Temples while the Guild was conducting its investigation. And I thought –'

'Thank you.' The wardstones in my hand seemed to weigh more than I remembered. 'For . . . all of it.'

'It wasn't unselfish,' Dace said. 'I still need an ally. There's going to be a lot to do now that you've managed to disrupt a couple of cults and reinterpret the Charter. I wasn't making all that up, during the tribunal. Bad times really are coming. Maybe war. I wanted your help. But I have no right to force you.'

'Ally?' I said.

He hesitated, then spoke quickly. 'Friend, if you like.' He cleared his throat. 'Well. You two might as well get comfortable on the boat. I still have to collect the others who will be travelling with us.' He took a few steps back towards the city before he paused, glanced over his shoulder and smiled. 'Don't run away, please.'

And with that, Brix and I were alone again.

We stepped on to the boat. It was bigger than the one we'd ridden downriver, with a cabin meant for at least six. Brix went inside. I followed and watched as she stood and ran a hand over the blankets on one of the bunks.

'I think it's going to be fun, seeing the Guild get turned inside out. By Corcoran Gray and a Tirnaal boy, of all things.' She exhaled. 'Gods, I'm tired. Maybe we can catch up on some sleep on the way home.'

'So now I'm supposed to turn the Guild inside out?'

She didn't look up at me. 'You want to, don't you? You just didn't want to admit as much.'

'I'm not fool enough to *want* this job. But . . .' I paused. 'It was what Dace said, about having knowledge under my skin that could help people. Save lives, even. Maybe it can be . . . I don't know. Put to some kind of use. The deaths last year, the dreams, all of it. Maybe there's more for me to do than hide at the cabin or rot in a Guild cell.' I turned the wardstones over, letting them slip between my fingers, cool and silky and inadequate. The stones twisted against each other. *Click.*

'I dream about dying every night,' I said, abruptly. 'About how it felt.' I didn't know I was going to say it until it was out, and then I couldn't take it back. A vigilant, nauseous sense of doom swirled over me like a fog.

'How *did* it feel?' Brix said.

I froze, startled by the question. Brix knew the inside of my head and every inch of my body, but it had never occurred to me to describe the dreams to her. In a strange way it almost felt too intimate. I knew this part of myself was unlovely and messy and sharp. But—

'Cold,' I said. 'Mostly. It hurt, but the cold was what bothered me.'

'And then?' She tucked her hands into her pockets. 'What happens next in the dream?'

'It varies. Anything that's been happening, it gets mixed in with the basic pattern of the nightmare. I die, and panic, and try to . . . not die.' It was absurd how difficult it was to get the words out, how ashamed I was of them. 'I fight. I make noise, I . . .'

'Cast spells,' she said. 'And then?'

I frowned. 'Then?'

She turned to me. 'What happens next, Gray?'

The wardstones pressed into my fingers. 'I don't know what I was thinking,' I muttered. 'We should go home. I'm not the kind of idiot who should try to fix the world, Brix. I can't help Dace reform the Guild, repair the relationship with the Tirnaal families—' *Click. Click. Click. Cl—*

'Wrong.' Brix cupped her hand over mine and stilled my fingers. 'When the dream ends, you *wake up*. We have choices, Gray. We choose to fight or not, to keep people alive or let them die, to burn things down or remake them.'

'I'll be taking drin every night to suppress the dreams, for a while at least,' I said slowly, feeling my way towards hope. 'It would always be a problem, which of the spells to use, which to try to forget. I'm not a monster, but I'm not exactly a normal man, either. I'd be—'

'Happy?' Brix tilted her head sideways. 'Doing good? How terrible. You have to choose which consequence you want.'

'Using drin is hardly a small consequence,' I said. 'Take too much and it'll kill you, over time.'

'So will magic,' Brix said. 'Since when has that stopped you?'

I winced. 'Gods, Brix.'

'It's been a hell of a week.' She shrugged. 'I'm too tired to be gentle with your nonsense, my love.'

I laughed, the tension in my muscles uncoiling with a rapidity that left me shaky. 'You're always saving me. It must be exhausting.'

'We're always saving each other. That's how this works.' She leaned forwards with great dignity and kissed me. 'Simple.'

'Simple,' I agreed, gathering her into my arms.

'We're staying in Varriel for a while, aren't we?' she said, with her lips against my mouth. 'You *are* the sort of idiot who will try to fix the world.'

'Dammit,' I said.

Because – well, I was.

ACKNOWLEDGEMENTS

Many thanks to my sharp-eyed editor Molly Powell, whose ability to get to the emotional core of a story makes my writing better over and over again, and to all the people at Jo Fletcher Books who have worked so hard to get this book in sparkling shape. Sequels are difficult, but you all made the process as painless as it's possible to be.

I'd like to thank my agent, Kurestin Armada, whose business acumen and gentle guidance always spur me to do my best work and take my writing seriously. I'd also like to say how much I appreciate my 'agent siblings' – colleagues who are always up for craft discussions, encouragement and support for each other's books. As always, the best part of this gig is getting to watch talented people do their thing.

To my husband, who has been unrelentingly supportive, and to my sister, who has read more drafts of the book than anyone except me: thank you, my dears. I couldn't do it without you. Sorry about not warning you about the claustrophobic bits (but thank you for reacting so well).

Kids, thanks for telling me that you think you might want to be book-writers when you grow up, for learning to make yourselves omelettes instead of eating all my expensive yoghurts and for only causing a flood while I was pushing a deadline that one time.

Fadz, I don't know how to write a book without your input, so you have to tolerate being thanked again.

Lastly, to all the readers who have come with me and Gray on the journey so far: thanks for giving my awkward wizard the privilege of spending some time with you. I hope we brighten up your day. You certainly brighten mine.

Help us make the next generation of readers

We – both author and publisher – hope you enjoyed this book.
We believe that you can become a reader at any time in your life,
but we'd love your help to give the next generation a head start.

Did you know that 9% of children don't have a book of their
own in their home, rising to 13% in disadvantaged families*?
We'd like to try to change that by asking you to consider the role
you could play in helping to build readers of the future.

We'd love you to think of sharing, borrowing, reading, buying or talking
about a book with a child in your life and spreading the love of reading.
We want to make sure the next generation continue to have access
to books, wherever they come from.

And if you would like to consider donating to charities that help
fund literacy projects, find out more at www.literacytrust.org.uk
and www.booktrust.org.uk.

Thank you.

*As reported by the National Literacy Trust